CHRONICLES OF A RADICAL HAG
(with Recipes)

ALSO BY LORNA LANDVIK
PUBLISHED BY THE UNIVERSITY OF MINNESOTA PRESS

Best to Laugh

Mayor of the Universe

Once in a Blue Moon Lodge

Chronicles of a Radical Hag

(with Recipes)

A NOVEL

LORNA LANDVIK

University of Minnesota Press

Minneapolis | London

Published by the University of Minnesota Press
111 Third Avenue South, Suite 290
Minneapolis, MN 55401-2520
http://www.upress.umn.edu

LIBRARY OF CONGRESS CATALOGING-IN-PUBLICATION DATA
Landvik, Lorna, author.
Chronicles of a radical hag (with recipes) : a novel / Lorna Landvik.
Minneapolis : University of Minnesota Press, [2019] |
Identifiers: LCCN 2018024155 (print) | ISBN 978-1-5179-0599-6 (hc/j) |
  ISBN 978-1-5179-0600-9 (pb)
Classification: LCC PS3562.A4835 C47 2019 (print) | DDC 813/.54—dc23
LC record available at https://lccn.loc.gov/2018024155

Printed in the United States of America on acid-free paper

The University of Minnesota is an equal-opportunity educator and employer.

26 25 24 23 22 21 20 19   10 9 8 7 6 5 4 3 2

To all dreamers and doers

PART ONE

1

July 15, 2016

Minus what that vicious lying mirror tells me, and the
knees that crackle like kindling every time I take the stairs,
and the ear canals that have muddied with silt of late,
eighty-one feels an awful lot like twenty-nine. Okay, maybe
fifty-three.

"You don't stop laughing when you grow old," George
Bernard Shaw is credited with saying. "You grow old when
you stop laughing."

If I liked those cutesy pillows cross-stitched with pithy
sayings, I'd cross-stitch what Mr. Shaw said on one, but I
don't, so I won't. It's not as if I'll forget something I agree
with so completely; really, I believe laughter is like collagen
for the soul. I myself try to have a good laugh at least once
a day, although in these trying times we're living through, I
wish there were a product, a "laffative" of sorts, I could take
to ensure mirthful regularity.

Having survived the hoopla of last year's surprise party,
I chose a quieter celebration yesterday with my friend Lois,
one that included a drive by the construction site of the new
downtown library (bigger than the old one by 3,000 square
feet!) followed by dinner at Zig's Supper Club, even though
Lois wanted to go to that big chain restaurant out on the
highway because they have two-for-one margaritas on
birthdays.

"They can afford to do that," I told her, "because they pay their workers so poorly."

Lois rolls her eyes as a default expression in response to much of what I say, but honestly, if I weren't around acting as her social conscience, she would always choose a free drink for herself over fair wages for the bartender pouring it.

My grand-niece Angela—she's the adventurer who's living in Paris and rides a little scooter that takes her along the Seine to her Pilates studio—sent me a lovely card, whose message was written in French because, well, she's in France.

"Joyeux Anniversaire!" are the words in the cat's thought bubble, and when you open the card, "le chat" is drinking champagne with a group of mice, one of whom (according to Angela's handwritten translation) is saying to another, "Drink up. Tomorrow the party's over and it's back to the same old cat and mouse game."

It's funny in that esoteric French way, *je suppose.*

Our server, guaranteeing himself a big tip, asked me to what I attributed my youthful appearance. Not wanting to give him a glib answer like Oil of Olay or "a diet of younger men," I expounded on the restorative power of humor.

"And curiosity," Lois said when I finally took a break to attend to my gin gimlet. "Haze here is the most curious person I know."

She was treating me to dinner, but this pronouncement was a little gift itself.

"Thank you, Lois," I said, and to the server I added, "I just want to know more."

More about him (he was studying environmental science at Bemidji State and was going to spend half of his senior year on the Galápagos Islands!); more about the couple whose heated argument about her out-of-control shopping and his inattention rose from their corner table like a storm cloud; more about Lois's date with her chiropractor's father, and whether she'll now be getting free adjustments.

As a gangly kid, I'd position myself on my sister Vivienne's bed, my finger idly tracing the patterns of the chenille bedspread while she sat at her desk writing love letters to her beau overseas. Before putting pen to paper, she always spritzed the thin airmail stationary with Jungle Gardenia perfume.

"It brings me close to him," she would say. "Harold can hold the paper to his nose and pretend he's holding me."

How did she know how to do something like that, I'd wonder, to send along with her words a little bit of herself to her boyfriend dodging torpedoes in the Pacific?

Vivienne's been gone for over ten years now, and my visits to Harold are getting harder and harder as he falls backward into that black hole of Alzheimer's, but I'm always heartened to see on his bedside table, along with the family Bible he can no longer read, a half-empty bottle of his wife's Jungle Gardenia.

Oh, pooh. This was supposed to be a celebratory column, and here I am doing what I've promised I won't do in my dotage—which is not to *be* in any kind of dotage!

July 18, 2016
DEAR READERS:

It is with great sadness that we here at the *Granite Creek Gazette* announce that Haze Evans suffered a massive stroke on Saturday evening, shortly after viewing a production of *Guys and Dolls* at the newly refurbished Lakeside Playhouse. After the show, she complained of a headache to friends but, typical of her generous spirit, made a point of assuring them it had nothing to with the actors' performance.

On the car ride home she slumped forward in her seat and was driven immediately to the hospital, thankfully just two blocks away.

Haze was hired by my grandfather ("one of the smartest moves I ever made," he told me more than once) and wrote her first column in 1964. I can't count how many people have told me her columns are their favorite part of the *Gazette* or how they consider her a trusted friend. She still receives the most mail, snail and electronic.

Haze has done much for our community, and it is our fervent hope that she will soon recuperate and continue to do more. We'll keep you posted.

Sincerely,

Susan McGrath

Publisher

"THE PHONE'S BEEN RINGING OFF THE HOOK," says Shelly Clausen, the newspaper's receptionist, her voice weary, as if she'd been toting barges and lifting bales instead of punching buttons and taking calls.

"I figured it would be," says Susan. "There's no one people care more about at this paper than Haze."

"It's beyond me," mutters Shelly, jabbing a lit-up square on the phone console and barking, "Granite Creek Gazette."

In the hallway, the publisher accepts a hug from Mitch Norton, the managing editor, who considers it part of his job description to always be the first one in the office.

"As you can hear, Smiley's got her work cut out for her," says Mitch, who has a host of nicknames for the dour receptionist.

The day before, just past dawn, he had been arranging his fishing lures in his tackle box, preparing for a sweet Sunday morning in his boat (he jokes that while his wife, Lucy, is a devoted member of St. John's by the Lake, he prefers to worship *on* the lake), when Susan called him with the news of Haze. Shifting into management mode, Mitch appeared at the hospital twenty minutes later, armed with a thermos of coffee.

"By the way," he says now, "Lucy and her garden club are wondering if they should send flowers, or would Haze even be aware of them?"

Susan shrugs, wincing as the buckled strap of her heavy bag digs into her shoulder.

"I don't think you can go wrong with flowers."

In her office, she shuts the door and sags against it, the energy she had summoned to get herself out of bed and to work used up. Staggering to her desk like a marathoner nearing the finish line, she collapses on the old office chair that had belonged to her grandfather. Its black leather is so worn and cracked that it's pale gray at pressure points, and a brocade throw pillow gives her the cushion its deflated seat cannot.

It's been a long weekend of snarly telephone conversations with a husband whose title may soon include "ex," of sullen texts from one teenaged son and an e-mail request for money from the other, with a hospital vigil and conferences with doctors, with the shock that she might lose not just the newspaper's institution but her dear friend Haze.

Even though it's squeaky, the chair is made so well that it still tilts back easily, and Susan rests her head in the basket of her entwined fingers and perches her crossed ankles on the desktop (her assistant, Caroline, once rightly noted that few women are able to relax in that classic executive pose, mainly because too few women are executives). The position, however, is not helping to generate any deep thinking; her thoughts are like fleas, jumping directionless, with no intention but to irritate. She is so rattled that in response to the short knock on the door, she nearly yelps.

"Susan," says Caroline Abramson, entering her office. "OMG. Are you all right?"

The chair squeaks as Susan flexes herself into a fully upright position.

"From the tone of your voice," she says to her assistant, who despite her occasional abbreviated text talk, is smart and canny and, best of all, *helpful,* "I gather you think I don't look so hot?"

"Forget hot—you look terrible." Caroline sits down and opens her iPad. "So what do you need?"

"Whoo. That's a loaded question."

Caroline levels a gaze at her. For being so young (twenty-six), she's a master at leveling gazes.

"Let's start at the beginning," she says. "First of all, any new news about Haze?"

Susan shakes her head. "I'm going to stop by the hospital after work. Unless I hear something before." She grimaces, not liking the implication of the word *something*.

"I'll go with you," says Caroline.

Bowing her head, Susan presses a thumb and forefinger against the rise of tears in her eyes. For the past thirty-six hours, she has been on the verge of tears, has passed the verge of tears, but as yet has not had the full-bodied cry fest into which her body and soul are ready to surrender. It would be so easy to give into it now, but there is too much to work to do.

Lifting her head slowly—it feels as if her skull were made of lead—she settles her filmy gaze at her assistant, whose warm and questioning face almost triggers a sob, but instead, Susan clenches everything that needs to be clenched and says, "I just can't believe it."

Caroline's head bobs in a nod. She too feels like crying but understands that it would be engaging in an unending game of tag— "You're it!" "No, you're it!"—that her boss does not want to play.

"So," she says, "you last saw her at Happy Tea. She was fine there?"

Susan's smile surprises herself. It's an expression that hasn't been in frequent rotation lately.

"When wasn't Haze fine?"

IN THE TUMULT OF THE LATE 1960S, the atmosphere in the newspaper office had become so rancorous (Betsy Colvin, the features editor, and Roger Czielski, the metro editor, regularly exchanging names like "Fascist" and "Bleeding Heart Ignoramus") that Haze had initiated in the conference room a Friday afternoon "Happy Tea," whereby staffers were encouraged to enjoy cheese and crackers, a selection of teas Haze brewed up in the office kitchen (by the third week, Bill McGrath had contributed two bottles of brandy, and Ed Dyson, the sports editor, had found an enthusiastic audience for the elderberry wine he made in his basement) as well as civil, and *only* civil, conversation.

"I don't mind debate," Haze had written in her interoffice memo, "but I do mind not giving each other simple courtesy."

It had been a big hit and went on for several months in the conference room until the cleaning crew complained that it was getting harder and harder to get the wine stains out of the carpet, and a suggestion was made that Happy Tea transfer to the nearby Sundown Tap.

Just as her mother, Jules, the original proprietor, had done, Chris Johnston still brewed a pot of nearly superfluous tea for the newspaper group who gathered every Friday after work, and it was she who greeted Susan and Haze at the Happy Tea just three days ago.

"Is this it?" she asked as the women settled into the center of the big, red semicircle booth. "Where's Mitch? Dale? Caro—"

"Seems everyone else has other plans," said Susan.

"Which means more scintillating conversations for us," said Haze. "As well as appetizers—Chris, why don't we start out with the CheeZee Bites—and by the way, I love the way you've done your hair. You look just like that woman in the insurance commercial."

Susan was once again amazed at the older woman's ability to give the perfect compliment. With her new updo, Chris *did* look like the woman in the ubiquitous ads, and Chris blushed, obviously pleased with the comparison, enough so that she announced the CheeZee Bites were "on the house." But a free appetizer was superseded by what Susan considered the real highlight: an hour of Haze all to herself.

As always, the columnist asked about Susan's boys.

"Jack's been pretty good about e-mailing," Susan said of her eighteen-year-old, who'd just left to spend his "gap" year traveling abroad. "He's only been gone a week, but I've heard from him four times already. Nice long e-mails too. He's *loving* London. He says he's got the "tube system" down pat."

"And Sam?" Haze asked, to which Susan shrugged.

"Honestly, Haze, he's either mad or sullen or eating a whole quart of ice cream."

"Well, he is a teenaged boy."

"He's taking Phil's and my breakup a lot harder than Jack is," she said and sighed before shifting the conversation to safer territory, to gossip about co-workers and mutual acquaintances: did Haze know, for instance, that Stanley Walpole, the bank president, had gone down to Minneapolis for a hair transplant *and* a tummy tuck?

"A tummy tuck! I didn't know men got tummy tucks."

"I read somewhere that men are having more plastic surgery than women," said Susan, pouring into her cup of tea a dribble of bourbon from the shot glass Chris had delivered. "Things like calf and bicep implants. No matter how old the man, he still wants to show off his muscles."

"No matter how old the woman," said Haze, "she still wants to show off her sex appeal. That's why I got my boob job when I turned seventy-five."

They laughed (the only time Haze subjected her body to a plastic surgeon's knife was to remove a mole on her shoulder), and Susan confessed that it was her goal to age as well as Haze.

"Age," said Haze. "I hate when that word's used as a verb. People don't describe kindergarteners as 'aging,' and yet we all are, I suppose, from the moment we're born."

When the Sundown Tap's most popular appetizer was delivered, conversation became secondary as they attacked the worth-every-calorie deep-fried cheese curds.

"Oof," said Haze, finally sitting back in the booth and holding her hands up in surrender. "Do not let me touch another one of those."

Susan pushed to the table's edge the small platter, whose two remaining CheeZee Bites slumped in sloughs of grease. "Out of sight, out of mind."

"Speaking of 'aging,'" said Haze, "did I ever tell you your grandfather wanted me to go into syndication?"

Susan in fact had heard this story but was always delighted to hear Haze's reminiscences about the newspaper—especially ones that had to do with her grandfather. She said, "Tell me more."

"He sent samples of my columns to a couple syndicates," said Haze. "One said, 'Too regional and *way* too confessional,' and another said, 'Is she trying to be Erma Bombeck or H. L. Mencken?'

"Frankly, I was glad, and told Bill I didn't want him to query any others because I thought syndication would have changed the way I wrote. I never wanted to sit down at the typewriter and worry about things like subscription demographics or tailoring my columns to this audience or that audience. I just wanted to write what I wanted to write."

"Okay," said Susan, "but just for clarity's sake, how does 'aging' fit into the topic of syndication?"

"Well, syndication would have given me more power, and power is one of the many things you lose when you get old." After a big sigh, Haze shook her head. "I guess I've just got the birthday blues. I'd like to think I'm not getting older, that I'm getting better—but am I? It's hard to think so when the world has such fixed opinions about older women."

"The world's going to *fix* their opinions about older women after the election," said Susan, a tease in her voice. "With our first female president!"

"That's right," said Haze, brightening. "When the Nation of Pantsuits rises up and demands to be counted!"

"I ALWAYS LIKED READING HAZE'S COLUMNS," says Caroline after hearing about the Happy Tea. "But now I want to go back and read a bunch more of them."

"I know," says Susan. "I've read every one since I started working here, but I've still missed years' and years' worth."

Their eyes widen as the lightbulb of an idea switches on for both of them.

"Let's go in the archives and read them," says Caroline, fingers moving on her keypad.

"No, not online," says Susan, as she stands. "Let's go into the real archives—Haze's office. She's saved *everything*."

OPENING THE BOTTOM DRAWER of one of several wooden file cabinets that crowd Haze's small office, Caroline says, "1964 to 1966. I guess it all starts here."

They unload the drawer and carry its contents into the conference room.

Seated at the long table, Susan takes out the manila folders that fill a speckled brown accordion file, and as she opens one, her eyes fill with tears.

"It's Haze's first column." She unclips an inch of papers attached to it. "And all the reader responses it got."

She passes half of the letters to Caroline, who peers at them like an archaeologist examining ancient papyrus.

"They actually *mailed* these?"

"That's what people did," says Susan. "They sat at their desk or kitchen table with pen and paper and *wrote*." She thumbs through the pages of onion skin, of flowery note cards, of monogrammed personal stationery. "And then they addressed an envelope, put a stamp on it, walked to the corner mail box, and dropped it in."

"So much *effort*," says Caroline.

"Oh my gosh," says Susan. "Here's a letter from the mayor at the time. Waldo Albeck. He wishes Haze good luck and hopes that she'll focus on 'the column-worthy business opportunities here in Granite Creek.'"

The conference room clock ticks away as they read letters written fifty years ago, grumbling about or praising the new columnist.

"I love all the different handwriting," says Caroline, when she gets to the last of her pile. "It sort of makes you know the letter writer a little better." She brushes her fingers along the engraved name on a piece of thick vellum stationery. "Like this, from Mrs. Paulette VanderVerk. I've never seen such beautiful handwriting."

Susan's shoulder presses against Caroline's as she leans in to look.

"It *is* pretty. And so was she. I remember her and her husband—he was a judge—visiting my grandparents. She had white-blonde hair that she wore in a French roll, and the pointiest-toed high heels I'd ever seen." She looks at the letter. "What's she say? Was she on the 'Yay, Haze!' or the 'Boo, Haze' side?"

"Yay," says Caroline.

"Most of the women were. Which makes sense, I guess."

It is past noon by the time they finish reading the contents of the first file, and the growl in Susan's stomach reminds her that eating hasn't been a priority in the hurly-burly of the past few days.

It reminds her assistant too, who asks, "Should I run to Rudolph's for some sandwiches?"

"That sounds great." She threads her fingers together and with her palms facing the ceiling, lifts her arms, her stretch long and luxurious.

As Caroline gets out her phone to call in their order, she asks, "So, turkey, tuna salad—"

"Oh my God," Susan says, dropping her hands to cap her head. "I just had the greatest idea."

2

July 16, 2016

EDITOR'S NOTE:

In her career, Haze Evans has won a fair number of prizes and accolades, but they were all "piffle" to her. Two years ago, I told her I was planning a big to-do to celebrate her fifty years' writing for the *Gazette*. It was a to-do on which she put an immediate kibosh.

"All I need," she said, "is for you to keep running my columns."

That's what we're going to do.

After five decades, Haze's columns still generate considerable reader feedback, but we were unaware of the volume of reader responses her long-ago columns inspired. Haze has kept meticulous files on every column, from readers' letters (noting which ones the paper printed), to interoffice memos. Until Haze can write for us again, we will be printing her old columns on a daily basis. Occasionally, we will include some of the letters readers wrote her in reaction to a particular column. Following is the very first column she wrote for the *Granite Creek Gazette*.

April 27, 1964

Cheerful Greetings, Readers!

I was thrilled when the peach organza prom dress I sewed won a blue ribbon at the statewide 4-H Career Day competition, thrilled when I graduated UND with a degree in journalism, and thrilled when the *Gazette* hired me away from the *Fargo Forum*. To be thrilled is a lovely state of being, one that I again find myself in now that I'll be writing a biweekly column!

Every year my bachelor uncle Ralph brought a different date to our family's holiday table, and one memorable Thanksgiving he was accompanied by Carol Bergeson. *Carol Bergeson!*

Thirteen years old and a recent graduate to the grown-ups' table, I was not only beside Miss Bergeson but *beside myself*. She may not be as well known here in Minnesota, but in the Dakotas and states west, she was the reigning Queen of the Rodeo, and throughout the passing of mashed potatoes, turkey, and candied yams, I deliberated over what sophisticated and witty words I might say to impress her.

"I saw you at the Dunn County Fair," I finally offered, watching her drizzle gravy over her generously filled plate. "You were wearing lots of fringe."

"I *always* wear fringe, darlin'," she said, "except at the dinner table, where it can get a little sloppy."

She was the nicest woman, with a big laugh and a headful of wild red hair, and she regaled us with tales of bucking broncos and rodeo clowns with drinking problems. Moreover, she had all the time in the world for a strangely pale teenager who thought she'd hidden a pimply chin and forehead with liberal pats of her mother's powder puff.

Uncle Ralph always whisked his dates away directly after dessert, not wanting, I suppose, to be part of the familial loosening of belt buckles, burps, and other noises repressed (and unrepressed), and when they were leaving, Miss Bergeson shrugged into her luxurious dark fur coat and pulled me toward her.

"Now remember, Haze," she whispered. "Everybody told me little girls didn't grow up to be rodeo stars. But I didn't listen to 'everybody'—I listened to myself. If you want something, chase after it, rope it, and pull it in!"

It is advice that has served me well, and after Walter Peterson announced his retirement, I thought, "That's something I want—his job! And so after it I went."

"Why should I give a features writer her own column?" asked Mr. McGrath, this paper's publisher. "A features writer who's only been with the *Gazette* for a year?"

"Because I love a good story," I said, practically ejecting from my chair. "I love hearing them and love telling them. And besides, I did a little research, and the *Gazette* hasn't had a female columnist since Ethyl's Kitchen Nook—and that was ages ago!"

"I believe it's been four years since Ethyl took her retirement," said Mr. McGrath, who went on to tell me how Ethyl had a point of view and how people who read her columns knew they were going to get tips for making moist pot roast and cute stories about who first dared to add grated carrots to their Jell-O salad.

"Just like with Ramblin's by Walt, they knew they were going to get a sportsman's slightly curmudgeonly view of the world as well as how the fish were biting on Flame Lake. What will they know they're going to get with you?"

"Who knows? We'll discover it together! I'll write what moves me, what riles me up or makes me sad, and just look at it from a business perspective—a column by a woman who could be the granddaughter of the columnist she's replacing—well, it could bring in not just younger subscribers but more women subscribers!"

The silence that followed was Grand Canyon–size deep, finally broken by the muffled rat-a-tat-tat of the pencil Mr. McGrath tapped eraser-side down on his desk blotter, and just as I thought he was going to tell me to get out of his office and pack up my desk, he sighed.

"All right. Have your first column on my desk Monday

morning. I'll give you a six-week trial run to show me what you've got."

So that's why I've written about Thanksgiving at the end of April. Because I'm really grateful.

Here we go. Wish me luck!

4/28/64
Interoffice Memo
FROM: JOAN DWYER

TO: HAZE EVANS

Haze—Thought you might be interested in your predecessor's reply to your column. Don't tell my boss I let you see this!

Bill—

What the hell was that? Maybe it should have been *you* who retired, because no offense, it looks like you've lost the discernment and taste that used to hold you in good stead as a newspaper man. What's with all those direct quotes— did you really say that stuff? And where was the blue pencil that should have cut this piece in half? The readership that I spent nineteen years building is *not* going to be happy with this shit! Send this twerp back to writing features on bridge parties and weddings!

Walt

P.S. And "Cheerful Greetings"? Here's my idea for her column name—"Puking on Paper."

P.P.S. Did you really call me curmudgeonly?

Susan had chuckled, imagining the office subterfuge of her grandfather's secretary passing on Walt's snide note about his successor, but out of all the correspondence Haze had paper-clipped to her column, she chose to publish only one response.

4/28/64

TO THE EDITOR:

My aunt gave my husband and me an "introductory" subscription to the *Granite Creek Gazette* when we first married. I always thought it was sort of cheap of her, because the "introduction" only lasted a month. What did that cost her—three dollars? But it was enough that we've kept up the subscription and the marriage (ha ha). My husband huffed and puffed while reading the new columnist (he *loved* Ramblin's by Walt), calling it a bunch of claptrap, but from what I've read, I hope she passes her trial run!

Sincerely,
Can't Use My Name Because My Husband Would Be Mad

"Then ditch the rat bastard," mutters Shelly. One of the many names Susan and Mitch call her is the Master Mutterer, although never to her face. Shelly does not go in for teasing, jokes at her expense, or heaven forbid, the tiniest inkling of what might be considered criticism. The area around her desk is carpeted in eggshells, or it seems that way, judging from the way everyone tiptoes through the reception area.

"She scared me half to death when I came in for my interview," Caroline once told Susan.

"She scares everybody," Susan had said, and even though she looked forward to the day when Shelly *finally* decided to retire, she was fond of the crotchety woman, who was one of the few holdouts from when her grandfather was still at the paper.

Now on her third Tums of the morning, trying to soothe a stomach agitated by a constantly refilled coffee cup and her own foul mood, the receptionist turns to the comics on page 12B. She supposes she feels bad for Haze, but not as bad as those who'd been fooled—unlike herself—by Haze's friendliness and bonhomie. It was her bitter joke that amid an office full of reporters, she was the only one who knew Haze's real story.

Shelly was hired in 1971, two days after her twenty-first birthday and exactly one month after she'd found scrawled on the magnetized refrigerator pad a note from her husband that read, "Bye Bye! I'm out of here—for good!" Shelly let herself believe for a few moments that maybe it was an April Fools' joke, even though it was already the fourth of the month, but the fantasy was short-lived when Ray called her that evening and offered an elaboration.

"I just got tired of you holding me back, Shel," he said from a pay phone in Des Moines. "Everything I wanted—from getting a little lake cabin to buying stock in General Mills to partnering up with Vern Anderson in his custom motorcycle business—you called a pipe dream. Your big problem, Shel—but it's no longer mine—is that you've got no imagination!"

Curling up like a salted slug, Shelly felt as if she were going to die and was surprised to find, by the sheer act of waking up the next morning, that she hadn't. Her first order of business as a jilted wife was to cut out pictures from the newspaper and *Life* magazine and use them to deface every photograph of herself and the rat bastard, starting with their Vegas wedding picture, in which they posed underneath a trellis threaded with plastic morning glories, he in a rented tux with a pink ruffled shirt, and she in the prom dress she had worn just months earlier.

"Is this imaginative enough for you?" she muttered, after gluing Steve McQueen's face over Ray's.

She smudged beads of Elmer's Glue on the back of a cutout cow's head and carefully pasted it over her own in a picture of her and Ray at a picnic table.

"So now you've got a thing for heifers, huh Ray?"

She found pictures of a heavily bearded gentleman, a basset hound, and an old woman with no teeth; these were all carefully pasted over her own countenance so that it appeared her rat-bastard husband had extremely bad and sundry tastes in partners. In other photos, the faces of movie stars were pasted over his, so that she appeared to have excellent taste.

She made a little album out of these reconstituted photographs, tying curly ribbon through the three holes she had jabbed into the construction paper with a paring knife, and kept it on her bedside table for years, until it was destroyed by a spilled rum and Tab, one of the three or four with which she tucked herself into the night.

SHELLY PICKS UP THE RINGING PHONE and in a voice pickled in vinegary sweetness agrees with the caller that yes, running Haze Evan's columns was simply a *wonderful* idea.

May 4, 1964

Hello from Haze!

Note to readers: I was up in Fargo Saturday for the funeral of a woman who was one of my first interviews when I wrote for the *Forum*. After our meeting, she revealed she had sudden concerns about her privacy and asked me not to write the story. I agreed, but now, after having learned of her recent death, I dug out my notes on our interview and decided to write what I hope is a tribute.

"My real name's Susan Elias," the costume designer told me in the slightly British accent the movie stars she worked with used back in the 1930s. "A perfectly fine moniker, but two weeks in Hollywood and I became SuZell."

Dyed an unnatural black, her hair was worn in a low chignon, like a ballet dancer's. Her face was pale, except for two feverish-looking spots of rouge. She held a cigarette in a foot-long ebony holder, given her, she informed me, by the Earl of Sussex.

"I was once given a ham on rye by the Earl of Sandwich," I said.

SuZell was not amused, her look implying that I had given her a sudden migraine. Stubbing out her cigarette in an onyx ashtray, she said, "Let's move on to my studio, shall we?"

The large room was filled with mannequins dressed in her designs.

"That was Roz's—*Rosalind Russell's*—favorite hostess gown. She told me she loved it so much she wore it to rags."

I replied that it looked brand-new.

Again the sudden, stabbing migraine look.

"She didn't wear *that* one. These are my original designs, *dear,* prototypes, as it were, from which I was commissioned others."

The clothing was beautiful; there was a business suit with linebacker shoulder pads she'd designed for Joan Crawford, a hoop-skirted ball gown for a Civil War movie, a pink blush of a dress whose silk seemed liquid. I could have spent hours examining the craftsmanship of the sewing, studying the way she set in a sleeve or draped a skirt on the bias, but touching anything was verboten and listening to SuZell rattle off the many testimonials she received to her genius . . . well, it got a little tiring.

"It's obvious you loved your work in Hollywood," I said, when we were back in her parlor. "What made you move back to Fargo?"

The migraine expression flashed on her face, and instead of answering my question, she said, "You sewed that blouse you're wearing, didn't you?"

Nodding, I flushed, wondering what misplaced dart or crooked seam had tattled on me.

"It's very well-constructed," she said, screwing a new cigarette into the end of her holder. "We designers are like architects, don't you think? Concerned with form and space and how it bests suits a person."

"I didn't design this," I said, tugging at my collar. "I used a pattern."

After lighting up, SuZell drew in what might be the longest inhale in the history of smokers, and her exhale put me in the middle of a fog bank.

"It might behoove you to learn how to accept a compliment," she said. "Especially from someone your superior."

It was then I thought my afternoon with the famous designer should end, and after I put my pen and notebook in my purse, the woman's rouged and powdered face did what it hadn't done before: became animated by laughter.

For a moment I wondered if I were dealing with someone who'd dropped a few marbles in the game of old age, and seeing my confusion, she laughed even harder.

"Have you had lunch?" she said finally, and when I shook my head, she added, "Fabulous. You can experience some more of my talents."

She served me a bowlful from a stove pot on slow simmer, and after my first spoonful of the orange soup, I said, "Oh, my."

"If I make something, I make it well," she said.

"What is it? It's so *good*."

"Sweet potato bisque. The sweet potatoes are from my friend Carl's farm. So is the cream."

I nodded, wanting to use my mouth to eat rather than talk.

"When I consider the damage canned soups have done to the American palate." SuZell shook her head. "Well, it's just like everything else. Convenience has overthrown quality as king."

The thick-crusted bread was homemade, and she used something called "a French press" to make our coffee. Dessert was light-as-air meringue cookies.

"I always kept a tin of these in my fitting room," she said. "Fairly low calorie, fairly big flavor. The stars loved them."

We talked through the afternoon, SuZell answering my questions thoughtfully.

Everything started, she said, when she flipped a coin in the chicken coop after she and her brother had finished collecting eggs.

"Heads was for New York. Tails was Hollywood. Tails won, and I packed a suitcase that night.

"You know that old song, 'How ya gonna keep 'em down on the farm'? My dad sang that at the supper table when I told them I was leaving." SuZell's face softened. "Dad and Mama were my biggest fans."

She talked about how the Hays Code put an end to the sensual gowns and dresses designers were making. "After that, the undergarments were like trusses." She talked about how confidence levels rarely went hand in hand with beautiful faces and figures. "In the end, it's all about feeling loved, isn't it? First and foremost by yourself."

When I asked again why she had returned to Fargo after all those decades in Hollywood, she shrugged. "It just tired me out. When they decided I was too old to work, what did that place hold for me? The family farm—now my nephew runs it—is only a couple miles west of town, so I see my brother and his family a lot—and I still have high school friends here. And of course, Helmer."

"Who's Helmer?"

The sudden migraine look flashed on her face, but it was quickly softened with a smile.

"Only the man who makes Clark Gable and Cary Grant *and* Gary Cooper look like two-bit stand-ins. The man the girl stupidly left behind, but the one the woman wisely came home to."

When I left, she gave me the kind of pin cushion you wear around your wrist like a bracelet.

"You always want to work smart," SuZell said. "Never take the shortcuts that will shortchange you, but if there's a shortcut that will get you there easier, take it."

May 6, 1964

TO THE EDITOR:

Having grown up in Fargo, I really enjoyed the piece on my old friend Susan Elias. We were chums from the time we first met in school, and I can't tell you how many fashion tips she dispensed throughout the years! "Why go for ordinary," she told me, when we were in the coat section at Orlandson's and I tried on a practical plaid mackinaw, "when you can go for extraordinary?" SuZell's success made all of us proud.

Mrs. Mildred Baccus

P.S. I wound up buying the plaid wool mackinaw anyway.

Among other reader responses was the one from the Ramblin's by Walt columnist, whose crabbed penmanship simply declared, "Still puking!" but Susan (who, Caroline teased, would be "SuMac like the shrub," if she combined her first and last names) chose not to publish it, nor did she print his response to Haze's following column—"This one drove me to the crapper!"

May 11, 1964
*Evans's Epistle**

In the small town in western North Dakota where I grew up, we had Crazy Days, a weekend set aside for all Main Street merchants to offer deep discounts, free samples, and giveaways. Anyone visiting Grudem's Shoes got a shoehorn, the five-and-dime gave children balloons, and Mr. Nelson of Nelson's Hardware handed out yardsticks. That was on Saturday; Sundays the stores were closed and instead replaced by kiosks selling ice cream and cotton candy, and there was a parade, whose participants were encouraged to dress, well, crazy. Playing in the bandshell were Cy Shelby and The Swingers, a quintet composed mostly of farmers, whose rehearsal studio was Cy's cow barn. (It was local legend that Cy's serenaded Guernseys produced extrasweet milk.)

As exciting as Crazy Days were, they could hardly prepare me for the launch of Granite Creek's first Nordic Fest.

Dreamed up by the civic-minded visionaries of the Women's Auxiliary and our local Sons of Norway chapter, the festival kicked off with a breakfast Saturday morning in the basement of St. Peder's Lutheran Church with lefse and the thick, rich Norwegian porridge that is rommegrot. The coffee was so strong that three days after the festival, I'm still up.

The Nordic Fest parade (more toned-down than that of Crazy Days) featured a contingent of women in their "bunads," the traditional Norwegian costumes representative of the area from which the wearer's ancestors came. Playing the fiddle, Ole Siggurson, served as a pied piper of sorts, leading the women, whose long skirts, jackets, vests and/or aprons featured beautifully intricate embroidery.

There was a bit of a lull after the parade, with no more events scheduled until the Swedish meatball supper that evening, hosted by Our Savior's, another of Granite Creek's Lutheran churches. Danish pastries were offered for dessert, which inspired one congregant to say, "Thank goodness, Denmark gets a little recognition in all this hullabaloo!"

Once the plates were cleared, we were encouraged to go into the sanctuary to hear Ardis Amdahl on the piano, accompanying her sister Gladys in a concert of Swedish folk music.

"Next year we hope to have more events for the children," said Avis Blake, president of the Ladies Auxiliary. "Maybe some clowns." At that point she turned to Dolf Romsaas, president of the Sons of Norway.

"Do they even have clowns in Scandinavia?"

*I'm having trouble coming up with a name for my column! All suggestions sent in will be considered!

3

"This is stupid," says Sam.

Susan breathes deeply—in her yoga classes she's learning the importance of breathing—before forcing her mouth into a fake smile.

"Sam, we've been through this. We—you and I—agreed you needed a summer job. It's already mid-July and—"

"I've been working at Dad's!"

"Yes," says Susan, trying not to react to his belligerent yet whiny tone. "On Saturday mornings, *occasionally*. That leaves you plenty of time for another job."

"Jack never had to work at the paper."

Susan smiles, to tamp down her simmering anger. "He was a paperboy for years, remember? But you're right, he didn't work in the offices, because he enjoyed working with your dad so much." She doesn't add, "And your father didn't find him napping in the RV he was supposed to be cleaning." Her smile grows bigger and more fake. "You'll see, it'll be fun. I've told you how much I enjoyed working at the paper when I was a teenager."

"Yeah, well, your idea of fun is a lot different than mine."

Again she chooses to smile rather than grit her teeth.

"And you're coming at the perfect time. We really need the help."

Sam rolls his eyes and rests his elbow on the passenger door frame. He and Jacob were going to ride their bikes down to the lake (whose narrow strip of beach is sure to be crowded with girls in bikinis) but no, he's got to go with his stupid mother, who's trying to ruin his summer vacation by making him work at her stupid paper.

WITH AN ALMOST SNARLED "Morning," the receptionist "greets" them, and this cheers Sam; he likes when adults don't try to cover up how miserable they feel.

He didn't tell his mother, but he's excited over the prospect of making money. Like Jack, he had been a paperboy, but Sam was not the wizard his brother was on a bicycle, riding no-handed as he flung papers on the steps of *Gazette* subscribers. No, Sam was much slower on his route *and* managed to get hit by a car—not hard enough to get hurt but hard enough to rattle his mother, who put an end to his delivery career.

His friend Jacob works part-time as a bag boy at the FoodKing, and Sam put in an application, or at least he told his mother he did. Jacob says it's easy enough and sometimes people tip him, but Sam doesn't like the stupid long red aprons the bag boys have to wear.

Stopping at the vending machine, he shoves in quarters, smirking at the annoyance his mother struggles to keep out of her voice as she says, "I'm sure there'll be water in the conference room." Out of the million things she bugs him about, she's been bugging him not to drink so much pop; all that sugar and empty calories, blah blah blah.

The *Gazette* has been running Haze's columns for only a couple days, and if Susan weren't aware of the crisis in the newspaper industry, she'd be convinced there wasn't one. Going by mere reader response, she'd assume the paper had a circulation with a couple more zeros added on to its actual number.

"Hey, Sam!" Caroline's voice is so bright and friendly it almost knocks him out of his sullenness. He can't quite bring himself to make eye contact with her (she's so pretty!) but responds with what he hopes is a businesslike nod.

Mitch, the managing editor, mimics his nod and says, "Welcome aboard, Sam!"

As she seats herself and nods toward Sam to sit down, Susan takes a yoga breath when her son takes his time settling into a chair opposite of the one she indicated.

"All right," says Susan, scooting her chair in closer to the conference table. "As you all know, the response to Haze's old columns has been phenomenal."

Mitch chuckles. "Shelly's about ready to unplug the telephone console."

Normally a few minutes might have been spent on joking about the sour receptionist, but not wanting to expose Sam to petty office gossip, Susan says again, with a little more emphasis, "all right," her preamble to getting down to business.

"The thing is, we have to figure out, where do we go from here? Caroline, you and I were talking yesterday about the order of the columns. So far, the few we've run have been in the order Haze wrote them—is that the way to go?"

Sam feels his ears redden as his mother looks at him. Does she expect him to *talk* at this stupid meeting?

"For me," says Caroline, "it's been really fun to read Haze writing as a young woman. Judging from what the readers are saying, they agree too. But I don't think we have to reprint every single column in order."

Susan chuckles. "Because that'd take us forever!"

Addressing Sam, who looks confused (or mad—it's hard for her to tell the difference), she adds, "Haze wrote two, sometimes three columns a week for fifty years."

Sam, who likes math, calculates the numbers in his head: two columns a week for fifty years would be fifty-two hundred; three columns a week for fifty years would be seventy-eight hundred. He can't help but say, "Wow."

"Wow is right," says Mitch. "She makes everyone else look like a slacker."

The phone on the console behind the table lights up, and after answering it, Caroline tells Mitch that Orin Mueller's stopped by to see him.

"Can't keep our biggest advertiser waiting," says Mitch, smoothing his tie as he gets up to leave.

"How about if we move ahead chronologically," says Susan, "but we can certainly skip weeks, months, even years. The content's the most important thing." She stands up. "I should say hello to Orin too. Caroline, why not get Sam started?"

Sam feels his face go red after his mother leaves and he's alone in the room with his mother's assistant.

"So, your mum's putting you to work, huh?" she asks, and Sam nods, knowing that whatever he said would sound totally stupid.

The only thing Sam can hear in the long silence that follows is the way-too-loud beat of his heart.

"Well, then," Caroline says, "how'd you like to work in an editorial capacity?"

"Huh?"

Caroline's smile is like an invitation, and Sam feels his muscles, which seem brittle with tension, ease just a bit.

"We could really use some help with figuring out what columns of Haze's to reprint. We've been reading the ones she wrote the first summer she was here, and we've picked some out to print. Did you read the one in today's paper?"

"Uh, no," says Sam, adding to himself, *as if.*

"She started off writing about the secrets contained in a woman's purse and somehow wove that into a story about a guy with a cello on a bus and then finished it by thanking readers for sending in names for her column. She listed a bunch of them—'From Haze's Hut,' 'Huddling with Haze,' 'Heavens to Evans'—but in the end she decided to just have her name be her column heading."

Sam can't think of anything to say so he says, "Oh."

"Believe me, it's a lot more interesting than I made it sound," says Caroline with a laugh. "So how about you read through some columns? You can jot down the subject of each one, and maybe which ones you especially like."

Sam takes a swig of his pop—too big a swig. It feels like a rock and takes a long time going down his windpipe.

"I don't know," he says finally. "I don't know if my mom would think that's . . . something I could do."

"Well, she told me to get you started, didn't she?" She pushes a file toward Sam. "This one begins in September. Enjoy!"

ALONE IN THE CONFERENCE ROOM, Sam texts, "HELP," to his girlfriend, Elise. "TRAPPED IN MY MOM'S OFFICE."

There is no response because he sends the text to himself. He knows it's stupid/psycho, although he's only doing what the counselor his mom made him see for a while advised—expressing his feelings. He's just not *relaying* them. He and Elise have gone to school together for years; they're acquainted, but only in his dreams is she his girlfriend. Still, he likes pretending he's having a conversation with her, even though it's totally one-sided. He also has occasionally texted/not sent to the singer Lorde, whose music he loves, and writers whose work he admires, and whenever he gets what he thinks is an innovative idea (like programming ice skates/roller blades to balance for kids learning how to skate), he'll text/not send to Steve Jobs, even though he's dead.

To lose his phone, to have someone discover these weird/psycho one-way texts is a fate he doesn't even allow himself to consider.

Leaning back in his chair, Sam puts his feet up on the conference table. Caroline had told him she had to get back to her office, and he worries that his supreme dorkiness sent her running. He sniffs his pits. Unoffensive (*in*offensive?)—whatever, they don't smell as far as he can tell.

He wonders what he'll do with his first check. Maybe he should start saving for a car? His dad's friend Mac keeps a classic 1967 Mustang blanketed in his garage—maybe he can buy that? He's got to wait until he's fifteen before he can get his permit—who wrote those lame stupid laws anyway? It's got to be a panel of mothers, he thinks, uptight, freaky mothers who have nothing better to do than worry about their kids rolling through a yellow stoplight or going two miles over the speed limit. He considers taking his shoes off—man, his feet are big! When did his feet get so big?—but his mother would probably run in with a can of air freshener, spritzing the room while yelling at him to try and act professional.

Sam sighs. His feet thump to the floor, and he leans forward, untying the string wrapped around a brown folder. His long sigh is a flag wave of defeat and surrender, and he opens a manila file and begins to read.

September 10, 1964
Back to School!
Her dress was red plaid, with a white bib bodice dotted with red buttons, and she didn't walk down the sidewalk so much as she skipped and hopped and danced across it.

"Come on, Petey! We don't want to be late!"

It appeared that's *exactly* what Petey wanted, lagging behind his big sister like a roped calf.

"Petey, come on! First grade's even better than kindergarten!"

Doubting this, the little blond boy burst into tears, and his sister put her arm around him, offering consoling words about a classroom gerbil and recess games of "Duck, Duck, Gray Duck" as well as a reminder not to eat paste, and then her voice was lost in the flurry of shouts, cries, and greetings of children racing into the school's entrance.

I hope Petey was entranced by the gerbil and recess games, and I certainly hope that if he did indeed eat paste, it was only a curious sampling and not of a quantity forcing a visit to the school nurse.

Never mind January 1; the first day of school has always been my first day of the year, when the possibility and excitement of whole new worlds crack open. There was an unofficial day, usually the last Friday of August, when my mother would take me to Engelman's five-and-dime for school shopping, an event I looked forward to with nearly the same anticipation as Christmas. My brother, Tom, and my sister, Vivienne, were older than me by ten and nine years, respectively, and so it was a holiday I celebrated only with my mother.

Oh, the delight of examining each notebook for quality of paper and uniformity of lines, of sliding open and shut the cover of a pencil case, of debating the merits of a pink rectangular eraser versus the little blunted-arrow ones you pushed onto the end of your pencil. Mother was a patient woman, but Job would get antsy with my methodical shopping, and she soon learned she was better served by situating herself at the soda fountain counter with a cup of coffee and an issue of *Photoplay* or *McCall's*.

After the selection of school supplies, I would pick out the special notebook to be used for the year's journal. No froufrou leatherette book with gilt-edged pages for me! I needed a workmanlike notebook to contain my deep and serious thoughts, ones I wouldn't address to "Dear Diary" but to a person I thought worthy of such deep and serious thoughts. (After all these decades, I still address my journal entries to this person, whose name shall remain anonymous . . . just because I don't have to share everything!)

Routine had it that my next visit was to the fabric section in the back of the store, examining the bolts of sturdier denims or corduroy for the gym bag my mother graciously sewed me every year. Once the morning had been whiled away in Engelman's, ritual called for a stroll across the street for lunch at Bertram's: egg salad sandwiches accompanied by a cup of beef barley soup for my mother, and a tin dish of chocolate ice cream for me.

Shoe shopping came next, and my long deliberation between patent-leather Mary Janes or brown Oxfords began to wear a tad bit on Mother, whose breaths became punctuated by sighs and whose fingers drummed a jittery tattoo on the arms of her chair. It was clever on her part that she spared herself the hours I would have spent shopping for a dress by sewing me one herself and surprising me with it the day before school. Knowing it was coming and that I would love it (Mother was an excellent seamstress with an eye toward the latest fashions) was the very best buttercream frosting on a rich chocolate cake.

I still get shivers thinking of the blue gingham dress with the white bolero I wore on the first day of seventh grade, so impressing the newly arrived from Chicago and oh-so sophisticated Loyce Denham that she lied, saying she'd seen the very same dress in the window of Marshall Field's.

So here I sit on a park bench directly across from an elementary school on its first day of classes, basking in the September morning sunshine, basking in all that excitement and promise of children ready to learn their ABCs, their fractions; lucky children who'll study about people like Newton and William Shakespeare and Betsy Ross, who'll be introduced to the mysteries of the solar system and a musical scale, who'll learn how to square dance and climb a rope and not to eat too much paste.

There are fourteen letters from readers clipped together, and Sam goes through them all. Most of them thank Haze for the walk down memory lane and the remembrances of their own school days it brought forth.

A man had written in faint, spidery penmanship:

I walked two miles to school in good weather. And in the winter my Pa would hitch up Sadie and pull me in the sleigh. Miss Monroe would greet us at the door, bell in hand. There was a wood stove in the back, and sometimes we spent recess gathering kindling. Ansgard Sonnestrom was pretty good about stocking the wood bin. Of course it was common knowledge the bachelor farmer had a crush on Miss Monroe. 'Course all of us schoolboys were in love with her too, I suppose.

The face of Miss Rosenblum, Sam's kindergarten teacher, flashes into his head; her pink full lips and her auburn hair that rolled softly at her shoulders, and her voice that always seemed on the verge of a laugh, as if she were constantly getting a charge out of her charges. Sam wanted to marry her when he grew up.

Lame, he thinks, feeling his face flush at the memory, and yet if he looked into a mirror, he would see that he was smiling.

Another letter reminds people that Mrs. Moutkis, the third-grade teacher at Granite Creek Elementary school for forty-five years, is celebrating her ninetieth birthday and all are invited to her reception at the VFW Hall on Second Street.

The next few columns he reads might be vaguely interesting—if he were an *old lady maybe* who likes to read about babies and popcorn makers and some television show called *Queen for a Day*. He sighs and turns to a column dated Tuesday, November 24, 1964.

My career in band lasted only through eighth grade (the clarinet is a beautiful instrument but not in my hands), and yet I've never forgotten the quote Mr. Baldry had taped above the chalkboard:

> *"Music expresses that which cannot be put into words and that which cannot remain silent."*
> *—Victor Hugo*

While not a talented performer of music, I am an avid listener, and yesterday I spent my lunch hour at Bonomo Records, flipping through racks of albums and 45s. Mr. Bonomo (any time I see him I want to break into the Bonomo's Turkish Taffy theme song) is the type of store owner who is amiable and knowledgeable, always willing to answer questions and help but also willing to sit behind the cash register, smoking his pipe and letting browsers browse.

I was doing just that, and needing to be cheered up, was in the rock 'n' roll section, comparing the black-and-white portrait on the *Meet the Beatles!* album with the orangish-sepia portrait of the quartet whose album was simply called *Kinks*. Whichever album I bought, I planned to play it loudly when I got home.

Sniffing a light and pretty perfume, I turned to see

a young woman wearing a Kingleigh College sweatshirt. Standing in front of the Broadway musical albums, she was sniffing too, and not in reaction to her own lemony fragrance, but because she was crying.

Going over to her, I asked if she was all right.

Her head bobbled, and I saw she was holding the cast album of *Camelot*.

"Oh," I said, immediately understanding the cause of her distress. "The record Mrs. Kennedy says they liked to listen to at night."

The young woman's lip trembled. "I was too young to vote for him when he first ran."

My eyes responded to her words by filling with tears, which surprised me because I thought after yesterday, I was all cried out.

"I'm majoring in elementary ed," said the young woman, "and the teacher I'm student teaching with? She said last year, when the announcement came over the PA system, her hands actually bled."

Seeing my startled reaction (was she talking about stigmata?), the young woman offered a weak smile. "She said the only way to keep herself from crying out was to clench her hands as hard as she could, and her fingernails actually broke her skin."

Still taken aback, I said, "Those must have been some pretty sharp fingernails."

"She files them pretty pointy. And I don't think she meant she was gushing blood or anything."

After an awkward silence, she added, "What a weird thing to talk about, huh? Sorry. It's just that I . . . well, I'm feeling so many things."

This I could understand. "Me, too."

A magical thing happened then; after a short orchestral introduction, the rich voice of Robert Goulet singing "If Ever I Would Leave You" filled the air.

The young girl and I moved closer to Mr. Bonomo and the *Camelot* album he was playing on the hi-fi near the cash register.

"My son Alan's in Colombia," he said. "Not the college— the country. He's in the Peace Corps. Helping build roads." He took a puff off his pipe. "It was all because of President Kennedy."

Mr. Bonomo moved the stylus back to the beginning of the album, and we listened to that entire album. Three other people came into the store, and they too gathered near. Nobody said anything, but there was an occasional sniffle, a clearing of throats.

Sunday marked the first anniversary of President Kennedy's assassination, and I spent it in my apartment, alone in my sadness. Yesterday I didn't feel so alone.

There are forty letters in this column's file, and Sam reads several that address various conspiracy theories; an unsigned one says the country is far better off without that rich SOB, but most are somber and sad in tone.

"Hey, Sam," says Susan, entering the conference room. She sits next to him, setting a can of sparkling water on the table. "I thought you might like a beverage."

Sam takes a sip, wishing it were Coke.

Regarding the piles of paper in front of her son, Susan asks, "Read anything interesting?"

Sam shrugs, his usual answer to many of his mother's questions.

"Okay then," says Susan, a trail of resignation in her voice. She turns to leave but freezes when Sam says, "Well, there is one thing."

Susan feels her shoulders tense, waiting for whatever snotty or whiny salvo he's going to lob her way.

"How come Haze's columns are all so different?"

It takes her a minute to process his civility.

"Well," she says finally, "she's a woman of many opinions and she observes—"

"No, I mean different size-wise. In length. Some are short, and others go on and on. Usually a column's about seven hundred words, maybe a thousand."

"How do you know that?"

Sam nods at his phone on the table. "I googled it."

Internally, Susan does a cartwheel. That her son noticed Haze's disparate column sizes and that he bothered to type in search words like "normal newspaper column size" thrills her.

"I'm surprised that you noticed that. It took me *much* longer—in fact, it wasn't until I'd gotten hired full-time after college that I figured out Haze didn't stick to a particular word count. So I asked my grandfather about it."

"What'd he say?"

Susan sips at her coffee, wanting to prolong this sweet moment when her son's voice is eager, *interested* in what she has to say. She's excited too that she has a piece of newspaper lore to share with him.

"He said that he used to publish her on the next-to-last page of the metro section, the same place he'd published the previous Ramblin's by Walt column. The weather was on the same page, and when Granddad realized Haze wasn't as strict with her word count as Walt had been, he'd adjust the page accordingly. For instance, if it were a short column, he'd list the temperatures in far-off places and maybe add a two- or three-line report on rainfall in Nepal or why the weather in Washington is so good for growing apples. If the column went long, the reader wouldn't know the temperature the day before in Berlin or Peking—uh, Beijing—because that would have been cut. I heard Granddad say this more than once: 'We just let Haze be Haze, because that's what our readers wanted.'"

Sam nods. "Makes sense." He picks up a letter. "Anyway, look at this—it's a letter from Mr. Dodd about a column Haze wrote about President Kennedy."

"Oh, brother. I can just imagine."

Harlan Dodd is their next-door neighbor, who several years ago declared himself a member of "The Tea Party" and who at the annual county fair will situate himself in a booth, wearing a tricornered hat, and rant about birth certificates and socialized medicine being the bomb that's going to blow up the country.

"No, that's the thing—it's not whack at all!"

Susan takes the letter and reads aloud:

"The day President Kennedy was murdered will forever be a stain on our national soul. We must all find a way as Americans to work together to fulfill the dreams this visionary president had for us."

Staring at the letter, Susan slowly shakes her head.

"I know," says Sam. "It's like some totally different dude wrote it."

4

August 10, 1965

I am not the only one writing about this story, but I feel more closely tied to it than the reporters who've come from Duluth and Fargo and the Twin Cities to cover it. How could I not feel proprietary; Connie Varner is married to Brian Varner, a news reporter who writes so eloquently for this paper!

"At first the doctor said twins," Brian said, still shaking his head over what's transpired. "A month or two later, he gave us the news that it was going to be triplets, and Con agreed, from all the activity, she was pretty sure there were more than two of them. But the fourth one! The fourth one waited for his birthday to let us know he was here!"

If you've fanned away the cloud of smoke that rose up from all the cigars Brian passed out, you've seen their pictures in the paper, but let me tell you, in person their darling-ness is off all recognized charts. Now that little Richard ("we'll see if he plays the piano as flamboyantly as *the* Little Richard," jokes his dad) is home from the hospital, the Varner household is a riotous and happy bedlam, filled with tag teams of friends and relatives helping feed, change, dress and rock four hungry, squalling, crying, sleepy babies.

Rita was my favorite, but only because I got to hold

that soft, warm bundle in my arms and she didn't make a fuss when I sang to her (although her face puckered for a bit when I tried to hit that high note). I'm sure Roxanne or Rhonda will be my favorites when I'm given the privilege of holding and serenading them with off-key lullabies.

Connie, who runs her nursery with an easy aplomb, told me, "If I think about all I have to do, I'd go crazy. So I don't think about it. I just do it."

That's a pretty good philosophy for almost anything, I reckon. And I took Connie's words to heart because I'm on a deadline with this column, and I had sat for too long in front of my silent typewriter, daydreaming and mooning over that sweet quartet of babies. But if Brian, their own father, can turn in a two-thousand-word prize-winning investigative report on taconite waste, surely I can tear myself away from my own daydreams and write something as well.

"I liked today's column, Miss Haze," says Mercedes Garcia, pulling open the blinds in the hospital room. "Four babies all at once!" She smooths the blanket over Haze's chest and begins to softly sing.

"You like that song, Haze? That was one my mother would sing to me. Mama had a beautiful voice, nicer than mine even, if you can believe that!" Mercedes chuckles. "I think lullabies are nicer in Spanish, don't you? More pretty. More soothing. English . . . better for traffic policemen! So hard, so bossy! Spanish is more . . . like a dancer's language, sí?"

Mercedes is the best kind of nurse, combining strength (she can lift—and has sometimes carried—patients heavier than herself) and softness. She will shave a man or help put on makeup for a woman when they want to rally for visitors; she'll sit bedside and listen to their complaints and fears, holding their hands if they want. Most always, they want.

She has lived in Minnesota for seven years, after accepting her daughter's invitation to join her in this northern state.

"Ay, it's so cold," she said to Christina, her first Thanksgiving holiday in Granite Creek. "I don't think I can live here."

She was serious: it was a cold that felt like an assault, and she felt cut up by ice that found its way into the wind, into the sleety snow, and onto the roads and sidewalks, making driving and walking perilous.

"Mama, you'll get used to it," said Christina, who had ventured from Los Angeles to attend the University of Minnesota on a full scholarship. "And you'll learn how to dress for it."

Manuel had been able to see his daughter collect her doctor of veterinary medicine degree, and during the ceremony had confessed to Mercedes that it was the proudest moment of his life.

"Next to when you got your nursing license," he quickly added.

They held hands over their armrests, and when they watched Christina stride purposefully across the stage to accept her diploma, he whispered, "She's just like you—wanting to help people."

"You mean animals," whispered Mercedes, and that caused a stutter of inappropriate giggles.

They had never said anything to Christina, but to each other they teased "as long as she's getting a medical degree, couldn't she get one that will pay more? In obstetrics or radiology or plastic surgery?" They did live in Los Angeles after all.

Four months later, Manuel was dead of a heart attack while watering a lemon tree in the lush backyard of a Bel-Air client.

"OH, I MISS MY MANNY," says Mercedes, running her fingers through Haze's lank hair. "He was always my partner in life, you know? My good things were his good things, and vice versa. We could brag so much about Christina, in a way we never would to anyone else, and then too, we could joke about her, the way we never would to a single other soul."

She sits down, drawing the chair close to Haze's bedside and listens for a moment to the old woman's breathing.

"Since I come here, I have been reading your columns, Miss Haze. I didn't learn English until I was seventeen and came to the United States. But ay, did I love learning it! It was hard for Manuel—

some people don't have that good ear—but for me English was a great adventure, and I, I was Ponce de León!"

Dr. Delancey scurries by the open door, but he doesn't look in.

The nurse shakes her head and whispers into Haze's ear.

"You're lucky Dr. Winner is your doctor. Might as well have a doctor with that name, sí? And he is good and kind. Not like Dr. Delancey, who thinks he is more important than any patient he might treat."

"All right," says Mercedes, standing up, eyes toward the monitors. "I must go check on Mr. Douglas, the old grabber who—"

There is a rap on the door frame.

"Hello, Mercedes," says Lois, mopping her face with a hanky. Haze teases her about being "such an old fussbudget with your hankies," but Lois inherited from her mother a drawerful of embroidered little cotton squares and can't see the point of not using them. "Whew, this air conditioning feels good. It's a sauna out there."

Mercedes nods sympathetically; it still surprises her how a place that can get so cold can get so hot.

"So how's our patient?" asks Lois.

"No change," says Mercedes. She raises her eyebrows, and her mouth bunches in an expression that conveys things could be better but they also could be worse.

After the nurse leaves the room, Lois sits next to her old friend. She won't use the hanky for tears—Haze would have none of that—but it takes her a moment to compose herself. If Haze *can* hear her, she wants to make sure she speaks in a strong and steady voice.

"I saw Janet Oakes at the FoodKing," she says. "Guess what was in her cart? Two steaks, two pints of cottage cheese and a carton of eggs! She's on some crazy 'all protein' diet, and she went on and on about already losing six pounds! My gosh, she can't be more than a size twelve to start with—what's the point? Well, we do know what the point is, don't we? She's man hunting, is what she's doing, afraid to be out in the world without a catch, even though once she reels 'em in, she doesn't know what to do with them!"

Lois shakes her head. "And then she has the gall to say how much she's enjoying reading your old columns, the ones you wrote when she was just a little girl! Ha! She may be younger than us but not that much younger!"

She sits still for a moment, imagining the wisecrack Haze would have had at the ready.

"Haze," she says, and a clog of emotion makes her clear her throat. "Haze, everyone's talking about your old columns! Susan— I was leaving your room just as she was coming in yesterday, remember?—anyway, Susan says young people are saying things like, 'They're so retro chic,' and older people are saying, 'Oh, it takes me back.' So come on, you've got to wake up and enjoy your expanding demographics!"

Lois studies her friend's face. It looks younger, in repose; instead of dragging her features south, gravity kindly settles on them. But her hair! Haze always had the best hair—thick and wavy, even as she was careless in its upkeep (unlike Lois, who attends her Thursday-morning hair appointment as reverently as a nun attends mass).

Now Haze's hair is greasy and plastered to her head, and Lois makes a mental note to talk to one of the nurses about washing it.

"I wonder if they'll reprint the column about our meeting—remember that, Haze?"

As it celebrated the beginning of their friendship, Lois'll never forget it, especially as she cut it out and framed it, and it's hung above the kitchen light switch for decades.

June 8, 1966

For any of you disturbed by my behavior at the Corcoran Veiber lecture Wednesday night, my apologies. I really couldn't help myself.

There was excitement in the air in the theater lobby—a famous author had come to town! I admit I wasn't familiar with Mr. Veiber's work, although once I saw his name on the Cultural Events calendar, I checked *Incident in Rhodesia* out of the library and had gotten halfway through it.

Once inside the theater, I took my seat, smiling at the woman next to me and remarking to her how I couldn't remember ever seeing so many men in the theater.

"Mr. Veiber has lived the sort of life Hemingway would have liked to live."

"Really?"

"That's what it says in the program," said my seatmate, shrugging. "I personally haven't read any of his books. I just like coming to these lectures."

After Mayor Albeck introduced "a man whose work has influenced and enlightened me and a generation of men with his huge appetite for life's adventure," the room exploded with applause, as the author appeared stage right.

"He looks like he has a huge appetite for life's *food,*" my seatmate whispered, as we peered over the rows and rows of men who'd jumped to their feet.

That caused our first giggle.

Mr. Veiber was certainly big-boned, with boulder shoulders and long legs that had a lot to do with his six-foot-two-inch height (also noted in the program), but it was that which had nothing to do with his bones that was truly awesome in size: his belly.

I mention this because it seems to me a man rarely apologizes for his excess girth and even seems proud of it (unlike women). Mr. Veiber wore a cape (indeed, it would be hard to try to button a suit jacket around that girth), and as he strode to the podium, he swirled that cape like he was preparing to dance the flamenco or fight a bull, igniting more giggles between my seatmate and me, which went unnoticed in the clamor of the standing ovation.

I wish I could say once Mr. Veiber began to speak, the adolescent behavior of Lois (we couldn't share all that laughter without sharing names) and me disappeared, but the fact is, the *more* the great man spoke, the harder it was to keep a straight face.

To begin a speech about how you "don't want to jinx anything, but you're reasonably sure the next time you're behind a podium is when you're accepting the Nobel Prize for Literature" sets a certain tone.

The writer proceeded to tell of his beginnings with a "slattern" for a mother, who'd married into wealth but whose soul was impoverished and whose life mission was that of sucking dry all creativity and daring in her son.

Along with frequent eyebrow raising, Lois and I quietly tsked and nudged one another.

"Multiply that with three dull sisters who followed the lead set by Mother and you've got a boy who has to fight to protect what is precious and good."

The giggles began in earnest when the writer began speaking of the only woman to understand him, to nurture and recognize his great talent, his Italian lover, the bella Luciana. On and on he went about a college semester spent abroad, and how this paragon of beauty and virtue helped convince him that it was literature, and not law, that was his destiny.

If he wasn't bragging about how he could see and feel things others couldn't, he was bragging about how he could make others see and feel things with his universal, yet singular style of writing. When he started bragging about his prowess as a ladies' man, "even though all the women who came after Luciana were trollops and gold diggers and murderous vixens, all" (yes, that's a direct quote), Lois and I could no longer contain ourselves. Our stifled giggles had grown too big to stifle and were the subject of many turned heads and disapproving looks, and finally we had to escape into the fresh air of the lobby.

We joined a man at the coat-check room and asked him why he was leaving early.

"Probably the same reason you are," he said. "I enjoy Mr. Veiber as a novelist, but as a person, he reminds me of a blow bag of an uncle I take great pains to avoid." He centered his hat on his head and gave the brim a quick tug.

"I'm sorry I had to sit through that, but it must have been especially hard for you trollops and gold diggers."

We all got a big laugh out of that one, and when Lois added, "Don't forget us murderous vixens," I knew I'd made a friend.

"Oh, Haze," says Lois with a chuckle, "remember all the letters you got after that one? Remember how Mr. Veiber's publisher even threatened a lawsuit and you were so proud of your own publisher standing up for you? How he said you had every right to offer your 'review' of his performance, just as a book reviewer had every right to write his or her opinions?

"I was so flattered, feeling like your co-conspirator, and I guess that's still how I feel."

Lois leans into her friend.

"I'm conspiring with you right now, Haze. Conspiring with you to get that feeding tube out of your nose, conspiring with you to heal that brain of yours, conspiring with you to come on back. I mean it, Haze. Come on back."

5

"'So it was cool getting a couple day's work, and they said I could stay on as long as I like, but I didn't come here to work in a hostel in Madrid! 'Course you'll probably wish I did when I run out of money and start asking you for loans. LOL Hasta la vista, baby!'" Phil stares at his phone for a moment, chuckling. "He's always been a go-getter, huh?"

Pretending to study the menu, Sam doesn't answer.

"He's taken some great photos too." Phil's thumb moves along the phone's screen. "I don't know—maybe that's how he could fund his trip, selling his pictures—have you seen this one?"

Phil holds out his phone, and Sam nods, thinking, Yes, Dad, I've seen your brilliant son's brilliant photos. They're all over his fucking Instagram page.

"It's amazing the quality of pictures these phones can take. I remember getting a Polaroid in the eighth grade, and I couldn't imagine anything getting any more modern—I mean a photograph that developed right before your eyes! But these things!" Phil looks at the phone again, shaking his head.

The server brings a coffee and a Coke, and they order—Sam chooses the beef burrito and a chicken taco—and he tries not to stare as the pretty young woman in her flouncy ruffled skirt bounces toward the kitchen.

"So how's the new job?" asks his dad. "Does it make you miss vacuuming out RVs? Or should I say taking a nap in one of the RVs you're supposed to be vacuuming out?"

Sam's face reddens—his dad'll *never* let him forget that one.

"So they've got you doing what? Making copies? Running errands? Getting people coffee? If I worked for the paper, I'd rather work down at the printing press than in the office—at least you'd get some physical exercise and—"

"I'm mostly helping with Haze's columns," says Sam, jabbing his straw in his pop glass.

"How can you help her with her columns? Didn't she have a stroke?"

"Dad, are you kidding me? We've been running her old columns from like fifty years ago, and people are going *insane*. They can't get enough of them."

His dad sips his coffee.

"You really haven't been reading them?"

"Sam, just because I'm married to the *Gazette*'s publisher, doesn't mean I read every single thing the paper prints."

Sam's heart thumps at his father's use of the present tense to describe his marriage.

"Especially something I know wouldn't be relevant to my own life."

"What do you mean?"

His dad laughs. "Come on, Sam. I'm a guy. What am I going to get out of an old lady writing about old lady stuff?"

It bothers Sam that he can't tell when his dad's joking or not, and he doesn't return his dad's smile, which makes Phil try even harder.

"And what kind of name is 'Haze' anyway?"

"You seriously don't know?" says Sam. "We just reprinted a column about it."

May 30, 1967

It's my brother, Tom, older than me by ten years, who dropped the *I* from my name and called me Haze.

When I was brought home from the hospital, legend has it that he held me in his arms and sang, "She puts us in a daze, our little Haze." He sang it throughout my childhood, and I can't tell you what I'd give to hear that playful little ditty sung by Tom.

He did not have the same good luck my sister's husband, Harold, or my cousin Stewart had. He did have the same bad luck his very best friend, Eddie Wilkes, had in that neither of them came home from the war. At least alive. Tom was killed in the battle of Saipan in 1944, two weeks after Eddie lost his life in the Normandy invasion.

Eddie had black hair and blue eyes and the whitest teeth I'd ever seen, and like every sentient female, I had a crush on him. He was a regular presence at our house and supper table, and his sense of humor often manifested itself in practical jokes, which were greatly appreciated by us kids, less so my parents. He was the first to possess a whoopee cushion, a joy buzzer, and rubber vomit and was suspended from school twice for his enthusiastic use of them. He had a beautiful tenor voice and a repertoire of popular songs and was happy to elevate Tom's less accomplished piano playing in impromptu parlor concerts.

Years later, I stood on risers at my high school choir concert, bewildered and frightened, watching my mother flee the hall as we sang a Gershwin medley.

Afterward, she fanned her face with the concert program and explained to me her exit. "It was 'You Can't Take That Away from Me.' Whew." Tears sparkled in her eyes. "I can't hear that song without remembering how lovely Eddie sang it."

And Tom! How did my parents ever recover from the loss of their only son?

Mother claimed that Dad installed a hoop above the garage door the day after Tom was born; he certainly passed on his love of basketball to their firstborn. Father and son joked that it was their office, with Dad issuing the stern command, "Tom, meet me in my office!" and Tom pretending to sulk, pretending to drag himself out of the chair from which he wanted to leap. "Oh, *all right.*"

The only time I saw my father strike my brother was when Tom came home the summer after his first year at college and announced that he had enlisted in the navy.

"I'm hoping to get a South Seas assignment," he said. "They say it's—"

Dad's palm slapped away whatever words "they said" out of Tom's mouth, and my mother called out, "Byron!" and I cried out, "Daddy!" and Tom stood staring at the carpet runner, his hand cupping his cheek, and Dad stood there looking like it was he who had just been slapped, and then he did something else I'd never seen him do: he began to cry.

He and Mother and Tom talked late into the night, long after Vivienne came home from a night out with girlfriends, whose beaus were also overseas, and long after I'd been sent to bed. The bedside clock had a luminescent face that read 12:42 when Tom came into my room.

"You up?" he asked, knowing I would be.

"Yes," I said in a small voice.

He sat down in the rocking chair that my grandmother had brought over from Norway, the chair that had wound up in the room of the last child to have been rocked in it. Next to it was a little basket that stored some of my toys, including a small rubber ball, and Tom picked it up and threw it to me.

It was our ritual, playing catch as we talked, and there were often long pauses between sentences when the only sound in the room was the splat, splat of a caught ball and maybe a "good catch" or an apology for a bad throw.

"Haze," he said after the ball had been passed between us dozens of times, "I'm sorry you had to see that. You know Dad loves me, don't you?"

"We all love you!" I said, and threw the ball with such wild aim that Tom had to flail his arm to catch it. He then dropped the ball in the basket, and coming to sit at the foot of my bed, he picked up one of the teddy bears who kept sentry there.

"You know he slapped me just because he was scared, right?"

Burrowed under the covers, I nodded.

"He doesn't have to be scared, Haze. If anyone knows how to watch out for himself, it's me! I just, I just feel like this thing, this war is like a forest fire or a volcano or something, and it needs every able-bodied man it can to help put it out, you know?"

"It could go out without you," I said, my voice muffled.

Tom addressed his next comment to the teddy bear. "I can't believe it—even Haze is against me."

I quickly assured him I wasn't and to cheer him up, suggested we "sing our song."

And so we sang "You Are My Sunshine."

Tom was usually the one to make me laugh, and I always tried to return the favor. A few years earlier, when I'd first heard the song on the radio, I asked him why anyone would name their son "Shine."

"Oh, Haze, you kill me," he had said, pretending my child's pun was a real knee-slapper.

I killed him in a good way; a torpedo killed him in a bad way.

Two songs that do our family in: "You Can't Take That Away from Me" and "You Are My Sunshine."

PFC Lance Tolan didn't enlist, but a low draft number sent him to Vietnam, and after reading his obituary last week, I called his family. Lance's mother and I talked for a long time, and when I asked her if she wanted me to write anything about Lance for my Memorial Day column, she said yes.

"Tell them that he had big dimples and everyone said he looked like a young Sean Connery as James Bond. Maybe that's why he liked to read spy novels! Tell them that he wanted to go into the FBI. Tell them that he could multiply big numbers in his head and that he was a talented cartoonist who always illustrated the letters he sent home.

Tell them that he had to buy a second *Pet Sounds* album by the Beach Boys because he wore out the first one playing it so much. His father and I listen to it every night in his honor."

Sam had been in the conference room reading Haze's column and the response letters paper-clipped to it. When he read the first letter, a flare of anger rose in him.

Are you kidding me? he thought as he read the letter by some jerk named Snell, who was in deep need of what last year's English teacher had pounded into her students: the importance of critical thinking. That's all you got out of this?

TO THE EDITOR:

I do not subscribe to the *Gazette* to hear thinly disguised antiwar propaganda. Hitler was a menace who threatened the world. What would your naive columnist do—let the tyrants and despots take over? A soldier's death is always hard, but let her be comforted by the fact her brother—just as young Mr. Tolan—died in glory, in the highest of service, to their country.

Sincerely,
Mr. Joseph Snell

He was shocked when he read the next letter.

TO THE EDITOR:

Sometimes I feel the world's gone crazy and I'm the only sane one, and other times I think I'm nuts too. Like Haze, I lost someone—an uncle—in the Normandy invasion. He was only twenty-nine, and he'd taught me how to ride a bicycle and, later on, how to change a bicycle's flat tire. My mother's best friend lost her husband in the battle of Okinawa. I thought that might be the war that ended all of them, but then along came Korea, and now I have a cousin whose son is listed as MIA in Vietnam.

What and when do we ever learn?

Harlan Dodd

As Sam tells his dad about the column and the responses it got, Phil wonders when he last saw his son so animated, so excited.

"Now, I'd read *that* column," says Phil when Sam finishes. "And I can't believe an old fart like Harlan Dodd could write a letter like that!"

"Right?" says Sam with a laugh. "Actually, it's the second letter of his I've read. And the first one was the opposite of the way he is now too." He leans over the burrito and taco he had ignored while telling his story. "That's the thing. I thought—like you—I was gonna be stuck reading a bunch of old-lady shit—uh, crap—and some of it *is* crap, but a lot is—I don't know, there's a lot of stuff that . . . that makes you think about stuff."

Phil resists the urge to reach across the table and ruffle Sam's hair and instead watches as his son attacks the food on his plate.

"Sam," says Phil, both amused and stunned, "slow down. You're going to choke."

The plate is clean in what seems like seconds, and Sam sits back, as if a little stunned himself. He swipes at his mouth with a napkin.

"I'd love to sit around and shoot the breeze, Dad, but I gotta get back to work. Muchas gracias for lunch."

AS HE ENTERS THE RECEPTION AREA, Shelly arranges her features into what she considers a smile but what looks to the rest of the world like a wince.

"I like your shirt," says Sam, and he flushes, feeling as if he had no control of the words that suddenly flew out of his mouth.

"Thank you," says Shelly, splaying her hand over her collar, as if trying to hold in a rare compliment.

Sam racewalks away, the word "awkward!" blaring through his brain. At the fountain by the vending machine, he laps up water like a parched dog and wipes what's dribbled onto his chin with his forearm.

Before she rounds the corner, Ellie Barnes announces her presence with her perfume, which to Sam, smells like a cherry juice box.

"Good afternoon, Samuel," says the features editor, who, like a skunk, has a white stripe in the middle of her black hair. "Say, I brought in a pan of sweet potato brownies. They're in the break room."

"Great!" says Sam, even though he's learned to avoid the treats brought in by Ellie, as she seems to follow recipes that confuse "healthy" for "tasteless" or "granular."

On his way to the conference room he passes Haze's office and is surprised to see his mother inside, sitting at the desk.

"Mom?"

Susan looks up, a dazed expression on her face.

"Oh . . . Sam! Did you . . . did you have a nice lunch with your dad?"

"It was okay. We went to Rosa's." Standing in the door's threshold, Sam folds his arms, not liking the thrum of anxious concern he feels. "Mom, were you crying?"

Susan pinches her nose with a tissue. "Oh Sam, I've just been reading all about Haze's marriage."

Relieved she wasn't crying over something that had to do with their family, he asks, "Haze was married?" and taking six steps across the small office, he plops himself in the chair facing his mother.

"*And* she wrote columns about it," says Susan. "Not enough, but what they lack in quantity they make up for in quality." She sniffs and blinks hard.

Not wanting to witness more tears, Sam leans forward and spins the file on top of the desk.

"'On Love and Marriage,'" he says, reading the yellowing label.

"I knew Haze kept a chronological file of every column she wrote, but I didn't know she had a special file reserved for the ones she wrote about her husband. I found it in there." Susan nods to a cabinet drawer still pulled out.

Sam reaches into the file and takes out a thin sheaf of papers.

"Don't!" Immediately Susan offers a sheepish, "Sorry. But I still haven't read those." She dips her hand toward the paper-clipped stack of papers to her left. "I want to know what happens in order."

He shrugs, and worried that she somehow offended him—she seems to have a special knack these days in offending her son—Susan asks, "So . . . tell me more about your lunch."

"Mom," says Sam, and as an idea blooms in his head, his eyes grow large. "Mom, you should run those columns in order."

"What columns—"

"the ones about Haze being married! I mean—they're making you cry! And Mrs. Athorn"—she was Sam's English teacher last year—"says that a good story always has a reader asking, What happens next? If *you* want to know, and it sure seems that you do, I bet lots of other people would too. I know I would." He feels himself color. "I mean, shi—sheesh. I didn't know she was ever married."

The circumferences of Susan's eyes widen as she mimics her son's earlier expression.

"Oh, Sam. That's a great idea."

"It is?" Sam says, and enjoying the compliment, he'd like her to expand on it, but Susan's already crossing the room, shouting for her assistant to stop the presses, and Sam doesn't care how lame a joke it is, he laughs.

6

"Haze Evans's fan base has never been limited to a certain age group," wrote Susan in the *Gazette*. "She hears from high schoolers as well as octogenarians, but only those who were reading her in the late sixties and early seventies were privy to a type of column she has not since written. Columns on marriage, specifically her own. It is our pleasure to reprint Haze's love story, as she wrote it."

December 31, 1967

I don't make many New Year's resolutions, having learned long ago that I seem to forget the root word of *resolutions* is *resolve*. The word should be changed to *considerations,* as in, "I'm considering not to eat my weight in chocolate this year." You can't break a consideration, you merely ignore it, which to me would lead to a lot less guilt and self-recrimination.

The one resolution I have remained committed to is that every New Year's Eve, I write in my journal a wrap-up of the year to which I'm about to bid adieu. I have remained committed to this practice since I was thirteen years old and, missing a childhood friend who'd moved away, I wrote him a letter recounting all the adventures we'd had together. The next year I recapped for him the ups and downs of 1948 and did the same thing for 1949, but the next year the letter was returned to me as "address unknown." Thereafter, my year-end summations were recorded in my journal. I submitted this column so that it will run New Year's Eve, but you can believe that before I attend this year's party, I will have sat down and looked back on the year, recording the high and not-so-high lights. But for you, dear reader, let me tell you about the year's highest light.

Two of the girls in my high school class got married the summer after graduation. Three more said, "I do" the next year (sadly, I've got the bridesmaids' dresses to prove it), and after that, it seemed a race to marry off all seventeen females of the class of '53. I may indeed be the last one, but I believe there's something to the saying, "saving the best for last."

On December 23, in my hometown in western North Dakota, I said, "I do," and in answer, a man said, "I do too." (Insert big whoop of delight here.)

Let me tell you a bit about my groom. Like me, he was his high school's valedictorian, although his class (he grew up in Houston) was slightly (ten times!) bigger.

He's kind and handsome and boasts a flashy name, which somehow fits this humble man. In his spare time, he likes to walk his dog (now *our* dog), snow ski and waterski, play piano, and sing in the St. John's by the Lake choir. Now here's the biggest clue: Some of you have had close personal contact with him.

Yes, my brand-new husband is Dr. Royal Kirby!

Our courtship may have not have been a secret to those who've seen us around town, at Zig's Supper Club (try their Chicken Kiev), in the audience at the Palace Theater (I'm still chuckling at Louis & Lewis—that comedy duo from Scotland), or picnicking by the falls. But when we started dating, Royal asked that we keep our personal life out of the paper, and it's an agreement I've kept, until now.

"I can't *not* write about getting married!" I told him, and he reminded me that I had already written our wedding announcement. (See the upcoming Sunday edition.)

"At least let me add my two cents' worth," he said.

"Okay, but a good writer tries to avoid clichés like 'two cents' worth.' "

Herewith, from the pen of my new husband, whose handwriting is much better than his prescriptions would suggest:

> *I have always been a lucky man. Lucky to know from a young age I wanted to be a doctor, lucky to have parents and teachers and ultimately funds to support that dream, lucky to land in this beautiful lake-filled state where I have learned to say "uffda," to eat lutefisk on Christmas Eve, and to love seasons, including—and especially—winter.*
>
> *In meeting and now marrying Haze, my good luck has magnified. I thought I enjoyed bachelorhood too much to give it up, but that was before I met my bride. I am older than Haze by fifteen years, and yet she makes me feel like a schoolboy. She makes me laugh, she makes me sing louder, she makes me want to be a better person. She is, for me, just what the doctor ordered.*

Yes, I cried when I read that. Who wouldn't? So here's to us, here's to all couples who find one another and hold hands through the rose gardens and brambles of life. My utter happiness is only slightly colored by the guilt of taking Granite Creek's most eligible bachelor off the market. Sorry—and Happy New Year!

"Oh," Susan had said softly while reading a memo note attached to the column. "Listen to what my grandfather wrote." She cleared her throat. "Haze, I had to call Royal to make sure he was still on board with this. He says, 'Fire up the presses!—she's worth any flack I get!' Just wanted you to know—Bill."

Susan's smile was faraway. "I'd forgotten what good friends my grandfather and Dr. Kirby were. Granddad had a picture of them on the golf course in his office. He told me that he enjoyed the conversations they'd have walking the course more than the game itself. In fact, if I remember the story, it was at my grandparents' New Year's Eve party that Dr. Kirby and Haze were introduced!"

Caroline had been reading a different sort of letter.

"It's from that same Mr. Joseph Snell," she said. "He writes that a doctor is a public figure and writing about his personal life 'trivializes his profession and the confidence of his patients—which I am relieved to say, I am not!'"

"Well, he's in the minority," said Susan, and indeed the pile of letters offering congratulations and best wishes dwarfed the two letters whose writers were not happy with the newlyweds' column.

"MY GOODNESS, WHAT A LOVELY WEDDING STORY!" says Caroline's mother, who reads Haze's columns online from her home in Winnipeg. "So romantic!"

"Wait'll you read tomorrow's." The phone slips away from its precarious anchor against Caroline's shoulder. "Hold on, Mum, I'm going to put you on speaker."

"So how is she doing?" Mrs. Abramson's concerned, amplified voice fills the kitchen.

"Still unconscious to the world," says Caroline. "I went to see her last night." She hiccups a little gasp.

"Oh, sweetie."

"It's just that . . . well, as old as she is, she's just so young, you know?"

"They can do wonderful things these days. Remember Midge Sedgewick was on death's door, and now with that new kidney she's back bowling!"

"Which you must have mixed emotions about," jokes Caroline, knowing Midge has always been her mum's number one rival in her bowling league.

"Honestly, Caroline, that's not funny," her mother says with a sniff. "Now come on, I want to know how things are in the romance department for you! Yesterday I saw your old boyfriend Dan

Merchant at Tim Hortons—he was sitting at the counter all by himself and—"

"Got another call coming in, Mum," lies Caroline. "Love you, talk to you soon!"

February 15, 1968

I wish I could write about the most romantic Valentine's Day a newlywed ever experienced . . . but if I did, I wouldn't be writing about my own.

It started off wonderfully. When I got up, Royal had already left for the hospital but had thoughtfully left a nice gushy card propped up against the toaster, and later at the newspaper there was a delivery of red roses (tip to men: you will earn big points by sending your wife flowers that she gets to accept in front of her co-workers!).

The plan was to meet at Zig's for a romantic dinner, and I was lavish with the perfume and the lipstick, and when Royal strolled in, my heart skipped so many beats I thought I might need to be resuscitated. (Thankfully, he is a doctor.)

It's a lovely thing to fall in love, especially when clocks and society are ticking and tsking, and you yourself wonder if that old-fashioned and ugly word *spinsterhood* is going to apply to you. The man of your dreams doesn't appear— but someone even better comes along, and defying logic, he thinks you're not so bad yourself, and you're a bride at exactly the time you were supposed to be.

I was aware that there were other life-forms around us, but our table was our very own candlelit universe. We ate shrimp cocktails, and I had a glass of champagne because after all, it was a celebration. Royal had soda water, because he was on call, but surely Cupid would conspire to prevent all medical emergencies.

Cupid wasn't cooperating. The hospital phoned just as we were about to order our entrées (I was debating between my old favorite Chicken Kiev or the Steak Diane).

Royal was apologetic, but duty called, and I assured

him that I understood, which was ninety percent true. Well, seventy-five percent. Okay, forty percent.

I watched him leave, and he hadn't taken two steps away from our little candlelit universe before his posture changed, and he took brisk and efficient strides across the room and out the door, and I knew that if I were a patient, I'd want that brisk, no-nonsense efficiency.

The good people of Zig's boxed up my dinner, and once home, I was all set to devour that Chicken Kiev, but when Brigadoon (once Royal's dog, now *our* dog) signaled that she wanted to go out, I decided that instead of a walk, I'd take her for a slide, and after changing into flannel-lined denim jeans and grabbing my skates, the hound and I were off to Kingleigh Lake. It was a cold night, and the moon wore a veil of clouds, and most of the frozen lake was covered in snow, except for the big rectangle the city always plows off for skating.

Brigadoon loves being out on the ice almost as much as I do. She runs at first, because of course dogs free of their leashes and fences will run, but remembering the surface she's on, she surrenders to it, stiffening her legs and sliding. Across the ice she slides, and if there's a picture that captures glee better, well, I'd like to see it.

There was a teenaged couple skating hand in hand and a hockey player shooting pucks into an unguarded net, but all of them stopped to watch this mutt skidding across the ice.

Like Brigadoon, I feel a joyfulness on ice, and when my blades made contact with that smooth, hard surface and I pushed off in a long glide, I thought, *ahhh*.

I skated around the perimeter backwards, the blades of my skates making the sound of industrious scissors snipping. No threat to Peggy Fleming and her gold medal, I am nevertheless a fairly good skater who can do a couple tricks, and as I spun and jumped, my lungs filling with that cold frosted air, the heaviness of being stood up (yes, I know I hadn't really been stood up, but I was feeling sorry for myself, okay?) on Valentine's Day lifted, and when Brigadoon slid into me as I was crouched down, leg extended in a Shoot the Duck* pose, I had to laugh. Hard. When I got home, I built a fire and made a cup of hot chocolate with a five-inch fluff of whipped cream on top, and sat sipping it, covered in the furry warmth that was my tired-out pooch, who'd been allowed up on Royal's big easy chair.

In grade school, onto the well of the chalkboard, we'd clip paper bags we'd decorated with paper doilies and red hearts, depositing our classmates' valentines in them, and I remember the thrill of taking that decorated paper bag home and reading every rhyme and studying every illustration on every valentine carefully, trying to discern who really, *really* liked me (what did it mean that Joel Morris and Todd Coons gave me the exact same Popeye valentine?).

It was just past eleven when Royal came home, with the good news that the emergency gall bladder surgery had gone well.

He promised me that next year he'd make a point to not be on call on Valentine's Day, but honestly, I don't care if he is. If someone needs their appendix out or their broken leg set or their baby delivered, I'd rather my husband is there to answer that need. I realized tonight that wherever he is, he's answered mine.

*I love that there's an official figure-skating trick named "shoot the duck"—so similar to the phrase my family used, although "Who shot a duck?" was a question asked not of an agile ice-skater but of someone suffering from flatulence.

The overwhelming majority of the reader responses attached to Haze's column were positive—many sharing their own Valentine's Day stories—although there were several who wrote in objecting to the asterisked sentence.

Sam laughed out loud reading the letter from, "Just Wondering" who asked, "Who shot a duck? Could it be the same person who cut the cheese? Maybe it was the one who dropped a rose! Who, oh who is that vulgarian ass flapper?"

May 5, 1968

If I had a nickel for every time someone asks me, "Why don't you use your married name in *your* column byline?" I could probably cash them in and buy something nice for the kitchen—maybe not a refrigerator but at least a toaster.

The other day a woman at the drugstore nearly accosted me as I was innocently pricing callus pads (hint: break in your new pumps before wearing them in the office all day), hissing at me that I dishonor my husband by "clinging to my maiden name."

Not wanting to break out into a fistfight by the foot care display, I politely thanked her for her opinion while inwardly screaming, "It's not my maiden name I'm clinging to, it's myself!"

As proud as I am to be my husband's wife, anytime I'm addressed as Mrs. Kirby, there's a split second of confusion, and I think, "Who's that?" Maybe it's a newlywed's reaction, although I think when Royal and I are celebrating our golden anniversary, the name'll still seem a bit foreign.

I asked Royal, "What would you think if you had to take my name when we got married?"

Granting me one of his charming, loving smiles, he asked, "What do you mean?"

"I mean what if that were the custom—that the man takes the woman's name instead of vice versa."

He looked startled.

"Well, I wouldn't do it. It's my *name*, for crying out loud."

"And how about, after you were married, you were referred to as 'the *former* Royal Kirby.' Wouldn't you think, 'Hey, I'm still here!'"

We stared at each other for a moment, and then

he said, "Haze, are you writing a column about this?"

"Maybe."

Now I'm not saying I have a vast readership, but still, my own name has been my byline since I published in my college newspaper, when I was hired at the *Fargo Forum*, and now here. When I told Royal I planned on keeping it for professional reasons, he assured me it was fine with him. So to any married woman reading this column, ask your husband if he'd ever take your name. To any married man reading this column, how would you feel if your name was suddenly changed and to the world you were no longer who you'd been?

This column garnered raucous response, both from the original letter writers as well as from Sam, Susan, and Caroline as they took turns reading the correspondence aloud.

They laughed after Caroline, who'd use different voices to better limn the letter writer, read a note signed "Mrs. Anonymous" because "that's how I felt when I had to take my big lug of a husband's name and especially when I couldn't seem to get rid of it even after the big lug and I divorced!" and continued to laugh when Sam, inspired by Caroline's interpretive rendering, huffed and puffed while reading a letter from the dogged Mr. Joseph Snell: "While having my morning coffee, I don't mind reading the light piffle that is this columnist's usual fare, but this morning's looney harangue was nothing more than a chronicle of a radical hag!"

"Whoa," said Caroline. "That guy's got a problem."

Sam flipped the notepaper over to see the memo stapled to it.

"Mom, it's a memo from your grandpa. Listen." He cleared his throat and lowered his voice. "Dear *Radical Hag*, Maybe you should add a recipe or a diet tip to soften your looney harangues, ha ha. P.S. There are so many readers' comments to choose from, I wouldn't give Snell the satisfaction of seeing this in print unless you'd like to do a little public tussling?"

"Oh, Sam, let me see that," said Susan, and after a quick perusal, she added, "So that's where it came from."

"What?" asked both Sam and Caroline.

"Every now and then when Haze would turn in what she knew would be a controversial column, she'd put a sticky note on it saying, "From the Chronicles of a Radical Hag."'"

Picking a typewritten page from the stack of papers in front of her, Caroline smiled. "Look—it's Haze's very next column—with a recipe!"

May 8, 1968

I could pen a long defense, but I won't waste precious time—especially the precious time of *men,* who by an overwhelming majority were the ones most offended by my last column about taking or not taking one's husband's name. (Jeepers, you would have thought I'd asked for an amendment to the Constitution to rip away men's names *and* their masculinity!)

Instead, I offer a recipe of my great-aunt Alma's cookies, with the suggestion that the baker in your household whip up a batch of these delectable cookies. I am certain I will then be forgiven for future hooey/baloney/radical haggishness that may appear in my columns. Really, they're that good. (The cookies, not the hooey/baloney/radical haggishness.)

Alma was the type of cook who didn't like to share her recipes, a parsimonious outlook, if you ask me. Why *not* spread a little goodness in each other's kitchens? In fact, Alma, had she read any of my columns, might have called me a name or two herself. But Alma's been gone for several years, and her daughter happily made and distributed mimeographed copies of this recipe for all the relatives who had coveted it over the years. So to all of those who wrote particularly angry missives, I ask that you put down your boxing gloves and put on your oven mitts instead.

P.S. In the spirit of what I seek, I've added an extra adjective to the name of the recipe.

AUNT ALMA'S GOODWILL CRESCENT COOKIES
Preheat oven to 325 degrees.

⅔ cup almonds, pulverized (I like to seal them in a
   plastic bag and go after them with a kitchen hammer,
   but you can pulse them in a blender.)
⅓ cup sugar
1 cup butter, softened
1⅔ cup flour
¼ teaspoon salt

After thoroughly mixing all ingredients in bowl, shape dough into disk, and wrap in plastic. Refrigerate one hour. Pinch off a bit of dough, roll in palm into ¾-inch ball, then into a log, and carefully bend, shaping into a crescent. Place on cookie sheets, an inch or so apart. Work fast or the dough will get too soft.

Bake 14–16 minutes.

Meanwhile, mix together ½ cup sugar and ½ teaspoon cinnamon in pie plate. When cookies are cool enough to handle, place several of them in plate, and shake mixture until cookies are covered in cinnamon sugar. Makes about four dozen.

Enjoy with coffee, tea, or milk, and let their buttery, almondy goodness melt away any misdirected anger from which you suffer.

"Mom," said Sam, "you should make those. They sound good."
Caroline elbowed the teenager. "No, *you* should. In the spirit of radicalism—and goodwill."

7

In downward dog, Susan's view of Olivia Shelby is framed by her slightly bent knees. Olivia wears a cobalt-blue tank top, and Susan can see the ridges of muscles in her back. When the teacher says, "Point your tailbone to the sky," Susan sees Olivia's pert and youthful hindquarters rise like a soufflé, while her own sag and droop, pointing not upward, but at best toward the window that faces the parking lot. She knows yoga is the last place you're supposed to feel competitive, but competition surges through Susan like an IV-administered drug that's not being carefully monitored by the nursing staff. More than mounting a successful crow pose or fully straightening her leg in bird of paradise, Susan wants to keep up with Olivia. Keep up ... and *best* her. When Olivia loses control of her breath and has to calm down in child's pose, Susan wants to power through with even, regulated breathing and easily work her way into a supported headstand.

But Olivia is not losing control of her breath, and not able (yet!) to do a headstand, supported or not, Susan shuts her eyes for a moment. She's heard there are yogis who go through their entire practice with closed eyes, but Susan is nowhere near that level and often loses her balance when her eyes are *opened*.

Tennis used to be her sport, and for years, she and Phil had played doubles against Gerri and Reed Albin every Saturday morning at an indoor court, and in the summer every Wednesday evening at the outdoor courts by Kingleigh Lake.

Susan had *loved* playing with Phil, a sentiment that seemed mutual, with Phil yelling out, "great shot!" and "fantastic!" during the games, and bragging about Susan's backhand or accuracy when they shared a postgame cup of coffee (Saturday mornings at Sweet Buns Bakery) or a pitcher of beer (Wednesday nights at the Sundown). But last September (Susan remembers the exact date because the next morning Jack was scheduled for a tonsillectomy) Phil had been mute during their game (which they lost), and on the way home from the Sundown, when Susan asked if anything was wrong, Phil had snapped, "I just wonder why you gave away the last two sets."

"I didn't think I gave anything away," said Susan. "But I do think the heat was getting to me."

The record-setting temperature and humidity had lingered into the early evening, and a peel of sweat had covered all four players.

"What'd you mean? Are you in menopause or something?"

Susan laughed, assuming he was kidding. "Phil, it's hot outside. And when I do enter menopause, I'll be sure to let you know."

The last game they had played was a Saturday morning in October. They'd opted to go to the outdoor courts because the day could have been a nominee for "Most Beautiful," with trees decked out in their red, orange, and golden finery and a sky so blue, science could have no explanation for its color.

Susan was hopeful that the bright beauty of the day might restore their game, which for weeks had been more chore than fun.

She was wrong. After she'd lunged for and missed Gerri's volley, Phil said, "Need glasses, old woman?"

They both were allowed to joke about each other's playing and had, but always good-naturedly, except for the past couple weeks. If there was any cheer in Phil's voice, Susan couldn't hear it under the disgust.

By the second set, the tennis ball wasn't the only thing Susan was intent on returning. When Phil hit Reed's serve with a high, out-of-bounds lob, Susan said, "Do you understand what those lines are for?" and when a tepid backhand of his sent the ball barely over the net, Susan advised that maybe he should lift weights.

They won the game but lost all that was important, and it turned out to be the last one they played. Several weeks later, Phil accepted his friend Mac's offer to go fishing with him in Mexico, and when he came back, he confessed to his affair with the dental hygienist and informed Susan that he was going to be staying at Mac's condo because he had some things he needed to think over.

Susan accepted Gerri's invitation to play the occasional game of singles, but for her, tennis was more fun with a partner. She hoped that one day her yoga practice would offer her more than physical exercise, but for now it was only a substitute for tennis, a way to relieve stress and burn a few calories.

After class, Susan changes in the locker room, trying not to notice how tanned and toned Olivia Shelby's thighs are. Susan's legs are a fish-belly white, but Olivia doesn't have a job that keeps her inside an office all day like Susan's does; no, Olivia's a landscape architect, who turns the yards of Granite Creek's wealthier residents into oases; she gets to go to work wearing a tank top and cargo shorts with lots of important pockets.

That's probably why her arms are so buff too, thinks Susan, lifting all those bags of mulch and potted plants. She's suddenly resentful that the heaviest thing she lifts at work is a pen.

"Jens tells me Sam's working down at the paper with you," says Olivia now, dabbing at her face with a rolled-up towel.

Pulling her T-shirt over her head, Susan nods.

"I've had Jens working with me every summer since he was ten," says Olivia of her seventeen-year-old son, who looks like a Calvin Klein model. "It's a great bonding experience. I hope the two of you enjoy your time together as much as we have."

"I hope so too!" says Susan, with too much emphasis—and apology—in her voice.

Lingering in the locker room after everyone has left, Susan scolds herself for the mélange of feelings that takes her back to junior high school, when her confidence was a frail bloom that got trampled on daily . . . or hourly.

She was a successful businesswoman who ran an award-winning newspaper, for Christ's sake! She was smart and well-informed and attractive and took care of herself and had a flair for fashion!

Okay, so she had inherited her position as publisher, and how could she not be well-informed being in the newspaper business? And her attractiveness certainly wasn't dazzling, and the backs of her thighs could never be called smooth, and a flair for fashion—who was she kidding? That she didn't wear the puff-paint appliquéd sweatshirts sold in Josie's Stylin' Boutique in the mini-mall where she got her hair cut only meant that there were worse dressers than she, but neither was she the type who could look chic in yoga class like Olivia Shelby. And Olivia Shelby still had a husband who lived with her in the same house, and her teenaged son certainly hadn't gained at least fifteen pounds in the past six months thanks to the upheaval of his parents' marriage and—

"Stop it!" Susan hisses to her blurred-by-tears reflection. Standing in front of the mirror positioned above the row of sinks, she collects herself for a moment before uncapping her lipstick and gliding the tube around her mouth.

"*Hi!* I know you!"

Startled by this greeting, Susan's hand jerks.

"Oh, sorry," says the young woman as in the mirror they both look at the slash of Muted Plum lipstick that now checkmarks the side of Susan's mouth. "I didn't mean to startle you."

"That's okay," says Susan. She wets a paper towel and rubs at the errant mark.

"It's just that I've seen your picture in the paper in the . . ."

". . . the masthead?"

The woman, hands clasped around the shoulder strap of her pink neon duffle bag nods. "And now to see you in the flesh—well, not the *flesh* flesh, which would be pretty easy to do in a locker room . . ." She laughs, embarrassed. "Sorry, I'm just a little nervous."

"Nervous," says Susan. "Why?"

"Because I just love those columns you're printing! The one of Haze Evans and her husband? I just got engaged myself, and, we—Brad and I—are taking premarital classes at St. Steven's, but really, I think I'm learning more from the columns!"

August 8, 1968

Not exactly blessed with mechanical aptitude, I nevertheless love to tinker with the two machines that mean the most to me: my typewriter and my sewing machine. Neither requires much maintenance, but I am filled with pride when I change a typewriter ribbon or a needle. It was while I was in the future nursery and current sewing room, seated in front of my Singer, that my husband entered.

"Do you think you could fix this?"

"Just set it in the mending basket," I said, using a voice a fair distance from cheerful. Surrounded by clouds of white tulle, pools of satin, and an invisible fog of anxiety, I was on a deadline, having promised my cousin Anne that I would indeed finish Sharon's First Communion dress before her actual First Communion. Which gave me thirty-six hours, if I didn't sleep.

My husband, who is sensitive to my moods (especially when smoke's coming out of my ears) politely backed out of the room, knowing that further aggravating me might result in tears or a pelted spool of thread.

Several days later, after Sharon had been successfully communed (I don't know the correct verb, not having grown up in the Catholic faith) and I had humbly accepted bouquets of compliments for the girl's beautifully sewn dress, Royal asked permission to use my Singer.

"Use it for what?" I asked, taken aback.

"Well, to sew, of course. I thought I'd fix that shirt pocket of mine. No sense you always having to do it."

Touched over his desire to lighten my housework load, I was about tell him that no, no, it was my pleasure to sew up his seams, when he added, "How hard can it be?"

To all and any married men reading this column: For marital harmony, avoid this phrase, especially when referring to a task/hobby/pastime/job of your wife's.

Seating himself at the machine, he stared at it for a while, finally asking, "So what do I do now?"

"You'll have to thread it," I said, my voice as chipper as one of his hospital's candy striper's.

"Well, doesn't thread just go through a needle?"

"Not just through a needle," I said brightly.

For a few minutes I enjoyed his struggle to figure out the Singer before graciously swooping in to give him a lesson. He was a good student, watching me carefully wind the thread around and through the various dials, hooks, and levers. After several demonstrations, he claimed himself ready to try, and try he did. Diligently. Until he finally, delightedly, got it.

"Okay, give me the shirt!"

"You have to thread the bobbin first," I said.

"What's a bobbin?"

Dear Reader, I did enjoy his befuddlement, almost as much as I enjoyed schooling him on presser foots and stitch length and thread tension and backstitching. He managed to sew a straight line; unfortunately it was one that fused the opening of his pocket to his shirt.

I could have passed him the seam ripper and showed him how to undo his mistake, but I could tell by his red face and colorful expressions that he'd had enough of the domestic arts and would confine his sewing to the operating room. Where by all reports, he does a sterling job.

August 10, 1968
DEAR HAZE EVANS,

You bet Dr. Kirby does a sterling job in the OR! I had hernia surgery last year, and a prettier scar you've never seen! And Dr. Kirby was so kind to me and so patient with my husband, who is sort of a know-it-all and likes to be the boss of every room, including mine in ICU!

Why I'm writing is that I hope Dr. Kirby isn't embarrassed by your column. If he is, I say, Put down your pen! We need good doctors more than we need wiseacre newspaper columnists.

I usually enjoy your work but not at Dr. Kirby's expense!

Yours truly,
Mrs. John Peltz

P.S. This is not for publication—unlike you, I do not get a kick out of publicly humiliating my husband.

October 8, 1968

My husband, Royal, has many talents, but dancing isn't one of them, and the times I forced him out onto a dance floor weren't fun for either of us (especially me, hobbling back to our table, a victim of my husband's rogue feet). Maybe something happens to a woman whose toes have been mashed, whose nylons have been snagged, whose insteps have been stepped on. Maybe she starts thinking her man owes her something.

To say Royal looked pleased when I informed him I had just purchased a dozen dance lessons would be grossly misrepresenting the word *pleased*.

"No," he said, after the "pleased" expression had further curdled. "I'm not taking dance lessons. One—I don't have time. Two—I don't want to."

"The teacher's flexible," I said. "She willing to work around our schedule. And besides, Ricky and Lucy and Fred and Ethel (names have been changed to protect the innocent—and our friendship) have signed up too."

I am pleased to report that I did not go stag to our first lesson, that my reluctant and grumbling husband showed up at the dance studio along with our friends and learned how to do a basic box step.

"That wasn't so bad," he said on the drive home. "When you're shown the steps, it doesn't seem so mysterious."

I wrote that down in capital letters in my notebook, because isn't that true for everything that challenges and/or befuddles us?

When I took my first clarinet lesson and I confessed to

my teacher that I wanted to play "Moonlight Serenade" for my mother's birthday in two weeks because it was one of her favorite songs, Mrs. Strom said, "How about we learn the scale first?"

In our second dance lesson, we spent the first half hour reviewing the box step we'd learned the week before and the next half hour learning how to cha-cha. Ricky was like Royal, adrift, but Fred was demonstrating a rhythm and grace previously unknown to us. ("We practiced all week," Ethel told Lucy and me. "Honestly, I think I might have unleashed a monster.")

That Royal and I were clunky in our execution of the cha-cha didn't bother him in the least, and when the lesson ended, he said, "Oh well, Gene Kelly wasn't always *Gene Kelly*."

We're having so much fun. I've introduced something into our marriage that I think will be a long-lasting source of enjoyment—I picture us doing a rhythmic rumba at our ten-year anniversary, a tempestuous tango at our twenty-fifth, and a stately waltz at our fiftieth.

After our second class, we decided to walk to Irv's for malteds, and as most of you know, this most wonderful establishment has jukeboxes at every table, and Royal put in a nickel, and a Tito Puente song came on, and my wonderful husband, right there in the middle of the linoleum floor of Irv's Ice Cream, cha-chaed with me.

If wonders ever did cease, it would sure take the fun out of things.

As was the new norm now that Haze's old columns were being published, the receptionist's console lit up with phone calls from readers who felt a need to bother Shelly with their inanities, including the warbly voiced woman who called in to say, "My Herb and I danced together, and let me tell you, my Herb and I romanced together!"

April 4, 1969

You can get lost in daytime TV. I watched a couple game shows in the morning and would have laughed at Paul Lynde on *The Hollywood Squares* if laughter were something that came easy to me. In the afternoon I watched one soap opera after another, comparing my troubles with those who got dizzy in *As the World Turns,* with those who desperately needed *The Guiding Light* as they were battered by *The Secret Storm* all the way to *The Edge of Night*. Assuring Royal that I'd eat something, I made a tuna salad sandwich, but it sat on the coffee table all afternoon, its bread hardening around the edges, its lettuce wilting. The phone kept ringing until I took it off the hook. I thought an actress on TV was screaming (all sorts of things happen on those soaps) until I finally realized it was the tea kettle I'd forgotten I'd put on. I had the lights on even though it was sunny outside.

I had a miscarriage. My second. The first one happened last year, and I just couldn't write about it. I can't believe I'm writing about it now; it's so personal, but writing's always been a tonic for me, and boy oh boy, a tonic I need. A little gin wouldn't hurt either.

This time I had tried so hard not to think of names, not to linger in those irresistible departments at Brady's — Maternity Wear and Infants & Babies — where I'd examine the bowed dresses (why are bows *the* accessory for expectant women?) and tiny pink and blue cotton onesies. The sewing room had already been painted a soft yellow in anticipation of our first baby, but the door's been shut since, and I haven't yet dared open it. And it will, for now, stay shut.

You wonder all sorts of things, first and foremost: What's wrong with me? Why can't I do what billions of women before me have done? Why does this body of mine destroy that which I want the most?

I am writing what Royal told me, because he is, after all, a doctor. He said it wasn't my fault, or my body's fault, that it was something that has no fault at all.

"Often it's nature's way of expelling a fetus that isn't viable. Other times it happens and we don't know why. There are women who smoke and drink and don't get enough rest or fall on the ice who deliver healthy full-term babies, and there are women who take meticulous care of themselves and miscarry. You cannot blame yourself. All you must do is be tender with yourself."

Oh, tears were shed! And the ache is still there, but I am trying to follow the doctor's prescription. Which yesterday meant eating a half pan of peanut butter bars. (I might need to further consult the good doctor as to what separates tenderness from indulgence . . .) Today I'll try to offset that pan of bars as well as some pain by taking Brigadoon for a walk so long it'll tire *him* out.

I know we all have our sorrows. We're taught to keep them private (ja, I'm talking to all you Scandinavians!) because their sadness would only be amplified in sharing them. I guess I feel differently. For me, a burden shared is a burden lightened. At least a little bit.

Along with Haze's column, Susan reprinted a letter that was written by a kindly, long-deceased man who invited classrooms of children out to his farm for hayrides in the fall and sleigh rides in the winter.

TO THE EDITOR:

Thank you for Haze's last column. I too have been childless and not by choice. But I bore the weight of it being my own fault. The doctors said everything was working with my wife but not with me. It makes a man feel diminished. I know my wife, God rest her soul, would have been a wonderful mother, and I denied her that. Still, she stayed with me for thirty-seven years. And we had a lot of fun. Traveled to all contiguous states and in '59—their first official year in the union—we visited both Hawaii and Alaska!

Sometimes, when we saw our friends go through problems and tragedies with their kids or grandkids, we'd think maybe we were lucky after all, being spared that kind of pain. But it really never erased the pain of not having children in the first place.

Once we sponsored an AFS student—a wonderful boy from Finland—and Genevieve would have welcomed a new student every year, but it was too much for me. I worried day in, day out over Arno's safety, imagining something terrible happening and how could I ever face his parents?

I know I'm nearing the end of the road what with this weak ticker of mine, and that's all right. I've had a long life, and Genevieve said she'd be waiting for me on the other side with her dancing shoes on and the shiny green dress I liked so well. Wishing children will happen for you and your husband, Haze. Any child would be a lucky duck with you two as parents.

Sincerely,

Robert Beckdahl
Leland Township

8

Tina wipes her eyes on her napkin.

"Oh, chica, that was sad."

"I know. Poor Haze." Caroline shakes her head.

"I can hardly believe they'd publish that all those years ago. I mean, it's so . . . personal!"

"And how about that Mr. Beckdahl? His letter was a lot different than the half dozen or so from readers who were 'outraged' that a family newspaper would run such a column." Caroline looks at her watch. "I'm surprised my mother hasn't called yet. That column'll hit her hard."

"My mother too," says Tina. "Most mothers, I imagine. Most *people*."

Caroline returns the coffee pot to the fancy machine that has turned her into a barista, capable of frothing up cappuccinos as authentic as any found in Italian espresso bars.

"Yeah, but my mother can really relate. She had a miscarriage. A couple months after my brother was born." Caroline turns around, leaning against the counter, her hands curled around its tiled edge. "She told me—just last year—that she was sad but also a little relieved, and that relief made her feel like a terrible person."

"Oh, chica," says Tina, getting up. She wraps her arms around the person she loves most in the world, and when she breathes in the scent of Caroline's shampoo—some organic brand with grapefruit extract—she feels tipsy.

In Caroline's world, she considers the glass not just full but brimming. That's why it kills her that she can't share with her mother that which makes her the happiest: her love for Christina. But the Abramsons—her mother, father, and brother—are all members in excellent standing of a church that believes in love, but only when it's parceled out to particular people. It is Caroline's great shame that she still feels she must lie to her family, but the idea of being cut off from them is too much for her to consider.

"I'm such a baby!" she had cried to Tina on their second date. "I love them just the way they are, and believe me, that can be a heavy load—I mean, my brother plays bass in a Christian heavy-metal band!—but I feel I have to protect them from loving me just the way I am!"

They had had dinner at the Sundown (Tina finding the Chee-Zee Bites both delicious and slightly horrifying) and sat afterward in the small gazebo on the north end of the town square, observing the hustle and bustle of a Friday night. A choice viewing spot, the gazebo allowed for a little privacy, plus its wrought iron bench was so small that its occupants had to sit close together.

It had been a soft spring night, and the college kids teeming into The Pylon for live music and cheap beer had their jackets off; one of the teenagers skateboarding down the courthouse's handicap ramp was wearing shorts. Two silver-haired men in suits took a smoke break outside the Palace Theater, where a touring opera company was performing *Tosca*, and a babysitter led a row of blond children out of Irv's Ice Cream, all of them focused on their cones.

The two women sat with their shoulders pressed together—about the only public touch Caroline dared exhibit to the world (much to Christina's exasperation).

"It's a big closet for me!" she joked, while being completely serious. "It's going to take a while to step out of it."

"*Hola*, Dr. Tina," said one of the blond children, whose Brittany spaniel had just that afternoon been in for its giardia vaccine.

"*Hola*, Tracy. *¿Cómo estás?*"

The child, who was in her first year of middle-school Spanish, blushed with pleasure.

"*Muy bien*," she answered, as her younger siblings nudged against her, asking her what she was saying.

After the parade of blondness had passed, Caroline sighed.

"How are you so comfortable being you?"

Tina laughed. "Who says I am?"

She felt the pressure of Caroline's shoulder against hers, and more than anything, she wanted to clamp her arms around this woman on this downtown night that smelled of lilacs and baked waffle cones, wanted to pull her close and kiss her until the far-off crescent moon bloomed into a half, a full, a blue moon.

"Well, you came out to your parents."

Tina nodded, remembering that bright morning when she was home on Christmas break and the sun spilled into their little house in Glendale as if poured by a bottomless pitcher. In Minnesota, where she was in her first year of veterinary school, it had been seventeen degrees below zero; here, the outdoor thermometer affixed to the backyard fig tree read seventy-three, a difference of ninety degrees! She had felt so warm and loose, especially after eating a plateful of her mother's huevos rancheros and drinking thick dark coffee, that she felt, well, now's the time, and had said the nine words that had been stuck in her throat for years: "I just want you to know that I'm gay."

Both parents stared at her for a long moment, and Tina felt lightheaded, her lungs filled with air she couldn't expel.

"Siempre lo supimos," said her father finally. "Pero esperábamos que no fuera cierto."

We always knew it, but we were hoping it wasn't true.

"Why?" Christina had asked, almost blind with the flood of tears that filled her eyes.

A sigh lifted her father's wide shoulders, so strong from decades of hefting shovels full of dirt, from hoeing, spading, from lifting trees out of the bed of his truck, gently patting their burlaped roots as he carried them across emerald-green lawns.

"Because we want your life to be easier," he had said, and that's when the tears breached their levee and poured down Tina's face.

"Father Renaldo thought he was telling us something we didn't know, but we did," said her mother, dabbing at her own tears with a paper napkin.

"Father Renaldo," said Tina, confused. "What has Father Renaldo got to do with anything?"

"He saw you kissing a girl at that retreat you went on. That one in the twelfth grade? He called us to say you must ask for forgiveness or you could go to hell."

A flush fueled by anger, embarrassment, and confusion heated Tina's face. She remembered that retreat to Big Bear and how she and a girl from a church in Simi Valley had formed a sudden attraction that had them sneaking out of a lecture featuring a nun advising a room full of teenagers how to live a virtuous life.

"But that was what, five years ago? Why didn't you didn't say anything to me then?"

Tina's father examined his fingernails (he was fastidious about his nails, scrubbing away all traces of dirt when he got home from work), and without looking up he said in Spanish, "We didn't think it was our place. We didn't think it was Father Renaldo's place."

"Like your Papi said, we knew a long time ago—" here Tina's mother looked at her husband—"by the time she was about eleven, twelve, right, Manny? But we decided we wouldn't say one thing or another until you told us."

Staring at the pretty blue coffee cup—her mother liked color in her kitchen—Tina shook her head, astonished by all that had transpired at the table at which she had only expected breakfast.

Her eyes grew round at the thought that came into her head.

"Is that why you switched churches?" Tina remembered coming home for Thanksgiving break and her surprise when dutifully accompanying her parents to mass, they drove to a different parish, all the way in Burbank.

"Maybe," said her father. "And of course we didn't like the grape juice."

"Sí," said her mother and then exaggerated her accent to a

"Cheech and Chong" level. "We give a lot of money to that church and still they can't give us a little stinkin' wine for Communion?"

"YOUR MOTHER'S SO FUNNY," Caroline had said after the first time she met Mercedes. Throughout her life, Tina's friends had expressed similar sentiments, only they had always said, "Your parents." Tina wondered how her mother's sense of humor would hold up after Manny died; after all, he had been not only her partner in life, but the two of them traded jokes and riffed off one another as if they were partners in comedy as well. But even in grief—and Mercedes's grief was deep—she didn't lose what was an essential part of her personality.

After she and Tina had hauled onto the brick patio over a dozen potted plants Manny's clients had sent over, Mercedes dabbed at the sweat under her nose and said, "They seem to forget the gardener died."

Tina's gasp preceded her laugh. Mercedes's laugh preceded her tears.

"OKAY, I'VE GOT TO GO," says Caroline now, reluctantly unwrapping herself from Tina's arms. "What time can I expect you?"

Dinner that evening with Mercedes is planned, and they are picking her up at the hospital, giving Caroline a chance to stop in and visit Haze.

"By six at the latest," says Tina. "Unless Lovie has her pups." A trucker had found the golden retriever mix limping along the county road and had brought her in. As well as having a broken hind leg and a sweet nature (earning her the name Lovie), she was pregnant.

Caroline leans in to kiss Tina. "If she does, call me. I'll be your delivery assistant."

"WOULD YOU LIKE A DONUT?" asks Sam, setting a white box on the receptionist's desk.

"What? I—"

"Pick out which one you want, and I'll get you some coffee."

"I—"

But Sam's already hustling off toward the break room, and so Shelly opens the box from Sweet Buns Bakery, which a traveling reviewer from the *Star Tribune*—the state's biggest newspaper—once claimed set a bar so high other bakeries could only limbo under it. There are a dozen donuts arranged in three rows, and iced and sprinkled, they look like pastry jewels. Reaching for a cake donut with chocolate frosting, Shelly changes her mind and takes a glazed cruller, just as Sam returns with a pot of coffee. He refills her mug and says, "Do you use cream or sugar? Because I'll go back and get it."

"Just black," says Shelly. "The only way coffee should be drunk."

"I don't know," says Sam. "Not that I've had a lot a coffee, but the few times I have, it seems cream and sugar only help it."

Shelly draws her lips in—it's a reflex of hers to stymie any rare smile—and considers the donut she's holding.

"Oh, let me get you a plate," says Sam. "Or at least a napkin."

He races off before she can tell him not to bother, she'll just set it on a tissue, and just as she's chewing her first bite, he's back, brandishing a small paper plate and a napkin.

"There you go," he says, setting both down on her desk. He grabs the latest issue of the *Gazette*—there are always several fresh-off-the-press copies of the paper on the coffee table in the reception area—and tucks it under his arm. "These'll be in the break room if you want more," he says as he picks up the bakery box and races off.

"Wait, I—" she says, but he's already disappeared down the hall.

The donut deserves the high praise the traveling food editor gave it, and with each bite Shelly's teeth break through the slightly crunchy top layer and into the smooth, near-creamy middle, and she wonders, why don't I eat donuts more often?

She would love to sit savoring her caffeine and sugar, but a phone light on the console goes on. There were calls before Haze's stroke and the publication of her old columns but only about a tenth—or maybe twentieth—of the calls she gets now.

"Granite Creek Gazette," she says, her voice sharp. The column on Haze's miscarriage was printed this morning, and as the caller jaws on and on about how moved she was, Shelly rolls her eyes, thinking, here it comes. Before the publication of Haze's old columns, the receptionist had plenty of time to do her sudoku and crossword puzzle and to read her cozy mysteries (always knowing who did it way ahead of the books' amateur sleuths).

"We appreciate the feedback," she says, when what she wants to say is, "Yeah, yeah, now may I *please* get back to my donut?"

Because Susan likes to keep track of the callers' opinions, Shelly marks a small tick under the "Like" column after she hangs up, and two seconds later, the phone rings again.

SAM'S ALWAYS BEEN INTERESTED IN SCIENCE (especially last year, when Elise sat ahead of him in class), and he thinks of Shelly as an experiment. How can a person be in such a bad mood all the time? What can he do to get to her crack a smile? Is she capable of laughing, and if so, could he make her?

"What have we here?" asks Mitch as Sam stands at the break room counter, shoving a chocolate donut in his mouth.

Sam swallows, hard, the wad of dough like an orange squeezing through a drainpipe.

"I, uh, I just brought these in for whoever wants one," he says when he can talk. He doesn't add, "in honor of me working here a whole month," which was his impetus.

"It sure looks better than what Ellie brings in," says Mitch, perusing the contents of the box. "Did you try one of those god-awful oatmeal raisin cookies she brought in yesterday? Oatmeal gravel's more like it."

He takes a shiny glazed donut and sinks his teeth into it.

"Hi, honey," says Susan, striding into the break room. "Uh, Sam." Her amendment is quick but not quick enough to erase the flush that's rising on her son's neck. He's told her, more than once, that in the office she is not to call him anything but Sam.

"Shelly told me you were here, and with donuts—how nice!"

She studies the contents of the open bakery box but doesn't take anything.

"Is Eldridge here yet?" asks Mitch, wiping sugar off his mouth, and Susan, pouring herself a cup of coffee shakes her head.

"Listen, Sam, do you mind working in Haze's office for a while? We've got a meeting in the conference room."

Sam shrugs. "Sure."

"You know the drill—get a file and start reading."

"Will do," says Sam, and although he wants to take another donut with him, he doesn't, and by the time he's sitting in Haze's office, the good mood brought on his bike ride *and* buying treats for his office mates (with his own money!) has deflated from a soufflé into something hard and burnt.

Whenever Sam stays with his dad, whose borrowed condo is only blocks away from the office, he rides his bike to work. It makes him feel self-sufficient and not like such a load. Last night, his dad had slapped Sam's belly with the back of his hand and said, "Guess you don't need your own inner tube down at the lake!" Sam thinks he was trying to be funny; he *used* to be funny, but since his parents split up, his dad's jokes make Sam cringe more than they make him laugh. For instance, jokes about his friend Mac.

"I think the lesson here," Phil has told his son, "is to go into medical equipment sales. Mac was never the brightest bulb in the socket, but man, has he done well for himself! And all from selling defibrillators!"

"Real nice," Sam had thought; after all it's easygoing Mac who's let his dad—and occasionally Sam himself—stay in his three-bedroom condo.

Sam had e-mailed Jack about their dad being a jerk and had been disappointed in his brother's short (as usual) response: "He's going through a lot. Don't make it worse for him!" He then texted/didn't send Elise: "DAD = A-HOLE." Not that he's had any deep conversations about family (or about anything) with her, but he knows her dad still lives with Elise, her mom, and two younger brothers and didn't have a stupid affair with another woman, a stupid affair that he couldn't even keep secret and wound up ripping their family to shreds. Not that his mother is perfect—not by a long shot—but he could never picture her getting her teeth cleaned by a young dude and thinking, Oh yeah, he's worth messing up my whole family for.

Pressing his fingers against his closed eyes, Sam shakes his head fiercely, like a wet dog trying to dry itself. His aim is to throw off all the crappy thoughts that get clogged up in his brain, that make him feel either sad or crazy, that make him want to eat a second, third, or fourth donut. He sighs and drums his fingers on the file folder he's supposed to open and whose contents he's supposed to read. He doesn't know why, but he feels all jangly, like everything's revved up inside. He opens the narrow drawer in the middle of Haze's desk and examines the neat compartments of the plastic organizer filled with paper clips, staples, pens, and rubber bands. He shuts the drawer, opens it, shuts it, opens it, and then, leaning back in the reclining office chair, he pulls the drawer out as far as he can.

In the back of the drawer, there are envelopes, stamps, a copy of *Computers for Dummies*, and a small round box painted with flowers. In sixth-grade art, they had had a two-week session on rosemaling, the Norwegian decorative painting, and he learned (sort of) how to paint those kinds of flowers.

Looking across the table at his friend Jacob's sloppy work, he had thought, "He's a rose-*mauler*," and even as he was pleased with his wordplay, he was more pleased when the teacher complimented his own precise brush strokes.

Sam twists the lid open, hoping to find candy. M&M's would be nice, or maybe Hot Tamales. But inside the box, there is nothing but cotton batting and on top of that, a key.

Two rows of drawers flank the desk's middle drawer, but only the top ones on the right and left sides have keyholes, and this key fits in neither.

Leaning back in the chair again, he surveys the room, wondering if there might be a safe behind the framed newspaper picture of Haze accepting an award, or behind the weird (or would his art teacher say "impressionistic"?) painting of maple trees, or behind the framed newspaper picture of Haze and some guy shaking hands (Sam doesn't recognize Lance LeRoi, star of the 1960s television hit show *Rowdy O'Doul, Cowhand*).

"Hey, Sam!"

Startled, the boy lurches up in the reclining chair.

"Caroline . . . hi."

The young woman smiles, and Sam's body feels like it's opening in response to that generous smile.

"So you're working in Haze's office today, huh?"

Sam bobs his head.

"Enjoy it—the light's a lot better here than in the conference room, which is where I'm supposed to be. Bye!"

"Bye," Sam answers, feeling his face heat up. He stares for a long time at the space Caroline had occupied, and sighing, he opens the file on the desk and begins reading columns.

September 15, 1969

When we were eleven, my friend Eunice and I were getting on the Ferris wheel at the Mountrail County Fair, and the man who loaded people on and off the cars was a Negro. He was the first Negro I had ever seen, and I was struck by how dark his skin was and how white his teeth were, whiter even than those of my brother's best friend, Eddie.

"He scares me," said Eunice as our car climbed slowly in a creaky arc.

"Why?" I asked, surprised. The carny who worked the ring toss booth, the one with the scar that crawled up his face, crinkling up the corner of his eyelid—now that guy was scary. This one was nice and friendly and had told us to enjoy the view.

"Because most Negroes are criminals," she said, a little tsk in her voice.

After the ride, I thanked the carney profusely when he lifted the bar and set us free, and as we walked into the small midway, I turned left when my friend turned right.

"Haze!" she said. "Come on! The cotton candy's this way!"

I wanted to keep walking left, toward the little tent with the flea-bitten circus ponies, toward the fun house with mirrors that made you look either two or ten feet tall, past the dirt parking lot, and into the dark night. Eunice lived on a farm, and I was spending the night at her house; her parents were going to pick us up by the bandstand at nine, and where did I want to go anyway?

My thoughts were all a jumble: Why would my friend—a kind and generous girl—say such a thing?

A boy in my class had gotten a lecture from our teacher about name-calling and generalizations after claiming "all girls are dumb." (This he had the nerve to say after Ella Lundberg knocked him out of a spelling bee round.) What would my teacher say to Eunice? I said nothing, but followed her to the cotton candy stand, and by the time we'd finished eating the sticky spun sugar off our paper cones, it was on to the next ride, the next thrill.

I'm remembering this on the sixth anniversary of the day those little girls were killed by that bomb in Birmingham. Killed walking into an assembly in their church basement. Killed by men who no doubt heard things like my friend and the boy in my class said, heard them over and over and believed them. That the Ku Klux Klan is full of grown men who wreak such hatred and destruction while hiding under sheets outrages and saddens me in a deep, soul-weary way. While it seems many of them are sick and fevered with hate, I'd bet there are others who just go along because they don't know how to stand up, because they're afraid, because it seemed easier to just get the cotton candy.

On this day, I'm thinking of my Sunday-best dresses my mother sewed for me, the ones she hand-smocked or trimmed with lace, and I imagine those four little girls in their flouncy skirts and shiny shoes, whose mothers had tied their sashes and combed their hair, and promised them an extra piece of cobbler if they paid attention during the sermon.

Sam takes a deep breath. His American History class had a whole unit on civil rights, and he remembered reading about that church bombing, but Haze's words make him feel as if it just happened. He unfastens the paper clip securing a stack of readers' letters. Most of them thank the paper for publishing the column, including Harlan Dodd, his nutzoid neighbor who apparently took a while to become a nut.

TO THE EDITOR:

Haze Evans's words make me think. And right now
I'm thinking that as much we have to be proud of to be
Americans, we also have to acknowledge our shameful side.
My little niece sang with the Cherub Choir this past Sunday.
About fifteen little tykes standing in front of the church
singing "Children of the Heavenly Father." Cute as all get
out. And now to think of that same scene, but imagining an
explosion bursting through the air, silencing the organ and
those little voices . . . well, you wouldn't ever imagine such
a thing. And yet those people down in Birmingham didn't
imagine it—they lived it. My heart is heavy.
    —Harlan Dodd

What happened to the guy who could write a letter like this, Sam thinks, that would turn him into the complete tool he was now? He reads through the letters and then comes across one that shakes him even more than Mr. Dodd's did.

TO THE EDITOR:

I usually enjoy Haze Evans's columns, but this one made
me really sad. Which is probably a good thing because I, like
many people, tend to run away from those kinds of feelings
instead of truly experiencing them, finding their cause,
and digging them out by the roots, etc. I admit the natural
prejudice (natural in the sense that it was almost assumed
a white person should have one) I had against Negroes
solidified when as a college freshman new to the city, I
was walking down Division Street in Chicago and my

purse was grabbed out of my hands by a "young buck."
(I was too refined for those words; these were the words of
the police officer who took my complaint.) Something worse
happened to me a year later when I was in my sophomore
year at Northwestern, but the perpetrator was not called a
"young buck" by anyone. The police, in fact, upon learning
the name of the white boy, whose family was well-to-do and
well known, told me it would be better for all to drop the
charges, because things could get ugly for me if I proceeded.

"Live and learn," I was advised, and because I was young
and afraid, I let this boy get away with a terrible crime,
which has shadowed me throughout my life. I left school
and was aimless and adrift for years, until I finally landed
here in Granite Creek, thanks to inheriting a relative's house.

The funny (in the sad sense) thing is that several years
ago while driving home late after attending a concert in
St. Paul, I got a flat tire and had to pull over. The first person
to stop on the quiet road was a Negro man, and afraid, I
nearly declined his offer to change my tire. But I didn't, and
he quickly and easily took off the flat and replaced it with
the spare and wouldn't accept the money I offered, only
saying, "Glad to help." Would I have felt that racing heart,
those prickles of fear if a white man had stopped? Even
though it had been a white man who had raped me?

What is the matter with us?

Marie Atherton
(And please use my name. I'm tired of feeling ashamed.)

Sam stares at the scratchy handwriting and faded ink. The letter's like
an antique, and yet it feels as immediate as a text. He wonders if the
paper published this letter. It's so . . . raw, and he feels both sorry for
and proud of the woman who wrote it, recognizing the act of bravery
it was to write it.

Jacob told him how boring his work days at the FoodKing are
and how he was going to hurl if he had to carry out the groceries

of one more old lady who asked him what grade he was in and dug around in her stupid coin purse for a two-quarter tip. Sam wonders how old Marie Atherton is now, if she's ever had Jacob carry out her groceries. Is she one of the old ladies digging around in her stupid coin purse for a tip?

He texts/doesn't send J. K. Rowling, "YOU KNOW SO MUCH, BUT DID YOU EVER THINK YOU DIDN'T KNOW ANYTHING?"

9

It's a hot, muggy August day, and Susan is in Des Moines for a "Women in Publishing" conference. She loves these annual gatherings but prefers when they're held a little farther away, to amp up the vacation factor. The hotel has an outdoor pool, but a group of loud and rowdy men spoiled the relaxing swim she had looked forward to after her first full day of speakers, panels, and breakaway sessions.

"Here's one for the Triple Alphas!" calls a man, slapping his big belly. He bounced on the diving board, hard, before cannonballing into the pool.

Swimming laps, Susan feels herself lifted in the wake in the man's splash. It's not the first time this has happened—the fraternity brothers gathered for their thirtieth reunion are partial to cannonballs—but it's the one that will finally make her, when she gets to the shallow end, climb up the little ladder and out of the pool.

A wolf whistle shrieks, and Susan ignores it, walking quickly to her lawn chair. When she puts on her hotel robe, one of the fraternity brothers yells, "Aw, don't deprive us!"

Picking up her towel and book, Susan walks across cement warmed by the sun. There are more wolf whistles and a juvenile invitation, and when she reaches the safety of the sliding glass door, she turns.

"You guys are the Alpha what?" she asks pleasantly, as if she hasn't heard their constant references to their fraternal name.

"We're the Triples! Alpha Alpha Alpha!" they shout, pride and belligerence in their voices.

"What did you say?" she asks, as if confused. "Alpha Alpha Ass-holes?" She slides the door open and makes her escape as the men lob back hurt corrections and angry insults.

SEVERAL OF THE FRAT BOYS/MEN are sitting in the bar now, but Susan hopes that in clothes and with her hair dried they won't recognize her.

"You really said that to them?" asks Maureen, a publisher of an alternative weekly paper in Tucson.

Susan sighs. "They reminded me of all the things I hated in college."

Shannon, who's the editor in chief of a national women's magazine, shakes her head as she pushes her straw through the pink sludge of her frozen strawberry daiquiri.

"Don't hold it against me, but I was president of my sorority. And *pinned* to the president of Tau Delta Phi."

"Pinned," says Susan as she and Maureen laugh. "I can't say I was sorry that weird ritual died out."

Again, Shannon shakes her head. "Yeah, one in several long steps on the way to matrimony. Which fortunately I didn't enter with the guy—I would have been the first of his *six* wives."

"*No*," said Susan, and as Shannon nodded dolefully, Maureen asks, "Are you married now?"

Shannon wasn't married but had been, and when she says the name of her ex-husband, her tablemates gasp, both having seen many times the hedge fund manager giving interviews on television or his name in the paper.

"I can't believe you were married to John Engval!" Susan says, "He was like a guru to my husband. He read both of his books and even went to one of his seminars in Chicago!"

"Mark my words," says Shannon. "He'll be in jail by next year." She shakes her head. "Pinned to a professional divorcé and married to a swindler. What happened to my radar?"

Maureen was celebrating her twenty-fourth anniversary with her husband, whom she'd met while working in Algiers.

"I'm not saying it's been easy," she said. "Mourad was . . . well, pretty sexist. No, make that *really* sexist. And I knew this when I fell for him, but I fell for him so hard that I thought I could change him."

"And did you?" asks Susan.

"No," says Maureen, shaking her head, and her countenance is mournful until a smile breaks through. "But our first daughter did. From day one, his eyes were suddenly opened to injustice and unfairness—especially when Deena turned out to be a soccer star!"

The women laugh, and the air around their booth swirls with the electricity of shared understanding and sympathy.

"Really, who do you think led the protest against the boys' team getting the best practice times out on the field? Mourad. And when Linnea, our second, started showing an interest in science, who do you think was the parent volunteering to chaperone every trip to the planetarium or the science museum? Mourad." Her smile is both warm and wistful. "He's a regular Gloria Steinem."

When it is Susan's turn to tell her story, she takes a long sip of her chardonnay before saying, "Well, my husband and I are separated, and I was hoping for a reconciliation, but I'm not holding my breath."

"If he was a fan of my ex," says Shannon, "maybe you're better off."

Susan manages a laugh.

"One of things I loved—love—most about Phil is his kindness," she says, "but for a while he was . . . mean, always *sniping* at me. It turns out he was having an affair at the time, with his dental hygienist!"

"And taking his guilt out on you," says Shannon, shaking her head. "Typical."

"Have you been in counseling?" asks Maureen.

Nodding, Susan says, "Couples counseling, although I can't say it did a lot of good. Phil dropped out after a couple sessions with the excuse 'he didn't need to talk, he needed to think.'"

"Is he still with the dental hygienist?" asks Shannon.

"No, and I hope he gets gingivitis." The women laugh at the joke Susan's surprised she was able to make. She takes a sip of her wine and then a second sip. "He claims they were only 'together' three times. As if the cheating wasn't all that bad because it was only *three times*. Anyway, he's living with a friend of his now, trying to figure out what he really wants."

She tells them about her boys and how the breakup has been easier for her son Jack than her son Sam. "He's always been the type of kid who just glides through everything.

"Then again, Jack's two closest friends have divorced parents, plus he was caught up in the excitement of his senior year of high school and making plans for his 'gap year'—he's globetrotting around Europe right now. Sam on the other hand is only fourteen, and well, it's understandably harder for him. He saw a counselor a lot longer than Jack did . . ." Susan shrugs.

"I hope everything works out," says Shannon.

Tears fill Susan's eyes, and Maureen reaches out and gives her forearm a squeeze.

"I don't want to cry," says Susan, "Lord knows I've cried enough." She dabs at her eyes with a cocktail napkin. "So why don't I tell you about the feature we're running instead."

HAZE'S STORY captivates the women.

"So what's her prognosis?" asks Maureen.

"Unknown," says Susan, thinking as she says it, what a sad word that is. "She could stay in a coma for a long time. She could wake up tomorrow and start chatting. She could wake up tomorrow and not be able to. They don't really know."

"To have been writing a column for a half century!" says Shannon. "We've got a couple who've been writing a column on parenting since I've been at the magazine, but that's only six years. How could she come up with so much material?"

"I don't know, but she did," says Susan. "And her voice . . . well, she's always written in a unique—and uncensored—way. Her columns really do feel like she's talking just to you."

"We had a political columnist who was pretty popular," says Maureen. "But I had to fire him when I realized as good as he was at pontificating, he was better at plagiarizing. And he'd only been writing for two years!"

"We just finished publishing all the columns Haze wrote about her husband," says Susan. "There weren't all that many, but the reader feedback has been phenomenal."

"Why do you think that is?" asks Shannon, holding up her emptied glass at the passing waiter.

"Because it was such a love story," says Susan, and she tells them about Haze's columns.

January 8, 1969

Brigadoon, as you know, is my dog through marriage, a mutt of indeterminate heritage (although there's some definite border collie and Lab, or maybe it's springer and retriever?), who'll bring me a ball whenever Royal's called away to deliver a baby or set a broken bone, inviting me into a game of catch to cheer me up. I read that dogs can smell about two hundred times better than humans; well, Briggy is also about two hundred times better than humans when it comes to reading emotions. She knows when she needs to comfort, when she needs to be playful, be protective, be encouraging, and as she adjusts her mood to better whatever one we're in, she's always adoring. Don't we love our pets for their unending love of us? We provide them food and shelter, sure, but they provide us with an excuse to believe we're worthy of their big loyal love.

You should see Briggy when Royal plays the piano. We allow her on the furniture (really, why not?), but when Royal treats us to a concert, Briggy doesn't sit on the couch but next to it. It's as if she wants no distraction. Her posture is straight, her ears perked up, her brown eyes fixed on the music maker. Van Cliburn, Glenn Gould, Jerry Lee Lewis couldn't ask for a more devoted fan.

Royal is modest about his talent, saying he plays "like a mildly talented fourth-grader," but to my—and

Brigadoon's—ears, he plays with a light touch and deep feeling. His "Clair de Lune" and "Für Elise" could make you tear up, but it's the song with which he closes every session at the piano that makes Briggy cry. Literally. It's a parlor trick they've worked on, and it's a good one. When she hears Royal pound out the opening bars, her tail starts wagging, and when he sings, "You ain't nothin' but a hound dog," she lifts her fine snout to the ceiling and lets out a plaintive howl, and she howls each time Royal sings the dastardly accusation.

I know most dog owners believe that theirs is the best dog in the world and that many wives are so inclined to think the same of their husbands, but I believe with this story I offer irrefutable proof that both Brigadoon and Royal are deserving of championship titles.

In celebration of them, and all good doggies and hubbies, here's a really tasty recipe.

SPREAD THE LOVE BANANA BREAD
¾ cup shortening (may use butter)
1½ cup sugar
1 teaspoon salt
3 eggs
3 cups flour
1½ teaspoons baking soda
2 cups mashed ripe bananas

Preheat oven to 350 degrees, and grease two loaf pans.

In large bowl, mix shortening and sugar. Add rest of ingredients, and mix well.

Spoon into two pans. Bake for 1 hour or until a toothpick inserted in center comes out clean.

(I don't mind when I don't get around to eating bananas and they get too ripe. I just put them in the freezer, knowing I can use them for this delicious recipe!)

March 30, 1970

Tomlinson's Tuxedos & Formal Wear must have had their biggest payday since prom night, considering all the elegantly suited men and women gathered to celebrate the opening of the new wing of Granite Creek Hospital. I was particularly taken by a certain handsome doctor who offered this quote to a local television reporter: "Our aim — every doctor's aim — is to provide care equal to that of the Mayo Clinic. This expansion and our new equipment will help us in that goal."

It was a gala celebrating civic pride and can-do spirit, and that the dance band was composed of three doctors and four nurses (Dr. Jill Halverson absolutely shone as a vocalist — she's probably been told not to sing to any of her patients, because none of them would want to leave!) and that the rubber chicken dinner was not rubbery at all but succulent and finely flavored were extra bonuses.

When we got home, after cursing the high heels I kicked off and the girdle I wiggled out of, I whined to Royal (the certain handsome doctor quoted above), "I wanted to dance with you! Why were you hunkered in the corner so long with that young man?"

I am pleased to tell you, my husband did not roll his eyes or sigh heavily but instead said, with a brightness of tone unexpected at one thirty in the morning:

"Haze, I'm so sorry, I should have introduced you. That was Joe (as I don't know if he'd mind being named, I'll protect his privacy); he just graduated with a double major in business and economics. The last half of his senior year was pretty tough — even though he'd always been a dean's list student — because his grandmother got sick."

I knew this was going somewhere so I just let Royal talk.

"He said he felt so helpless watching her suffer, that he could tell her to invest in gold or diversify her portfolio, but since she wasn't an investor and didn't have a portfolio, he felt pretty useless."

Here Royal stared off, fiddling with his wedding ring, and after a moment he told me he was the grandmother's doctor.

"Joe told me how much he appreciated me taking the time to sit and listen to her, how he couldn't believe that when I learned his grandmother played Scrabble, I set up a board, and we'd make our plays during my rounds. As if that were any hardship on my part!"

(Royal's an avid Scrabble player.)

"Joe thanked me for, quote, making his grandmother's last weeks a lot nicer than they could have been. I told him I was just doing my job, to which he replied, 'That's what I'd like to do.'"

"So he's going onto medical school?" I asked, quickly adding the very relevant question: "What if he gets drafted?"

"He dodged that bullet—or should I say bullets." said Royal. "He enlisted right out of school and luckily was never sent over."

(To all of you potential letter writers admonishing my husband's patriotism; let me remind you that Royal is a veteran whose experiences in Korea have molded his position that war should only be a very last resort.)

Royal then went on to say that Joe had accepted a position at an investment firm in Chicago.

"And he told me that he wants to doctor his clients the way I doctored his grandmother; he wants each one to know they matter. He was a very thoughtful young man. We talked about everything from emerging markets to cancer treatments to Sophia Loren."

"Ooh," I said, "what'd you say about her?"

Royal shook his head. "Privileged information."

I went to bed thinking about that young man and how lucky he is to have figured out such an important thing already. Imagine the kind of a world where everyone believes everyone else matters. It'd be the end of war (oh, when will the one we're in stop?) of famine, of persecution; the end of everything that imperils this beautiful place. Oh my. I luxuriated in thinking about this brave new world for a good long time, but then my shallow side surfaced through my deep thoughts, and I wondered, what *did* they say about Sophia Loren?

August 14, 1970

Our state bird is the loon, our state flower is the lady's slipper, and our state motto is "L'Étoile du Nord" (which is a pretty fancy French motto for modest Minnesotans). Do you notice I say "our"? Yes, my allegiance has officially switched from my home state to the one I now call home.

Growing up in North Dakota, where the earth was spread out like a smooth and endless carpet, I never paid much mind to the beauties of the prairie, but I do appreciate them now: the way the nap of that carpet—grass, wheat, soy and corn fields—changes in the wind, how dawn and dusk play out on that vast, endless horizon of sky, the wide-openness of the place.

But Minnesota, ahh, Minnesota with its bounty of trees, of pines and spruce and birch and ash and oaks and elms and maples, with a lake to the left of you and a lake to the right.

Our big "official" honeymoon has not yet been taken (it's been over two and a half years, but who's counting?), and so we continue, when our schedules work out, to take our little honeymoons, hereafter known as our honey (*crescent*) moons. We recently packed up the car with gear and provisions and drove to Grand Marais, a charming little town that huddles alongside Lake Superior. We climbed along what's called (the things you learn!) a tombolo, an island connected to shore via a gravel bar. This particular tombolo (I love that word—it sounds like an Italian brass instrument) is called Artists' Point, and rightly so as there were several artists, canvasses set up on easels, capturing the landscape—or waterscape—with their oil paints and brushes.

We puttered around the Ben Franklin store there, and Royal bought me a new notebook (I'm writing this in it now) with a picture of a black bear on its cover. I bought him a T-shirt with a loon whose speech bubble reads, "I'm Crazy about Grand Marais."

We drove up the Gunflint Trail, a gorgeous scenic byway that meanders from Lake Superior's North Shore to the banks of the Boundary Waters Canoe Area. Readers, heed my advice: take this drive through dark green forests, past lakes that were dug out by glaciers. If possible, take it with someone who will sing—as Royal did—songs that hail the beautiful outdoors: "I've Been Everywhere," "This Land Is Your Land," "The Happy Wanderer," and "God Bless America."

Royal didn't object to me joining in, although my voice is one that is always in search of a key; he was more about sharing the joy of voices raised. In fact, his strong and lovely voice was like a hand, pulling up my more feeble one.

One song we improvised, to the tune of a Christmas carol, was inspired by the wildlife we managed to avoid hitting (whew!) as they leaped, jumped, and ran across the two-lane road.

"Five golden deer! Four sly raccoons, three hopping rabbits, two skittering skunks, and a moose with a rack of huge antlers!"

It was a little vacation hour-wise but a big vacation experience-wise. We paddled a canoe on two deep blue lakes, we fished successfully, eating our northern pike on an open campfire, we skipped rocks, hiked trails, and at the Gunflint Lodge, played a rousing game of Texas Hold 'Em with a couple from Bristol, England.

My niece and her bridegroom got so sunburnt on their Mexican honeymoon that they came back home two days early. My old college roommate got her passport and

money stolen in Paris on her honeymoon and spent too
much time at a place that wasn't on their initial itinerary: the
American Embassy. I'm not denigrating honeymoons. It's
just that our honey (crescent) moons are working out just
fine, thank you.

"Compliments of the gentlemen in the corner booth," says the
waiter, placing another round of drinks in front of Shannon, Maureen, and Susan.

The women look across the bar to see three men waving.

"Oh no," says Susan. "It's the Alpha Alpha Assholes."

"Tell them thanks but no thanks," Shannon instructs the waiter,
adding, "Put this round on my tab."

"Okay," says the waiter, trying to hide his smile. He'd waited on
the same men the night before, and they had tipped him about 5
percent.

"So tell us more," says Maureen, helping herself to the skewered
cocktail onions in her just-delivered martini.

"Well, he was often mentioned in her columns—you know, as
having accompanied her to this performance or on that trip to the
Twin Cities—but she really did want to respect his privacy, and so
she didn't write all that many columns specifically about him."

"Did they ever take their 'official' honeymoon?" asks Shannon.
"And did she write about it?"

"No. She never wrote about an official honeymoon because she
never got to take one."

"She didn't?" says Maureen, her voice soft.

Taking a sip of her chardonnay, Susan shakes her head.

April 18, 1971

When it rains, it pours . . . and sometimes a typhoon
sweeps in. Most of you are aware of the two-hundred-mph
gales and crashing waves that threatened to drown me and
pushed me way out to sea, where I bobbed up, far from
shore, clinging to the lifesaver not of my making, but yours.
Yes, your many kindnesses—from your cards and letters to

your offers to chauffeur/shop/clean, to the many hot dishes swaddled in dishtowels, to the pies, cakes, and canned tomatoes and peaches delivered—thank you. (And to Mrs. Melvin Henke and Doris Dussault, a special thank you; grief stepped out into the hallway anytime I helped myself to your Famous Chinese Chicken Casserole and your Lemon Dream Pie, respectively.) And how to thank my mother, who tended me so carefully these past weeks?

Yes, as it's been reported in this paper, Royal, my dear husband is dead. (I can just hear Mrs. Cullin scolding me, "It took you a whole paragraph before you introduce your topic sentence!") But you see, I don't want it to be my topic sentence, I don't want it to be my topic, I don't want it to be true.

My slim, nonsmoking husband felled by a heart that should have beat for decades longer, but according to the autopsy couldn't because its left anterior artery was totally blocked. They call the kind of heart attack he had a "widow-maker," and they called it right, because it made me a widow.

Winter has reluctantly stepped aside, and yesterday I opened the kitchen windows to let in the toddling infant that is spring. Air so fresh I could clean my countertops with it burst in, and the polka-dot curtains flew up with a gasp, like skirts in a mischievous wind. When we first moved into our house, Royal insisted we keep the yellow-and-white curtains the previous owner left because they made him smile.

I didn't tell him that I thought they were gaudy—the polka dots were nearly as big as tennis balls, and one of the first items on my "to do" list was to "sew new kitchen curtains!"

I hadn't gotten around to it, and I'm glad the curtains are still here, and in them, one of the stories of our married life together. A short life—we just celebrated our third anniversary in December—but still, it seems our house sings with his songs. I know I should close the fall board to keep the dust out of the piano, but I just can't, wanting it ready for him to sit down and play, wanting to hear his and Brigadoon's "Hound Dog" duet.

Royal always got up before me and always whistled when he shaved, and I'd holler out a sleepy, "Don't cut yourself!" to which he'd holler, "Ouch!" A little joke. So many little jokes funny and dear to no one but us. He was a meticulous man (which you want your doctor to be), and the brush in his shaving mug is rinsed clean, but I still hold it to my nose and smell his shaving cream on it. To me, it's a perfume I could get lost in.

I have asked, "Why me?" a hundred thousand times, but I asked the same question, albeit with less rage and more awe when I fell in love with Royal and he asked me to marry him. "Why me?" It had been my luck for a long time that the coin landed on heads. Now it's clattered to the floor, landing on tails.

Susan has just finished telling the women about the column when the fraternity men stumble past them.

"Hope you're enjoying your drinks," slurs one of them, and to his friends he says, "Buncha lezzies."

10

Sitting on his bike, his fingers curled around the chain-link fence, Sam watches a backhoe dig up dirt and a bulldozer push it around at the new library construction site. It is only when he looks up and sees the big digital sign in front of the Granite Creek Savings & Loan flashing the time and temperature—11:14AM 84 DEGREES—that he pushes off.

Now after the twenty-minute ride to Kingleigh Lake, he pulls up his T-shirt by its hem and swabs his face with it.

"Geez, it's hot," he says, positioning himself on the beach towel.

"It's summer, my friend," says Jacob.

"Oh . . . so that's what it is," says Sam, irritated by Jacob's new habit of ending sentences with phrases like, "my friend," "old chap," and worst, "guv'nor." Sam is further annoyed that Jacob is bare chested and doesn't have to hide his body behind his T-shirt the way Sam feels compelled to do.

Both boys, stretched out and propped up on their elbows, gaze out at the lake, past the shoreline where little kids fill buckets with sand or splash around in the shallow water, to the floating raft where two girls in bikinis are practicing their dives.

"Man, that one in the pink sure has nice tits," says Jacob. "I wish I had some binoculars."

"I wish I had x-ray vision," says Sam.

"Let's go in," says Jacob. "And get a better look."

"Go ahead. I'll be in in a minute."

Jacob runs frog-legged into the water before diving in, and Sam watches as he swims out to the raft. When he hoists himself up the ladder, both girls dive off, and when they start swimming to shore, Sam laughs. Jacob considers himself a ladies' man, and while Sam envies his friend's confidence, he can't help enjoying when the ladies themselves aren't impressed.

Sam leans back and closes his eyes, letting his other senses luxuriate in the hot summer day; he feels the sun on his face, hears the sounds of splashing, the laughter, and shouts, smells suntan lotion and lake water and grape popsicles. He licks his upper lip and tastes the salt of sweat.

That morning at the office, he had brought in a file of Haze's columns with his notes as to each one's subject and which ones he thought should be reprinted, and after Caroline, his boss while his mother was away, thumbed through them, she told him to take the rest of the day off.

"Why?" he had asked, afraid he'd done something wrong.

Caroline had laughed at the look on his face. "Because it's such a beautiful day. And because you've been doing such a good job."

"But my mom might—"

"It'll be fine with your mom. She likes to reward hard work. Really. Go have some fun. Go to the lake or something."

He had texted news of his unexpected freedom to Jacob, who texted back: "ALREADY HERE."

Sam's mother will be coming back tomorrow from whatever conference or panel or convention she's been at, and he wonders vaguely what they'll have for dinner. It used to be that whenever Sam's mother returned from a trip, she'd bring him and his brother a present—often a Hot Wheels car to add to their collections but sometimes souvenirs (plastic beehive banks after her visit to Salt Lake City, rubber crocodiles from Florida). When Susan realized that not just Jack but Sam too had grown out of the toy/hokey souvenir stage, it had been her policy to make a special dinner when she returned.

It recently occurred to Sam that maybe *he* should be the one making dinner—after all she would probably be tired from the travel—but it's another good intention of his that fails to leave the starting gate.

A hip-hop song blasts from a car radio in the parking lot and fades away as the car drives off. He hears a kid whining about sand in his sandwich and his sister's rejoinder: "Maybe next time you'll stay on the blanket like Mommy told you."

Maybe his mother will make stir-fry, Sam thinks—he loves her stir-fry. Or maybe they'll grill hamburgers out on the deck. For the thousandth time, Sam thinks, Thanks a lot, Dad, as another memory fills his head of how things used to be—this one of his dad wearing his "Kiss the Chef" apron and calling out, "Prepare for magic," every time he lit the charcoal.

Sam feels droplets of water on his face before a hand pushes his shoulder up and down. He hears laughter and opens his eyes to see Jacob looming above him.

"Come on, Sam, wake up!"

"Huh?" asks Sam, and when his frame of vision widens to see the two bikinied girls standing behind Jacob, he pushes himself up, feeling clumsy and babyish. He can't believe he'd fallen asleep, and he pretends to scratch his chin, although he's really checking for drool.

Rolling up his towel, Jacob says, "Sam, this is Lena, and that's Shauna. Lena works at the FoodKing with me. We're going over to Nick's to party—he's the head cashier—so, come on."

Sam feels fat in his T-shirt and stupid for having been napping like a baby.

"Oh man, I wish I could," he says, "but I've got to get back to work."

"I thought you had the day off," says Jacob, stuffing his towel in his backpack.

"Nah," says Sam, trying to sound casual. "I'm supposed to be back there by one."

"Where do you work?" asks Lena or Shauna, Sam can't tell who's who.

"At the paper," says Sam. "The *Granite Creek Gazette*?"

"Then you'd better hurry," says Lena or Shauna, whichever one is looking at her phone. "It's quarter to."

Riding back, Sam mutters and swears at himself: What is his

problem? He'd heard Jacob talk about the eighteen-year-old Nick and how he supplemented his cashier income by selling weed and Ecstasy, and how he lived with his older brother and threw rad parties, and not only did Sam decline an invitation, but he lied about having to work? What kind of loser was he?

A car honks at him from behind, and Sam veers closer to the side of the road.

He salutes with his middle finger just as a boy, sitting in the car's passenger side, waves to him.

Recognizing the kid as a fifth-grader he was paired up with at last year's tri-school field day, Sam quickly readjusts his fingers and flutters them in a wave.

"YOU'RE BACK!" says Caroline, surprised when he returns to the office. Sam's pretty surprised himself—he had planned to just chill at his dad's, maybe play some *Grand Theft Auto*, but when he went to the condo to change, Mac was there, back from a weeklong sales trip to the West Coast. Mac was a nice enough guy, but it was, after all, his condo, and whenever Sam was there, he tried to be respectful of his host's space.

"Yeah, nobody was at the lake," lies Sam, "so after I swam for a while, I thought I might as well get back to the grindstone."

"That's quite a work ethic you've got," says Caroline. "I'm impressed."

Sam shrugs elaborately. "Feel free to tell your boss."

They both laugh, and a tiny bit of Sam's anger and frustration lift.

It had been decided that since the conference room was often in use, Sam should now use Haze's office, and he reads a couple of Haze's columns, setting aside one paired with Mr. Joseph Snell's usual out-of-joint response to show Caroline for possible publication. He shouldn't have come back to work—what kind of loser goes back to work when he could have gone and partied with *girls*? He drums the lip of Haze's desk with his fingers, rocks back and forth on her office chair, and swivels back and forth, looking to the file cabinets to the left and right of the bookshelf. When he stops swiveling, he leans his head back in his hands and stares at the bookshelf while chastising himself for being such a dweeb, such a loser, such a *fucking* loser. He wonders what Jacob and Lena and Shauna are doing now. Probably getting high and making out, two recreational activities Sam has yet to do. His eyes are fixed on the highest shelf of the bookcase, and a long moment passes. Sam squints—maybe what he's staring at is a book spine without any print on it, maybe a dictionary or something. Squinting again, Sam sees—what, hinges?—on one side of it. He gets up, and on his tiptoes he can just reach the top shelf, and he grips the mystery rectangle and pulls it down.

Setting it on the desk, Sam stares at it, like an archaeologist studying a dug-up bone.

Stained so its grain shows through, it's not a book but a wooden box, with the words "Pirate Booty" etched into it. Its lid hinges are brass, and so is its keyhole. Keyhole. A flare of excitement spritzes in Sam's chest as he remembers the key in the small rosemaled box, and he retrieves it from inside the desk drawer. Taking a deep breath—he's enjoying the drama of the moment—he takes the key that's inside the little decorated box and puts it into the other box's lock. It fits, and as he turns it, his heart hammers. He opens the lid.

His shoulders slump with disappointment. He didn't know what "pirate booty" he was expecting to find: unmarked bills? narcotics? a gun? *Something* more exciting than a bunch of papers and a notebook. With one finger, he flips down the lid, but a moment later he flips it back up, and with a roll of his eyes, as if he's performing to an audience, he reaches for the papers. He pulls off the paper clip and begins to read.

> Darling, I wonder if that's a new dress? It must be, for I like to think I keep a close eye on all the beauty that is just down the hall. If it's not a new dress, know that it looks new to me, or is it that I'm just so dazzled by you that all your finery looks new and sparkling?
>
> Darling, do you realize it's our anniversary? One year since my dream of you became a reality. I know silver represents

twenty-five years, and gold fifty—as short as our time has been together, it's all platinum . . .

> *Haze, A Poem*
> *Haze, Haze, Haze*
> *I'm in one*
> *Because of you*
> *A soft haze*

Sam has a flicker of conscience that warns him he's treading on private property, that reading Haze's long-ago written columns is one thing, but reading love letters written to her is another thing entirely. But conscience is weak and puny when challenged by a mighty curiosity, and he keeps reading.

PART TWO

11

After Royal's death, Haze didn't know if she could lend the possessive "her" to the word "sanity." Shock and numbness had gotten her through her husband's funeral; had allowed her to stand up straight in the receiving line, accepting the handshakes and hugs of hundreds of people; had allowed her to take a few bites of the luncheon the Ladies' Circle had provided in the church basement; had allowed her, over the following weeks, to express her grief in a semblance of a column and send her mother to the paper with it; had allowed her to write over two hundred thank-you cards and affix stamps to them; but as she dumped the last stack into the mailbox, she leaned against the cold blue metal, afraid to step away because she was sure she would fall and keep falling.

IT WAS BILL MCGRATH, Royal's best friend, who pulled Haze away from the precipice. Not with a sudden yank of her shirttail but with slow and steady signs of concern.

She was burrowed under the covers of her bed, the place she had decided to stay for the rest of what she hoped would be her brief life, when one afternoon Bill gently knocked on the shaded window and told her not to be scared, but he was coming in.

He sat in the chair in the corner of the room, the chair Royal always used to sit in when he tied his shoes.

"Haze, we're worried about you." After sitting in silence for a long while, he added, "and I know you're not sleeping."

"I'm going to start locking my door," said Haze, her voice muffled.

Bill's laugh was soft. "See, I knew you weren't sleeping."

Another silence moved in, settling in the room like a cold front. Finally, sighing, Haze emerged from the covers, pushing herself up and leaning against the headboard.

"Your mother left?" asked Bill.

"She would have stayed longer, but I sent her back home. Just because I don't have a life doesn't mean she shouldn't."

"Oh, Haze," said Bill, and his chair became an ejector seat in response to the hurt in her voice and on her face.

Sitting on the side of the bed, he took her hand between his.

"I know it doesn't seem possible right now, Haze, but you are going to get through this."

Haze shook her head, and when she spoke, her voice seemed to come from far away.

"I don't see how."

Six weeks after Royal's death, a pale and gaunt woman opened the door to the *Gazette* offices, startling the young, newly hired receptionist so much that she rocked sideways in her chair, nearly falling off it.

"I know I've looked better," the woman said in a rusty voice, "but I usually don't get such an . . . honest reaction."

"No, I just . . . I get here early, and I . . . I just didn't expect anyone yet."

"Never mind," said Haze, offering her hand and introducing herself. "And you obviously are not Berta."

"No, I'm Shelly. Shelly Clausen. Berta's replacement."

"Oh, yes, Berta retired." To herself, she muttered, "I'll have to call her."

Shelly wished that the phone would ring, and when it didn't, she scribbled something on her memo pad. She had read about the columnist and her recent tragedy and wanted to say something, but nerves and shyness were like a trap in her throat, permitting no words to exit.

"Well, then," said Haze, rapping her knuckles on the reception-ist's desk, "Welcome aboard, Shelly."

In her office, Haze sat straight in her chair, hands lightly resting on the leather border of her desk blotter. This space was her sanctu-ary, her favorite place in the world next to the home she and Royal had shared, but now she felt like the new girl, seated at a school desk with no one to tell her where the bathroom was, what time the lunch bell rang, whether the teacher was mean or nice.

But then Joan Dwyer came into the office, and after her, a steady stream of people, all offering sympathy, welcome, and the odd gift. After Roger Czielski gave her a hug and a can of macadamia nuts— "They're from Hawaii!"—Haze shut her office door, which was al-ways her signal that she was working.

"Which I might as well do," she said to herself, feeding a piece of paper behind the platen of her Selectric typewriter and pressing the return key. She had no idea what she wanted to say, but her fingers didn't care, and they began jumping across the keys.

May 23, 1971
Garret Powell, a boy in the grade ahead of me, accidentally shot his twin brother to death with the rifle they had gotten for their fifteenth birthday.

The sheriff was quoted in the paper as saying, "The boys were just horsing around!" and anyone who knew Garret and his brother, Gilbert, thought, "of course they were." They were big, strapping, fun-loving boys who staged elaborate practical jokes, who greeted the world with laughter and an eager attitude of "what's next?"

Garret's grief was dark and deep, and after two attempts on his own life, his parents had him committed. He was in the state institution for a long time, and when he was released, he went home to help run the family farm.

Several years ago when I was visiting my mother, I was shopping on Main Street, and out of Major's Bar I saw a figure stumble, weave, and then fall to the sidewalk.

I rushed over and saw that it was Garret, who had not aged at all well.

"Thank you, miss," he said, not recognizing me as I helped him up. "I'd ask you"—his words were slurred, and yet he had that careful, affected posture of someone trying to hide their drunkenness—"I'd ask you to excuse my condition, but I know it's inexcusable."

I don't want my condition to be inexcusable. I know people suffer, brothers accidentally shoot their twins, young mothers get diagnosed with inoperable cancer, first-graders get run over by their own school buses, leaving, of course, their loved ones behind at an intersection of despair and grief.

I am at that crossroads. I took the luck that brought Dr. Royal Kirby into my life for granted, thought it had a shelf life of, oh, at least fifty years. We were married for only three years and four months, and I can honestly say I was still in the "madly in love" phase. My heart would speed up when he'd come through the door, and I'd open my arms and rush to him.

Royal laughed at my jokes as if I were a Vegas headliner. We planted together our vegetable garden, but he weeded it, because he knew how much I hated that chore. After I forced him into dance lessons, he became an eager partner, and our first dance at Zig's was to Tony Bennett's "Fly Me to the Moon," and that song title became our catchphrase.

"Would you like scrambled eggs for breakfast?"

"I'd rather you fly me to the moon."

"Royal, where should we go for vacation?"

"Fly me to the moon."

Like all private jokes and passwords shared with those you love, they were banal and stupid, precious and dear.

Today the one thing that made me get out of bed, that made me get here into my office and at my desk, is that I was loved. My husband died, but that can't take away the absolute fact that I was loved.

And if Dr. Royal Kirby had anything to say about it, he

would say (in his deep, sonorous voice), "Haze, here's my prescription for you: just keep going. I'm so sorry I can't be with you as you keep going—we had such plans!— but that's what I'd do if I had to face the indescribable, unimaginable idea of life without you. I'd try to find a way to just keep going."

So that's what I'm doing now. I don't want to be like Garret Powell, stumbling out of a bar and apologizing for my condition. That wouldn't honor my husband, Dr. Royal Kirby, who not only would have written me a prescription to keep going, he'd have called the drugstore to make sure the pharmacist had filled it.

HAZE DIDN'T EVEN PROOFREAD THE COLUMN but yanked it out of the typewriter and marched down the hallway to Bill's office.

"Hi, Joan," she said, slapping the pages on his secretary's desk. "Give this to Bill, will you?"

"Of course, Haze. Oh, I'm so glad you're—"

But Haze had already turned around and was jogging back to her office, trying to outrun emotions she didn't even know were in the race. She wrote another column about Royal that afternoon, ignoring the rainfall of tears on her fingers.

WORK WAS A BALM FOR HER. In the daytime, among her friends in the office, or out with pad and pen in hand, interviewing a quilter, a bird-watcher, a National Merit Scholar, she was able to bob above that riptide of grief that pulled her under at night. For five solid months after Royal died, she cried herself to sleep, waking up an hour or two later with a start, scared out of sleep by nightmares. She had been told of Royal's last minutes by a sobbing Carol Meyer, the pediatric nurse who on her way to her station wagon in the hospital parking lot saw Royal stagger out of his car, clutching his chest, falling to the concrete, but Haze never dreamed of this scenario; instead she chased her husband down narrow bazaar corridors or stood in a crowd in front of a tall building, calling up to Royal through a megaphone, pleading with him not to jump.

The first time she slept all through the night, she woke up feeling not refreshed but guilty. Royal had died suddenly, painfully, and the least she could do was to be wracked by nightmares—what kind of wife was she anyway?

The first time she laughed, she immediately burst into tears. She'd been with Lois at a garage sale, browsing through a dusty collection of salt and pepper shakers displayed on one half of a ping-pong table.

"Look," said Lois, picking up a squat figurine wearing a crown and holding a scepter. "It's Myra Willouby." This was the garden club president known for her imperious air. Lois shook the figurine, and a flutter of pepper was released from its crown.

"Always fertilize!" said Lois, her voice shrill. "One must always fertilize."

Haze offered a chuckle at Lois's impression, and the chuckle grew until both women, hunched over with laughter, made their way past Avis Stephens, the garage sale host, who'd been forced by her husband to sell a third of her collection, pleading with her, "How many damn salt and pepper shakers does a person need anyway?"

Haze and Lois laughed all the way to Lois's car, but when Haze slammed shut her door, the tears that had risen through laughter changed their inspiration.

"Oh, Lois!" she cried. "How can I laugh? What right do I have to laugh?"

ON THE FIRST ANNIVERSARY of Royal's death, Bill had said, "absolutely," when Haze asked if he'd drive up Highway 61 with her to honor Royal's wishes of having his ashes scattered on Lake Superior.

"I just couldn't give him up any earlier," Haze said as they stood on a rocky outcropping by the Split Rock Lighthouse, watching the last cloud of ash dust the dark water.

It was a raw, windy day, and after a long, forlorn silence, Haze said, "I almost wish I would have buried him. At least I'd have a tombstone to visit."

"What would it say?" Bill asked.

Haze stared out at the cold expanse of gray.

"'Dear, Beloved Husband.' 'Man O' My Heart.'"

"I'd add, 'True friend,'" said Bill solemnly. "'Respected Doctor.'"

"I don't know if I could afford all those letters," said Haze, and they chuckled weakly, the way people do at old memories and regrets.

THEY STOOD SENTRY FOR A LONG TIME, and then as if they'd both received an invisible nudge, they turned away, making their way up the rocks to the path and the car.

On the second anniversary of Royal's death, Bill stuck his head in Haze's office and mouthed, "See you tomorrow night?"

She nodded in answer.

HAZE WROTE TO MAKE SENSE OF THINGS, so of course she had to write about the wild turn her life had taken. As was her decades-long habit, she addressed her thoughts to a woman whose high, halting voice she had heard on a radio broadcast, whose story her mother had told her, and whose books she later read. How the woman had fought as a child to communicate and how she learned to do what Haze herself loved to do—to read and write, albeit in different ways—inspired Haze as a girl to direct all journal entries not to "Dear Diary" but to "Miss Keller." It made her feel her words were more substantial, more considered. By the time Haze got to high school, she had dropped using the formal title, feeling the person who helped her collect her thoughts wouldn't mind the more familiar greeting.

June 18, 1973

Dear Helen,

My columns have served as my public journal; I get to write about what interests me and share it with readers. I am so glad I can share my private feelings here; I'd go crazy if I couldn't vent with pen and paper.

Oh, Helen, I am torn between dancing a jig and breaking all laws of science by evaporating from the face of the earth.

I have fallen in love with Royal's best friend and my publisher, who happens to be married to a very lovely woman named Eleanor, who is a credit to the community and an impeccable hostess who graciously welcomes people (including me) into her home for elegant dinner parties. I feel shame and guilt and disgust over my actions, but the actions don't stop because trumping all these feelings is love. I talk to Royal a lot, and although my mind hasn't deteriorated to the point where he answers, I know he's rooting me on. That sounds ridiculous as I write it, but one thing I learned from my good doctor was that contained within the utilitarian muscle that is the human heart, there is untold mystery.

"People can't help their feelings, Haze," he said. We'd been talking about his hospital administrator—a staid, personality-free guy as far as I'd been able to tell—and the gift shop volunteer, who'd both left their spouses to run off with one another. I, righteous in my morality, had sniffed and said, "People might not be able to help them, but they don't have to act on them, especially when others will be directly hurt."

I still believe that . . . but now I also understand actions like people leaving their spouses to run off together.

Oh, how to explain what seems unexplainable? It's just that Bill was so . . . so good to me. I started to rely on him. Not for anything romantic or sexual—that was the farthest thing from my mind—but for his kindness, his helpfulness. When I could barely get out of bed, he had groceries delivered. He hired a high school boy to weed the garden and mow the lawn in the summer, and after the first snowstorm of the season, he sent the same kid over to shovel me out. And then his kindnesses started meaning more . . .

What the hell am I doing? The sad but exhilarating truth is, I don't care.

12

Judging from the look on Bill's face, their first kiss was as much a surprise to him as it was to Haze. Pulling apart as frantically as they pulled together, they stared at one another, eyes wild, their breath ragged.

My Year of Yodeling was an amusing book about a young American woman working at a Swiss ski lodge, but it quickly became apparent to Haze that while the author was funny on the page, she decidedly was not on the dais, and not wanting to nod off as it appeared many audience members had, she slipped out during the presentation. Coming out of the dank basement bathroom, she gasped as she and Bill McGrath, coming out of the Palace Theater's men's room, nearly collided.

"I didn't know you were here!" said Haze at the same time Bill said, "Haze, what a surprise!" and after they shared a laugh, Bill said, "I haven't read Miss Fredlund's book yet, but if she writes the way she speaks . . . I believe I'll skip it."

"It was much livelier than you'd think," said Haze, but she might as well have said, "You drive me wild, Bill McGrath," because a second after her words left her mouth, she and Bill flung their arms around one another, and her mouth became occupied with an entirely different enterprise.

"What . . . what," began Haze after the suction of their lips loosened and they staggered apart, staring at one another.

"I . . . I'm sorry," said Bill.

Haze fumbled in her purse for her lipstick. "Don't be sorry," she said, taking off the tube's grooved gold cover and turning the base so that a bullet of red rose. Gliding it over her mouth, she pressed her lips together.

"Okay?"

Not quite sure whether she was questioning the state of her lipstick or offering reassurance for what had just happened, Bill nevertheless nodded, and because he believed himself to be a man of action who seized opportunities, he said, "Could I come over later tonight?"

"Lois and I were planning to go to the Sundown after this," said Haze, but before disappointment had a chance to settle on Bill's face, she added, "but I should be home by ten."

They heard footsteps on the marble stairs, and they exchanged another wild-eyed look before Bill ducked into the men's room and Haze patted her hair and smoothed her skirt, and as she ascended the stairs, she said to the woman descending them, "How are you enjoying the lecture, Mrs. Snell?"

"Thankfully Joseph got free tickets through the Rotarians," said the over-rouged woman. "So it wasn't a total waste of time *and* money."

HOURS LATER Haze opened her kitchen door, and Bill stepped onto the little coir mat as he had done dozens of times before, but this time his arms were empty of crossword puzzle books or a pie or hot dish Eleanor had made. This time, they opened and Haze stepped into them.

Their embrace wasn't tight so much as it was steadfast, the way two people would hold each other after surviving a storm, and they stood that way for a long time, until Haze pulled away. At the same time, she took Bill's hand, and he quietly followed her.

THEIR LOVEMAKING had a seriousness to it, their sounds of pleasure soft and subdued, and when Haze climaxed, she didn't shudder so much as pulsed.

Haze wasn't a smoker, but Bill was, and when he asked if she'd mind if he had a cigarette, she shook her head.

"It reminds me of my dad," she said, watching Bill as he got up and fumbled in the pockets of his sport coat, draped over the sewing table chair.

There was a click, and then a flare of light rose against the shadowy light, and Haze leaned over to get the ashtray that was in the nightstand drawer.

"Here," she said, handing him the metal dish that sat atop what seemed to be a plaid beanbag. "I keep this for when my sister and her husband visit. They smoke too."

"It's a filthy habit," said Bill, and exhaling, he added, "Most of the good ones are."

Haze chuckled and held out her fingers in a V.

Bill passed her the cigarette even as he protested that she didn't smoke.

"I'm not going to inhale," said Haze. "It just seems a good way to mark the occasion." She puffed quickly on the Pall Mall and just as quickly blew out a puff of smoke.

Leaning against the headboard, Bill drew one arm behind his head. When he took back the cigarette from Haze, he took a long drag and released the smoke in a row of wavery rings, which they watched until they deflated and disappeared.

"Haze, whatever happens after tonight, is up to you. I have my hopes, of—"

"What are your hopes?"

Bill studied the glowing end of his cigarette for a moment before he tapped the cigarette, the ash falling with soundless resignation into the tray.

"Well, I thought this was a pretty big 'occasion,' and my hopes are that it's the first of many."

"Why?" asked Haze, her voice as small as a girl's.

"Because I think I love you."

His words were true, but he didn't know it until he said—and heard—them out loud.

"Oh God," he said.

"That's how I feel too, Bill." Tears welled in Haze's eyes. "I'm both thanking Him and asking for forgiveness."

Bill nodded, his head so heavy his chin grazed his chest.

IT WAS SURPRISINGLY EASY to carry on their affair. Bill had a decades-long habit of taking long, late-night walks, explaining to Eleanor that it not only helped soothe his insomnia, but he liked to think about the day's news and how the paper had presented it. After their two sons were grown, Eleanor occasionally joined him, but although he was a good sport about it, she could see that her presence defeated the whole contemplative idea of the walk, and besides, she was an early-to-bed-early-to-rise person and was often under the covers and softly snoring by the time he laced up his walking shoes.

"DO YOU THINK ELEANOR SUSPECTS ANYTHING?" Haze asked, the fourth time she and Bill slept together. It was a question she didn't want to ask him, even as she had asked herself a million, zillion times.

"I don't," said Bill, his voice clear but flat. "It would never occur to her to even wonder."

"That sounds so mean."

"That's not how I meant it," said Bill, rolling his broad-shouldered body so that he faced Haze. "What I meant was Eleanor's a trusting person, and I've never given her a reason not to trust me—until now."

"You never had another affair?"

Bill laughed. "I don't know if I like your tone of voice."

"Well, according to Marilyn Sagerstrom all successful, attractive men do." Seeing the look on Bill's face, Haze added, "The entrepreneur from Taylors Falls who was in my column last week? The one who invented that quick-dry fabric? She spent about a third of our conversation on what cheating bastards successful, attractive men are."

"Was she married to one?"

Haze nodded. "She asked that I not write about him, but really, she's so bitter, I don't know if she can enjoy her success. And she just got huge contracts with the air force and the coast guard!"

"Well, for the record," said Bill. "I've never been unfaithful to Eleanor . . . until now."

Haze's eyes blurred with tears. "I don't want to hurt her."

Bill enveloped Haze in his arms and whispered into her hair, "Neither do I."

September 12, 1974

I don't think the little head shot that accompanies my column flatters me, but apparently it's a good-enough likeness that people recognize me now and then. Even though our paper's circulation has a wider radius than you'd think, being recognized outside Granite Creek is uncommon (make that extremely rare). I had spoken at a Women in Business luncheon in the Cities, and driving home, I decided to get a little grocery shopping done at the supermarket near my highway turnoff (it's always a little exotic to shop at an unfamiliar store), and it was in the cereal aisle that I had a little bumper-cart incident with a woman.

We both apologized, and then, with a big smile, she said, "Say, I know you! I never miss one of your columns!"

Her smile was gracious but fleeting, and she wagged her finger, saying she had a bone to pick with me.

"I have children," she said, her jaw now tight, "and some of the subjects you write about are not for kids! Your last one, for instance, where you railed against our new president—how am I supposed to teach my kids respect for our country and its leadership?"

I could have just offered a weak, "I'm sorry you feel that way," and vamoosed, but her cart blocked my exit, and besides, sometimes I just like to *engage*.

"How old are your children?" I asked sweetly.

"Mikey's ten, and Penny and Pammy are twelve." Her chest puffed out. "They're twins."

"And they read my columns?" My voice was as sugary as most of cereal surrounding us.

"They read the Sunday funnies, but that's about it."

"Then why do my columns bother you if your children aren't even reading them?"

"Because they might someday!"

Instead of doing the sane thing, which would be to offer a cheery ta-ta and barrel past her on my way to the frozen foods aisle, I said, "All right. Say they did read my columns— even if you disagreed with them, don't you think it might incite some interesting debate? A good exchange of ideas?"

"No—they don't need to be exchanging ideas!"

(Readers, I may be guilty of paraphrasing now and then but always strive to capture both the flavor and intent of conversations. These words, however, were verbatim.)

"And my latest column," I began, "the one about President Ford's pardon of Nixon?"

The woman nodded her head, her nose wrinkling as if she'd just taken a whiff of sour milk.

"You thought it didn't show respect for our country and its leadership?"

"*Exactly!*"

"But Nixon was charged with high crimes and misdemeanors! What respect did he show? He should have gone to jail!"

"He resigned—isn't that enough for you people? What good would it do us as a country to have our president in jail?"

A gangly stock boy heading down the aisle toward us abruptly turned around, like a witness fleeing from the scene of a crime.

"As I said in my column, it would have shown us all that no one—not even the president—is above the law!"

"This way we can all move forward! Like President Ford said, it's in the best interest of the country!"

"And I happen to disagree," I said, and finished with the

debate, I shoved my cart, not so that I would bang into hers, but close.

"And you know what else?" said the woman. "You should print more recipes! Less columns and more recipes!"

"The recipes are an occasional dessert! The columns are the regular meals!"

I don't know why I was so rattled, and if that woman in that particular supermarket reads this (although she may never read me again, but at least I hope she appreciates that I changed the names and sexes of her children), I apologize.* Not for the views I expressed in that—or any column—but for my parting, unnecessary shot.

"Here!" I said, "If you won't treat your kids to different opinions, to new ideas, give 'em these!" My aim was good; next to the two boxes of bran flakes and canister of oatmeal in her cart landed my well-aimed box of Lucky Charms. "They really are magically delicious!"

*Please take note of my largesse in giving this woman what she wanted: another recipe. It's not for a dessert, but these, hot out of the oven and served with butter and jelly, are delectable in their own right.

My mother would have tsked at my additions to the recipe name, but then she would have laughed.

MOM'S UPRIGHT (AND NOT UPTIGHT) POPOVERS

    2 eggs
    1 cup milk
    1 cup flour
    1 T butter
    ¼ t salt

Beat eggs, milk, and butter. Sift flour and salt; add to egg mixture, beating until smooth. Pour into well-greased muffin or popover tin. Bake 15 minutes at 475 degrees; reduce heat to 350 degrees, and bake 25 minutes. Prick with fork before serving to let out steam. Enjoy!

13

Haze and Bill's affair lasted more than three years, and no one, as far as they knew, ever got hurt. Except Haze, and she would never admit it to anyone, because she had no right to. Which made her think Bill might feel the same way, which in that case made two people who got hurt.

Haze wrote in her journal:

> But Helen, I got hurt loving Royal. Love doesn't exactly immunize you from hurt, in fact it sort of ensures it. But at least Eleanor never (as far as we know) found out. As far as we know, we were as clever as John le Carré spies, not doing anything to raise suspicion, covering all tracks that needed to be covered . . .

Susan, Bill's granddaughter, came from California to spend the summer with her grandparents, but her curfew was fairly early, and she was asleep—or at least in her room—by the time Bill indulged in one of his late-night walks that led to Haze's house.

Bill put Susan to work in the office, and she eagerly assumed her duties as an all-around gofer. A curious and inquisitive girl, she had a reverence for the written word, which of course endeared her to Haze.

"She loved my column about old radio programs," said Haze one night as she and Bill lay in the guest-room bed. "I wonder how many other thirteen-year-olds would have read that column!"

"She's a jewel," said Bill. "If her dad had showed a tenth of the interest Susan seems to show for the paper, well, I wouldn't have to worry who I'm going to hand the reins to."

"So it's okay to end a sentence with a preposition?"

"What?"

Haze laughed. "That's what I heard Susan ask Mitch. We were in the break room, and she was reading aloud that story about the fire at Belgum's resort. One of the sentences ended with a preposition."

Bill chuckled. "What did Mitch say?"

"The perfect thing. 'Rules of grammar are beautiful things, but they're also flexible things.'"

"I'm going to give that man a raise."

HAZE HAD TAKEN SUSAN UNDER HER WING. She took her out for lunch at the Sundown, answered her questions about where she got her column ideas and what she did when she didn't have any.

"I go outside," Haze had said. "I look around and find someone to talk to. Oops—there's a preposition at the end of my sentence."

The girl blushed. "Sorry. That comes from my English teacher, Miss Chavez. She's sort of hard-core."

Susan McGrath's presence was like higher-wattage bulbs in the light fixtures; everything brightened up. She was even able to get the usually dour receptionist, Shelly Clausen, to laugh once in a while (an odd, unexpected sound as it was heard so rarely). Most importantly, her enthusiasm reminded everyone why they were in the newspaper business in the first place, and it was always nice to remember that what you were doing was necessary, needed, and sometimes even noble.

Susan came back the next summer, when she was fourteen, the summer Eleanor was diagnosed with ovarian cancer.

Haze herself had been focused on her own ovaries, which weren't cancerous but had been busy doing their job, which was to excrete eggs . . . one of which happened to be fertilized and decided to stick around.

When her first period stalled, she didn't pay much attention; Haze's cycle wasn't strictly bound to any exact calendar number, and she and Bill were meticulous about using condoms, but when her second period failed to make an appearance, she began to wonder ... *Could I be?*

She gave a fake name at a clinic in Minneapolis (not that they'd recognize the small-town columnist, but why take chances), and when her pregnancy was confirmed, she drove home, entertaining herself with fantasies of what life was going to be with this new baby, so excited that when she got inside her house, she almost called Lois, but she had kept her affair with Bill a secret even from her best friend and didn't think she could spring news of a baby, let alone its parentage, in one phone call. If a hidden camera had been installed in Haze's home, it would have shown a woman dancing through rooms, cackling, would have shown a woman who looked like she was starring in a training film for DEA personnel—she obviously was high on *something.*

Bill had been in a series of meetings the next day, and Haze was glad; it eased the strong temptation of waltzing into his office to announce, "Guess what, Bill? I'm having your baby!"

When he joined a half-dozen *Gazette* employees at the Sundown for Happy Tea, Haze was tickled to be in a booth full of people with him, sitting on her secret like a hen warming an egg. When everyone had gone home, leaving them alone in the big red booth, Haze practically thrummed with excitement, but before she could tell Bill her big news—*their* big news—anguished words rushed out of her lover's mouth.

"Haze, Eleanor's got cancer. Ovarian cancer. We just found out."

Watching him take a big slug of beer and feeling everything inside her crumple, Haze whispered, "Oh, Bill. Oh, I'm so sorry."

"She's really going to need me now."

"Of course she is," said Haze, and unable to touch one another in the public place, they slouched in misery.

"Hey, what's the matter with you two?" asked Jules, bussing their table. "Somebody get fired?"

"You will be," said Haze, "if you keep serving those deep-fried mushrooms."

"Ha ha," said Jules. "They're one of our biggest sellers. And I can't be fired, I own the joint."

"A lucky technicality for you," said Bill.

Making little jokes was all they could do, and their pretense of mild good cheer continued until the bill was paid.

"I should get home," said Bill, as they stood out in front of the Sundown, trying to look like casual co-workers saying their good-nights.

"Of course," said Haze. "Of course."

SHE CRUMPLED ONTO HER BED—not the guest-room bed she and Bill shared, but hers and Royal's bed, the one she always slept in and the one Briggy always slept next to.

How could she have been so stupid? A baby with Bill. A genial divorce for him and Eleanor, who would understand Haze and Bill were powerless in the power of their love. Maybe they'd build a house out near Kingleigh Lake, one whose backyard faced the east so that Haze and the baby could watch the sunrise during early morning feedings, and with a big porch on the west side so she and Bill could watch the sunset, quietly discussing what astonishingly smart thing their baby had done that day—how pretty she was (Haze knew it was going to be a girl), how they would start her on piano for a musical foundation, but if she wanted to switch to saxophone or guitar, they'd certainly let her!

But now, after hearing that terrible news about Eleanor, Haze realized how silly, how girlish, how utterly rickety and unsustainable her fantasies had been. She lay in her bed as panic ebbed and flowed in her like a rapacious tide, but before that tide threw her against rocky shoals, Haze, understanding her therapy, sat up, took out her notebook from the nightstand drawer and began to write, her pen scratching against the paper as if it were trying to dig up something hidden, which of course is why she wrote.

July 3, 1976

Dear Helen,

It's been so easy to carry on with Bill. Okay, I'm feeling wild, feeling like control is something I'm aware of, but not something I'm necessarily possessed of, but even in this crazy, scary state, my editorial eye squints at my first sentence. "So easy to 'carry on' with Bill"? "Carry on"? What does that mean?

I knew it was wrong from the start. At least I thought I should know it was wrong from the start, but it's awfully easy to rationalize something that seems so right. And honestly, I know Royal would approve! (My heart races as I write that, not as some sort of fluttering lie detector needle indicating "liar! liar!" but as the reverse: it's beating hard at the truth.)

If our love was a pie chart (okay, now I know I'm crazy) divided into three parts delineating why it should exist, the first part would be "Because it would make Royal happy."

As absurd as it sounds, that is a deep and incontrovertible truth. I knew Royal as my husband, and Bill knew Royal as one of his best friends, and we both knew that his heart was wide-open and willing to accept love in all its beautiful, messy manifestations. Royal loved me, and he loved Bill, and he'd only want what made us happy.

"But adultery is wrong," I said to Bill in one of the many discussions we had about what we were doing. (The sex was nice—okay, *really* nice—but even nicer were all the long, deep, and meandering conversations we had. Sometimes I was happier when we finished making love, just so we could get to the pillow talk.)

"It is," Bill had agreed. "But sometimes it's okay to be wrong."

On my side of the bed, there was a pillow on the floor, thrown off in the hurly-burly of what we'd been doing under the covers, and I grabbed it and smacked Bill with it.

"I'm just quoting Royal," said Bill. "Who did add this caveat—'of course, not in the operating room.'"

The second wedge on the pie chart would read, "Because it makes us happy."

After Royal died, happiness was a state of being that I wasn't sure I'd ever again experience, but when it came to me, I welcomed it with open arms. I felt like a person near drowning who manages to paddle up through the dark, dank water and, bursting through, takes a big gulp of air and shouts, "yes!"

The third wedge of pie would be called, "Unknown." But really, when I think of it, maybe that's really what the whole pie is made of. I've always thought I had a strong moral compass, where you know there's a true north, but what happens when the needle points to "Are You Sure?" or "What about This?"

I know Eleanor didn't deserve to be cheated on, but I also know I didn't deserve to be widowed, and I did deserve to find love where I found it.

(I wish Bill had left his Pall Malls here; after reading that last sentence, I have a need to fire up a match and breathe in the cigarette's noxiousness and exhale it out.)

We are all such tender flowers—some of us are perennials (and for the longest time, I thought I was one) who get to bloom year after year, unimpeded by drought or bugs, too much sun, or too much shade—and the rest of us are annuals—so pretty and confident as we unfurl our petals, unaware that next season, we might not come up at all. This is all I know: I was lying fallow and was convinced that I was going to be weeded out of this garden of beauty, and then Bill came along and said, "Hey, I'll tend you, I value your poor withered leaves, I'll help them grow." What would you do? Would you think, "Nope, I'll just die here on the vine," or would you think, "No, no, I want to live!"?

I looked at Eleanor as a flower too, with Bill tending to her, but I also thought, hey, that gardener can take care of more than one plant! Of course I had to then think, what would I have done if Royal felt a need to take care of more than one garden?

I have no answer. There is no answer. I've been terribly wrong, and I've been terribly right.

More than anything, I want a baby. I wanted Royal to be the father of him/her but he wasn't. That never happened. But now there's a baby and her (I just know it's a her) father is married, *and* he's got teenaged grandchildren! But somehow we'll make it work, because more than anything, I'm our baby's mother.

SHE DIDN'T TELL BILL the next day at work because he didn't come into work. She was going to tell him and in fact had it all planned out; at five thirty, after everyone had left, she would go into Bill's office. She wouldn't sit on his desk, as she often did—that was too flirty, too suggestive. Instead, she'd sit on the black leather chair facing his desk and, hands folded primly on her lap and in a clear and unwavering voice, she would tell him that she was carrying his child and that she hoped he would be happy about it, but if not, she understood. She didn't know where their relationship would go from here; she wasn't expecting him to divorce Eleanor—especially not now, when she was so sick—but she also hoped he'd acknowledge the baby as his own . . .

What Haze really wanted was some magic, happy-ending solution that would erase scandal and hurt, a happy-ending solution that would make everything all right.

"As if that's going to happen," she muttered to herself, throwing the vinyl cover over her Selectric, and as she exited her office, she jumped, hand splayed out over her chest.

"Goodness, Susan, you surprised me!"

"Oh, I'm sorry, Haze, I was just getting my purse. I was halfway to Grandma and Grandpa's house and I realized I forgot my purse! Pretty dumb, huh?"

"Who hasn't forgotten their purse at some—" began Haze, but her words were cut short by the girl's wail.

"Did you hear about my grandma? Did you hear she's got cancer!" The last word Susan managed to cry out in two different octaves.

Haze nodded, and uninvited but certainly welcomed, Susan fell into her arms.

"DO YOU LIKE CHIPPED BEEF ON TOAST?" asked Haze.

"I don't know," said Susan, "I've never had it."

"Then it'll be a pleasant surprise." With a wooden spoon, Haze pushed the puffed-up plastic bag under the boiling water. "My mother used to make it from scratch, but this Stouffer's isn't too bad. Did you call your grandparents?"

Susan sniffed. "Grandma said it's awfully nice of you to make me dinner. She also said I should mind my manners and offer to help."

"With frozen food, there's not much to do. Although you could get some bread from the bread box and put it in the toaster."

All Haze could think to do when Susan had crumpled in her arms was to take her home and offer her dinner, happy to provide aid and comfort to the girl, even as she needed aid and comfort herself.

They sat at Haze's small dinette table, eating chipped beef on toast and sliced garden tomatoes, talking about Susan's school in Santa Monica and how they took field trips to the oceanside and celebrated birthday parties on the pier.

"I've never been to California," said Haze.

"Oh, you'd love it," said Susan, licking a spot of cream sauce off her upper lip. "We've got a grapefruit and a lemon tree in our backyard, and it's only an hour to Disneyland, and when I get my permit, my dad's going to let me drive up the Coast Highway all the way to Santa Barbara!"

"Santa Barbara," said Haze. "I'll bet it's as lovely as it sounds."

Except for the scrape of silverware, they ate quietly for a while, until Haze closed her eyes and moaned in response to the perfect red freshness of her tomato slice.

"They are good," said Susan, delicately cutting a neat triangle of tomato. "My friend Mandy—her mom writes for the TV show *Harry's Home!*—have you seen it? It's kind of funny, about a guy whose family sort of takes advantage of him . . . Anyway, Mandy eats her tomatoes with sugar—ick! Why would you do that when it's so good with salt?"

She offered a lopsided smile that held both hopefulness and apology.

"Sorry. I know I sound like a jerk, babbling on and on about dumb stuff. I just—if I don't talk about dumb stuff, I'll talk about my grandma, and I'm just too scared to do that."

Haze nodded. "I only knew one grandmother, my mother's

mother, and she was . . . well, she was sort of mean. She was the first in her family to ever go to college—a teacher's college—and she taught until she got married. Then they wouldn't let her teach anymore."

"Why?"

"Teachers used to have to be single. Just like airline stewardesses. When they got married, their careers were over."

"That's crazy!" said Susan.

Haze nodded. "And she was always bitter, I think, because of that. She'd *loved* teaching. My mother said Grandma often told her it was the happiest time of her life . . . which didn't make my mother feel too good."

"I can see why."

"My brother and sister and I hated going to her house," said Haze. "It felt like punishment. Fortunately, she lived a state away—in Montana—and we only had to see her twice a year."

Haze smiled, but her emotions took a sudden sharp turn, and tears sparked in her eyes.

"Sorry," she said, dabbing the corner of her eye with her ring finger. "It's just that now I can see why she was so unhappy—she didn't get to choose her life."

"We studied the suffragette movement in school, and one day Sherri Clark—*the* most popular girl in my class—said that women's lib was nothing but a bunch of angry, bra-burning women who didn't shave their pits." Susan rolled her eyes. "And everyone laughed."

"I bet you didn't."

"It felt like I was *supposed* to, but I didn't."

"Good for you." Haze patted her mouth with her napkin. "You give me hope for the future."

"Are you scared about the future?"

The girl asked the question with such intensity that had she still been eating, Haze might have choked. As it was, she swallowed hard.

"Not scared . . . but sometimes . . . worried."

Susan nodded. "I know. It makes you not believe in evolution."

"What do you mean?"

"Well, isn't evolution like a march—step by step, moving

forward—toward improvement? And sometimes it seems like we step backwards. Or not just step backwards but fall backwards."

Tapping her fork against her plate, Haze regarded Susan.

"You're a precocious one, aren't you?"

Susan shrugged.

"But I'm sure you've heard that before, haven't you?"

"Yeah."

"I like that about you," said Haze. "And I agree with you about evolution. I thought we would have been much further along by now."

14

"Haze, I have missed you more than I can say," wrote Bill in a letter he sent to her house, a letter Haze read sitting in the big high-backed wing chair, Royal's chair.

I'm finding some things out about myself that I'm not especially proud of—number one being that I am not very good at being the husband of a sick woman. As I write that, I see how heartless it sounds, but what I mean is that fixing things is my standard m.o., and when I don't know how to fix things, it seems I sort of fall apart. Really, Eleanor is the strong one here, patting my hand before she went into surgery, assuring me that of course everything will be all right, while I'm blubbering like a lost little boy.

I know that's not the sort of thing you want to hear: what kind of man would write such things to his lover? What sort of man has a lover when his wife is ill? Haze, I'm all tied up in knots, and I don't know whether I'm coming or going.

Would you see me this Saturday? Susan's parents are flying in this weekend as well as my other son and his wife, so I can go for a "walk" knowing that Eleanor will have plenty of company.

I'll be in the office briefly Friday afternoon—just give me a nod . . .

Yours,
Bill

"*Mine?*" Haze said aloud, staring at the letter's sign-off. "You really consider yourself *mine?*" Her brain was firing a barrage of signals, to laugh, to cry, to holler, and she did all three, and when she was done, she apologized to Brigadoon, who had been giving her worried looks throughout her tirade. She sat for a long time in Royal's chair, the letter lying on her lap like a dinner napkin.

It had been two weeks since Haze had heard the news of Eleanor's diagnosis and her own. She and Bill had had a few stolen moments in his office—brief, violent embraces that would break apart suddenly, punctuated with anguished whispers of apology and longing.

Haze knew there was no perfect moment to tell Bill about her pregnancy, but she also knew that these moments were too imperfect; she could wait until things had settled a bit, until Eleanor got through her surgery, until Bill seemed a little less *stricken.*

And now I can't tell him, she thought, and picking up the letter with a weariness that suggested it was written on lead rather than paper, she shuffled off to the kitchen like an arthritic octogenarian to put on a kettle of water.

Why had she thought this time would be any different? *Because the fathers were different.* She was ashamed that she had thought this, that she was buoyed by the thought that maybe her body would hang on to an egg fertilized by Bill when it couldn't hang on to eggs fertilized by Royal. She had been cruelly wounded by what her body had done to her and assumed it was all her fault; now she had tended to this tender shoot of hope—maybe it hadn't been just her, maybe the fault was hers and Royal's together, maybe this one would hold.

But as much as her mind was willing, no, *desperate,* her body was not, and that Tuesday—a mere two days ago, a lifetime (literally) ago—she had woken up in sticky, bloody sheets, woken up to the same deep, thudding failure.

She had called Lois then—she had to—and her friend picked her up and drove her to the clinic in Minneapolis.

"I'll tell you everything on the way home," Haze had said, white-faced as she climbed into Lois's car. "Please don't make me say anything until later."

Lois had turned the radio on, and they listened to farm reports and disc jockeys prattling on about weather and baseball scores and to Neil Diamond singing "Cracklin' Rosie," and Rod Stewart singing "Maggie Mae," and Mick Jagger singing "Angie."

All these men singing about all these women, thought Haze, and then Carly Simon came on singing "You're So Vain."

The same avuncular doctor who'd confirmed her pregnancy examined her and told her he was sorry and prescribed "a couple days of pampering," and Haze, true to her word, told Lois the story of her ongoing affair with Bill McGrath and the child that they weren't fated to have together.

Once Lois had to slam on the brakes to avoid rear-ending a car she'd inadvertently been tailgating, and another time, she almost swerved into a van in another lane.

"Let's get something to eat," she said, pulling onto an exit ramp. "I can't drive and listen to this at the same time."

Over a pot of coffee and "Our World Famous Caramel Rolls!" at Junie's, a bustling truck stop whose waitresses wore white nylon tiaras and frilled handkerchiefs in their uniform breast pockets, Haze finished her story, and when she was done, she sat back in the booth, exhausted.

"I am *done*," she said, so softly that Lois said, "What'd you say?"

Haze's eyes widened. "I just realized that it's over."

Lois reached her hand across the table for her friend's.

"Oh Haze, I'm so sorry. Sorry for everything. You know that whatever you need from me, you've got."

Haze picked up the check the waitress had set on the table. "Including this?"

If she couldn't make a joke—no matter how small—she was going to slide down the booth cushion and join the rest of the crumbs on the restaurant floor.

HAVING JUST PUT THE TEAKETTLE ON THE STOVE, Haze saw Brigadoon go to the back door, just before she heard the light knock. Willing herself not to run, willing herself to breathe, she walked slowly across the kitchen, not just hearing, but feeling, the pounding in her chest.

Before the door was a third open, Bill slipped inside like a cat burglar, and the couple held each other for a long time.

"Oh, my Haze," whispered Bill into her hair, "Oh, my Haze."

"I . . . I've made some tea," said Haze, finally extricating herself. She knew the longer she stayed in his arms, the harder it would be to get out of them.

They sat at the dinette table, the table she and Royal considered a far more romantic place to eat dinner than the heavy walnut dining-room table Haze had inherited from her great-aunt Eileen. The married couple could easily lean across the small span of Formica to kiss, barely raising their backsides off the padded flecked-with-silver vinyl chair seats. And too, a chalkboard had hung nearby, and sometimes they whiled away a breakfast or dinner, taking turns writing terms of endearment or salacious invitations. Haze still regretted that she'd erased the chalkboard the morning of Royal's death to write a reminder to him to pick up gardening shears; how she would have loved to have seen one of his doodled hearts still there, or one of his scrawled messages, "Meet me in the bedroom—clothing optional."

She had taken the chalkboard down after Royal died and stuck it under the kitchen sink, next to a bottle of bleach, and where it had once hung, there was now only a nail hole.

"Hey, your hand's shaking," said Bill as Haze poured them cups of tea. "What's the matter?"

"Well, obviously I'm nervous," said Haze, surprised at the snappish tone in her voice. So was Bill.

"Oh, Haze. Darling. Please don't ever be nervous with me. But . . . I know. I know it's been a long, hard couple weeks and a bear of a situation and—"

"Bill," said Haze before allowing the censors that were a fraction away from clamping down her words. "Bill, I don't think we should see each other anymore."

As far as his reaction went, Haze didn't know what she expected, but she did not expect him to sit slumped, staring at his folded hands, blinking as if he had something in his eyes. For the first time, he looked old to her.

She wanted to talk, to fill that murky, silent space that they were huddled under, but it seemed formal rules had been established, and it was Bill's turn.

He finally took it, his head tilting as he raised it, as if it needed more support than his neck offered.

"Haze," he said, the word coming out like the creak of a rusty-hinged door. He cleared his throat. "Haze, I wish to God I wasn't in agreement with you."

The couple stared at each other for a long moment, both of them breathing hard, competitors facing one another after a hundred-yard dash.

"But your letter," said Haze, confused. "Your letter didn't sound like you were ready to break things off. It sounded like you couldn't wait to see me."

Bill's mouth bunched up in inverted U, and Haze thought what a handsome man Mr. William McGrath was, with a head of hair gone to silver and eyes the cobalt-blue color of the bottle of Phillips' Milk of Magnesia her mother had kept in the medicine cabinet. He had at least four inches in height and thirty pounds on Royal, and while her husband had delicate, surgeon's hands with long fingers, Bill's were big and thick-fingered, a whorl of silver hair filling the space between the lower knuckles.

"I couldn't wait to see you, Haze. I couldn't wait to get out of the house. I think—I pray—Eleanor's going to get through this—but right now it's like the whole place is shrouded in this gloom. This *fear*. Really, it's like a fume I'm choking on. Christ, I'm glad the kids are here."

Bill bowed his head and studied his cup like a tea-leaves reader trying to read the future. Haze cleared her throat, signaling him to go on.

"All I really wanted, when I wrote the letter, is to see you. To hold you. But walking over here, I couldn't get out of my mind something Susan said tonight at the dinner table."

"Which was?" she said, ignoring the heat that was rising in her chest. She really liked Bill's granddaughter, but at this moment she hated her.

"Eleanor wasn't eating with us," Bill said, his voice thick. "She makes a real effort to get to the table, but tonight she was just too bushed. So we're there, passing around the buckets of fried chicken and coleslaw my son had picked up, and Susan says, 'Grandpa, I wish I didn't have to go back to school because more than anything, I want to stay here and help you help Grandma. But even without me, I know you'll do a good job. I hate what Grandma has to go through, but at least she's got you to go through it with.'"

Two perfectly synchronized tears rolled down the man's eyes, and he stanched them with his thumb and forefinger.

"Even though I know I'm a cad for loving you, I can't say I feel like one. But I realized that it's just too much. I *want* to be with you, but I *have* to be with Eleanor."

Haze's head was bobbing like a horse's with an ill-fitting bit.

"So," she said, her voice squeezing around the lump in her throat, "so what happens at work? Should I quit?"

"Aw, Haze," said Bill, reaching across the table and taking her hand. "No. No, you can't quit. You love your work—everyone loves your work! Your work has nothing to do with . . . with us."

"Yes, but we'll see each other every day. How will we do that?"

Bill's fingers tightened around Haze's. "We just will."

"It'll be so hard."

Bill drew her hand to his lips and pressed his lips against it.

"It will be hard, Haze. But it'll be all right."

"Bill, there's something . . ."

The resolve to not tell him about her miscarriage was being snuffed by the sudden rage that flamed up in her, the scream that filled her head: Why do I feel I have to protect you from this? Who protected *me*?

"Well, see, it happens that I . . ."

His head was slightly cocked, and he furrowed his eyebrows, and Haze could tell he was both puzzled and concerned at her tone of voice.

"I, I was . . ."

As fast as the rage had flared up, it was extinguished. She couldn't tell him. The man was already dog-paddling in a Slough of Despond—did she want him to drown in it? What good could it possibly do him to have this information? Haze knew it was over between them, but she still loved Bill McGrath, and why would she want to hurt someone she still loved?

"I just wanted you to know how"—there was a pause long enough to fit Hamlet's soliloquy inside it—"that however wrong it was, it was right for me. You lifted me up from a dark place, and I'll always be so grateful to you for that."

His eyes leaked more tears, but Haze's did not. She had held back her secret. Holding back her emotions was a piece of cake.

"I guess I never thought of the word *grateful* to explain how I felt about us, but that's it exactly, Haze. I'm as grateful as you are."

He squeezed her hands, and with the agile grace that belied his age, he was out of his chair and standing.

Haze rose too, but Bill held up his hand like a crossing guard.

"I'll see myself out, Haze. *Thank you for everything.*"

HAZE DIDN'T SLEEP in the bed she and Bill had shared or the bed she and Royal had shared; instead she lay down on the couch, pulling the crocheted afghan draped over its side, inhaling its loops and nubs of old yarn, woven and tied together years ago.

"Mama," she whispered, to the afghan's creator, and after a moment, she repeated the same word but with an urgency, born out of a sudden realization. "Mama! I'll never hear anyone ever call me that!"

Her howl filled the living room, and if sound waves had force, it would have knocked the walls down.

With Brigadoon serving as witness, her furry, loyal head resting on her master's hip, Haze wailed, sobbed, cried, and whimpered, and when she was wrung dry and mute, she stared up at the ceiling. She saw molecules and atoms pulsing and dancing in the fuzzy gray light, or maybe she didn't—what did it matter? What *did matter* even matter? Her life had been riven apart once, and she'd managed to pick up the jagged pieces and piece together a whole, or patchwork semblance thereof, but twice riven . . .

"I know," she said aloud, to herself, to her dog, and to a God she hoped, but wasn't sure, was listening, "I know that on a scale of human suffering, I'd rate, but not as much as a hollow-eyed child starving to death, or as an earthquake victim searching through rubble for her family, or as a . . ." She hiccuped a little sob. She had compassion for the millions—no, billions—whose suffering was at a primal level not understood by herself, but as trite and silly as it sounded, it was all relative. Her world—the only one she could *attempt* to understand—had more than enough of the needed essentials . . . and still, she wondered where the nearest rock was because she'd like to curl up under it and die.

She was surprised, but not flabbergasted, when after an hour or so of marinating in her misery, she sat up, wrapped the afghan around her, and turned on the end-table light. Squinting against its glare, she got up and retrieved from her purse hanging on the kitchen doorknob a pen and a notebook. She had to do what she'd done all her life: write it all down.

SHELLY NEVER PARTOOK of the office Happy Tea; when her work week was done, the last thing she wanted to do was yuk it up with her co-workers at the *Gazette*. She couldn't be bothered with the office gossip she was certain was a large part of the gathering, and she didn't like drinking in public, preferring to host her own happy hour, which was never really happy, but at least the drinks were generous.

Still, knowing what she knew, she was tempted to slide into a booth next to Mitch as he unspooled one of his convoluted, unfunny jokes, or listen as Ed, the sports editor, droned on about the North Stars playoff chances; she was tempted to tell a piece of news that would have had all of them bug-eyed and gape-mouthed: the news that their revered and married boss, Mr. Bill McGrath, was carrying on an affair with their revered and widowed co-worker, Haze Evans.

One Friday evening, Shelly got so far as the door of the Sundown, but as soon as her hand reached for the handle, she drew it back as if someone had shouted, "hot!" and lurched away in a giant step, nearly breaking into a trot. She was breathless when she got to her small house, whose repairs Ray used to keep up on but which now seemed to sag under the weight of worn roof shingles and her own disappointment.

Shelly didn't allow herself to feel deeply (her TV favorites were shows like *The Man from U.N.C.L.E.* and *Mission Impossible*—heavy on the action and light on emotion), cocooning herself in bitterness and resignation, but when she saw Mr. McGrath and Haze Evans locked in what her romance novels described as "a torrid embrace," the shock she felt was so strong, it felt electrical.

It had been after five, and Shelly would have left the offices like everyone else, but as she was locking her desk drawers (she was not about to let the cleaning staff paw through her things), she was seized with an urgent need to get to the restroom *ASAP*, and she raced down the hallway, sweaty and flushed, thinking she might not make it in time.

She did, but a brutal case of diarrhea kept her on the toilet for at least ten minutes, and cursing when she left the stall, shaky and weak, she washed her hands and splashed cold water on her face and leaned over the sink for a long time, breathing slowly and wondering if she were sickened by a random bug or the spiced ham sandwich she had had for lunch, made from lunch meat that tasted fine, even though it'd been in the refrigerator for nearly a week.

She lobbed the crumpled paper towel into the waste basket, and after rearranging her purse straps on her shoulder, froze, hearing a high-pitched squeal of laughter, followed by a lower echo. It traveled down the hall, and slowly, carefully, Shelly opened the door a crack.

Haze—she knew it was Haze because of the tacky print dress she wore—was pressed against the wall of the hallway, and doing the pressing, and much more, was Mr. Bill McGrath, whose tossed-off suit jacket lay crumpled on the floor.

Shelly, whose general opinion of the human race was fairly grim, nevertheless was stunned. Bill McGrath struck her as one of the few men whose natural reaction to anything *wasn't* to zip down his pants; truth be told, she harbored a little crush on him. It was safe to have a crush on him; his age, his courtly masculinity, and his obvious dedication to his wife made him untouchable.

But not to Haze. The thought was so bitter that Shelly thought she actually felt a rise of bile. She was tempted to storm out into the hallway just so that Haze would know she wasn't getting away with this . . . *adultery*, but instead, when the couple nearly collapsed into Mr. McGrath's office, she carefully slipped down the hallway into the reception area and out the door.

At home, she found her copy of "Minnesota Movers!" in the coffee-table drawer and proceeded to deface the brochure put out by the governor's office, one that Joan Dwyer had ordered for everyone in the office because it featured her boss on the cover.

Pressing deeply into the slick paper, Shelly proceeded to give Bill McGrath's smiling visage a cross-eyed gaze, devil's horns, and the letter A on his forehead. The ink was dark blue and not scarlet, but the point was obvious.

Dinner was a can of SpaghettiOs with a rum and Tab for an appetizer and one for dessert, and when she washed the dishes, her glass wasn't included in the cleanup because she wasn't done using it.

With one of the mysteries she'd checked out of the library, she settled herself on the forest-green corduroy couch Ray had insisted they buy, even though it wasn't on sale (she had hated that he was a spendthrift; although the couch had certainly held up far longer than their marriage), but she couldn't concentrate and didn't care who in fact had killed Reginald Tromley, the village vicar, and tossed the book aside.

Squatting by the television set, she spun the dial, but there was nothing on any of the eight channels broadcast in Granite Creek, and she bumped the on-off dial with the palm of her hand, agitated and angry.

"I should call his wife," Shelley muttered, but upon seeing the notepad next to the phone, she had a better idea. In her round and bloated script, she wrote:

Dear Mrs. McGrath,

Who I am is not important, but what is is that your husband is having an affair with Haze Evans, yes, the same happy-flappy columnist who's so popular and who everyone says is "just so wonderful" and "so insightful" and "someone who makes me think about my life." Ha! I used to think all these compliments were a little over the top when they'd call into the paper (oops, have I given you a clue as to who I am?). Little do all those readers know what I and now you know—that that "wonderful" and "insightful" columnist is a big, fat fraud who happens to be banging her boss! (Sorry for being so crude, but that's the truth.)

I hope you'll let the world know about your husband (I can't, I need my job) and that big, fat fraud who yammers on about love or loyalty or honor or her dead husband. Remember that column she wrote last week about her youth pastor back in Podunkville, North Dakota, and how he taught her how "faith is a verdant field that can tolerate seeds of doubt" or some bullshit? Wonder what that youth pastor would have to say about adultery?

Wonder what you'll say?

Shelly addressed an envelope and even put a stamp on it, but by the end of the night, she had ripped it up into tiny pieces, not wanting to be the messenger of such life-changing news.

PART THREE

15

Trembling, Caroline sits next to Haze's hospital bed.

Although she will admit to feeling fury when she opens her cable bill, reading her mail does not usually elicit such strong emotion in the young woman, but the day's delivery has included a letter from her mother. While an avid and enthusiastic user of e-mail and the telephone, Mrs. Abramson will occasionally collect her deeper thoughts in a letter (i.e., a notecard busy with bees, butterflies, or flowers) and send them to her daughter in the States.

This particular letter, however, does not contain her views of another government blunder or news of their neighbor's backyard bacchanalia that brought a visit from the police, or the analysis of a Bible verse; no, what makes Caroline shake is the news that her mother's coming to visit.

"Mercedes," says Caroline, and standing up, she opens her arms wide and drapes them around the nurse, the gesture surprising both women.

"I'm sorry," says Caroline, pulling away.

"No, no, don't be sorry," says Mercedes, who is genuinely happy that her daughter's reserved partner has greeted her so enthusiastically. "That was nice." As the young woman sits back down next to Haze's bed, Mercedes asks, "Carolina, what's wrong?"

Like a child thinking she can stop crying by scrunching up her face, Caroline does just that, but the muscle contractions don't work, and tears leak out of the sides of her eyes.

"Oh, *mi querida*," says Mercedes. "What is it?"

Several soggy tissues later, Caroline has composed herself enough to tell Mercedes about her mother's visit.

"I *wish* I could tell her," says Caroline. "I mean, I know she loves me, and I love her, but she and my whole family—they're pretty religious. I mean *really* religious."

"Ey," says Mercedes. Christina has told her about Caroline's fear of coming out to her family, but to hear the anguish in the young woman's voice makes her angry and sad at the same time. "Can I do anything to help?"

Caroline's smile is quick and wide, and she dabs at her eyes with her fingertips.

"Well, would you mind being over when I tell her? It'd probably be a good idea to have a nurse around."

MANUEL HAD ALWAYS BEEN THE MORE GOD-FEARING of the two, and while Mercedes respected his deeply held feelings, she couldn't say she shared them. Her first indication that the church didn't value her occurred when she asked her mother when she might be an altar boy like her older brother Ernesto.

"That is not a girl's job!" said her mother, her voice an exclamation and a scold.

It didn't take long to realize that she was a second-class citizen in the eyes of the church, and as she grew, she understood she held the same status in society and government, but it was the church's failure to celebrate and honor who she was, who all girls and women—except the Virgin Mary!—were, that hurt and angered her the most.

Manny's faith in the church had begun to falter when he understood how much it was opposed to the person his daughter was.

"God gave us Christina," said Manuel at one of their kitchen-table conferences. "So how can we tell God He was wrong?"

"God is not wrong," said Mercedes, "but the church is." She didn't add, "Haven't I been telling you that for years?"

After Manny died, her friends at Holy Rosary provided solace, but when she moved to Minnesota, she joined no church and in fact spent her Sunday mornings working at the hospital, which for her was a form of worship.

SHE WOULD HAVE LIKED TO STAY and talk with Caroline, but she had other patients to attend to, and after checking Haze's vitals and tucking the blanket around her—Mercedes was convinced it comforted sick people to be cocooned in their covers—she hugged the young woman.

"Whatever you need from me, let me know. If you want me to talk to your mother, make her tamales—anything—I would love to help where I can."

Caroline's eyes continued their tear lubrication, and she hugged Mercedes back, hard.

"Thank you."

June 27, 1976

Well, the big news* around the news office last Friday was the Granite Creek girls' volleyball team playing in the state tournament, right on the fourth anniversary of the enactment of Title IX, which supposedly will level the playing field between boy and girl athletes, or at least level the field on which they play. Don't get me wrong; I'm thrilled that that which was denied for girls so long—the opportunity to participate on school teams that play against other school teams—is now available. Maybe there truly will be some parity in junior high and high school sports programs, but when the girls get to college, I sincerely doubt that their sports will get the attention and, most of all, funding, that boys' sports do. I hope I'm wrong.

I for one was a very good ball player. In grade school, all the boys wanted me on their team because the balls I hit were often home runs and the balls I fielded often resulted in a double play, or at least an out. In summer, we'd gather at the park and play until supper and then after supper until it got dark. I have fond memories of walking home with

Andy Pruitt and discussing, with great seriousness, our dream teams to play on—he loved the New York Yankees, while I was enamored with the Boston Red Sox. Even if he thought, "What are you, crazy—girls can't grow up to be pro ball players!" he never expressed it, because he knew, at that point in time, I was just as good as he was.

Things began to change, of course, in junior high when we all started seeing one another not just as fellow human beings but as BOYS or GIRLS, and the boys started puffing out their chests and braying, and the girls started hunching their shoulders and giggling. I was still allowed to play ball but began to hear comments that had no place among teammates and certainly no place in a family newspaper, and by high school, well, forget it. If you were an athletic girl, you could try out for the cheerleading squad or the dance line.

I did play on an intermural basketball team after school, our schedule determined by when the boys needed the gym to practice.

It's true, our physiology is different, and hips and less muscle mass and a lower center of gravity affect us so that in competition with a man, we'd come in second, but in the sports world, someone always comes in second, or third, or fourth . . .

And we're in the midst of baseball season, and I'm a proud rooter for the Twins, but am I the only one disheartened that something that is supposedly "America's Pastime" is only represented by men?

There is such a long list of Things Girls Aren't Supposed to Do, and I celebrate that one item is crossed out. So to Title IX, I'll raise a glass of the elderberry wine that Ed Dyson puts out every year (I'm no sommelier, but this stuff's good!) and toast to girls given an opportunity to come in first, second, third, or fourth. To at least be in the game.

*I exaggerate. Another female staffer mentioned that the weather seemed to get more coverage.

TO THE EDITOR:

I am so tired of these feminist tracts from your columnist that I'd cancel my subscription if there were another local paper I could read! Honestly, what is her problem? God made men, and God made women, each with their own strengths and weaknesses. Why does Haze Evans feel women's strengths aren't enough?

Please stop this continual pollution of your paper by this radical hag's screeds.

Mr. Joseph Snell

MR. SNELL HAD BEEN PARTICULARLY BUSY in the 1970s, responding to nearly every column Haze wrote with a letter explaining why the column was (a) stupid, (b) a waste of time, or (c) the product of an out-of-control feminist and/or radical hag. In response to Haze's column about the premiere of the late-night comedy show *Saturday Night Live*, Mr. Joseph Snell wrote, "What's a bigger waste of time—reading about an inane, smug comedy show, or reading an inane, smug column about it?" After her column about the averted nuclear catastrophe at Three Mile Island, he wrote, "The clean and efficient benefits of a nuclear-powered world far outweigh the cries of 'we're doomed!' by a left-wing/anti-science contingent that think the sun and wind can solve our energy problems!" And even when Haze wrote about Mother Teresa winning the Nobel prize, her harshest critic was outraged by the recipe she included.

HEAVENLY HONEY MUFFINS
    2 cups all-purpose flour
    ½ cup sugar
    ½ t salt
    3 t baking powder
    1 egg
    1 cup milk
    ¼ cup butter, softened
    ¼ cup honey

Preheat oven to 400 degrees. Combine the first four ingredients in a bowl. In another bowl, whisk the last four ingredients, and stir into the dry ingredients until just moistened.
Spoon/pour batter in greased muffin cups until three-
quarters full. Bake 15–18 minutes or until inserted toothpick comes out clean. Remove muffins from pan to a wire
rack. Serve these heavenly muffins warm or cold—food for
angels either way!

TO THE EDITOR:

I appreciated that Haze Evans devoted a whole column to
the holy work of Mother Teresa, and I would suggest that
the columnist do herself a big favor by trying for one day
to exemplify Mother Teresa and dedicate herself to serving
others rather than serving herself. And her use of the words
"heavenly" and "angels" in her recipe was childish and
unnecessary.

COMING HOME EARLY that evening from the conference, Susan
had thrown together what she thought was a not-so-special dinner of
salad and reheated chili, which they'd eaten out on the patio. But the
fact that all through the meal Sam had been as solicitous as a maître d'
("Can I get you some more water, Mom?") and was now helping her
do the dishes *without being asked* makes Susan think she should put
chili on a more regular dinner menu rotation.

"Mom," Sam says, putting away a handful of silverware. "Why
do you think that Snell guy hated Haze so much?"

Washing a serving bowl, Susan laughs. It's not that the question
is so funny; she's just near-giddy that Sam continues to be engaged
in a conversation with her.

"I don't think he hated her so much as disagreed with her
opinions."

Along with one of Haze's old columns, they'd published one of
his many rejoinders in the paper that day.

"Yeah, but the names he calls her, like 'radical hag'? I mean, shouldn't he attack the ideas and not the person behind them? And would he be calling her those kinds of names if Haze was a guy?"

My boy's growing up, Susan thinks, stifling her urge to hug him (she doesn't want to scare him off). She passes him a rinsed bowl and notices how tall he's getting.

"I think most of the time 'Mr. Joseph Snell,'"—Sam smiles at her exaggerated intonation—"tried to only argue his point, but you're right, that he resorted to name-calling—and *sexist* name-calling— was beneath him. I think that's why Granddad chose to publish only a small percentage of his letters."

Nodding, Sam wipes the bowl, and then he continues this evening of surprise by asking his mother if she'd like to go back out on the patio, because it's so nice out there and would she like him to make her some coffee?

It's Susan's ritual to end dinner with a cup of decaf, and that Sam has offered to make her some (does he even know how?) *and* wants to spend even more time with her renders her mute for a moment. Finally, staring at the draining sink water, she says, "That sounds good."

Outside, after he serves her coffee, he clears his throat, and says, "Mom, I've got something to show you."

So that's it, Susan thinks, her heart thudding. He's been softening me up for the blow.

Her son's voice is so serious, deeper than usual. Is he going to pull up his shirt and show her a baseball-sized lump pressing out of his rib cage? Or a devil tattooed on his bicep? Or will he slap down, like a resigned Vegas blackjack dealer, photos of Phil and his dental hygienist attending to more than teeth?

With a sheepish smile and a flush to his face, Sam says, "I'll be right back."

And he is, holding under his arm a wooden box, which he sets on the iron-mesh patio tabletop.

Susan stares at the words *Pirate Booty* etched into it before looking up at Sam, who answers the question in his mother's eyes by saying, "It's filled with Haze's stuff. Letters. A journal. I found it in her office."

Now Susan's forehead tamps down, furrows.

"I probably shouldn't have read what's inside it," says Sam, nearly breathless. "But I did. I was sitting in her office yesterday—I mean, I was working, not just sitting—anyway, I was looking up at her bookshelf and saw this box that . . . well, that wasn't a book. And I found a key too—in her drawer—and it fit."

Not knowing what to say, let alone think, Susan stares at her son.

"I know, I know, it's kind of like a break-in," says Sam, opening the box. "I thought that the whole time. But I also thought, well, she left this stuff in her office . . ."

He hands his mother a journal and a packet of letters. "It's all about Haze and your grandpa. They were . . . well, here, read."

Susan watches openmouthed as he lurches out of his chair and runs inside the house before she can say anything. After a moment, she closes her mouth and unfolds a piece of lined white paper. The first two words under the date make her gasp.

Darling Haze,

She stares at those words. They're written in the same slanted, angular penmanship her grandfather used when writing her notes and letters when she lived in California, but her grandfather never addressed her as "Darling."

She reads on.

You were absolutely splendid at last night's banquet—my God, woman, your wit is as deadly as your looks! And where did you get that dress? It was a faithful servant, complementing your curvature and making you look even more radiant than ever, and you know I love when you wear your beautiful brown hair up. You look like a sexy Gibson Girl.

Your speech was fine and funny, but I'm sure you recognized that by the many laughs that filled the room. I had to sit on my hands to stop them clapping after your every word, to press my lips together so I wouldn't offer up well-deserved but inappropriate wolf whistles.

All I could think of was how much I wanted to get out of my tuxedo and into your arms. Made it a little hard to give my own speech after yours—know that my mind was on you instead of excellence in journalism or whatever the hell I gave my speech about.

Yours, of course,

B

LIKE AN ARCHAEOLOGIST holding a piece of ancient papyrus that's revealed to be a love letter from Mark Antony to Cleopatra, Susan states at the paper, stunned. Her breath is shallow in her chest, and she feels flushed. She wants to swallow, but how can she when her throat feels completely blocked?

"Honey, bring me another beer, will you?" The voice of her neighbor Jeff Larson carries over the hedge as well as the voice of his wife, Laurie, who calls back, "Not until you unload the dishwasher like you promised!" If Phil were there, he'd call back to them, making some sort of joke like, "And Jeff, when you're done, will you bring me a beer too?" Phil was King of the Block; he knew everyone in the neighborhood much better than Susan and told her juicy gossip about people she waved to but barely knew.

She closes her eyes, as a pang of missing Phil skulks through her, and when she opens her eyes again, she reads the next letter and the next. When she gets to Haze's journal, she feels nearly paralyzed, *stupefied*.

The summer sun is setting when Sam comes out, and when he flicks on the patio light, Susan realizes how long she's been reading.

She sighs and closes the journal.

"You okay, Mom?" asks Sam, sitting next to her.

Susan's nod doesn't last long before switching direction, shaking side to side. She blows out a sigh and shrugs.

"Honestly, Sam, I don't know what I am."

"So you . . . you didn't know all about this?"

"No! No, of course not! I'm absolutely shocked." She sits for a long time, biting her lower lip.

"Mom?"

Her son's face is hurt, quizzical.

"Oh Sam, I just feel so, well, hurt! Hurt and left out! I mean . . . oh, what do I mean?" With her lower lip extended, she exhales so that her bangs flutter. "I just feel bad that Haze didn't tell me! She's not only been a mentor, but she's been like . . . well, an aunt to me. An aunt who's always on my side. And right now, well, right now—oh my gosh, I just realized if she'd had the baby, it would be my aunt! Or my half-aunt . . . or uncle!" She flutters her hand in front of her face, her eyes filling with tears. "Now I feel like I hardly know her. Like I hardly knew my grandfather." She shakes her head. "He and my grandmother always had—I *thought*—such a loving relationship."

Sam is listening to his mother the way a top student listens to his tutor.

"It seems like they did, from everything I read," he says, his hand fanning out toward the box. "I mean, it seems like he loved Haze but he loved your grandma too."

She knows he's right as soon as she hears the words, and because she doesn't seem able to hold it up, Susan bows her head.

"Sam," she says finally. "That is so . . . big of you to think that. So adult."

"Mom. Come on. I'm not a total moron."

Mother and son look at one another, and Susan thinks she will always remember the fullness of this moment, the lingering smell of charcoal from the Larson's backyard grill, the barking of another neighbor's beagle, the night air, soft as a baby's blanket, but most of all the sense that all the struggles Sam and she have had over the past year have graciously stepped aside for a moment, allowing for something new between them.

"I have to tell you," she says, speaking without censorship, as if to a friend, "my mind is sort of blown."

Sam nods. "You and me both. I didn't know old people did stuff like that."

A laugh blurts out of Susan, and seeing Sam's face, she regrets it immediately, but not being able to help it, she laughs again.

"Sam, Haze was only"—she does some quick calculations—"in

her late thirties when she and my grandfather had their . . . affair." The words sound strange coming out of her mouth, as if they were spoken by someone else.

"Yeah, but your grandpa was *old*."

"He'd have been in his sixties, that isn't—" she stops herself, realizing the lens through which Sam looked at age was a different prescription from her own. "You're right he *was* old."

"Then again, Haze likes older guys."

Puzzled, Susan looks at him.

"Royal, remember? Wasn't he like a bunch of years older than her? And wasn't Haze's dad a bunch of years older than her mom? Maybe it runs in the family."

When Susan's expression doesn't change, Sam says, "Mom. She wrote about it, remember? In her columns?"

"Oh, yeah," says Susan, her surprise at his memory stretching her words. She takes a sip of her decaf, the fact that her son made it helping her to tolerate its triple-than-usual strength. "But you've got to remember too, your grandfather was a pretty dashing guy."

"Guess *that* runs in our family," Sam says, one eyebrow cocked, his voice smarmy.

FOR SO MANY MONTHS, Susan's big California King has been as wide and lonely as a raft whose fellow shipmate mutinied, but when she's in bed later that night, she feels something she hasn't felt in a long time: contentment.

Contentment expands into buoyancy. When was the last time she and Sam talked so much, laughed so much, shared so much?

Good old Haze, she thinks. She knows in the morning and in the days to come she'll have to fully process what it means that her beloved grandfather cheated on her beloved grandmother, but for now she's grateful for Haze, the adulterer who brought her so close, at least for an evening, to her son.

In his own room, Sam texts/doesn't send to Lorde: "HERE'S A SONG TO GO WITH YOUR 'ROYALS'—'LOYALS'—WHEN IT COMES TO LOVE AND SEX, WHO ARE WE LOYAL TO? JUST ASKING."

16

May 20, 1980

Oh my, the world throws tantrums, and we can do nothing to rein them in.

I have a high school friend, Wilma (I could write a whole column about how much she hated her name), who ventured westward right after graduation, winding up in Portland, Oregon, where she worked for a spell as a telephone operator. In one of those hard-to-believe, this-could-only-happen-in-a-movie occurrences, a gentleman caller (not the Tennessee Williams kind, but one who dialed "O," needing a connection) complimented her on her voice, which led to a conversation, which led to a date, which led to more, and eventually a walk down the bridal path. Wilma's husband is a rancher, and she writes me periodically about the goings-on in her neck of the woods, which happens to be thirty miles from Mount St. Helens, which erupted in a major volcano last Sunday, spewing lava and ash and gases. You've probably seen some of the television coverage—the destruction is vast and dark and reminds us of how it's so easy to think of ourselves as big shots until Mother Nature reminds us how puny we really are.

I haven't heard from my friend; I telephoned, but the lines were down. I've sent a letter, but this is no rain or sleet or snow that the valiant post office must push through; this is lava and deep ash and asphyxiating gases.

Wilma told me once that she loved North Dakota, loved the unending expanse of prairie and its deep quiet, but the breakup with a boy she thought she might someday marry made her buy a bus ticket west.

"There are all kinds of places to love," she wrote me once (I save all my letters, and I've been rereading the ones she sent). "I still think North Dakota is beautiful, but my gosh, Haze, to live near mountains *and* the ocean is really something! Jed's favorite cousin lives outside New Orleans, and we visited him last year, and I thought I was in another world, let alone another country, and it made me think, I could love this too, this swampy place where logs float in bayous except they're not logs—they're alligators!"

Wilma was born with a shriveled left arm; it dangled from her shoulder like an afterthought, but she was not the type to ask for pity or special favors.

She moved to our town in the fifth grade, and during show-and-tell she stood in front of class and said, "This is my arm." With her right hand, she batted at her shrunken arm and laughed at the audible gasp that rose in the room. "I didn't do anything wrong to get an arm like this, it's just the way I was born. I love to play basketball and with an arm like this, it's a little harder, but my mom says everyone has something that makes things harder for them than it does for other people. So don't feel sorry for me, or if you do, feel sorry for my eyes because I hate that they're blue. I wish they were green. It's much more mysterious."

I can quote her fairly well because when I got home from school, I wrote everything down so I wouldn't forget. This show-and-tell presentation topped even Rod Kjelberg's, who once brought in the litter of puppies his dog Moxie had.

So I'm thinking with all that strength of character and presence of mind that Wilma has—surely she'll survive a volcano. I'll let you know when I hear from her.

CAROLINE'S MOTHER, who has instructed everyone to call her Sarah ("except you, Caroline! To you I'm still Queen!") dips another tortilla chip into the bowl of guacamole.

"We have some good Mexican restaurants in Winnipeg but nothing like this. This is so good!"

Caroline is physically seated at Mercedes's dining room table, but mentally she is floating in the Sea of Tension, off the Isle of Worry. She had asked if she could help—practically pleaded—but Mercedes and Tina are a competent team in the kitchen and insisted that Caroline and her mother sit back and relax; after all, they are guests.

At first, after introductions had been made, small talk had been small, touching on weather, Sarah's changing planes in Fargo, and the bumpy little commuter plane that got her to Granite Creek, and Caroline's toenails.

"I've never seen anything like it!" said Sarah of the alternating colors with which Caroline had adorned her nails. "And look at yours!" she said, noticing Tina's sandaled feet that sported the same alternating colors on her toenails. "Did you plan that?"

Caroline had offered another fake smile, thinking, No, after we got out of the shower one day, we decided to paint each other's toenails and got a little wild.

"They are fun, yes?" said Mercedes. "Next time I will paint my own toes with ten different colors!"

Laughing, Tina draped her arm around her mother and pulled her close. "I'll bet you don't even own a bottle of nail polish—and if you do, I'll bet it's clear."

"That's what I like too," Sarah said, fluttering her modestly manicured fingers.

Now at the dinner table, Caroline can barely eat, even when Mercedes serves her daughter's requested favorites, mole chicken and chile rellenos, dishes that Caroline has eaten with gusto at this same table at least a dozen times.

"Sarah?" says Mercedes, holding a bottle of wine, and to Caroline's great surprise, her mother nods.

She winks at Caroline.

"I'm on vacation."

After her and her mother's second glass of cabernet, the evening begins to loosen up.

"I've never been to Mexico," says Sarah, "but after eating this food, I *have* to go."

"Oh, the places I could take you," says Mercedes. "My *tía*, my aunt Consuelo, is the best cook I have ever known. All children learn how to love vegetables when Tía Consuelo makes them!"

"Where does she live?" asks Sarah.

"In Tampico. Most of my family still lives there."

"Are you not allowed to visit them? Because of your immigration status?"

Caroline rolls her eyes. "Mum, Mercedes has been a U.S. citizen for decades."

Sarah offers a little shrug to Mercedes. "I only meant . . . I know they make things a lot harder for you people down south than for us people up north."

The moment of tense silence is short-lived when everyone realizes Sarah wasn't making a politically incorrect statement (of which, thought Caroline, she'd already made plenty).

"It was no big deal, legally wise, when Caroline moved down here," continues Sarah. "I'll bet it was a different story when you moved to California."

Suddenly recognizing that her mouth is open and half full of half-chewed chicken, Caroline closes it, staring at her mother.

"I think the prejudice comes from the language," says Mercedes, pouring more wine into Sarah's glass. "It's easier to be afraid of someone who doesn't speak the same language."

"It's a good thing you're not from Quebec!" says Sarah to her daughter.

Caroline laughs, and her heart beats in a sped-up rhythm. She's not used to feeling so comfortable, so *good* in her mother's presence.

Sarah turns to Mercedes.

"Have you ever been to Canada?"

"Yes, to Vancouver, once with my husband. Manny had a client who asked him to work on the landscaping of his second home. Or maybe it was his third. Or fourth—he had a *lot* of money."

They laugh.

"I hear how pretty it is from Caroline," continues Mercedes, "but I am still not used to the cold here—I don't know how I would do in an even colder place."

"Actually, where we are is not much colder than Minnesota," says Sarah. "Maybe not colder at all." Shrugging elaborately, she spills a little wine and then giggles and says, "Whoopsie."

Caroline raises her eyebrows and smiles at Tina. The knot in her stomach seems to have unraveled.

They are still raving about the flan dessert as they repair to Mercedes's little patio.

"Christmas lights!" says Sarah. "I love that you've strung Christmas lights out here!"

"Manny always liked many lights. He said they make everything look festive, and I agree. Although Tina would sometimes say, 'Mama, we're not living in a cantina, you know!'"

"Well, we could decorate our houses like Versailles," says Sarah. "And our kids would still think our taste was awful."

"I can see it!" says Mercedes. "The children of Louis XV whining and crying about the ostentatious throne room!"

For years, Mercedes has kept a "Word a Day" calendar and studies each day's entry, bringing it into her vocabulary like a welcomed guest. It's not anything that thousands (millions?) of people who buy that same calendar do, but nevertheless Sarah gapes at her.

"Mercedes, the day I know the Spanish word for 'ostentatious' is the day I know the Spanish word for 'dog'!"

"I think what she's saying," says Caroline after a brief and confused silence, "is that Mum doesn't speak a word of Spanish. And she's impressed by your command of English."

Sarah nods, and Mercedes, who has also helped herself to the evening's wine, says, "I like to be a commander, in command of things. And it's *perro*."

Tina howls. It's one of the things Caroline likes best about Tina—her wild and uninhibited responses. She'll laugh hard at a comic on the *Tonight Show* and a minute later be sobbing over a commercial for pet adoption.

"Mamá," she asks, "¿estás borracha?"

"Of course not," Mercedes sniffs and to Sarah says, "My daughter is wondering if I am drunk."

"I'll bet you're wondering the same thing," Sarah says to Caroline. "And in answer to that wondering, I say, No." She took another sip of her wine. "But ask me in two minutes."

The years, decades, disappear as she and Mercedes laugh like two junior high school girls, and Caroline and Tina sit back in their webbed plastic patio chairs, feeling as if roles have been reversed and they are the mothers watching the antics of their silly daughters. The mirth is contagious.

It's beautiful and balmy, and a few bold stars have poked through the shroud of a summer night's sky that tentatively explores darkening. Half of Mercedes's backyard is devoted to a vegetable garden, and while the air isn't exactly redolent with the smell of snap peas, tomatoes, and zucchini, there is a scent of soil, of green growth, of offering, and Caroline is so filled with love for her mother, who seems to have unbuttoned a couple top buttons, so filled with love for Mercedes and her deep graciousness, so filled with love for Tina, the woman who is at her side to both battle and embrace life, that words slip past the usually vigilant censor squad, and she says, "Mum, I need to tell you something. Tina is more than my friend. She's my everything."

What has happened in the backyard? Was there a sudden eclipse?

The four women, two in their twenties, one in her late forties, and the other in her midfifties, sit at a patio table draped in a floral plastic tablecloth, a big red candle sputtering its flame in the center, twinkles of multicolored lights scalloped across the rectangular wood frame Mercedes had paid a nursing student who was good at carpentry to construct around her patio. There might have been peripheral noise: Mercedes's next-door neighbor was a fan of country and western music and often played Dolly Parton and Tammy

Wynette at decibels that floated down the block, and her neighbor two doors down liked to rev his Harley before he roared off to whatever sports bar or symphony (Mercedes didn't like to make assumptions) he was attending, but right now no one heard anything but the words just spoken, clanging in everyone's ears.

"I'm a little confused," says Sarah finally. "What do you mean by 'my everything'?"

A panic has caught in Caroline's chest like a sudden burst of heartburn, and she looks wildly at Tina, who looks back at her gravely . . . and then winks.

The surprise of it—and her nerves—makes Caroline laugh, but it is a laugh that's extinguished nearly as soon as it's lit, and Caroline faces her mother and says quietly, "It means I love Tina. Someday I'd like to marry her."

Sarah gapes at her daughter as if Caroline is suddenly speaking in tongues but obviously not the Pentecostal Christian kind. (Once a woman from Regina spoke at their church's monthly program and, suddenly seized by the Holy Spirit, began to babble nonsensically; at first Sarah thought she was having a seizure.) She looks at Tina and Mercedes, and from the look on her face, it's obvious she's looking for some sort of answer; when no one provides it, she pushes her chair back with a force that the flimsy aluminum legs can't handle, and she topples backward.

Everyone else is out of their chairs in seconds, with Caroline calling, "Mum!" and Tina calling, "Sarah!" and Mercedes calling, "Are you all right?"

"My shoulder," moans Sarah as Caroline and Tina help her to sit up on the cement patio floor. "I think I've done something to my shoulder!"

"We'll get you to the hospital," says Mercedes.

"No," wails Sarah. "I don't think my insurance is good down here!"

"Mum, don't worry about it," says Caroline. "Now put your good arm around me, and we'll boost you up."

The other women lend their hands in support and help lead Sarah down the walkway and to Caroline's car in the driveway.

"THE X-RAYS don't show any break, Mercedes," says the ER doctor, who just yesterday in the hospital cafeteria had thanked her for steering him away from the chop suey special. "But she's torn her rotator cuff. We stabilized her arm, and she can decide what sort of further treatment she wants when she gets home to Canada."

In the car, Sarah informs her daughter she wants to stay in a hotel.

"Mum, no!" says Caroline. "We've got a nice bed all made up for you and—"

"I will not stay in your house," she says.

From the back seat, Tina says, "I can stay at my mother's house, Caroline."

"Better yet," says Mercedes, "why don't you stay with me, Sarah? I've got a spare bedroom, and I'm a nurse. I can take care of you if you need anything."

"HERE'S SOME TEA," says Mercedes, setting a tray carefully on the lap of Sarah, who is perched up on the pillows of her guest-room bed, one arm in a sling.

Sarah holds the mug under her nose for a long time, breathing in the rich peppermint-scented steam.

"And these are *churros*. I was just about to serve them before . . . your accident."

"I'll tell you right now," says Sarah, setting down the mug. "My Christian values are very important to me."

Mercedes nods. Her hands are clasped at her waist, and she feels awkward, standing next to the bed in the small room. She has been at the bedside of hundreds—thousands—of patients, but in the hospital, not in this bright-turquoise room with the big framed Frida Kahlo print Tina gave her.

Sarah takes a bite of a *churro*, and a dusting of cinnamon sugar settles on her lower lip.

"Umm. Good." She finishes eating the deep-fried cookie and takes a sip of tea. "Too bad it's not my right arm in a sling."

After Mercedes smiles uncertainly, Sarah adds, "I'm right-handed, and if I were forced to eat with my left hand, maybe I'd lose a little weight."

"Lose a little weight? You are thin already!"

"You're a good nurse," says Sarah. She gestures to the plate of cookies. "Have a *cholo* with me."

Mercedes can't help but laugh. "*Churro. Cholo* is slang for a gangster."

A pink flush washes over Sarah's face. "I'm so dumb," she says quietly.

"Ey—no. You should have heard all the words I messed up—still mess up in English!"

Sarah sighs. "Will you sit with me for a while, Mercedes? Unless you were on your way to bed?"

"It's not even eleven yet," says Mercedes. "And I am a night owl."

She returns with a cup of tea and a dinette chair and helps herself to a *churro*, and the two women sit companionably, sipping and nibbling, but when the last cookie is gone and Sarah dabs at her mouth with a napkin, Mercedes expects the mood to change, and it does.

"I don't know you well, Mercedes, but I know that you're a nice and generous person. I can see you love your daughter very much but . . . but how can you support what she's doing?"

"You mean like loving someone like your daughter?"

Sarah's flush this time is darker. "Someone like my daughter? My daughter's a wonderful person! Anyone would be lucky loving someone like Caroline!"

Mercedes presses her lips together as Sarah glares at her, and then watches as Sarah's eyes soften and a trace of a smile lifts her lips.

"That was a trick, wasn't it?"

"I am not that clever."

"Like heck you aren't," says Sarah. Her smile broadens, but seconds later it flattens, and tears spill down her face.

Mercedes takes the tray off Sarah's lap, and because the small nightstand has only room for a lamp and her own tea cup, she sets it on the floor and takes the woman's hands in her own.

"I know this is a . . . well, a shock for you. And it is never nice to be shocked."

"I can't believe it's true!" Sarah wails. "It has to be a phase or something—my Caroline is not gay! In high school, in college, she had lots of boyfriends! Just look at her—she's lovely!"

Mercedes nods. "That she is. She is a lovely, *lovely* person, your Caroline."

Wincing as she removes her hands from Mercedes's, Sarah sniffs, wipes her eyes with her hand, and says, "I don't know what your religious background is—I assume it's Catholic, because most of you Mexicans are Catholic, right? And let me know if I've gotten this wrong, but isn't it true that the Catholic Church denounces homosexual relationships?"

Even though it's a medical impossibility, Mercedes feels her blood begin to boil. First of all, Tina long ago schooled her in the word *assume*—"Mama, it makes an 'ass' out of 'u' and 'me'!" and second, don't get her started on the Catholic Church's—with so many church's—problems with human sexuality.

With a mouthful of tea, Mercedes swallows down the words she wants to say, and after placing her cup on the nightstand, she levels at Sarah the kind of gaze a disappointed corner-store owner might give to a repeat teenaged shoplifter.

"Sarah, yes, I was raised Catholic, like 'most'—or at least, many Mexicans. And I know millions of people are . . . fortified by that faith, but for me, no. That is not to say I do not believe in God or goodness or love or understanding, but anyone, any padre or priest or pastor who tells me my daughter is wrong to love—*love*, not hate!—whom she loves . . ." Mercedes shakes her head. "I have no time for that."

"But Mercedes, it's wrong! It's wrong and it's a sin!"

Mercedes has folded her hands in her lap, and she studies them now. Her fingers are squat, and she keeps her nails short and unpolished, but she loves her hands, cherishes them, for their strength and capability. They have stroked the fevered brow of countless patients, tucked in blankets, shaken thermometers, and searched for good veins; and for those she's loved, especially Manny and Christina, she's used them the way a conductor uses a baton, to conduct the tempo and tenor of their lives. She presses her hands together now, squeezes the impulse that makes one hand want to shoot out and slap this *mujer loca*.

"My husband and I," she says, in a slow and measured voice, "we knew for a long time that Tina was 'different,' that she might like girls more than boys. And I admit, we were scared and worried. Life is not easy for those who are different. But I think life is even harder for those who are different but cannot be their different selves." A long moment passes, and Mercedes adds, "*¿Comprendes?*"

More tears meander down Sarah's face. Most of the iridescent-blue eye shadow she had so carefully applied that morning is long gone, except for a smudge that inexplicably sits high above her eyebrow like a shiny bruise. She had given up on mascara—a beauty consultant at Hudson's Bay department store told her women of her age didn't need it as long as they had a good eyeliner—but her eyeliner and lipstick had worn off hours earlier. Without her makeup her face looks both older and younger.

"I don't know what to do, Mercedes. I love Caroline."

Mercedes breathes in deep, her chest puffing up.

"I know, Sarah. I love my Tina too."

"This is just going to kill Jerry. And Blake—that's Caroline's brother—he's always looked up to his sister! And *my* sisters! Penny's already a grandmother, and Barbara's planning a big wedding for her daughter—what am I supposed to tell them?" Her voice raises in a wail. "That my own daughter will never be getting married and the only way she'll ever have kids is with the help of a turkey baster?"

Mercedes almost blurts out a laugh, but the anger that rises up at the same time stifles it.

"Sarah, calm down."

"And God!" wails Sarah. "Surely God is going to punish her!"

Again, Mercedes's blood does the biologically impossible and heats up, but she takes a deep breath, a breath that fills her lungs to capacity. She wants to be kind and understanding—it's her nature

to be kind and understanding—but she is tired of the woman's ig-
norant and mean-spirited whining.

"I think I hear my kitty," she says. "I'll be right back."

In the living room, her calico cat, Pancho, is perched on the wide
arm of the sofa, regarding Mercedes with his usual implacable and
slightly bored look. He had made no noise—he's too regal to make
noise—but Mercedes thought it better to make up an excuse for her
departure than tell Sarah the truth, that if she stayed in that room
one more second, she might do something she'd later regret.

She sits down and scratches the cat behind the ears, muttering
all the while about the crazy woman who's taken up residence in her
guest room. "I know it's hard for her," she whispers as Pancho turns
his head, uninterested in any secrets, "but she makes it *so much*
harder!"

She returns to the bedroom, where Sarah is propped against the
headboard, her eyes closed. Mercedes is relieved, thinking semicon-
sciousness is the best thing for her (and for everybody), but as she
bends to pick up the tea tray on the floor, Sarah says, "I'm not asleep."

In silent but emphatic Spanish, Mercedes swears to herself.

"I just feel so . . . lost," Sarah says, her voice high and thin. "I don't
know what to do."

Of all the good and learned professors and doctors and nurses
who taught Mercedes her profession, her favorite all-time teacher
was her community college speech teacher, who sometimes had her
students debate each other just by asking questions. Her common
refrain was "You can learn things you didn't even know you were
asking about."

"What do you think you should do?" Mercedes asks, sitting
down.

Sarah stares straight ahead and waits so long to answer that
Mercedes stifles two yawns.

"I think I should do the right thing," says Sarah finally. "I *want
to do the right thing.*"

"What do you think the right thing is?"

Sarah sighs. "There are lots of right things, although the right
thing for my church might not be the right thing for my daughter."

"What do you think the right thing for Caroline is?"

Sarah's head tips to one side, as if its weight is suddenly too heavy for her neck.

"I don't know."

"You don't know?"

Mercedes hears Sarah's deep inhale, her deep exhale.

"What she would *want*," she says, and her voice is hurried and tinged with petulance, "is that I 'accept her for who she is' and give her my undying support."

Now Mercedes takes a full breath and sighs.

"Don't you think that's something a child should have from a parent?"

"Of course!" says Sarah. "But not when they're ... they're engaged in a lifestyle that is morally corrupt!"

"I will tell you this," says Mercedes, who is through asking questions. "There are many things that are morally corrupt. I for one think war is morally corrupt. I think killing and hurting others and not taking care of each another is morally corrupt." Her accent gets heavier; it always does when she's excited or agitated. "I could go on and on about all the things that are morally corrupt, but I will say only one more thing: I think it is morally corrupt for a mother to punish a child because that child *loves.* Loves someone who loves her back. Your Caroline and my Christina have a beautiful and full relationship. God makes all kinds of people, Sarah, and I don't think He—or She!—made a mistake making our daughters!"

Her throat is clogging up with anger and sadness, and she can barely get the last words out of her mouth, and when they are out, she doesn't leap out of her chair, but close to, and she strides the few steps it takes to get to the door, which she closes behind her, not slamming, but not unduly concerned of any noise it may make when it shuts.

17

November 6, 1980

Well, apparently Edith's gone and died. I usually leave the television reviews to our esteemed arts and entertainment editor, but watching the first episode of *Archie Bunker's Place* left me so bereft and out of sorts, I thought, How can I not write about this?

Millie Siefert didn't have a television set, and she wouldn't know what I was talking about. Before she moved into a nursing home in Minneapolis, she lived on my block, and over the years gave me counsel on when to plant tomatoes, the difference between a blue moon and a harvest moon, and what's best for the complexion (she swears by Noxzema). She got her entertainment from the radio, which she tells me, "is better than television because you get to make up the pictures in your mind."

You probably saw her belated obituary in the paper last week; she was ninety-six and had never been married, because, as she told me, "I don't have time for that foolishness." She would have said the same thing if she'd heard me mourning a made-up television character.

Millie was born in 1884! She lived through two world wars; she was allowed to vote for the first time at the age of thirty-six; she saw the beginnings of air travel and a man walk on the moon. (She told me she did go to her brother's to watch Neil Armstrong on television because "it was just too unbelievable. My mind couldn't conjure the pictures.")

I think I was upset by Edith's demise because it happened "off air"—a new television season begins, and we're told Edith's gone. This viewer felt bereft; we weren't allowed to properly say goodbye to such a beloved character.

Again, Millie would have mustered a sniff of contempt and pity for my reaction, but it's Millie's death that had caused my overreaction to Edith's. She was as independent a woman as I'd ever known, and lived in her house down at the end of my street until last year, when a niece moved her into a senior citizens' home down in the Twin Cities. Millie did not want to go, claiming she could still do just about everything but drive, and who needed to drive when there was "such a thing as passenger seats!" I'd take her to the FoodKing every Monday evening, and it was always fun to slowly cruise the supermarket aisle with her, both of our hands on the shopping cart handle, and listen to her complaints, which had a habit of turning into jokes.

"Oh, that's too high!" she'd say when I'd quote a price stamped on the bottom of a can of peas. "Especially for vegetables that taste like baby mush! Of course baby mush is the only kind of food you can eat when you've got bad choppers. By the by, don't ever shop for dentures at the Goodwill!"

It turns out Millie died two months ago.

Last weekend, I was planning to spend an artsy weekend in Minneapolis, seeing a play at the Guthrie, visiting the Walker, and the Art Institute, and I called Millie's "home," wondering if I could take her out for lunch in between all my "cul-chah." The person answering the phone, after a brief moment and sounds of paper shuffling, said, "Millie Seifert died September second. In her sleep."

Why this is unsettling to me, why the character of Edith's death was unsettling is that it just seems like an unraveling thread that no one cared to knot. So that those of us who cared would know it was done. Over. That the double knot had been tied.

P.S. There wasn't a sweet tooth in Millie's mouth (not even when she got dentures!), but she was partial to these cookies, which I've renamed in her honor.

MILLIE'S NO-NONSENSE MACAROONS
1⅓ cups sweetened shredded coconut
⅓ cup sugar
2 T flour
⅛ t salt
2 large egg whites
½ t vanilla or almond extract (your choice)

Mix together the coconut, sugar, flour, and salt in small bowl. Add the egg whites and vanilla (or almond) extract, and mix well. Scoop out teaspoonfuls, and drop onto greased baking sheets. Bake at 325 degrees for 18–20 minutes or until golden brown. Cool on wire rack.

"Hey, Grandma. Hey, Grandpa," says Susan, settling herself in front of her grandparents' shared tombstone.

It's a muggy evening, and she smells of the mosquito repellant she's sure is less toxic to those miserable flits of biting creatures than it is to her future neurological health (she doesn't doubt that one day she'll publish something like "Alzheimer's and Chemicals" or "Dementia and Overuse of Furniture Polish"). But the skeeters have been relentless this overlong season, and she has scratched 'til they bled too many bites and now has coated herself with a thick spray of insect poison, willing to risk the death of a few hundred thousand brain cells so she can sit on the grass, at dusk (she might as well be wearing a sign that reads, "Bite me") and talk without constantly slapping herself.

She has felt off-center, no, off-*kilter*, which is much worse. She feels she hasn't lost her balance so much as tumbled down a hill she didn't even know she was on.

Uncapping the thermos she's brought, she raises it and says, "To you, Grandma." She takes a long sip, and her jaw bone tingles from the sweetness. Her grandmother wasn't much of a drinker, but when she did imbibe, she was partial to pineapple daiquiris. Susan had made a blender full using her grandmother's recipe, which along with canned pineapple in syrup, called for a spoonful of brown sugar.

"I'm wondering," she says and looks around, conscious of her voice's volume, but there is no one else paying respects to dearly departed. She takes another long swallow. "What I'm wondering is, did you ever know? Did you ever know that your husband—that would be *you*, Grandpa—that your husband cheated on you with Haze Evans?"

Her back straight, she sits on her plaid blanket, sipping her tropical drink out of a plaid thermos, looking—if the tombstones had been erased out of the picture—like a picnicker in a *Town & Country* ad.

"And if you knew, did you do anything?"

Susan was too rational a person to think she'd hear an answer, but she was open to signs: an owl hooting, or the wind stirring through the nearby weeping willow, tossing its leaves the way a young girl tosses her hair, but there were no chatty raptors or whispering trees, and the evening was still as a Red Cross shelter during a P.A. announcement.

"And Grandpa," she says finally. "How could you? You *loved* Grandma. Everyone loved Grandma."

What she says is true, but even as she says it, Susan knows that even if her grandfather were to speak to her from the Great Beyond or the Press Room in the Sky or wherever he may have landed, his answer would be as simple and profound as, "it just happened."

Susan knows Phil loved her and also knows that she took their love for granted, paying more attention to the demands of her job and of parenting than the demands of her marriage. She's not blaming herself for his affair, but she does blame herself for the ease with which she put him second, third, fourth.

Susan has learned some things about herself that are not fun to learn, that like a bookie, she keeps tabs on what she's paid out and what's owed her. She expects those she loves to act the way *she* wants them to act, *and why can't they see that what she wants is what they should want?*

Once early in their marriage, she and Phil lay on their bed, post-sex, slick with sweat and satisfaction.

"If I could, I'd marry you every day," Phil had said, and while Susan thought it was romantic, she also thought it was childish, a tad *needy.*

"Let's not get carried away," she had joked.

He had been so proud of her when she took over the paper, talking her through her many fears and doubts. For the longest time Phil had been her biggest cheerleader, and she sees now how seldom she shook pompoms for him. He loved selling recreational vehicles and was good at it, but her ownership and running of the newspaper was the career in the family that really *mattered*, that changed people's lives. (Although she had been approached many times by someone telling her what fun they'd had on the speedboat or snowmobile Phil had sold them, and just last week the Sawyers in their motor home named "FancyFree" had pulled up next to her in the bank parking lot, and Mr. Sawyer had leaned out his window to gleefully announce, "Tell Phil we're on our way to Phoenix, and then we're taking this baby all the way to Orlando!"). People had *fun* with the products he sold them, and yet she knew in her heart of hearts, she had subtly (or not so subtly) given out signals that while he made a good living, there was something *unserious* about it.

Tears dribble down her cheeks.

"But Grandma never did that to you!" she hisses, slapping the top of the tombstone. "She never made you feel small!"

Of course Susan doesn't know this; no one knows what happens within a marriage unless one is *in* that marriage, but still, she has a pretty good idea.

What she remembers about her grandmother is how she *adored* her grandfather. All those summers Susan spent at their house, she was always struck by how right before her grandfather was due home, her grandmother would put on a Henry Mancini album, spritz her favorite perfume (Seven Winds) behind her ears, and pat her hair.

"Got to cast my spell," she once told her granddaughter.

Susan can't remember ever putting on a Bruce Springsteen album (Phil's favorite) or spritzing on her favorite perfume (Chloé) in anticipation of his coming home. Her feminist side argues, did he ever put on an album by The Pretenders (her favorite) or spritz on his favorite cologne (Paco Rabanne) in anticipation of *my* arrival? She feels bad, thinking how nice, and how easy, it would have been for her and her husband to have celebrated one another like that.

"But you didn't," she says to the name engraved on the left side of the marble stone. "You didn't celebrate Grandma, did you?"

Her tears aren't dribbling now, they're running, and even as she says (shouts) the words, she knows they aren't true.

She knows they're not true because she knew her grandfather, knew her grandmother, knows Haze. And she knows Phil. And knows that people can love each other and still make mistakes. Susan knows her grandfather didn't sleep with Haze to purposely hurt his wife, and she doesn't think Phil slept with that stupid dental hygienist (she can't—or won't—remember her name) to purposely hurt her.

"It's just so mixed up!" She flings the thermos at the tombstone, and daiquiri splashes across it. Both mortified and slightly awed by her gesture, she looks around and is relieved she's still all alone. She staggers a bit as she stands, not from the alcohol but a cramp in her leg. Gathering up her blanket, she murmurs a quick apology to the gravestone splotched with liquor, and after tucking the thermos and blanket in the handlebar basket, she mounts her bicycle and rides out of the cemetery.

18

"How about that game last night?"

Sam looks up from his desk. "Huh?"

"The Twins," says Dale Jacobsen, the paper's sports editor, who seemed incapable of starting a conversation without a reference to a team's score or amazing hit or dunk or goal or ref's bad call. "They won last night. Pulled it out in the ninth inning."

"Wow, sounds great," says Sam.

"It was," says Dale. "Three runs. It was great."

He stands in the door's threshold for a moment before he shakes his head, mutters, "See ya," and wanders down the hall, hoping to find someone with whom he can rehash the game's highlights.

Sam's just glad Dale hadn't seen him bawling, which he was close to doing. He'd been reading a column on the subject of spring flowers; at least the first paragraph had been about yellow crocuses "poking up from their soil beds, like curious little blond toddlers after a long nap." The second paragraph startled him so that he had to read it again.

This is a spring I won't discover with my dog, Brigadoon. No more walks with her pulling at the leash as she sniffs all the new things growing; no more watching her run around the backyard birdbath, scattering those newly returned robins, who only want to clean themselves up; no more of her interrupting my planting of annuals over and over by proudly delivering her ball to me, then gleefully chasing after it.

181

Brigadoon, my dear pal, died last night in her sleep. She lived eleven years longer than her original master, my late husband, Royal, whom she loved enormously. She grew to love me enormously; dogs are loyal, but they're also pragmatic, and after she understood Royal wasn't coming home and that I now doled out the Alpo, I was the recipient of that big dog love.

She had slowed down, and her muzzle had long gone white, but still, she'd wag her tail and wiggle her hind end like a puppy every time I came through the door. She loved snuggling next to me as I read a book or watched a television program (yes, she had couch privileges), laying her head on my thigh, sighing with contentment when I'd scratch behind her ears or pet her furry skull.

"Hey, Sam."

Looking up, Sam is much happier to see his mother in the threshold than Dale Jacobsen, and after he answers "hey" back, she asks where Haze has taken him now.

Sam understands immediately what she means, and he offers a big smile, which to Susan, is like a present, a bouquet.

"Back to when her dog died. Listen to this."

As Susan sits on the wooden chair facing Haze's desk, Sam reads, "Brigadoon always sensed what I needed. If I needed cheering up, she was suddenly the comic, pouncing at a squeaker toy and pretending to get angry that it squeaked, or rolling on her back and pedaling her back legs as if she were on an invisible unicycle. If I were *really* low, she became my own personal bodyguard, following me around the house (waiting patiently outside the bathroom door), sitting next to me whenever I sat, or pulling her leash, always draped over the back-door doorknob, and carrying it to me, with the prescription 'Come on. You need a change of scenery.'"

Susan stares at her son with a mixture of pride and wonder: he has such a nice speaking voice—when did it stop cracking? Again, she's startled by how much taller he's gotten, or is it just that he's not slumping? He looks almost, well, she couldn't say "regal," could she? Sure, she could, she's his mother.

"Mom?" says Sam. "Why are you looking at me so weird?"

"Was I?" says Susan, with a laugh, and as she stands, she says, "We'll run that one, okay? Are there many reader responses?"

Sam looks down at the sheaf of papers. "A bunch."

"Pick out a few, and we'll run those too. Everybody loves a good dog story."

"How long will she be like this?" Sam asks Mercedes.

"We don't know," says the nurse, her eyebrows circumflexed over her brown eyes. "It's no fun for her though, is it?"

Sam shakes his head, embarrassed that the sudden lump in his throat makes it impossible for him to talk. He'd ridden his bike to the hospital on his lunch break, and now he wishes he were anywhere else. To kill time as he composes himself, he slowly shrugs off his backpack, and setting it next to the bedside chair, he sits down. After clearing his throat, he says, "So. When did you, like, decide to be a nurse?"

The question surprises both of them. Sam doesn't know why he asks it, other than trying to make conversation.

"Well," says Mercedes, touched that this teenaged boy has even an inkling of interest in her. "Ever since I was a little girl. I always had my little brother Ramon pretend he was sick so I could take care of him. It was not his favorite game."

Sam smiles.

"But he'd play with you anyway?"

"He had to. I was older than him, and until we were teenagers, bigger and stronger. But he was never good at pretending he had a broken leg or a concussion."

"What's he doing now?"

Again, Mercedes feels a flush of surprise. When has anyone been interested in her brother? "Ramon is in Mexico. In Monterrey." Her chest swells with both pride and homesickness. "He's an attorney. Much better advising clients than he was pretending to be a patient!"

They both laugh, and then Sam asks, "Do you have any brothers and sisters here in America?"

"One. My brother Ernesto lives in California. But my sisters, Rosa and Lupe, live in a place called Tampico. In Mexico." A picture of her siblings as kids flashes in her head. Ramon, arms crossed over his chest, wearing his usual smirk. Ernesto with his arms around her and Rosa's shoulders, always their protector. Lupe, the youngest, her face turned, dreamy, always looking elsewhere.

Warmed by the memory Mercedes asks, "You have a brother, yes?"

Sam nods. Through his mom's standing in the community, he's used to people he doesn't know knowing about him.

"He's traveling through Europe."

"Yes, your mother told me about his trip. She's very proud of him, of both of you."

"Uh . . . she might be a little prouder of Jack," he says, feeling the tips of his ears grow hot. "He's like SuperSon."

The nurse smiles. "Does he fly?"

"Just about."

When Mercedes leaves to attend to other patients, Sam sits in the strange quiet of the hospital room, where equipment whispers and hums.

"Hello, Haze," he says finally. "Sam here. Sam Carroll? Sorry it took me so long to visit . . ."

For the longest time, it hadn't occurred to him to do so; previously Haze was just the nice old lady who always seemed happy to see him the few times he was in the office, but now, after reading so many of her public and private writings, he feels he knows her almost as well his friends. Maybe even better.

"I just wanted to tell you I know about you and my great-grandfather. Wow. I know it was kind of snooping—you did have those letters and stuff locked up—but . . . I couldn't help myself. Well, I *could* have, I guess, but I didn't."

He finds himself directing his gaze at the foot of Haze's bed. He doesn't like looking at Haze's face, which looks like a pale mask, doesn't like looking at the tube in her nose.

"And my mom read them too. I figured I sorta *had* to share them with her, you know? We were both wondering though, why you kept them in your office—not just the letters from my great-grandfather but the journal too. My mom thought maybe it was because you wanted to keep him close to you. Although he'd be just as close to you at home, right? Anyway, I'm sorry . . . but in a way, I'm not. I don't spend a lot of time thinking about old people's love affairs—no offense, and I guess you weren't *that* old when it was going on—but I like the idea that a relative of mine made you happy for a while and vice versa." He takes a deep breath and pursing him lips, expels a long stream of air. "Wow. I don't know, reading all that and reading your columns . . . you just, you just seem to *know* so much. About how people feel and stuff. And you make me think about stuff too. And so I just wanted to come in here and say thanks. 'Cause who knows—maybe you can hear me, right? Maybe you'll wake up in a couple days and say, 'Hey, Sam, glad you came to see me. And no prob that you read my all my private personal shit! And your girlfriend Elise is right—you do have a beautiful voice! I was hoping you'd sing to me!'"

Startled by what he's sharing with her, especially his claim (yearning) that Elise is his girlfriend, Sam shifts his gaze to Haze's mask/face. Tears rise in his eyes, and he begins quietly, almost whispering, to sing a song his mother often sang to him when he was little, "You've Got a Friend."

His ears suddenly go red when he hears, "That's pretty," and he has an intense wish that there were such things as Harry Potter's invisibility cloak, which he would immediately plunge under. He jumps up and mumbles that he was just leaving, but the tall, skinny old woman entering the room says, "Oh, don't go on my account. You're Susan and Phil's boy, aren't you?"

Sam nods, again not surprised that someone he doesn't know knows him.

"I'm Lois. Haze is my best friend." Ignoring his gesture toward the chair he now stands beside, the woman goes around the other side of the bed and strokes the patient's cheek. "Hello, gorgeous."

Embarrassment over his serenade fades, and curiosity takes its place.

"Oh, yeah," says Sam, "*Lois.* I've read about you in her columns. You guys met at that . . . that writer guy's lecture."

"We certainly did." To Haze, Lois says, "This is the young man who's helping his mother with all your old columns." She looks up. "Susan and I often run into each other here."

"Are you sure . . . are you sure you don't want to sit down?"

"No, but you go ahead," says Lois, and holding the bed's safety rail, she stands on her tiptoes before bending her knees and executing a small squat. "I sit way too much. And when I do my little exercises, I figure it might inspire Lazybones here. Right, Haze? Or are you going to lie around forever?"

Sam sits down as if her words have pushed him, and the woman laughs as she rises again on her tiptoes.

"Haze insists we keep up the jokes." As she slowly squats, she says, "And she insists all company talks about her, so tell me: what's been your favorite column so far?"

"Umm," he says, feeling his ears grow red again. "Let me think . . . well, today I read about when her dog Brigadoon died. We're going to print that one."

"Oh yes," says Lois. "Good old Brigadoon. She was a real friend to Haze."

"We . . . we had a dog. Well, it was my brother's dog, really; we got him right before I was born. He named him Mario—after the Mario Brothers video game? He was a goldendoodle, half golden retriever and half poodle? They're supposed to be really smart dogs, only I guess Mario didn't get the memo."

Still executing her slow bends, Lois chuckles.

"He died a couple years ago, got hit by a car. He'd get loose and run all over the place." Sam swallows hard. "We never got another dog after Mario."

"That's not saying you won't," says Lois briskly. She brings her hands to her hips and stretches to the right. "You thought you'd never get another dog after Brigadoon, didn't you, Haze?"

Sam is fascinated, both by the old woman's agile moves and by what she's saying.

"Did she? Get another dog?"

Lois stretches to the right. "*Dogs.* She's had a couple since Briggy.

I'm taking care of the one she's got now—Polly. In fact, I'm trying to figure out a way how to sneak her in to see Haze."

"Maybe we could dress her like a candy striper."

Lois hoots.

"That might be just the thing that would wake Miss Lazybones up—seeing Polly in a candy striper's uniform!" She leans over the bed rail and strokes Haze's cheek. "But I'll never forget the day she got her first dog after Brigadoon, because I was with her. It was the same day we saw that awful Elm Street nightmare movie, remember, Haze, and I was so rattled?"

RIDING BACK TO WORK, Sam thinks of Mercedes and Lois and how weird it was that he had not only had but enjoyed conversations with both of them. Two women old enough to be his grandmas (he doesn't know that Mercedes is only a few years older than his mother; to him anyone with graying hair qualifies as grandmotherly) who not only interested him but made him laugh and vice versa. Go figure!

Back in Haze's office, Sam, who one weekend with Jack watched a whole marathon of the *Nightmare* movies on cable, googles the date of the first one released, making it easy to find Haze's column about the new dog in her files.

November 19, 1984

Well, I went and did it. I know the repercussions might be long-lasting, that my freedom has been compromised, and that I will often question my sanity, but I got another dog, or I should say, he got me. It's the craziest thing, after having seen a matinee movie, my friend Lois and I were walking around Kingleigh Lake, me more for the calorie-burning exercise (I always ask for extra butter on my popcorn), and Lois more to calm herself, as the movie's villain had really spooked her. I was reminding her that she was the one who chose *A Nightmare on Elm Street* over *The Terminator* (note to the new cineplex owners: why do most of your movie selections cater to teenaged boys?) when a dog was suddenly in step next to us. Really, neither of us saw him dash out from behind a tree or a parked car; it was as if he appeared out of thin air.

"Where'd you come from?" I asked the scruffy, collarless canine, but being a canine, he of course didn't tell me, although his mouth did seem to offer a smile (really!), a greeting of "Howdy!"

"You'd better go back to your owner," Lois said, now firm and scolding, where a minute earlier she had been nervously jabbering about an upcoming blind date her cousin had set up for her—"Just my luck I get someone like Freddy Krueger!"

The dog offered another crazy smile (had he been listening to Lois?), and showing him our seriousness, we sped up, arms pumping. He kept apace.

Then Mother Nature intervened, deciding to throw a quick sleet shower at us. The dog sprinted along with us toward my car, and when I opened the driver's side door, he jumped in with the assurance of a medal winner hopping up to the awards podium.

He politely sat in the passenger's seat, and Lois, grumbling about how she thought *she* had dibs on that, got into the back seat, and I, a bit flummoxed, did the only thing I could think to do: I turned the ignition key.

At home, he didn't squirm or fidget as I toweled him off in my kitchen, and I could hardly eat my dinner without offering him some of last night's meat loaf.

He snuggled by my side on the couch as I read about what Reagan's reelection means to America in *Time* magazine (I'm still steamed that our Minnesota boy, Walter Mondale, AND the first female vice-presidential candidate didn't win), and later, as I was brushing my teeth and slapping on cold cream, he let me know with one single yip that he needed to go outside.

I placed a cushion at the foot of my bed and didn't give

into that goofy smile, which I knew was a request to hop on up, and after a few wags of his tail, which I failed to be seduced by, he settled onto the cushion, where he slept the whole night.

We visited John Draper, the vet on Summer Street, who after calling the pound (there were no reports from an owner of a lost dog matching this one's description), examined the pooch, gave him a few shots, and had his assistant Jody engrave a dog tag that said "Howdy."

He texts/doesn't send to Elise: "I'M GOING TO ASK MOM FOR A DOG."

19

July 14, 1985

Today I turned fifty! Throughout the years, I've taken note of famous people who share the same birth year—1935—as me. It was a pretty good year, one that produced people with all sorts of voices: musical, Elvis Presley *and* Julie Andrews; literary, Ken Kesey; comic, Woody Allen; and enlightened, the Dalai Lama.

Fifty sounds so old, and how did it get to be the mideighties when it seems the seventies were just a couple months back and the swinging sixties swung only a year or so ago?

This is the first birthday I've had without the person who's responsible for bringing me into the world all those decades ago—my mother. As I've previously written, she died last winter after a long illness. Because it was her desire to be the first to wish me a happy birthday, I always got a 5:30 a.m. phone call from her. I'm a fairly early riser but not *that* early. Yet even when my birthday fell on a Saturday or Sunday, I loved getting that call.

There are so many things you miss about a loving mother, especially on the first birthday you have without her.

She was a master cake baker, and her creations were not just oohed and aahed over by other kids at my birthday parties, but requested by those kids' mothers for their own celebrations. Butterflies, ballerinas, panda bears, fancy hats, a miniature farmyard—she not only accepted any request I made but far exceeded my own ideas as to how it might look. She was an artist who sculpted in cake and painted in frosting. I've written about what a fine seamstress she was and how she'd create me Paris (or at least Fargo) runway-suitable clothes; now there are TV shows about cake artists and fashion designers, both of which my mother was, although her artistry was confined to her bedroom, where her old Pfaff sewing machine was, and the kitchen.

The Creative Arts Building is the first place I visit when I go to our wondrous state fair, as it displays hundreds of handmade quilts, embroidered tablecloths, hand-smocked baby clothes, knit sweaters, hand-painted plaques and mailboxes, latticed blueberry pies, sprinkled cupcakes, and crumbly coffee cakes. I love these exhibits because they honor the impulse—the need—to be creative and artistic.

As my birthday present to you, here's

MOM'S THREE WAYS TO ENJOY CHOCOLATE

2 cups sugar
4 tablespoons cocoa
½ cup milk
¼ scant cup corn syrup
pinch salt
1 teaspoon vanilla

In a saucepan, mix the first two ingredients; add everything but vanilla. Cook to boiling, then boil for 3 minutes, being careful not to scorch. Remove from heat, stir in vanilla.

Variations

1. Ice cream topping: It's ready as soon as you stir in the vanilla! Pour over ice cream; it'll harden.

2. Sheet cake frosting: After stirring in vanilla, beat with a wooden spoon for two to three minutes before spreading thickened frosting on cake.

3. Fudge: After stirring in vanilla, beat with a wooden spoon
   for three to four minutes or until your biceps cry "Uncle!"
   Spread out on a large platter, and cut into squares.

"Happy birthday, honey!"

"Happy birthday, son!"

"Yo, Jack. Happy birthday!"

Sam can't believe it. He's on the verge of tears; what a wuss! But it's been so long since he's sat so close to both of his parents, and now, watching his happy, world-traveling brother wave, he has to swallow hard and yell at himself to "man up!"

"Thanks!" says Jack. "A bunch of people sang 'Happy Birthday' to me at the hostel—all in English, even though there's only one other American!"

"Where are you now?" asks Sam.

"Prague," says Jack. "Just got in yesterday. It's beautiful!"

"So are you, honey!" says Susan. "I love your hair!"

Jack poses, patting his longish, curling hair, and thanks them again.

"I love yours too, Mom!"

It had been Sam's idea to stop at GC Marine & Recreation so that they all could wish Jack a happy birthday together.

"Come on, just think how much it would mean to Jack—and to Dad."

They had found Phil not in the trailer that served as his office, but cleaning the cockpit of a cabin cruiser. His look of surprise quickly changed to worry, and he asked if everything was all right.

Now they're all facing the phone, propped up on the boat's (sparkling clean) windshield, Sam squatting between the leather seats on which his parents sit.

"Where're you off to next?" Phil asks. Sam notes with some amusement that like his mother, his dad leans toward the cell phone when he talks, his voice raised, the way older people think they need to when talking what they call "long distance."

"I don't really know," says Jack. "There's this German guy who's got a car and is heading up to Warsaw . . . but I think I'll be going south. Working my way toward Greece."

"Please be careful," says Susan.

Jack laughs. "Really, Mom? You want me to be careful? Huh, I've never heard that before."

Sam looks at his mother, whose big smile and flushed face make her look . . . well, pretty. He wonders if his dad thinks the same thing.

Jack goes on about the clean and efficient trains, about the gypsies that hang out at the stations, about an Italian girl he met who's going to Purdue University next year.

"She's the most beautiful girl I've ever seen," he says. "And she's going to study aerospace engineering! She wants to be an astronaut!"

"Do they have Italian astronauts?" asks Susan. Even though it seems a perfectly valid question, it sounds like a dumb one.

When they hang up—Jack's idea because he's going out to a club with new friends—Sam stands up from the squat he's been in, stretching his arms over his head.

"Hey, can I go down below?"

"Be my guest," says his dad.

After Sam descends below deck, Phil thanks Susan for including him in on the birthday call.

"It was Sam's idea," says Susan. Surprised at her tone of voice—why did she have to sound so snippy?—she apologizes.

"That's okay," says Phil, and after a moment, he adds, "Sam's a good kid."

"He is," agrees Susan. "He, uh . . . well, I think the job has really been good for him. He even asked if he can work at the paper after school starts."

"What'd you tell him?"

"I said sure. I mean, I think he could handle both his schoolwork and a little part-time job. Don't you?"

Staring, as if mesmerized by the speedometer gauge on the boat's dashboard, he finally nods.

"Phil," says Susan, reaching out to touch his arm. "Are you okay?"

When he turns to her, his face is sad.

"It's just that—well, Sam didn't tell me he wanted to keep working at the paper. He . . . he doesn't tell me much of anything."

"You just have to keep asking him things." Again, Susan hears a tone of impatience in her voice that she doesn't like, and adds, "At least that's what works for me. I keep bugging him until he finally talks just to shut me up!"

Phil gives her a grateful smile.

"That is the truth," says Susan quietly. "At least partially. But I find what's really made a difference between us—what's sort of opened up the line of communication—is Sam helping with Haze's columns." She swallows hard. "Did he tell you about her and my grandfather?"

Phil shakes his head, and his look of surprise increases as Susan tells him about the love affair between Haze and Bill.

Below deck, there's not much floor space in between the berth and the door, but enough for Sam to get down on it. He does twenty-five sit-ups and six (up from four!) push-ups before flipping over, lying on the carpet patterned with anchors. Not wanting to interrupt any conversation (hopefully a good one, but he's heartened that they're having one at all), he won't go back on deck until his parents call for him. With the pillow of his entwined hands under his head, he stares up at the ceiling.

Who invented the technology, he wonders, that lets him see his brother on a phone screen all the way from Prague? (Where the hell is Prague anyway?) Should he grow his hair out like Jack's? Would his be curly too? What makes hair curly anyway?

He imagines the beautiful Italian girl who wants to be an astronaut and reminds himself to look up whether Italy has a space program.

Sitting up, he digs in his pocket for his phone, and fingers flying over the screen, he texts/doesn't send Elise, "BELOW DECK ON BOAT. WANNA COME SAIL AWAY WITH ME?"

PART FOUR

20

"So I shouldn't be worried that Sam got Al Henning for history?" asks Susan.

"Why should you be?" says her friend Liz.

"Sam says he's a really tough grader. He says the highest grade he's ever given was a B minus."

"High school mythology. Al's tough, but he's a good teacher. Sam's got history right before my class, and I haven't noticed him coming in traumatized." She pauses for a moment. "How's your face feeling?"

"Really tight," says Susan. "If you could see me, you'd see that I'm barely moving my mouth."

"What'd you say? I can hardly understand you—you must barely be moving your mouth."

"Don't make me laugh," says Susan. "My whole face will crack if I do."

The idea of their faces cracking of course cracks them up, but they try to temper any damage by pursing their mouths, their laughter coming out in a volley of tight-lipped "ho ho hos."

Wearing masks of hardening blue clay, they are in a dimly lit room, lying under thin lavender-infused blankets, spending the two-for-one spa day certificate that Liz won in a PTA silent auction fund-raiser. After massages and mani-pedis, they are finally alone, away from the earnest staff, whose names are stitched in pretty calligraphy on the breast pockets of their white doctorly coats.

"So tell me again how I have nothing to worry about with Sam," says Susan.

"You have everything to worry about," says Liz. "He's a freshman in high school!"

Susan warns her friend not to make her laugh again, as she wants the full "revitalization and renewal" benefits the esthetician promised the facial would give.

"But really, Susan, you'd be so proud of him. He was like a student teacher Wednesday, practically leading the whole discussion. I was . . . *superfluous*, I could have gone down to the teachers' lounge for a smoke."

"If you smoked," says Susan, and tries to corral the smile that wants to break through her clay mask. She had been thrilled that Sam got her good friend as his English teacher, and more thrilled when Liz called her three days into the start of the school year.

"I'd asked the kids to bring in an example of a writer with a strong voice, and Sam read a column Haze had written. I tell you, Susan, the kids were so engaged, not only listening to Sam but discussing the topic afterward. It was beautiful."

That had led to her incorporating Haze's columns into their journalism curriculum, and the two "Radical Hag Wednesday" readings and discussions they had had so far had proved to be fifty-five minutes of thoughtful, passionate, and illuminating debate.

The music in the spa room is low and new-agey, and Susan can't tell if she's listening to gongs or whales, and when she expresses this to her friend, Liz says, "I think it's gongs. Or maybe monks chanting."

Whatever it is, and despite the shrunken-head tightness of her face, Susan feels more relaxed than she can remember.

"Liz," she says, "I'm going to tell you something, something in confidence, that Sam found out about Haze."

"I'm all ears," says Liz, and as she hears about the affair Haze had with Susan's grandfather, her eyes grow as wide as the mask will allow.

When Susan's finished telling the story, there is such a long silence that she says, "Liz? Please tell me you're awake."

"Of course I am," whispers Liz. "I guess I'm just . . . well, stunned."

"Imagine how I felt. And please know this is just between you and me."

"Of course. My God. What was Sam's reaction?"

Blinking hard—Susan doesn't want the salt water of her tears to somehow undo any of the mask's "revitalization and renewal"—she says, "Of course, we were both shocked. But honestly, Liz, Sam seems to have gotten so mature lately. I can't believe that we've been able to talk about something so . . . intimate. And he's been so sensitive; he really seems to understand how betrayed I felt for my grandmother. He's a lot more forgiving, but of course he never knew either of my grandparents. They were gone long before he was born."

"Sam's always been a thoughtful kid."

Susan nods and again feels the prickle of tears; of course he has been; it was just hard for her to remember that when he acted out all his hurt and anger over Phil's and her split. She takes a deep breath.

"And then after Sam read a column about Haze's dog dying, he wondered if she wrote anything about when my grandfather died. She *did*, and he brought the column into my office yesterday."

"Oh, wow! What'd it—"

Liz is interrupted by the door opening and a chirpy voice saying, "Good afternoon, ladies. Time to unmask!"

October 11, 1994

The pews at St. John's by the Lake filled up early, and ushers had to set up folding chairs in the narthex to accommodate all the mourners. It was a beautiful funeral, befitting a man much beloved, admired, and respected in our community, Mr. William Adam McGrath, the former publisher of the *Granite Creek Gazette*.

"He understood the seriousness of providing readers with a diversity of voices," said Pat Gaines, who had run the op-ed page for four years before moving on to the *Sacramento Bee*. "Bill thought everyone's voice was worthy of, if not agreement, then at least respect."

Louis Hagman, who'd served on the downtown council with Bill, said, "Every time you sit in the little gazebo on the south side of the square, think of Bill. It was his idea to build it—and how many marriage proposals have taken place there? Every time you see a show or concert at the Palace, think of Bill—he spearheaded the fund-raising that allowed us to refurbish it. When you think of Granite Creek's motto—'The Town That Can'—think of Bill, because he came up with it."

I did not know that, but there were a lot of things I realized I didn't know listening to the eulogies. Bill McGrath cut a wide swath.

Susan McGrath gave the final eulogy, and in it, she described the man who was not only her grandfather but her mentor, guiding her with patience and love but "unafraid to crack the whip when the whip needed to be cracked."

As many of you know, Bill remained at the helm of the *Gazette* for nearly fifty years, and although he'd long retired by the time his beloved granddaughter Susan took over, he sent her daily e-mails.

"Sometimes he'd send jokes, sometimes inspirational stories, sometimes profiles of people he admired, what was new in technology, or medicine," Susan said. "They were never intrusive; I was always happy to open an e-mail with the subject line he always used, 'You're Doing Swell.'"

With a change of tense, his family, his many friends, colleagues, and fellow citizens say the same to the great and good man that was William Adam McGrath: You did swell.

Both Susan and Sam had sat quietly for a long moment before Susan leaned back in the same chair her grandfather had sat in and Sam pushed toward her the box of tissues on her desk.

"Thanks," said Susan, wiping her eyes.

"I didn't know he sent you daily e-mails," said Sam.

"I think he was probably first in line to get an e-mail account." She blew her nose, an indelicate little honk that made them both laugh. "I saved them all."

"Could I read them?"

Susan nodded. "I printed them all out and saved them in a folder, just like Haze."

"It's weird reading that column knowing what we know about them, isn't it?" asked Sam. "I tried to, you know, read between the lines, but I didn't see anything that would make me know that they . . . well, about their past."

"I know! And that Haze stayed on at the paper, that she didn't want to work somewhere else, that she didn't want to *move* somewhere else . . . it must have been so painful for her."

"Did she ever have another boyfriend?"

"Not that I know of," said Susan. "But then again, she was pretty good at hiding her extracurricular affairs."

They laughed again at the truth of the statement as well as Susan's choice of words, but the frivolity was short-lived for Sam.

"I wish I had a grandpa like you did," he said, sighing. "One who was interested in my life."

AFTER ACCEPTING THE RECEPTIONIST'S COMPLIMENT that they both look "super!" Susan and Liz leave the spa. Even as it's mid-September, the late afternoon air is warm, and they decide to take a walk.

"Let's go by the library construction site," says Liz, taking her friend's arm, "because I want to hear all the wolf whistles we'll get on account of our poreless skin."

"Yours docs look good," says Susan.

"Yours too. But did that esthetician really have to say, 'For upkeep, you might want to schedule regular appointments'?"

"I'm sure she recommends that for everybody."

"Yeah, but the word *upkeep*. That's what you use to describe lawn care."

Their spa day inspires them to take a long walk, and as they turn onto a residential block, they return to their earlier conversation, with Liz saying, "I never knew any of my grandparents," just as Susan says, "I know the relationship I had with my grandparents was pretty special."

They laugh, and Liz posits that great minds think alike.

"But you go ahead," Liz continues, and Susan tells her that after her and Sam's conversation, she had been moved to call *his* grandfather about his delinquent role in Sam's life.

"How'd that go?"

"Dad was defensive at first, as he always is when he thinks I'm criticizing his parenting/grandparenting, but honestly, if I didn't contact him, I'd never hear from him."

"Do you ever talk to your stepmother about it?"

Susan shakes her head. "She's busy with her own kids—she's got eight, you know. And at least twice that many grandchildren!"

"Eight kids! Can you imagine having eight kids?"

Like Susan, Liz has only a quarter as many, a son and daughter, both in college.

"And I think all but one lives in Southern California, so they're *really* in each other's lives." Susan sighs. "So after Dad says he's gotten several postcards from Jack, he complains that he never hears from Sam, and I tell him, 'Dad, Sam never hears from you. Make the effort like Mom would have.'"

Susan's mother had often talked about having the boys come out to Mission Viejo for the extended summer vacations Susan had enjoyed in Granite Creek, but talk was as far as it got, Sam being only two, and Jack six when Donna McGrath died early from cancer. When her father remarried two years later, he told Susan that while he welcomed visits from her and her family, he hoped she'd understand that they'd have to stay at a hotel, seeing as Elaine's three youngest children were still at home and they had no extra room.

Susan sighs again; it's a pattern her breath reverts to when thinking/talking about her father.

"But less than a week later, Sam got a letter from him. I tell you, Liz, he was thrilled. I forget—because I hardly get them anymore—how much a letter can seem like a present."

"Did you get to read it?"

Susan nods, and an old, white-faced collie lumbers toward them, wagging its plume of a tail, and they both lean over the picket fence to pet it and praise its "good-doggedness."

"I told him I totally understood if he didn't want me to," says Susan as they resume walking, "and he made a joke about the two of us having a history of reading private correspondence. But I knew he wanted me to read it."

"What'd it say?"

"First of all, I'd forgotten what beautiful handwriting my Dad has. Really, he's an artist."

"And some schools don't even teach cursive anymore," says Liz, shaking her head.

"In the letter Dad told Sam a little bit about the view of the ocean from his deck, about how he'd played hockey when he was a kid in Minnesota, and that he has season tickets to the Kings games, and he asked if Sam knew the first NHL team in California was the Oakland Seals."

"The Oakland Seals? I never heard of them."

"Neither had I. The franchise didn't last long." Susan shrugs. "Dad spent about a page and a half writing about hockey. But then he wrote that he's happy to hear Sam's doing good work on the newspaper. He wrote how his own dad—my grandfather Bill—was disappointed in his sons' lack of interest in the paper and how hard it is feeling like a disappointment to your own father."

"Oh, man. He said that?"

Susan nods. "Which is more than he ever told me. So anyway, Sam wrote him right back."

"Did he show that to you?"

"Nope. But he asked me for a stamp. And then Sam got another letter from Dad."

Susan answers the questioning look on her friend's face.

"I believe their correspondence is now 'officially private'; at least he hasn't shown any more of it to me. I just hope it continues, because I can tell it means a lot to Sam."

Liz smiles. "I'm glad. And by the way, you're glowing."

Susan *is* happy, talking about this budding relationship between her son and father, but she reminds Liz that any improvement in her complexion is due to the clay mask whose guarantee was to revitalize and renew.

21

Class had begun with Sondra reading a column Haze had written about the *Challenger* space shuttle explosion, which ended:

> We were watching the miracle of pioneers "boldly going where no man (and women too!) has gone before," and within seconds, a giant cloud with two shooting plumes left us awed and confused, not knowing exactly what we were seeing. It didn't take long before we were told. The miracle of this space mission was tragically earthbound.

"Hey, Ms. Garnet—are you crying?" asks Dylan, and Liz, wiping her eyes, nods and says, "Sorry, I just remember that day so clearly. I was a new teacher and just so excited that one of our own was going up in space."

May 28, 1985
Today I had a root canal. Although my dentist is kind and sympathetic and doesn't take personally the enmity his patients feel toward him, it still, despite his best efforts, was an unpleasant experience. I was shot so full of novocaine that I felt my mouth, chin, and tongue were made of blubber, but still, I was *aware* of the pain, aware that something was being done to the nerves of my teeth that seemed almost sacrilege, and I vowed right then and there to never, ever go to bed without brushing and flossing. (So far, the vow is being upheld!)

I took a long nap when I got home, and this evening did what a lot of people do when they want to enter a vegetative-forget-about-everything state; I invited Howdy up on the couch to watch TV with me.

There was a documentary about a bunch of musicians singing a song called "We Are the World," and I watched it, fascinated. That's the way to do it, I thought, raise voices in song to raise money for good causes—this one for famine relief in Africa.

One tear after another streamed down my face, and after I dried them, I wrote out a check. Will my money matter? Maybe not a lot, but maybe a little. And sometimes a little to someone in need is a lot.

I wish I could sing—I mean, in a way that people enjoyed. Eddie—I've written about him before; he was my brother's friend and like my brother, was killed in World War II—he could have been a professional singer along the lines of Frank Sinatra and Dean Martin, or for you younger readers, Prince or Michael Jackson. Really, he had a voice that took you places, a voice that could make you cry, sigh, and dream. I think Eddie, had he lived, would have tried to make a living out of singing. I don't think he would have pshawed and apologized for his talent. I think he would have realized, hey, I've been given something, and I'm going to use it! And why not, it sure beats sorting nails (the job he had before he shipped out) at Nelson's Hardware! Why are we so easily talked out of our dreams, think our talents are too puny to water, to let bloom?

So a day darkened by my petty fears of dental intrusion and pain turned into a night of hope and pride that I'm part of this human choir, despite a certain inability to stay in tune.

"I like how it started off one way," says Charlotte, who sits down after reading the column aloud to her classmates. "I mean I can *so* relate to hating being in the dentist's office."

The other kids laugh, as does Charlotte, revealing a mouth filled with a scaffold of braces.

"But then she kind of turns, you know, and the column's about something else. And then something else. I like that I get surprised. And I wish Eddie wouldn't have died . . . so that he could have been a singer."

Now as a blush stains Charlotte's face, and afraid she's revealed too much and that she sounds stupid, she stares down at her hands.

"I've got a cousin who's a great singer," says Kyle, and because he's several castes above her in the high school hierarchy, Charlotte feels her blush begin to wane.

"He's in a band, and they write their own songs and everything." Kyle smiles at Charlotte, which makes her feel fizzy as a shaken can of soda. "And I like that video," Kyle continues. "Of all those other people—not my cousin—singing that 'We Are the World' song. You can still watch it on YouTube."

"What do you think of Haze writing about feeling hope and pride that she's part of 'this human choir'?" asks Liz, standing at the front of the classroom. "What other metaphor could she have used?"

"Well, she *is* talking about a group singing together," says Stacy. "So that kind of makes sense."

"Yeah," says Abdi. "Like she could write about being part of the human zoo if she was like at the zoo or something."

Burbles of laughter rise up, and Dylan says, "Or part of the human wasteland if she was like at a garbage dump or something," and Grace says, "Or part of the human circus if she was like at a clown convention or something."

"Okay," says Liz as the laughter threatens to take over the discussion. "Let's move on. Claire, why don't you read the next one?"

The girl, taller than anyone in the classroom, stands and begins to read.

June 4, 1988

Reading stories about the ACT UP action in New York City and the arrest of protestors gathered to bring attention to the lack of AIDS research and drugs, I thought of an old pal.

Of all my childhood friends, I think the most fondly of

Richard. His dad was president of our town's bank, and he and my father were good friends as well.

In the summer, we were part of the same neighborhood gang that played hide-and-seek or kick the can on summer nights, and skated down at the pond or slid down the big hill behind the library in the winter. But my dearest memories are of playing with Richard inside, at his house or mine.

That boy had the most fabulous imagination. We'd spend hours on the high seas, the brocade sofa in the front room our sailboat, warding off marauding pirates or man-eating sharks. The same sofa was our train car, and we were hoboes, riding the rails all the way to California, where we'd pick our breakfast off trees and swim in the Pacific. We'd play Americans versus Nazis, although neither of us ever wanted to be the Nazis.

At my house, we played different games. Up in my room, we'd spend hours playing house. He loved playing dolls as much as I did, and our play—thanks to him—was much more fun and detailed than when I played with my girlfriends. There was always a crisis going on; his doll might be dying from scarlet fever, or she was deaf, and we had to invent sign language for her, or we had to amputate her toes because she'd been lost in a blizzard searching for her runaway pony.

We played dress-up too, and he was as—no, more—extravagant as I was, digging into the trunk stuffed with my mother's and sister's cast-off paraphernalia. I was always Ruby Redman, and Richard was always Olivia Oliver.

You might gather that Richard was "different." He knew it too and confided in me how good he was at hiding it.

"Can you imagine what my Pop would do if he saw me playing with these?" he asked once, after my mother's voice calling "Supper" ended our afternoon of play and we tucked our dolls away in their crib. "Or not just my pop—*anybody*. Please don't tell anyone, Haze."

When my brother, Tom, died, and my parents were in their dark cloud of grief, Richard helped me a lot, always willing to listen (over and over) to my stories of Tom and sitting quietly, holding my hand, when those stories inevitably brought forth tears.

"This is the thing, Haze," he told me one afternoon, walking home from a Saturday matinee at the Prairie Rose Theater, a movie that had been preceded by a newsreel about General Eisenhower and his steady command of U.S. forces. "War is fun to play, like cowboys and Indians or cops and robbers, until you figure out what the real stuff is. I mean, think of all those cowboys who got scalped or the Indians who got smallpox from infected blankets, or the robbers who got shot, or the cops who got killed by robbers who didn't really want to kill them but needed money to feed their dying neighbor's baby or something."

Richard's thinking was always so much more layered than other kids'; he never stopped at what was in front of the curtain but always investigated what was behind it, above it, below it.

"If there's a war going on when I grow up, I tell you what—I won't be in it. I'll be a conscientious objector. Or I'll say to the president, 'Instead of a war committee, start up a peace committee.' And I'll be on it."

I had to laugh. "How will you even get the president to listen you?"

Richard shrugged. "I'll figure it out."

He would have too.

I never did tell anyone about Richard, but as the years passed, it became more and more obvious that he was "different."

In the schoolyard, boys threw words at him like "Pansy! Sissy boy! Faggot!" as casually as they threw footballs and baseballs to one another. Torment was a daily part of his life, but he bore it all with a strength to which those boys were blind.

His family moved to Detroit when he was in the eighth grade. I gave him a bag of penny candy for the long car ride; he gave me a wooden box he had handcrafted (one more of his many talents!). He had etched with a wood burner the words "Pirate Booty" on it, and he explained it was for my dearest treasures. I had lots of good childhood friends, but none of them had the imagination, the pizazz, the heart of Richard.

I lost touch with him, but I hope he's doing well. For all I know, he is on a secret presidential committee, working on peace. Peace for everyone, including people like him.

The classroom is silent when Claire finishes, and she looks up, an expression of sadness on her long face.

"Should I read the letter they printed with it?"

At Liz's nod, she does.

TO THE EDITOR:

Haze Evans's most recent column brought back memories of my cousin Gerry, who was made to suffer all his life because of who he was. It is my shame that I didn't stick up for him as much as I could have, but his flamboyance, his difference, frightened me. I thought it might be catching. The poor kid—I'll never forget at a big family reunion, Gerry was called those same bad names as Richard was, at a family reunion! By his relatives!

Nobody knows what happened to Gerry; he lit out the day he graduated high school. I hope he found someplace where he could be himself, hope he made a new family of people who welcomed him in.

Harlan Dodd

Claire sits down, looking as if she might cry. Some of the other kids in class do too, Liz notices.

Sam feels both thrilled and frustrated that he can't tell his classmates how he himself found that box Richard gave Haze and what "pirate booty" he found inside. Instead, he responds to the letter Claire just read.

"This is the weird thing," he says. "Harlan Dodd is my next-door neighbor, and he's this real right-wing tool—"

"Sam," warns Liz. "Let's keep it respectful."

"But he's so hard to respect!"

"Yeah, he yells at us if the toe of our shoe happens to touch his precious lawn," says Jacob.

Liz restrains her smile; she's heard stories from Susan, and she can bet that the toes of shoes belonging to Sam and his friends often find their way "accidentally" onto the old crab's lawn.

"In the summer, my mom has to ask him to turn down his TV 'cause it's always blasting Fox News—"

"My grandpa listens to that too," says Elise. "My grandma hates it—she says it's turned him into an 'angry old buzzard.'"

Liz is about to interrupt, explaining that they'll be covering Fox News when they explore Trends in Media, but then thinks, fuck it, and she smiles as she imagines the reaction her students would have if she'd vocalized that particular thought.

"There sure seem to be a lot of 'angry old buzzards these days,'" says Sam, and the class hoots when he makes his voice sound like that which he's just mentioned.

"But still," he continues, "it makes me kinda sad . . . just like that column did."

There's a shift in the classroom, and once again Liz notices (and will later tell Susan) how Sam has directed it. Since their Radical Hag Wednesdays began, his classmates have looked to Sam as their leader—he, after all, gets to read Haze's columns as part of his job at the newspaper. Nobody else works at a newspaper; only Charlotte Henry comes close to having such a cool job. (She lives on a horse farm outside town and leads tourists on trail rides.)

"My mom says how scary a time it was," says Brianna. "She says before, the only AIDS anyone heard of were these diet candies—I think they were spelled different—that she and her sister used to eat. When they heard about all these strange sores gay men were getting, and then dying . . ." Her voice fades to a whisper. "She says everyone started getting afraid. You didn't know if you'd get infected by swimming at the Y or kissing somebody!"

"My grandma says she loved President Reagan—she voted for him twice—but she thought he totally blew it when it came to AIDS," says Patrick. "She says if he would have addressed the problem earlier, then maybe—" The boy's voice cracks, and he stops speaking for a moment. "Then maybe her brother—my great-uncle—wouldn't have died."

"My dad was on his college golf team," says Grace. "And their best player died of AIDS. My dad never even knew he was gay, and he felt bad that he—I think his name was Mark—never felt comfortable enough to tell him. He said the only reason they got to nationals was Mark."

Liz feels as if her heart is physically reacting to sadness, feels as if it's clenching up like a morning glory under the hot afternoon sun.

"When the column first ran," she says, "so many people wrote in. When Susan—uh, Mrs. McGrath, the *Gazette*'s publisher—ran it again, she printed a few of those letters, which are included on your hand-out. Jacob, do you want to read the last one?"

Sam feels himself tense. Jacob always gets embarrassed when he has to read aloud, his ears baking red as he fumbles over words, and Sam's surprised when his friend stands up—when has he stood up when he's asked to read aloud?—and begins, in a clear, confident voice, to read.

TO THE EDITOR:

Regarding Haze Evans's most recent column on the AIDS epidemic: I would say cancel my subscription, but then where would I get my news? Maybe I'll just declare here and now that I'll never read another column of the radical hag, whose employment at your paper continues to baffle and disgust me. AIDS is a scourge, brought on by people whose minds are perverted and twisted, and what they are getting is an answer to their sick and anti-God choices. She professes compassion for this small minority; I profess compassion for the vast majority who live their lives as God intended them to, loving their partners in the holy matrimony God intended. I am sickened.

Sincerely,

Mr. Joseph Snell

Again, Sam breaks the silence.

"Haze wrote a column about him when he died," he tells his classmates. "In fact, it's the column I brought in today."

While they discuss the columns and letters reprinted in the *Gazette*, Sam occasionally brings in one that hasn't had a second appearance in the paper.

"I think the letter Jacob read is the last one Mr. Snell ever wrote in to the paper, because this is dated June 16, 1988."

"Well, let's hear it," says Liz, and Sam stands and reads the column.

I renew my season tickets every year to Palace Theater Presents, and I often will travel down to the Twin Cities to see a play at the History or Guthrie Theaters, or a comedy revue at Dudley Riggs. I am a big fan of stage presentations, from musicals to Shakespeare to improv to heavy dramas and to everything in between. When I read a review that describes a production as "provocative," I think, oh, goodie, I'll see that. I like to be provoked, to think, to find a new way of thinking, or conclude that my old way was just fine. But traveling down to St. Paul to see *You Itch, I Scratch* was not just a waste of travel time but a waste of the playwright's time, a waste of the actors' time, and most certainly a waste of the audience's time.

"Bare my soul, you sole bear!"

"Jump higher or risk stubbing your toe!"

I kid you not, these were actual lines said by the hapless actors portraying the circus trainer/philosopher Jean Paul Sort-of and his pogo stick–wielding acrobat lover. That the play was only an hour was a blessing, but no one that I saw leaving the theater looked blessed.

Speaking of provocation, I seemed to provide plenty of that to one very faithful reader (and responder), who often called me a "radical hag" and who thought I had an anti-American/leftist/amoral agenda. His letters angered me, but they also made me proud of myself—and of him—for caring so much. His obituary was in the paper last week: Mr. Joseph Snell, age seventy-four.

He was an insurance man, who after retirement became a prolific oil painter, whose work is displayed around town (check out his *North Shore Sunrise* in the First Bank lobby and *The Beauty of the Lilies* in the narthex of his home church, St. Matthew's). In the past few years, he was a regular exhibitor at the Granite Creek Art Fair, and we shared a laugh (somewhat) when I bought his painting *Autumn Maples*.

"I'll take it for sixty," I said, teasing him, as the price tag was seventy-five.

"For you," he said, "one hundred."

Whenever I'd receive a particularly critical letter (which most of them were) from Mr. Joseph Snell, I'd look up at the lovely *Autumn Maples,* which hangs in my office. Sometimes I have a hard time squaring what came out of his pen versus what came out of his paintbrush, but I guess that's because we're all really puzzles inside enigmas inside mazes.

After Sam finishes reading, his classmates say things like, "Whoa," and "He painted? I can't believe it!"

"I've seen the picture," Sam says, "It's, like, abstract but . . . cool."

"I can't believe she was so nice writing about him," says Charlotte, "when he was always so mean to her."

"My mom says that the percentage of reader letters was about 80 percent loving her stuff, and 20 percent not. Joseph Snell was definitely on the 'not' side, and there's no one who wrote as many anti-Haze letters as he did." Sam holds up the paper he's just read from. "After the column she even included a recipe in his honor!"

"What'd she call it?" asks Stacy, "Crab Apple Cake?"

"No," says Charlotte, "Crusty Old Coot Cookies."

"No," says Dylan. "Big Bastard Biscuits."

"No," says Caleb, "I'm a Douche Donuts."

Amid the laughter and the shouting, Liz calls for order with a single word.

"*Class.*"

THANKS FOR CARING BUTTERSCOTCH/PB BARS

½ cup butter

1 (1 ounce) square unsweetened chocolate

⅔ cup packed brown sugar

1 egg

1 teaspoon vanilla extract

1 cup all-purpose flour

1 teaspoon baking powder

dash of salt

1 cup butterscotch or peanut butter chips

Melt butter and chocolate in a large saucepan over low heat. Remove from heat. Stir in brown sugar until dissolved, and cool to lukewarm. Add egg and vanilla, and mix well. Combine flour, baking powder, and salt; stir into chocolate mixture until blended. Stir in chips.

Spread into a greased 9-inch-square baking pan. Bake at 350 degrees for 22–27 minutes, or until a toothpick comes out clean. Cool on wire rack. Cut into squares, and serve after dinner or arguments.

22

"Mama, why not go out with him?"

"Ay," says Mercedes, and Tina laughs as a blush colors her mother's face.

"But really, why not?" Tina kisses the head of the sleeping puppy in her arms and says, her voice softer, "Papi wouldn't mind. He'd like to see you not so alone."

"I'm not alone!" says Mercedes. "I've got you, I've got Caroline, I've got my friends and my colleagues at the hospital, I've got—"

"Mama, what could it hurt? I can tell every time Mr. Wilkerson brings his cat in that he's a nice guy. *Very* devoted to Fluffy."

"Ay," says Mercedes again. "I can just hear Manny—'You can't go out with someone who calls their cat Fluffy!'"

Both women laugh, loud enough to wake the puppy, whose transition from sleep to tail-wagging wakefulness is abrupt.

"So you agree, eh Cesar?" says Tina, petting the wriggling dog, "That Mamacita should go out with the good Mr. Wilkerson even though he calls his cat Fluffy?"

"You want me to take him out?" asks Caroline, coming into the living room with a tray bearing mugs of hot chocolate.

"Nah, I'll do it," says Tina and leaves the room with the puppy, cooing, "Shall we take a little walk? A little walk so you can tinkle?"

Mercedes thanks Caroline as she takes a cup of hot chocolate.

"We always just plopped marshmallows in our cocoa, but Tina tells me this is how you made it for her when she was little."

Thanking her, Mercedes dips her spoon into the whipped cream adorned with chocolate shavings, and with spoon in mouth nods her approval.

After enjoying their beverages for a moment, Mercedes says, "I suppose Tina has told you about my predicament?"

"Predicament?"

"About my invitation from Mr. Wilkerson."

"You call a man wanting to take you out for dinner a predicament?"

Mercedes smiles, but to her—and Caroline's—surprise, her eyes fill with tears.

"Oh, Mercedes," says Caroline, moving closer to the woman on the couch and putting her arm around her.

"Tina . . . Tina thinks I'm foolish. But I . . . Manny was the love of my life. How could I go out with another man?"

Caroline squeezes Mercedes's shoulder.

"Tina doesn't think you're foolish. She knows how much you and Manny loved each other. She just doesn't want you to be lonely."

"I'm not—"

Caroline cuts off her protest by asking, "If it were reversed, if it had been you who died, well, wouldn't you want Manny to be happy, to find companionship . . . or love?"

"No! I'd kill him!"

It's the look on Caroline's face that makes Mercedes laugh, and realizing Mercedes was kidding, Caroline laughs too.

Taking a big sip of hot chocolate, Mercedes tongues the whipped cream that remains on her upper lip.

"If I had been the one to die first," she says, "yes, yes. I would definitely want Manny to find someone else. He would *need* to find someone else. But men are like that, I think. They need someone to take care of them more than women do."

"Still," says Caroline. "A dinner date is only a dinner date."

Mercedes nods. "And I do hear they have really good food at Zig's Supper Club."

"I know it was a favorite of Haze's," says Caroline.

"Guess who peed *and* pooped?" says Tina as Cesar charges into the room. "This little wonder dog!"

January 28, 1988

While in the Cities just after the fifteenth anniversary of the Roe vs. Wade decision, I witnessed a demonstration outside a clinic that had antiabortion protestors carrying signs reading, "Murderer!" (and worse) and shouting the same things to anyone entering the clinic.

Some biographical details in the following stories have been changed to protect the innocent or guilty, depending on how you look at it.

I knew "Jane Roe #1" in high school. She sat next to me in English . . . until she didn't. When we took turns reciting "The Raven," everyone laughed when she lowered her voice and read her section in a spooky, Boris Karloff–like voice. Our teacher called on her more than anyone to read aloud, because she'd use all kinds of funny accents to bring life to the text: when she read Emily Dickinson, she'd use a high, melancholy voice; when she read Keats, she'd do it in a stuffy British accent; and her Russian accent while reading Chekov was uncanny . . . and funny.

She was the peppiest member of the pep squad and as a member of the student council, had lobbied for recess, saying that even high-schoolers should swing and teeter-totter. I used to think it was a shame my old friend Richard had moved out of town, because he and Jane Roe #1 would have really hit it off.

I didn't think anything of it the day she didn't sit next to me in English, or when she was absent the next. Then the weekend came, and the party lines were buzzing with the news that this bright, funny star (who always had the lead in class plays) had died. The whole town was stunned.

Her death was attributed to "complications due to an emergency appendectomy," but her best friend told me she had traveled with her boyfriend (Mr. BMOC, who was going to UND on a full academic *and* athletic scholarship) to "see someone in the Twin Cities" to get rid of her pregnancy.

I had no idea what she was talking about. As a (naive)

junior in high school, I knew about pregnancy but had no idea people sometimes got rid of them; all I knew was the ache and loss as well as shock (Jane Roe #1 had had sex!) I felt.

"The poor girl," I heard my mother say, her voice choked, to my father. "The poor, poor girl."

Jane Roe #2 was a girl at college. I didn't know her well, but Rose, a bohemian who lived in my dorm, did. Usually it was the jazz records she played at full volume that had people banging on her door, but this time it was her bellowing that caused me to timidly knock, asking, "Rose, Rose, are you all right?"

Rose was a girl whose take-no-prisoners persona was either feared or admired, and to see her tearstained and shaky when she opened the door was to see her in a previously unseen way.

"Dorothy!" she cried. "Dorothy!"

She had an illegal hot plate in her room, and I turned it on and made us a pot of tea while Rose sat on her bed, sobbing.

I handed her the cup of Earl Grey, and she sat holding it a long time before she was able to speak.

"Dorothy," she said, a final sob shuddering through her. "Dorothy dropped out of school!"

Admittedly, dropping out of school is a big and often regrettable decision, but Rose's reaction seemed, to put it mildly, a bit over the top.

"Dorothy the writer?" I asked, of the girl who wore a beret as regularly as most of us wore headbands.

Rose nodded. "The editor of *Cardinal's Song*!"

This was our college's biannual poetry journal, which had been the first to publish a student who'd gone on to become a fairly well-known (relatively speaking) poet.

"Oh," I said. "Why'd she drop out?"

"Her modern lit prof got her pregnant! She went home to Milwaukee on spring break and paid this woman two hundred dollars to get rid of it, and she couldn't stop bleeding! She just called me—from the hospital! She said the doctors there are telling her she's lucky to be alive! And her parents aren't letting her come back to school!"

This is what I remember: The black bedspread under which Rose huddled (where'd she find a black bedspread anyway?), trembling as if it had a life of its own; the Emma Goldman poster above her bed, whose curled right corner needed more tape; the muffled shouts and laughter from the field hockey game on the athletic field her window faced.

"What's going to happen to the teacher?" Rose wailed.

"Nothing! She told her parents it was him, but they don't want a 'scandal'! So they're making *her* drop out!"

I know I'm not the only one with these stories. And the fact that I'm not makes me think, thank heaven for Roe vs. Wade. Now people can go to real doctors, in real clinics.

The thing is . . . I always wanted to be a mother, but I could never carry my pregnancies very far. Even though logically I knew it wasn't my fault, I still felt it was. And I think women who have trouble conceiving babies or miscarry them are often antiabortion: how could anyone be so cruel as to get rid of something we want so badly?

I've spent a lot of time thinking about this, and these are my personal conclusions: Your story isn't mine. No woman owes me her baby. If you believe you can't have a baby, I shouldn't have the power to say, "You must." For too long, men (and some women) have thought they have control over women's stories, not understanding that every single person has the right to have power over their own story.

I know there are those who ask, what about the baby? I understand that. I ask that question myself. I desperately wanted my pregnancies, hoped that they'd grow and become babies I delivered, but there are women who desperately, for many reasons, do not want their pregnancies to grow, who do not want to deliver a baby.

At the clinic, I heard antiabortionists shouting at a young woman, "God will punish you!"

What gives them the divine insight to know what and why God punishes? And how is the punishment that God does or doesn't mete out to someone else any business of theirs?

Long ago I wrote about my own miscarriages, and many readers wrote in, saying things like, "Oh, don't worry, you'll have another," "It was meant to be," or this: "It's Nature's way of expelling something that wasn't right." Most people were truly concerned, but some, probably thinking I was being overdramatic, reminded me that it was no big deal, after all, I could just try again! It's funny, some of those people who thought my miscarriages were nothing to get upset about and that I only lost "a couple cells" are the people I know who most oppose the legalization of abortion. When a miscarriage is natural, it's God's will, and it's "all for the best," but when a woman chooses to lose "a couple cells," it's murder.

Liz gets a kick out of chaperoning school dances. She likes seeing the kids all dressed up, perfumed, and cologned, likes the mix of shyness and bravado, likes watching the awkward moves a cool kid can make and the smooth moves a nerd can make on the dance floor, likes the decorations (lots of orange and red crepe paper and glittery leaves taped onto the walls in celebration of Fall Fest!), likes whatever disco-ball lighting effects the AV club comes up with, likes (even while missing the live bands that used to play) hearing the music the DJ spins. What she definitely does not like is being yelled at by a parent.

After a bathroom break, she's on her way back to the gym, when a woman marches toward her, her face nearly as red as her dress.

"What exactly are you trying to prove?"

"Hello, Mrs. Bancroft," she says, having met the same woman at open house earlier in the school year, although her voice then had been much more modulated.

"There are many of us who believe in the sacredness of life and don't believe a teacher should be brainwashing her students to think otherwise!"

"I'm not brainwashing my students, but I hope I'm encouraging them to *think*."

"We don't believe in abortion in our family!"

"I'm not asking anyone to change their beliefs," says Liz, her hands splaying outward. "I'm only offering one woman's opinions on all sorts of subjects."

"Well believe me, I'd transfer Blake out of your class if he didn't like it so much!"

March 27, 1989

The Lutheran church in our town was at the end of the block. Pastor M lived next door, in its old white parsonage, along with his wife. Mrs. M was an avid gardener, who planted everything from snap peas to snapdragons, pumpkins to pansies, zucchini to zinnias. Mrs. M welcomed us kids into the parsonage yard, understanding that its towering oak tree practically begged children to climb its leafy, expansive arms, and in the spring and summer, we were happy to help her in the gardens, as she often rewarded us with her homemade caramels wrapped in wax paper.

Mrs. M was lighthearted and fun, and my friend Richard, who always saw more than the rest of us, wondered what she saw in Pastor M.

"I mean, it's not like he's a barrel of laughs," he said to me once as we walked home after a morning helping Mrs. M pull weeds and lay mulch. I had to agree there; when it came to his sermons, he was more a droner than an orator, and my mother's elbows, warning us to stay awake, were kept busy poking both me and my father. "Plus he's so much older than she is!"

"He is?" I asked. My own dad was my mother's senior by many years, but I never was aware of it as a kid. Unless someone had old-age giveaways, like gray or white hair, stooped posture, or a shambling gait, my young mind categorized all adults as in the same vague age.

"By at least ten years," said Richard. "Which wouldn't really matter, but he acts like he's *a hundred and ten* years older."

Apparently the young-hearted Mrs. M shared similar opinions, boarding a train west and never coming back.

It was quite the scandal in town; Pastor J came out of retirement to stand in for Pastor M while the latter went off to retrieve his wife. Three weeks later, he came back. Alone.

The next Sunday he preached a sermon about the sin of temptation and not living up to one's vows. I don't know if he felt any regret or remorse—certainly none was expressed, and I honestly don't think he was a thoughtful-enough man to consider any point of view other than his own, certain as he was that it was guided by God.

Several years later, after retrieving the sweater I'd left behind in confirmation class, I pushed open the church door and saw Pastor M in the backyard, staring at the tumble of weeds that had replaced Mrs. M's flower garden.

Not wanting to disturb him *or* talk to him (I'd just spent an hour in the plodding tedium that was his lecture on the Nicene Creed), I tried to make myself invisible, crouching a little as I passed the lilac hedge, but my stealth proved not so stealthy.

"Hazel?"

(Even teachers called me by my nickname, but true authority figures, like Pastor M and the school principal, still insisted on this address.)

Pulling at the hem of my cardigan, I said, "I left behind my sweater," and planned to offer a wave and keep walking, but the expression on the minister's face was a rope that pulled me toward him.

"Pastor M? Are you all right?"

It was a rhetorical question—obviously he wasn't—but the only one I could think of asking.

He didn't answer for a long time but stared at the garden of horseweed and bull thistle and witchgrass.

"I should have cared enough to have kept this up," he said, his voice so soft I felt I was eavesdropping. "The circle ladies volunteered to help out, but I told them no. I said they could keep up all plants on church property, but the parsonage gardens had been planted by . . . by Mrs. M. Planted and tended to with great devotion." His voice broke a little, and I forced myself not to obey my instinct, which was to run, especially after he'd lifted his eyeglasses to wipe away tears.

"Maybe if I had paid attention to her the way she paid attention to these flowers . . ." He cleared his throat. "She said she always planted annuals because she liked a new garden every year, but I think it's because she knew one day she'd be gone. And it was easier to leave something that wasn't going to bloom again."

When I got home, I wrote down in my journal what Pastor M had said; it was the only time I'd heard him speak with any sort of emotion.

The pictures on the news of the Exxon Valdez oil spill, that massive blackness spreading out over the waters and shoreline of the Gulf of Alaska like a malignant liquid tumor, are shocking and sickening. How did that tanker run aground? Who's responsible? I thought this column was going to be about this devastating environmental catastrophe, but the words that came out on the old Selectric were about Pastor M. Same theme, I guess. Carelessness. So easy to excuse, but really, isn't carelessness the beginning of all disasters?

After reading the column on Radical Hag Wednesday, Kyle says, "I don't really get that last line."

Liz raises her eyebrows and purses her mouth, an expression that asks if anyone cares to comment.

Grace does.

"I think it means that we don't really take carelessness seriously, 'cause it's so easy to be careless about simple stuff, like not brushing your teeth good or writing a book report on a book you didn't really read." She glances quickly at Mrs. Garnet. "I'm not talking about myself."

Liz smiles. "Go on."

"There are different degrees of carelessness is what I mean, and they can lead to different degrees of disasters—if you're careless about brushing your teeth, they might rot or abscess or whatever, and—"

"Okay, I get it," says Kyle, nodding. "That preacher dude was careless in how he treated his wife, so she finally left—"

"But was it carelessness that caused that oil spill?" asks Stacy. "Something the captain did wrong?"

"Maybe not. Maybe it was a mechanical error or something," says Dylan. "You know, something wrong with the ship."

"Then wouldn't it be carelessness of like the maintenance crew?" asks Jacob.

"All good points," says Liz. "But we've got to move onto the next column."

April 20, 1995

My friend Lois, Bruce Schneeman, and I stood watching a bank of TVs, our arms folded tight across our chests, protecting us.

"My wife's family's from Oklahoma City," Bruce said (note: I spoke this morning to Anita Schneeman, and all her family members are thankfully fine), as we tried to make sense of not just the carnage but how the carnage came to be.

Lois and I had been browsing at Schneeman's Furniture. I need a new couch (and have for about a decade), and Lois was looking at an accent rug, as she had finally had her molting seventies shag carpet pulled up to reveal the pretty blond wood floors underneath.

We were more distracted shoppers than serious ones and were testing out two side-by-side recliners, pulling their levers like we were race car drivers and they were our stick shifts, whooping as we were sent in varying degrees backward.

When Bruce rushed into the showroom and called, "Ladies!" we thought for a moment we were being scolded for our rambunctious recliner test-drive, but as he navigated the maze of sectionals and ottomans and chairs, he said, "There's been a bombing in Oklahoma City!"

We followed him into the small-electronics room and watched the news on a half-dozen television screens.

I didn't go into the office, where I knew I could get all the latest incoming news. I didn't want all the latest incoming news. I didn't know *what* I wanted. I was just so discombobulated that in this world I live in, also live people who can plan and execute such barbarity.

The perpetrators are unknown right now, but when they're caught (and they will be caught), I'm sure we'll hear the heinous drivel that they believe explains their motives. But that's all it is: the same heinous drivel that's always espoused by those sick enough to commit acts of terror, those evil ideologues who believe that causing death and destruction somehow glorifies their cause.

"I had to ask my mom about the Oklahoma City bombing," says Claire. "I'd never even heard about it before."

"My dad said when he heard it was an American who did it, he couldn't believe it," says Patrick. "Especially an American who'd been in the army, like he was."

"Your dad was in the army?" asks Dylan.

Patrick nods. "In the Persian Gulf War. Same one as the guy that did it, that McVeigh."

There is a silence in the classroom, and Liz watches emotions flit across her students' faces.

"I like how Haze writes about the little things in her own life," says Elise, "and then about big things in the world."

A weird warmth radiates in Sam's chest. He could listen to Elise all day.

"I think that's the gift of any good writer," says Liz. "By bringing us into their own world, they bring us into the whole world."

"My grandma tells me stories," says Stacy, "and I've started writing them down. Plus I write down things that people say, like Haze did, if they impress me."

"Is it full of things I've said?" asks Dylan.

The classroom laughs, and even as Stacy reddens, she says, "Uh, that page is pretty blank."

Liz has been complaining to her husband how stupid testing regulations are taking the fun out of teaching, but on Radical Hag Wednesday she's reminded what makes her profession the best in the world. Her kids are engaged, thoughtful, willing to offer their opinions and listen to others; they're *excited* about learning. She's had numerous e-mails from parents about the discussions the "Haze homework" has sparked around the dinner table, in the car, while doing dishes.

Pride rises in her as Blake, a boy whose florid acne has exacerbated his natural shyness, raises his hand and says, "I've started reading some other columnists online. Have you ever heard of a guy named Dave Barry? Or Carl Hiaasen? They're pretty funny."

23

Countless times, Susan has said (and meant), "What would I do without you?"

Caroline believes in herself, but her belief isn't as constant as she'd like, often giving way, like a rotted pier, to the crashing wave of doubt whose cry, as it batters to shore, is "You're a fraud!"

The first time she confided this to Tina, her girlfriend laughed and said, "Chica. All women—probably most men too, if they're really honest—feel that way."

"You don't! You're the most *unfraudulent* person I know!"

Wrapping her arm around her and drawing Caroline close, Tina said, "My first operation? On Doobie, a big old retriever who'd eaten a sock? Ay. After I'd scrubbed up and was putting on my gloves, I thought, What am I doing? Whose beloved dog am I about to kill?"

"Those were just nerves," said Caroline, kissing the velvety lobe of Christina's ear. "Deserved nerves—I mean, my God, you're dealing with life and death. Me, I'm only dealing with schedules and appointments and correspondence, and I still feel sometimes like I don't know what I'm doing."

Propping herself up in the bed, hand supporting head, Tina said, "Caroline, it's the easiest thing in the world for us to feel like we're never good enough at what we do. And it doesn't matter that I'm a vet or you're a journalist—"

"Ha! An assistant!"

Tina frowned, more with her eyebrows than her mouth.

"An assistant who thought she wanted to write for a newspaper but is finding out she might like the administrative side even better. How many times have you told me that yourself?"

Caroline can't help a small smile. "About a million, probably."

"And let me tell you, whether you wind up writing for a paper or running a paper, you might still feel like a fraud, because that's how women are raised to feel."

"Even you, with your mom and dad believing in you?"

"Of course. Because they were 'just my parents.'" Rolling her eyes, Tina shook her head. "It was the rest of the world that I thought really mattered! And the rest of the world thought I was just a little Hispanic girl who'd gotten lucky with affirmative action scholarships!"

The silence fell on the air like a cloud bank and pressed on them for a while.

"That's what we have to fight," Tina said finally. "All those 'no, no, nos' that we've heard since we were little girls. All those nos that tell us we're wrong to think what we think, to do what we do, to be who we are."

WHEN CAROLINE WALKS into the reception area, she asks, "Is Sam here yet?"

He's off from school because of teacher conferences, and to Susan's delight, he announced that he wanted to spend his vacation at work.

Shelly, who's angry that she used a pen on today's especially hard Sudoku puzzle, nods.

If she wonders about Caroline's strange, hunched-over posture, she says nothing but directs her attention back to the bedeviling puzzle.

As Caroline heads down the hallway, arms cupped low around her squirming stomach, she giggles, both from nerves and giddiness. She passes the conference room but hearing her name, backs up and looks in.

"Oh, hi, Susan. I'm looking for Sam."

"Look no further, he's in here."

He is, along with a small group of people gathered around the table, all of whom stare at her.

"Why am I reminded of the movie *Alien?*" asks Aaron Pimsler, the news editor.

Unzipping her jacket, Caroline laughs, as the bundle of fur she's corralled inside scrambles up her chest.

"Oh, it's a puppy!" says Susan, and a chorus of words tumble after hers: "He's adorable!" "What's his name?" "Can I hold it?"

Sam has asked the last question, and Caroline obliges his request by placing the wriggling pup into his hands.

"Dude!" says Sam, laughing as the dog attacks his face with his tongue.

"Is he yours?" asks Susan, and as she reaches out to pet the puppy's head, she laughs too when the animal decides her hand is as delectable as Sam's face and licks her fingers.

"No, he's the last puppy from Lovey's litter. The stray dog that broke her leg? That Tina fixed up?"

Caroline swallows hard.

"That my *girlfriend* Tina, the woman I love, fixed up?"

Her voice cracks, and in the short silence that follows Susan thinks, Finally, it's about time. Dale, the sports editor, and Mitch, the managing editor, both think, whoa. Aaron, the news editor, who was working up his courage to ask Caroline out, thinks, Damn. Ellie Barnes, the features editor, thinks, I wish I were more interesting. Sam thinks, *Is she saying what I think she's saying?*

She is. Caroline had made a very specific plan to come into the office and admit to Susan and Sam—and whoever else was around— her real self. It was her Coming-Out Party, only she wasn't dressed in strapless tulle, announcing that she was ready to take her place in high society; she was in her office-appropriate black slacks and a turquoise cowl-neck sweater, telling the people in her world that she was gay.

"Well," says Susan, seeing the tears sparkle in Caroline's eyes, "I think we've covered everything. Ellie, yes, I'd love an interview with that dance company head. Pat, I'd like at least one more source on that financial advisor scandal. The rest of you, we'll talk further over lunch. Thank you."

Susan closes the door after most everyone shuffles out. Remaining are herself, Sam and the puppy in his arms, and Caroline, who is sitting with her head in her hands.

"It's all right," says Susan, putting her hands on the young woman's shoulders. "It's all right."

Sam's emotional circuit board is so lit up it would be hard to identify one prevailing feeling—he can't stop giggling at the puppy's persistent kisses—and yet his mother's assistant, who's appeared in more than one of his jerking-off fantasies—has just declared herself not just out-of-bounds but on the wrong team!

From her slightly shaking shoulders, Sam can tell Caroline's crying, and he's surprised at the thickness in his own throat.

"Mom, can I keep him?" he says, as the puppy confuses his earlobe for a chew toy.

"I . . . I brought him for you," says Caroline, looking up, her pretty face streaked with tears. She turns to Susan. "I know I should have asked you, but I just thought Cesar would love Sam and vice versa."

"Cesar?" says Sam. "Is that his name?"

"That's what we've been calling him. But if you . . . if you keep him, you can call him whatever you like."

"Come on, Cesar," says Sam, as he walks across the room. "Let's go see what's happening outside."

His hands aren't free to text/not send to Elise, but if they were, he would have typed, "CAROLINE'S GAY, BUT THE BIG NEWS IS: I GOT A DOG!"

After Sam leaves, Susan sits down and asks, "Was the puppy to distract from what you were saying or vice versa?"

Caroline shrugs, and her expression looks as if she's trying to hold in a laugh or a sob.

"A little bit of both, I guess. You're not mad at me, are you?"

Susan cups her hand over her assistant's. "For what? The puppy? Ten percent mad to ninety percent glad. I mean, Sam's been wanting a dog for a long time. Thanks for providing the kick in the pants."

Caroline breaks their long stare by looking at their hands.

"And you're not," she whispers, "you're not mad that I didn't tell you I was gay?"

Now Susan's face looks as if she's trying to hold in dual emotions: surprise and exasperation.

"Zero percent mad. Fifty percent sad that you'd think I was mad. And fifty percent glad that you finally told me."

"It's funny that all your emotions rhyme," says Caroline.

"I'm a poet—"

"I know it."

The women smile, but Caroline punctuates hers with a "whew!" and adds, "I feel so much lighter."

Susan leans back in her chair to survey her, and nodding, she says, "You look like you've lost about . . . two ounces."

"Maybe I could write a feature about it: 'How to Lose Weight by Confessing Your Deepest Secrets.'"

"I do feel bad," admits Susan, "that you felt it had to be one of your deepest secrets."

"'Bad.' Another rhyming word!"

When she speaks again, after a long moment, Caroline's voice is lower, heavier.

"I feel dumb that it *was* one of my deepest secrets—I mean, who hides that they're gay anymore? But . . . well, I've told you about my family. They were always so *certain* in their beliefs that it made me uncertain in mine. I never wanted to hurt them, but"—she exhales a chestful of air—"I finally figured out it hurts more to lie about yourself. Although my mother might disagree."

"You told her?"

Caroline nods as a tear slides down her cheekbone.

"And I figured once I let Mum know, I could let everyone know."

"I'm glad," says Susan, squeezing her assistant's hand. "Now let's get to work."

September 2, 1997

I met Cliva in college and learned quickly that she wasn't just an Anglophile but a Royalphile. She was in the dorm room next to mine and decorated her door with a sign that read, "Here within are the Quarters of one Dame Cliva Adams." She held "high tea" parties in our commons room, introducing us rubes to scones (ugh—not my cup of tea, or should I say not my cup of tea accompaniment—I prefer muffins), which she baked in the home economics kitchen. Cliva was from New Mexico, but her ancestry was English and Scottish, and she claimed that her great-great-grandmother was a distant cousin of Queen Victoria.

"Big deal," said Rose, another girl on our floor, who was fond of wearing black and would play her jazz records really loud, only responding to about the fourth or fifth shouted request to "turn it down!"

"Who'd want to be related to royalty anyway?" she'd say. "What makes a person 'royal' anyway—a marauding, conquering temperament or a luck of birth?"

Anytime I hear the word *anti-establishment*, I think of Rose, who would show up to these high teas in an old sweatshirt and what were then called dungarees, speaking in a smarmy British accent and crooking her pinkie with great exaggeration as she slurped her tea.

Finally Cliva told her if she considered the teas such a joke, she didn't have to come, to which Rose answered, "The teas aren't a joke—I love free food—what is a joke, however, is your fascination with royalty."

She went on to suggest that fascinations often led to compulsions and other neuroses and that "come to think of it, I have noticed a twitch in your right eye."

The girls around the table protested—Cliva had no such twitch—Rose simply smiled, pocketed several little triangular sandwiches and bowing deeply, bid her adieu.

I was thinking of both these old chums today when I heard the shocking news of Princess Diana's death.

While I wasn't enamored of monarchy as Cliva was, neither was I like Rose, disdainful of it. Fact is, I'm rather neutral, not really following or caring about the lives of those who live in castles and have little to do with the day-to-day goings-on of my life.

But a little pomp and circumstance never hurt anyone, and I enjoyed watching the pageantry and spectacle of the princess's wedding to Prince Charles and always liked seeing Diana's open, lovely face on magazine covers or watching her on TV, speaking in that low, slightly breathless voice. More than her stylish fashion sense, however, I was impressed by what seemed her genuine empathy and concern for people, and my respect for her grew when I learned the sadness and betrayal with which she lived.

And now she's gone, so young, so vital, the victim of a stupid, senseless car wreck.

I think why I'm feeling so bad is that Diana, despite all that was thrust upon her and all that was taken away, was so much more than a princess.

July 25, 1999

It's easy to get cavalier, thinking we have things figured out and life goes a certain way and then: boom. Our own arrogance slaps us in the face, reminding us—hollers at us—that we might be in charge of what clothes we choose to put on in the morning or what brand of toothpaste we squeeze onto our brushes, but that's about it.

When I heard that John F. Kennedy Jr.'s plane was missing and then, days later, that his, his wife's, and his sister-in-law's remains had been found on the bottom of the Atlantic Ocean, I thought, No. *No.* This goes against all that should be right and good.

I've written before about his father, his uncle, about those bright and beautiful Kennedys cut down in their prime, and once again, as I did hearing the news of their deaths, I feel all curled up, curled up to protect my wounded heart. Why is it that—

Shelly pulls back, surprised by two splats on the newspaper in front of her. For a millisecond, she wonders if there's a leak in the ceiling. Looking furtively around the reception area like an employee who's just pocketed a box of staples or a roll of stamps, she daubs her eyes with a tissue. In her closed-down world, crying was something rare as a white peacock, and it would take time to cull her memory and remember the last time she had been so moved to shed tears.

A tiny sob hitches up her chest as her eyes fill again.

"Hey, Shelly," says Sam, and the receptionist jumps in her chair, banging her knee against the edge of her desk.

Not meaning to startle her, Sam is quick to apologize, and seeing the distress on her face, he asks, "Are you all right?"

"Just had a coughing fit is all," says Shelly, faking a cough to buttress her fake claim. "What are you doing here anyway?"

Sam flushes at the snarl in the woman's voice.

"I . . . uh, I've got the morning off from school—Mom signed a note—I've got a dentist's appointment, and I just thought I'd stop in for a while before I . . ."

The embarrassment on the boy's face irritates Shelly; at least she assumes it's irritation she feels, until she collapses onto her desk, sobbing.

For a moment, Sam stands rigid like a Yosemite hiker coming across a grizzly, but then adrenaline kicks in, and he rushes to the receptionist, placing his hand on her heaving back.

"Shelly? Shelly, what's the matter?"

To Sam, calling her by her name and asking this question feels as intimate as having his hand on her back, and he wishes more than anything that he'd slept in before visiting Dr. Arnowitz for the stupid biannual checkup his mother insists on. He was worried too that someone would come in at any minute—Mitch always comes in early, and often Caroline—and Sam was sure Shelly would not like her mental breakdown (his diagnosis) witnessed by anyone else.

"Shelly," he says, his voice soft, "would you like to go into the break room? Or the bathroom? I can—"

"Yes," she gasps, rolling back in her chair (one wheel grazing the tip of Sam's shoe) as she opens a lower drawer. Grabbing her purse, she rushes out of the room as if a fire alarm's been pulled.

Standing watching her, Sam's body feels rubbery, like he's gotten off a ride that's spun him too fast. When he thinks his legs are up to the task, he walks out of the reception area, deciding not to work after all. It would be *way* too weird to stay in the office. He'll go early to his dental appointment and read about Goofus and Gallant (and think how Goofus always seems to have more fun) in the old *Highlights* magazines that are always splayed out on the waiting-room end tables.

IN A BATHROOM STALL, Shelly is posed like Rodin's *The Thinker,* only her perch isn't a bronzed rock but a porcelain toilet. She has long since stopped crying, yet an occasional little soblette twitters up her throat, reminding her of her outburst, and she presses her face harder against the knuckles of her fist. She feels foolish—what that boy must think of her!—but she also feels something so foreign she can't even name it. In her chest, there is both a weight and a softness, as if her heavy heart has been wrapped in a soft, fuzzy baby's blanket.

Shelly has never been one for reflection, self or otherwise, but now, in the confines of this gray-walled stall, she asks herself, What the hell? What the hell happened out there when she read those columns? Why the hell should she give a good goddamn about the deaths of British and American royalty?

Because . . . because of so many things, she thinks. Because of how she had thought the nickname John John was the cutest thing she'd ever heard.

"I was named after my father," her ex-husband had told her when they were watching a television documentary about the Kennedy kids. "And no one ever called me Ray Ray. In fact when my old man called me anything, it was usually, 'Hey, stupid.'"

Ray's tone had been light, as if the story were a joke, but Shelly saw the pain in his eyes, pain he tried to hide with his tough-guy squint.

"Did you know JFK had such a bad back that it was hard for him to pick up his own kids?" Shelly had said.

"That came from his war service," Ray said. "Guy could have easily used his daddy's connections to get out of serving, but he didn't. I admire that."

They had been sitting on the green corduroy couch they had bought on credit at Montgomery Wards and that would be theirs after only four more payments, holding hands during the telecast, and when there was a commercial, Ray was the one who got up to help himself to a beer and make her a rum and Tab.

Shelly knew there was a trove of sweet memories of Ray—even if the bastard had left her, he was a good guy—but it was easier to keep it hidden away in the dusty attic of her mind, unopened.

Still, I'm not the only one whose husband left her! thinks Shelly as tears wet her knuckles. That poor Diana, a princess in so many ways, was treated like dirt by a man who's no prince in my book!

"Shelly?"

The receptionist freezes, her eyes widened into circles.

"I didn't quite understand what you said. Are you all right?"

Blood rushes to Shelly's head. Did she actually say what she was thinking *out loud*?

"Fine, fine," she says, her voice gruff. She forces a cough. "I just . . . I was just talking to myself is all. Reciting my grocery list."

Her face flames red at the inane words that come out of her mouth, and with great effort, she hoists herself off the toilet, flushes it, and barrels out of the door and to the wash basins.

"I'm . . . uh, I'm making a princess cake tonight. Old family recipe of my mother's." She still sounds gruff, her voice an octave lower than her normal speaking one, and she bangs the soap dispenser with her palm while turning on the faucet full blast with her other hand.

"Sounds good," says Caroline, who seeing her own puzzled reaction in the mirror, quickly turns toward the stalls.

24

Sticking her head in her assistant's office to say hello, Susan says, "Just what I like to see. Hard at work, and it's not even nine o'clock yet."

"So there *is* such a thing as a princess cake," says Caroline, peering at her computer screen.

Standing in the door's threshold, Susan says, "I assume you're going to elaborate?"

"Morning," says Caroline, looking up at her boss. "I was just . . . it's just that I was in the bathroom, and I heard Shelly saying something about Princess Diana. Only she told me she was just reciting her grocery list out loud, because she's making a princess cake."

"What?" says Susan, confused.

"I walked into the bathroom, and I heard Shelly talking about Princess Diana and what a rat her husband was to her. And she was crying. When I asked her what was wrong, she said she was just thinking of the ingredients she needs to buy because she's going to make a *princess cake*."

Susan stands still for a moment, thinking.

"So do you think it was a reaction to Haze's columns today?"

"Must be, but I wouldn't have thought the one about Princess Diana would be the one to do her in." Caroline shrugs. "I guess I thought she was incapable of been done in."

While Susan would like to spend more time pondering Shelly's odd behavior, she's got a paper to run, and after muttering, "Very strange," she asks Caroline to meet her in her office to go over the morning's agenda.

"Oh, I . . . should I come back?"

Mercedes looks at the sharp-featured woman standing in the doorway and smiles.

"Oh, no, no. Come on in. I'm all finished up in here."

Putting the clippers on a tray, she places one of Haze's hands on top of the other and says to the patient, "All done with your manicure, Madame. Tomorrow we'll go after those toenails of yours."

Smiling, she looks up at Shelly, who has not moved from the door frame.

"Please, come on in." She gestures to the chair next to the bed. "Haze loves company."

Shelly gives a quick nod, which seems to trigger a flush that softens her natural scowl.

"I'm, uh . . . I'm Shelly," she says. "I work with Haze. I'm the receptionist."

"Nice to meet you," says Mercedes, and she means it. It's not her place to ask who Haze's visitors are, but she always appreciates when they introduce themselves. It makes everything . . . friendlier. She introduces herself, and before she leaves on the rest of her rounds, she says, "Please, make yourself comfortable."

Hard to do that in a hospital room, thinks Shelly after the nurse leaves, settling herself in the plastic molded chair. Bringing her purse to her lap, she notices that the topstitching on a pocket has frayed. Next she examines her fingernails and reminds herself to pick up a bottle of polish on her way home. Shelly doesn't have many creative outlets, but giving herself a manicure is one of them, and she is proud of her nicely shaped and groomed nails. Attractive hands are an important asset for a receptionist, she reasons, seeing as how they're on public display as she handles the phone, writes out messages, gets coffee for advertisers and visitors, and so on.

Forcing herself to look up at Haze, Shelly blurts out, "Sorry. I'm just so nervous."

Haze's face is serene, if masklike, and the phrase "when it rains, it pours," enters Shelly's head as she feels, for the second time that day, tears flood her eyes.

"Whoo!" she says, digging around for a tissue in her purse with the frayed topstitching. "Whoo, I—"

She shakes her head, her words stopped by emotion damming up her throat. The tissue is rendered useless after a moment, and standing, Shelly drops the sodden mass into the nearby wastebasket and yanks two, three, four tissues out of the box on the patient's nightstand.

"Haze," she finally manages to say in a choked whisper. "I'm so sorry."

The truth of her words spoken aloud—when was the last time she apologized for anything?—presses her back down into the chair.

Her eyes travel the length of Haze's inert body.

"So sorry this happened to you, so sorry I haven't been to see you earlier . . . so sorry I've been so cool to you all these years, I . . . I . . ." She blows her nose and shakes her head, a warning to herself that she will no longer tolerate this sniveling. "But your affair with Bill . . . it was just so wrong! He was a married man!"

The sensation Shelly feels in her chest almost makes her laugh—she's got literal heartburn!—and she breathes deeply to calm herself.

"I bet you're surprised that I knew about it, but really, Haze, not to brag, I know about *everything*. At least everything that happens in the office." She stares at a display of get-well cards hanging from a cord someone draped across the wall and then begins to count them. There are sixty-two cards, and she is ashamed that not one of them is from her.

"Oh, Haze," she says finally. "What do I know about love and its rightness or wrongness, for cripe's sake? I couldn't hold on to the love of my life, for the simple fact I wasn't the love of his."

Shelly puts her hand on the spotty mound of knuckles and fingers that are Haze's, and more than making an apology, she is shocked by this gesture. How many years—decades—has it been since she held someone's hand?

"Haze," she whispers, "Susan McGrath was so smart to rerun your columns. I didn't realize what a . . . force you were before—I don't know, maybe it is true that you don't know what you've got 'til it's gone." She squeezes Haze's hands. "Not that you're gone, I don't mean that.

"Today they ran two columns together, the ones you wrote after Princess Diana's and John F. Kennedy Jr.'s deaths, and I don't know . . . they just made me think. Of so many things. I don't know where Ray—he's my ex—is now, or if he's even alive. He's been out of my life a lot longer than he was ever in it. But for the short time he loved me, he really loved me. He made me feel like a princess, and not in that icky, put-on-a-pedestal way. Just sort of honoring me as a person, you know? He'd make me pancakes on weekends and shape them like flowers—like tulips. He'd put about three of them on a plate—he made them small—and then he'd draw on stems and leaves with the syrup! Wouldn't that make anyone feel like a princess, or at least special?"

Shelly sits for a long moment, thinking of those bouquets of pancakes served to her on the unbreakable Corelle dishes she, always practical, had insisted they buy over the china Ray liked.

She could have sat there all evening, but her stomach, used to its six o'clock can of ravioli or microwaved turkey potpie, lets out stutters that swell into growls, and squeezing Haze's hands one more time, she rises, thanking Haze for listening and wishing her a good night.

IN CURATING THE COLUMNS they chose to reprint, it seemed logical not to skip back and forth through the years but to present them in a chronological order, even as one year might be represented by only one or two columns, and the following year by five or six. Occasionally they reprinted a column that mirrored something currently happening in the community. When social media trolls excoriated the chief nurse at the Granite Creek hospital, who was entering treatment for opioid addiction, they reprinted Haze's nod to a president's wife and her bravery for publicly going into treatment.

"I never even heard of Betty Ford before," Sam had told Susan.

He, by choice, came to the office at least three times a week after school. He never told his mother he'd do it for free (he wasn't that stupid), but it seemed like both deep work and somehow play to sit at Haze's desk in the late afternoons, reading her words and those of her readers (although from the mid-1990s on, thanks to e-mail, there were far fewer handwritten or typed letters in the files).

He might laugh at a column spotlighting a circus acrobat who'd estimated he'd done forty thousand backflips, and blink back tears of sorrow and rage after reading what Haze wrote after the Columbine high school shooting. And while the early part of the 2000s featured lighthearted personal interest stories (the kid who overcame dyslexia to become a spelling bee victor; Haze's increasing dismay when standing in front of dressing-room three-way mirrors), almost as many were impassioned and angry.

She wrote about the integrity—or lack thereof—of the 2000 Florida election debacle ("Hanging chads? Sounds like something you'd see a dermatologist for!"), she wrote about the "shock and grief that has knocked me to my knees" after 9/11, and about "the screech of hawks drowning out the coo of doves" in the run-up to the Iraq War.

"RIGHT ON!" "Total drivel!" and "Get over it!" were some of the responses readers had regarding Haze's Inauguration Day column, and Susan reprinted it, followed by the recipe Haze had originally included.

January 20, 2001

Oh, my. It's really happened. Our new president was sworn in today. The Supreme Court majority who aided and abetted Mr. Bush's entry, and who in my opinion sacrificed a concise, thoughtful, and analytical decision to blind partisanship, will forever after (one can hope) have to explain the unexplainable, which is why they let their version of the story trump the real story.

I'm particularly disappointed in Sandra Day O'Connor. I was transfixed by her story—growing up on a Texas cattle ranch as a rough-and-tumble young girl, armed with a rifle, shooting jackrabbits for food. She ultimately went on to Stanford Law School and found it hard to find employment but ultimately had various positions as an attorney. While people (of the male persuasion) were trying to pull her down, down, down, she worked her way up and up and ultimately reached the pinnacle of her law profession, becoming a Supreme Court judge.

There were four other wrong votes besides hers, but as she had been a swing voter of late, seeming to regard her rulings on a case-by-case basis, I thought she'd swing right this time. *Right* meaning correct, not *right* meaning political leaning. I thought this because she's a woman, and I always hold women to higher standards. Because in truth, we seem to want to do right more: right for everyone, not just for ourselves. Even as I type that, it seems an over-the-top statement, but really, isn't it true? Aren't the mothers on the block always looking out for all the children, aren't our first teachers (mostly female) the ones negotiating for fair play, teaching us empathy and how to get along?

And then those gifts are dismissed as slight, unrealistic, and, worse, feminine.

I'm furious at Judges Scalia, Rehnquist, Kennedy, and Thomas, who proved that impartiality and fair-mindedness is not the rule of law, but I've swallowed an extra dose of disappointment over Judge O'Connor, because as a woman, I expected her to be on the right side.

I feel so helpless and unheard right now . . . you may too. Or you may not. In either case, enjoy these bars, which *have* earned their title.

SUPREME LEMON BARS

Preheat oven to 350 degrees.

    2 cups flour
    ½ cup powdered sugar
    1 cup softened butter

In a large bowl, combine above ingredients until crumbly. Press into bottom of ungreased 9″ x 13″ pan. Bake for 25–30 minutes or until golden brown.

Combine in large bowl:

4 slightly beaten eggs
2 cups sugar
¼ cup flour
1 tsp baking powder

Stir in ¼ cup lemon juice. Pour over warm crust. Bake for an additional 25–30 minutes until top is light golden brown. Cool completely.

In a small bowl, combine 1 cup powdered sugar and 3 T lemon juice (use more juice if you want thinner consistency), and drizzle over cooled bars. Optional: Sprinkle with blueberries or other fruit.

Makes about 36 bars.

TO THE EDITOR:

Haze Evans's recipe does me no good as I don't bake. But here's a little recipe I'd like to pass on to her:

1 cup personal interest stories
½ cup wit
½ cup insight
1 T local flavor

Mix well, and serve to an appreciative public. Meanwhile, toss out all political rants and smart-aleck recipe titles.

    Sincerely,
    Harlan Dodd

While it wasn't as biting as the letters Joseph Snell had written, it was the first letter from Harlan Dodd that sounded like the Harlan Dodd Sam knew, and it was printed in the paper on Monday. On Tuesday, they printed another politically charged column but with no accompanying recipe.

October 29, 2002

There are some pretty sights to see on the ride down from Granite Creek to Minneapolis, but those of us in the van were so lost in our thoughts that even when we looked out the windows, I doubt we really saw the lakes, the last colorful hurrahs of the deciduous trees, the golden bristle of harvested farm fields, scenes I've witnessed during countless autumn drives. Although we were traveling in a journalistic capacity, it was more a pilgrimage we were making, and inside the van it was as quiet and somber as a funeral cortege, which I suppose it was, even as we lacked a hearse or a riderless horse and weren't in a line of cars with their headlights on.

It has been a hard four days. When the first reports came in about a small plane crash, I felt that flick, that flick of a black shade being yanked down on my normal, sunny, smiley day. "No!" was my inner shout (or maybe it was outer, as I was home with a cold and heard the news on the radio, and when I'm alone, I may occasionally talk aloud to myself): "A private plane carrying Senator Paul Wellstone, his wife, daughter, and campaign aides went down in a small northern Minnesota town."

I've had conversations/arguments/shout-fests with plenty of people, but I knew many Republicans who loved our senator as much as Democrats did. He was the rare politician who *cared,* who went into politics for the best reason, for what should be the only reason: to help people.

"We all do better when we all do better," was one of his many true and pithy sayings, and he worked hard every day in his sly, good-humored way to bring this particular philosophy to bear. I loved him as much as you can love a politician before worrying about your mental health.

The van drove past the exit that would in normal times lead us to Junie's, the best truck-stop restaurant in the world, but none of us had an appetite, and besides, we didn't want to be late for the memorial service.

"I'm going to pay tribute to Paul Wellstone, and in my suitcase I'm bringing . . . Affection."

I don't know what compelled me to break the somber silence with a riff on the old car-trip game that kids play, and Susan McGrath, who sat next to me in the back seat, threw me a sharp and puzzled look but seconds later said, "Well, I'm going to pay tribute to Paul Wellstone, and in my suitcase I'm bringing Affection and . . . Bravery."

"I'm going to pay tribute to Paul Wellstone," said Mitch Norton, our paper's managing editor, who was driving, "and in my suitcase I'm bringing Affection, Bravery and . . . Commitment."

We played the game all the way to *Z,* and I don't remember all the words said and who said them, but I do remember "honor," "love," and "sorrow."

It was an emotional, sometime raucous service, attended by national politicians, including Senator Ted Kennedy and former president Bill Clinton. There were some in the arena who booed politicians who stood for things opposite of what Wellstone stood for, and I found that booing disrespectful—at least they showed up!—but when emotions are running high and raw, manners are sometimes forgotten. There were musical performances and eulogies given not just for Paul Wellstone, but for his wife, daughter, and aides, eulogies that ran the gamut from humorous to anguished to long-winded. Later some television and radio pundits who weren't even at the arena—weren't even in the state!—were outraged by the "incivility" of a memorial service that often seemed more like a political rally (well, Senator Wellstone was, after all, a politician), made the ridiculous claims that the audience had to be prompted to applaud, that the overflow crowd packing the arena included busloads of people paid to attend.

None of them mentioned the man being honored, wondered why over twenty thousand (unpaid) people felt a need to go to his memorial service (it's the only senator's funeral *I've* ever felt a need to attend). None of them thought to talk to all those whose faces were etched with sadness, whose hearts, if x-rayed, would have shown breaks. None of these pundits were curious enough to let go of the story *they* wanted to tell.

This was the thing about Paul Wellstone: he believed in stories, in yours and mine and ours, and his job was to do everything he could to make those stories better.

EVEN AS SAM'S FINGER PUSHES THE DOORBELL, he tells himself, there's still time to go, and after hearing the three-note ding-dong-ding and waiting a respectable two seconds, he is ready to turn around and flee.

The door opens.

"What?" shouts the old man, as if Sam were a persistent Jehovah's Witness.

"I . . . I brought you some cookies."

"Cookies!" says Mr. Dodd, and although he sounds as if he were scolding Sam, he motions him in with a furious wave of his liver-spotted hand.

Following the man through the living room and into the kitchen, Sam is compelled to remark, after the man's motioned him to sit at the small dinette table, "It's so clean in here!"

Harlan Dodd looks at the boy as if all marbles he might have possessed have been scattered.

"Why does that surprise you?"

Not knowing the answer himself, Sam shrugs.

"Do you drink coffee?" barks Mr. Dodd, "because I personally can't eat a treat without coffee."

That the man uses the word *treat* makes Sam smile, but whereas Mr. Dodd might have asked, "What's so funny?" he doesn't, because he's opening a canister at the counter, and as he makes coffee, Sam looks around the neat kitchen, marveling at the precise rectangle of the dish towels hanging from the oven handle, at the gleaming white-tiled counter whose only occupants are the coffee maker and a toaster. A television in another room is on, and Sam hears agitated, albeit muted, voices squabbling about Obamacare.

As the coffee brews, the old man sets china cups, saucers, and dessert plates on the table.

"Uh, can I help you?" Sam asks.

"Do I look like I need help?"

Sam cringes at the man's sharp tone.

"It's . . . it's just that these are my wife's things," says Mr. Dodd, his voice still gruff but slightly softened by apology. "I don't want anything to break."

Mr. Dodd had been long widowed when the Carroll-McGrath family moved in next door, and it's hard for Sam to imagine he was ever married.

"You must miss her," he says after a long, awkward pause.

"Of course I miss her!"

"What was her name?" The words are out of Sam's mouth before he can censor himself, something he immediately thinks he should have done, judging from Mr. Dodd's apoplectic face.

"Katie!" he says with the same sneer he might say, "Idiot!"

He busies himself at the refrigerator and a cupboard and returns with a matching china creamer and sugar bowl. Cloth napkins and heavy silverware are taken out of a drawer and placed on the table, and finally, when the coffee's brewed, Mr. Dodd serves it and sitting across from Sam, helps himself to a cookie.

"Katie—of course her real name was Kathryn," he says. "She would have said, 'Harlan, you've got company. Put those treats on a proper plate!'"

Looking at the table set with the kind of dishes his mother keeps (but rarely uses) in a hutch in their dining room, Sam says, "I'm surprised you let me sit here, let alone bring out all this nice stuff."

"And why's that?"

Sam wishes he had a switch to turn off the blush that warms his face. It's one thing to feel stupid but another to *show* that you feel stupid.

"Well, you don't exactly like me much."

Mr. Dodd chews for a moment and takes a sip of coffee.

"I don't know you enough to like or dislike you. Although I'm fairly sure you like to visit me on Halloween—even though you and your friends seem to prefer the trick part over the treat."

Another wash of color rises on Sam's neck and face as he thinks, *busted*, and he mumbles, "Sorry."

"Silly me—I thought putting bags of dog excrement on people's doorstep and setting them on fire was a thing of the past! I was so glad to see you boys brought back the tradition."

Sam looks up, surprised at Mr. Dodd's joking tone.

"And the—what was it, lard, Crisco—on my door handle the year before? Priceless. Whatever will you do for this Halloween?"

Sam smiles and says helpfully, "Well, we could always TP your backyard."

It appears joke time is over when Mr. Dodd says with gruffness back in his voice, "Don't you dare," but seconds later he laughs, and Sam, relieved, joins him.

Minutes pass as they enjoy their "treats," which Sam's coffee also turns into, thanks to all the cream and sugar he pours into it.

"You say you made these?" says Mr. Dodd, examining a cookie, and when Sam nods, he says, "What shape are they supposed to be exactly?"

Sam shrugs. "Crescents, but it was hard rolling them out."

Taking a bite, the old man chews, swallows, and says, "They taste better than they look."

"Thanks. They're one of Haze's recipes."

"Katie always enjoyed those, and her columns."

"So did you. At least you used to."

Mr. Dodd looks at him oddly, and Sam explains.

"I've been working for my mom . . . at the *Gazette*, reading Haze's columns and all the letters from readers. She saved them all."

Mr. Dodd nods, his gazed fixed on the cream pitcher in front of him.

"Katie was the one who introduced me to Ms. Evans's columns," he says, emphasizing the "Ms." "When she and I were first married, we'd sit here at this same table, and she'd read them aloud to me, and then I'd read aloud the funnies to her. *Mark Trail* and *Hi and Lois* were her particular favorites."

Sam stares at Mr. Dodd; he can't picture the old man reading the funnies to anyone.

After a moment he says, "I noticed that you seemed to like her columns, at least by the letters you wrote in, but then you changed, and you started writing letters like the one we reprinted the other day."

Not content with a mere bite, Mr. Dodd pops a whole cookie in his mouth and chews for a long while, and after a generous slug of coffee he says, "Haze Evans is a fine storyteller—when she's content telling just a story. But her political rants and raves got to be a bit . . . much."

Sam listens for a moment to the televised voices, one of which is hollering about "Benghazi!"

"Like those?"

Boy and man stare at each other for a long time.

"So tell me more about your wife," says Sam finally. It's a peace offering the man accepts, and twenty minutes pass as Dodd tells Sam of the love of his life, who had the mind of a judge ("she easily could have been one, but she ran her own business instead—Interiors by K. D.) and the looks of Connie Stevens ("not that you'd know who that was, but believe me, my Katie was favored as physically as she was intellectually), a woman who died far too young of "that scourge, cancer."

When Mr. Dodd offers him a third cup of coffee (he had never before finished even one in his life!), Sam declines, sensing that as a good guest, he should be on his way.

"I've got to study for a history exam."

"It's important to know your history," says Mr. Dodd and standing up, adds, "Thank you for the cookies. Thank you for the visit."

"You're welcome," says Sam. "I wouldn't mind doing it again."

"Coffeepot's usually on," growls Harlan Dodd.

25

"You don't have to keep calling me Mr. Wilkerson," says the silver-haired man sitting across from Mercedes. "You *could* call me James."

"Only if that's your name," says Mercedes. Her reaction to nervousness is to joke, and a little tension evaporates when he chuckles.

"Could I interest you two in any dessert?" asks the server, a young woman whose easy graciousness will take her far in the service (or any) industry.

"What do you recommend?" asks James.

"My favorites are the chocolate mousse—it's really rich but really worth it—and you can't go wrong with the warm raspberry cobbler served with our homemade ice cream."

Mercedes and James exchange twin raised-eyebrow looks.

"Let's try both," says James.

It's several degrees from being a balmy autumn evening, and James asks Mercedes if she'd like to walk a bit.

"A walk would be nice," she says as he helps her put on her coat. "Especially after all that dessert."

Zig's Supper Club is on a hill, situated in a neighborhood Mercedes isn't familiar with, and she enjoys the stroll that takes them alongside a dark expanse that is the golf course, its fairways and putting greens not illuminated by the streetlights.

"Are you a golfer?" asks James, and Mercedes shakes her head.

"No. The only club I've ever held is a sandwich."

James laughs. "You're funny."

A sudden gust of wind adds chill to the October air, and Mercedes's hands find her pockets.

"I could take you," says James. "Golfing that is. I'm a member at the club, and it's . . . it's an enjoyable sport."

Mercedes's immediate response is "no, thank you," but she surprises herself by not voicing it. They continue walking as she ponders the invitation, wondering what Manny would think of her out on a golf course, with people who had money and leisure to spend. She doesn't have to wonder long, as Manny's voice in her head is as loud and clear as if he were beside her, and it says, *Está bien.* It's okay.

Tears well in Mercedes eyes, and although she feels a little sad, she feels a lot of other things too.

"Well, I suppose I could try it," she says, looking up at the man who's at least a foot taller than she. "Who knows—I might be good at it. I've got a lot of upper-body strength."

She takes her hands out of her pockets and stops to flex her arms. Chuckling, James reaches out and pats her bicep.

"I'm impressed," he says, feeling the hard muscle under her coat sleeve. "It's bigger than mine."

He flexes an arm, and Mercedes pats his bicep, and when he moves his arm, inviting her to keep her hand in the crook of his elbow, she does.

October 13, 2016

Wassup, Dudes?

For extra credit in history, I watched the presidential debate a couple days ago with my mom and dad. My dad kept laughing at everything that guy from *The Apprentice* said, and my mom just sat there with her arms crossed, shaking her head and sort of muttering, "Oh my God!"

My mom is a background kind of person, even though she does a lot. Sometimes it seems like the people in the background get more stuff done than the people who are jumping up and down for attention. My mom's like SuperMom, always checking out these recipe websites and making things like

Mexican frittatas and Moroccan stews, so it's always kinda cool to eat dinner, plus she drives me and my little brother to our soccer practices in the fall and our hockey practices in the winter, and everyone loves when she's in charge of snacks because she'll bring homemade stuff like chocolate chip or gingersnap cookies and not fruit or crappy granola bars. She checks our homework, well, more my little brother's because I don't really need it (LOL), and takes us shopping when we need stuff and made us go to that language camp every year that we didn't really want to go to, but it is pretty cool knowing how to speak Swedish. (Think of all those supermodels I'll be able to talk to!) I mean, sometimes I think, Mom, chill! Don't make waiting on people your life's goal, although she does work part-time at Dr. DeMaris's office, taking calls and filing and stuff. But she was like a different mom watching that debate. My dad said he wouldn't mind a beer if she was going to the kitchen, and she said she wasn't, which was kind of surprising 'cause she'll always jump up if any of us have a request. She'll even jump up when we don't even say anything, like, "Anyone want a soda or some popcorn?" but that night, she just sat there laser-eyed on the TV. It was like the rest of us were invisible.

I heard her arguing with my dad, which she never does, and it made me feel kind of weird but kind of proud too. I mean I never really know what my mom thinks because mostly what she thinks of is me and my brother and my dad, but I was brushing my teeth and heard my mom say, "Mike" (that's my dad's name), "What about that tape of him saying those disgusting things about grabbing women? I'm scared to death! Please tell me that you can't be supporting him! He doesn't know anything!"

"He knows how to be a billionaire!" my dad said, and he laughed again, and then I heard a door slam.

Dylan sits down and jams his fists into his face, pressing up his cheeks so that his eyes are nearly closed. He wonders why, *why* he ever wrote such a stupid-ass thing let alone read it aloud and is waiting for the laughter to fill the classroom, but after what seems like a year—or at least an hour—he lifts his head slightly. There's no laughter.

"Lois," says Sam, "that's Haze's friend, you know the one she's written about? She says if Haze doesn't wake up in time to vote for Hillary, it'll kill her."

Now, there is laughter, from both Liz and her students.

Sam laughs too and says, "Lois can say some pretty rad stuff."

"Dylan, good job," says Liz. "Would that be your column heading, 'Wassup, Dudes?'"

Nodding, the boy thinks again how totally lame he is.

"Wish I would have thought of that," says Caleb, "but I couldn't think of anything better than, 'How Ya Doin?'"

"I know, thinking of a good heading is almost as hard as writing the whole column," says Elise.

"Well, remember how Haze struggled with that and finally just decided to have her name at the top of her column?" The teacher surveys the class. "Abdi?"

The tall, thin boy stands. Liz doesn't require that her students stand when they read, but it seems most of them want to when reading their columns.

"Pull Up a Chair and Set Your Carcass Down."

When the class laughs, he says, "Nah, that's not my real heading. This is."

He begins to read.

Citizens of the World,
I was in Minneapolis this weekend to visit my cousins. They live in this big, tall apartment building that is full of Somalis. People say it's Little Mogadishu. It's weird when everywhere you look there's another person who looks sort of like you, unlike here in Granite Creek. Still, I'm glad my parents came here, even though some kids on my traveling soccer team called me "Terr," short for "Terrorist," until I became like the top goal scorer.

I don't like cities, they're too crowded, and they're too many buses and cars that stink, and the park near my cousins' place has a basketball court with no nets on the hoops and broken bottles and garbage and plastic bags and litter smashed against the fence. There're a lot of pretty girls though. My parents want me to go to college in Minneapolis, or maybe even a bigger city. But why do we always have to go to something bigger? My parents tell me all the time, they want me to make the most of my opportunities. Yes, I know how much they sacrificed for me and my brother and sisters. Yes, I know their lives have been hard, they haven't even seen their own parents since we came here, but still, why do parents always want what *they* want for their kids? Instead of what the kids want? Like I love to draw and paint, and my parents have a lot of my pictures framed and hanging in the house, but they laugh when I tell them I'd like a career in art. Then they get mad. They want me to be a doctor or a lawyer or an engineer like my dad.

You probably have no idea what it's about. Neither do I. Sayonara.

"Kids really called you 'Terr'?" says Sondra. "What a bunch of jerks!"

"That's nothing compared to the names my dad's been called," says Abdi. "And by grown-ups. I was going to write more about that but then . . ." he shrugs elaborately.

"It was a hard assignment," says Liz to the class. "When you're writing a column, you have to figure out all sorts of things—not just your topic but your angle on the topic. And what's your particular voice, your style? All and all, I'm impressed enough by all of your efforts to ask you to write another one."

There are a few scattered groans, but Liz sees some expectant, excited faces looking back at her.

"But this time," she says, taking out of her desk drawer the small cloth bag that until this morning held Rummikub tiles but is now filled with slips of paper, "you won't have to think of a topic. You will, however, have to choose one."

Handing the bag to a student, she says, "There are twenty ideas in there. Pick one, and pass the bag down your row."

Unfolding his slip of paper, Kyle says, "I got 'Who's Your Hero?' Oh good, I get to write about myself!"

Liz joins the class in laughing, although she's not sure Kyle is kidding.

As the bag is passed among the students, there are excited and not-so-excited announcements. Sam's is in the latter category.

HE'S GETTING HIS JACKET out of his locker when he feels a tap on his shoulder.

"Piss off, hoser," Sam says, giving Jacob one of their usual insults/greetings, but when he turns, it isn't to face Jacob.

"Hey!" He says, a flush announcing his embarrassment. "I thought you were someone else."

"Nope," says Elise. "Just me."

Sam sets his backpack down and shrugs into his jacket, while his mind races to say something witty.

"I was just wondering if you always take the bus home," says Elise, and the wittiest thing his mind can come up with is "No. Sometimes I walk."

"Good! That's what I was hoping." Now it's Elise's turn to blush. "I was just wondering if maybe you'd like to walk with me. I mean 'cause it's so nice out."

Sam nods eagerly, although to his mind the fall day's gloriousness has nothing to do with the weather.

By the time they've walked two blocks on sidewalks confettied with orange- and rust-colored leaves, the awkwardness that was at full boil in Sam has settled down to a weak simmer.

It figures that when they talk about Radical Hag Wednesday, Sam feels the most at ease, his words delivered for no reason other than to express his thoughts.

Elise has said she wishes she could read all the columns that Sam has.

"I mean, you've read so many. *Lucky.*"

Sam nods, he does feel lucky.

"I really liked the ones about the Obamas in last week's packet," says Elise. "Talk about a power couple—when Hillary gets elected she should nominate Michelle to the Supreme Court!"

Elise has a pink POTUS pin on her backpack strap, and Sam thinks how much Haze would like her.

"And the one about Barack Obama's parents not living to see how far their son went in the world?" she continues. "I felt so bad for his mom—I mean, she's the one who raised him and everything—but at least she got to see him grow up."

"Yeah, and I liked how Haze made us feel bad for the dad, because of the choices he made."

"Don't remind me."

"Huh?"

"Life Choices," Elise says. "That's the topic I picked today." She shakes her head. "Sort of a big one, don't you think? Like something you write a book about, not a column."

"Guess you have to figure out your angle," says Sam, remembering Mrs. Garnet's advice. "Is it going to be about a choice you made, or someone else—"

"You're so smart."

This literally stops Sam in his tracks.

Elise laughs.

"I mean it. The stuff you say in class is just so, I don't know . . . thoughtful."

"I guess when you're a nerd, you have a lot of time to think."

"Who says you're a nerd?"

"Anyone who's not one."

They both laugh.

"I'm not a nerd," says Elise, "at least I don't think I am. And I don't think you are either, and even if you are, what's the matter with being a nerd?"

"If that was a compliment," says Sam, "I accept it."

At a corner house whose boulevard is edged with hearty marigolds, Elise says, "Well, this is where I turn. Thanks for walking me home."

"Well, technically," says Sam, "I haven't walked you home since we're not at your house yet."

"But it's another three blocks," says Elise.

Sam sighs as if put out.

"Oh, I'll manage," he says, and he hunches as if his backpack weighs a ton and drags his feet like a nomad on a cross-continents trek.

What he really wants to do is skip, but even he has standards.

When they get to her house, Elise says, "I'd ask you to come in, but I have to watch my little brothers, and believe me, you don't want to do that."

Sam's about to say he doesn't mind, that he'd like to be around when Elise watched *anything*, but she's taking her phone out of her pocket and says, "Here, I'll give you my number, and you can, you know, call me. Or text."

"I already do," says Sam. He has no control; it's as if the words have been projectile-vomited out of his mouth.

Elise cocks her head, and before she can say, "What is the *matter* with you, weirdo?" words gush out of his mouth.

"I . . . sometimes I text you."

Elise frowns, puzzled. "I've never gotten them."

"Because I don't send them to you. I mean, I don't even have your number. I just type them and then send them to myself."

The heat rising up his neck and into his head is almost enough to make him pass out, and yet he can't seem to stop doing what it is that makes him feel so faint: talking.

"Sometimes I text other people too. Like famous people I'd like to talk to, even if they're dead. Haven't gotten any answers back though!"

Sam's laugh is high and tinny as he shouts to himself, Shut up! What's the matter with you? Your life is over, dude!

But Elise is not running to her front door, hollering, "Help!" Nor is she backing away slowly, hands out in appeasement, telling him in a soft, soothing voice that everything's going to be all right. She is, in fact, looking at him with a full-on smile.

"Tell me some of the famous people," she says, and blushing

furiously, Sam answers, "Well, Lorde sometimes, and sometimes writers, like maybe J. K. Rowling . . . Philip Pullman? And a couple times, Steve Jobs."

"I'm flattered to be in such good company," says Elise, still smiling as she talks. "What's your number?"

Sam answers, and her fingers fly across her phone's keypad, and his phone chirps.

He looks down at it and sees in the message bubble: "SO TEXT ME. OR CALL."

26

"Wow," says Phil.

"That's kind of what I thought," says Susan.

They sit there silently for a long while, at the kitchen table that holds their family's history of breakfasts, lunches, and dinners (they rarely ate in their dining room, its table most often used for either company, class projects, or folding laundry). Now bare of crumbs, of spilled juice, of peanut butter jars, of silverware and plates, the table holds only their wine glasses and a homework assignment.

"I didn't know he could do this," says Phil, and his hand smooths a piece of paper marked with a big red A.

"Liz had told me how . . . well, what a force he is in her class—a force!—but this came as a surprise to me too."

"Thanks for letting me see it."

"I couldn't *not* let you see it," says Susan, and she takes a big gulp of wine. "I mean, he's our son."

Phil raises his eyebrows and offers a cockeyed smile; it's Phil's signature look when he doesn't know what to do with his feelings.

When Sam had left to spend the Friday night at Jacob's, Susan had called Phil and asked him to come over so she could "show him something."

Not knowing what to expect, Phil had brought a bottle of Susan's favorite merlot, and they both laughed when he presented it to her.

"It's not a date—" she began just as he said, "I know it's not a date."

They had stood awkwardly in the entryway, which Phil had

always teased Susan for calling a foyer, until Susan had laughed again and told him to follow her into the kitchen.

Sam I Am.

"True Love." Sigh. (And not a good sigh, more like an "I can't believe it" sigh.) If I had been given the topic "True Love" to write about a year ago, I still probably would have had the same reaction (*@#&!$#@!!—why couldn't I have gotten an easy one like Jacob did—"Best Vacation Ever"). Still, it wouldn't have taken me very long to figure out that I'd write about my parents. It's not like I thought they were Romeo and Juliet or anything (as if!), but this topic made me look at them not just as my mom and dad but as two people who started off as two people in love. Or it did at first. Like I said, if I'd written this a year ago, I would have talked about how to me true love is like being on the same team as your partner and always wanting to stay on that team, cheering each other on in both good times and bad. How it's like being amazed at plays they make ("I made your favorite banana cream pie in celebration of you selling that RV to the Olsens!" or "Congratulations on the newspaper award—let's go out to Zig's!") or helping each other off the field after a bad game (like when my dad's friend Jim got sick, and my dad would come home from the hospital all jacked-up and worried, and the only way he could get to sleep was if my mom read to him aloud, which she'd always do no matter how late it was. Sometimes I'd sneak down the hallway and sit outside their bedroom door to listen, first to her voice, and then to him snoring!).

But they're not together anymore, so what I thought was true love doesn't seem so true anymore.

So I'm looking at another angle. Not thinking of true love as only a thing between people but maybe between you and something else—like a dog (I think Cesar's the best thing on four legs, and he thinks I'm the best thing on two), or a sport, or a hobby. This is kind of a surprise to me, but I'm really getting into writing in a way that seems to matter way more than a hobby. Not like I'm good or anything at it, but I really like—no, I love doing it. Love trying to put down what I'm thinking and feeling. (Not everything, don't want to scare anyone, LOL!) Working at the paper and reading all those columns of Haze's have given me this love, which feels true right now, but hey, who knows, maybe next year I'll really get into toe wrestling or playdough sculpture. And also, what I've learned is that true love might not always be permanent but that doesn't disqualify it for being true at the time. Which kind of invalidates my argument about writing about my mom and dad, because I think for a long while their love was true.

P.S. I know Sam I Am is kind of a stupid column name, but I couldn't help myself.

Phil sits for a long time, staring at the paper in his hand as if it's a hypnotist's pendant and he can't look away.

"And he got an A, huh?" he says finally, seeing the red grade circled at the top.

Susan crumples a bit inside, thinking, What an asinine response! but then Phil adds, "It deserves it."

Crooking his forefinger, he wipes at the corner of his eye, and his sigh is long.

"God, I miss Jim. I forgot how you used to read to me when he was dying. That meant a lot to me."

"We got through all of Lonesome Dove, remember?"

Phil nods. His shoulders are hunched, as if all of his feelings are centered in his chest and their weight pulls everything in.

"Would you . . . would you like some more?" asks Susan, holding up the bottle.

Phil holds his hand above his glass.

"Still don't have much of a wine palate, I guess." He smiles, but it doesn't have a lot of mirth in it. He looks, Susan's startled to see, like he might cry.

"Phil?" she says at the same time he says, "I just wish—"

They stare at one another for a long moment.

"What do you just wish?" Susan asks softly.

"That . . . that things were different." He sighs and discovers a hangnail that needs his attention. Picking at it, he says, "I'm sorry for everything, Susan."

Susan's head bobbles in a nod. "Me too."

THE LITTLE GIRL LAUGHS when Shelly raises her voice and says, "Not by the hair of my chin chin chin," and laughs when Shelly lowers her voice and says, "Then I'll huff and I'll puff and I'll blow your house in!"

"Read it again!" says the girl.

"But I've got all these other books," says Shelly, indicating the pile on the window seat.

"I like *The Three Little Pigs*! They're funny."

So Shelly reads the worn Golden Book again and makes her voice go even higher for the pigs and lower for the wolf, and when the girl laughs, it feels to Shelly like a standing ovation.

"Sounds like we're having a lot of fun in here," says a nurse, entering the room. "Here, Ariel, I brought you some juice."

"She does really good voices!" says Ariel, and Shelly, who doesn't beam, comes close.

VISITING HAZE one day after work, she'd nearly collided with a candy striper pushing a cart. It was a feat for Shelly to not upbraid the young girl to "watch where you're going!" but she held her tongue and accepted the girl's sincere apology, albeit delivered with a nervous giggle.

"Say," said Shelly, a lightbulb of an idea blinking on in her head, "do they have an age limit for candy stripers?"

The sweet-faced girl, whose cheeks were so rosy they looked freshly pinched, looked startled before saying, "Umm . . . I don't know. I mean the candy stripers I know are all like my age . . . but there's a volunteer coordinator you could ask."

And so Shelly had found her way to the blue-haired woman's office, had her interview, and began coming on Monday and Thursday evenings to read to children. Sometimes it was hard—there was a bald little boy hooked up to wires and IVs who was so weak he couldn't open his eyes but who smiled as Shelly read his favorite *Clifford the Big Red Dog* stories and who always whispered, "Thank you," when she was finished—but she inherently knew to swallow down any lumps in her throat or warbles in her voice, knew that the last thing these children needed was that sort of nonsense.

Shelly found herself practicing different voices she might use—how the kids loved different voices!—mostly at home and once in the employee bathroom at the *Gazette*, where a startled Ellie Barnes, responding to the gravelly "Fee, fi, foe, fum" emanating from a stall had asked, "Who's there?"

"GOOD BOY," Sam says when he lets the puppy in from the backyard.

His wagging tail a blur of motion, Cesar wiggles in reaction to the praise and adds several hops as Sam sets his food on the floor, practically burying his muzzle in the bowl full of tiny brown pellets.

"Slow down," says Sam with a laugh.

Tasked with making the salad, he washes his hands and resumes his place at the counter.

"Isn't he the best dog ever?" he asks his mother.

Susan smiles, thinking how he sounds about eight years old.

"He sure has been house-trained fast, thanks to you."

She agreed to let him keep Cesar, but only if Sam took full responsibility for him. It was the kind of blustery directive most parents give to children when it comes to a new pet, but much to her surprise, one that her son obeyed, diligently. For the first couple days, the puppy had a few indoor accidents, but not once had Susan cleaned up a mess or wiped up a puddle, and although she did buy the puppy chow, Sam was in charge of dispensing it. It was nice coming home to a being who greeted you with delight, nice to have a furry little creature snuggle between you and your son when you watched TV on the couch. With Cesar the whole house felt warmer, softer.

"Routine," said Sam sagely. "That's what Christina told me. Dogs respond to routine." As he takes the lettuce out of the salad spinner, he's about to expound more on what he'd learned from the veterinarian, but in the non sequitur way a teenaged conversationalist takes, he asks instead, "Hey, Mom, what's up with Shelly?"

"What do you mean?" asks Susan, who's just sampled the spaghetti sauce, trying to figure out if it needs more oregano or less.

"She's like so much nicer!" he says, ripping up lettuce leaves. "I mean, I doubt she could ever be *really* nice, but for her, she's a lot nicer!"

"Mitch was wondering if she's got a boyfriend," says Susan. The sauce definitely needs more oregano, as well as a lot more garlic and a little more pepper. "I told him she's got some new friends and some are boys, but little boys." She laughs. "He didn't know about her hospital work."

"She even asked me if I could recommend some books for a nine-year-old patient she's reading to. I was gonna say Harry Potter, but then I thought, one of those books takes a long time, and you'd hope no kid would be in the hospital long enough to hear the whole thing. So I told her about the Lemony Snicket books and those *Wimpy Kid* ones."

Spooning more oregano into the pot, Susan chuckles. "Somehow I never pictured Shelly reading a Lemony Snicket book."

"I know, right?" Sam laughs too. "What a world."

The cell phone on the counter chimes. Susan used to uphold a "no phones at dinnertime" rule, but now that Jack's abroad, her phone is always on and available, and she asks Sam to see who's calling.

Handing her the phone, Sam says, "It's Mrs. Garnet."

"One second, Liz," says Susan into the phone. She samples the sauce and places the spoon on its ceramic spoon rest. "Man, I make good spaghetti. What's up?"

"Well, I've just got to tell you what when on in class today," says Liz with an urgency that makes Susan turn to look at Sam. Only he's not there.

May 4, 2010
Ahhh, glorious spring. I do like to walk, and I'm convinced a walking habit has caused my body to believe it is far

younger than the birth date stamped on my driver's license says it is. Today's walk home was a real treat, surrounded as I was in the majesty of everything blooming and budding. Hyland Park is on my route, and occasionally I'll take a little break, sitting on a bench to observe and listen to all that can go on in its playground.

A curly-haired boy climbed to the top of the jungle gym, a feat that inspired him to shout, "Ta da!" A curly-haired girl pumped her legs on the swing, singing a song whose primary lyric seemed to be "nobody's perfect!"

Their mother (ditto on the curls) was on the bench across the playground from me, holding something in her hands that held her complete attention.

Throughout the years, I've seen plenty of mothers with their children at park playgrounds. I've seen mothers sit next to one another, gossiping as they watch their kids; I've seen mothers reading paperbacks or newspapers (always engrossed in my column, ha ha); and I've seen mothers, their faces tilted upward and smiling into a sunny sky, opening their eyes every now and then to check on junior. As involved in gossiping, reading, or sunbathing as they were, however, it always seemed they were aware and engaged, ready to leap up if Susie was climbing too high on the monkey bars, or to break up a sand-throwing fight between Billy and Bobby. I'm not saying mothers are more delinquent now, but it does seem their "devices" (I can't help but think of that old truism that warns of no good when someone is left to their own devices . . .) enthrall them to almost the point of hypnotism. What words and pictures are they reading/viewing that are so interesting?

I don't have a "smart" phone myself, although the one I have I wouldn't call dumb, seeing that it's portable and I can take/make calls on it.

Bells and whistles are fine, but sometimes their clanging and shrieking gets in the way of the real hearing, the real seeing, the real being.

After Elise read aloud Haze's column, Liz had been prepared for a lively discussion—when weren't the discussions lively?—but she wasn't prepared for Brianna blurting out, "Left to their own devices is right! My mom found out my dad and his secretary have been sexting for the past year!"

A bell jar of silence clamped down on the classroom.

Hoo boy, thought Liz, and while she was figuring out what to say, Linnea, a girl who only speaks in class if called on, said, "My mom took my brother's phone *and* computer away because he's watching so much porn."

As if an arctic wind had swept in, her students sat frozen, staring at Liz with wide eyes.

"Well," she said ineffectually, "maybe we—"

"I'll bet there are guys in this room who should have their phones and computers taken away for the same reason," said Charlotte.

The blushes on several boys' faces deepened.

"Yeah," said Elise, "Haze writes about mothers paying too much attention to their phones, but I bet they're not watching porn or playing stupid games like *Mortal Kombat* on them!"

"Yeah," said Sondra, "you don't see my mom taking away my phone or computer because I'm watching porn or blowing people's heads off!"

"Help," said Kyle, sliding down in his chair. "I'm surrounded by a roomful of radical hags!"

The silence that followed was as potent as a collective gasp but was quickly broken by shouts of outrage, over which Kyle cried, "Kidding! I'm just kidding!"

SUSAN STANDS AT SAM'S DOOR for at least a minute, and just before she knocks on it, he says, "I hear you out there, Mom. And yes, you can come in."

"The sauce is ready," Susan says, standing in the threshold. "Shall I put the noodles on?"

"I guess," says Sam, who's sitting at his desk. He closes his computer. "And I wasn't looking at porn, by the way."

Taken aback, Susan's mouth drops open.

"I . . . I didn't, I . . ."

Her son pushes himself away from the desk.

"It's just so hard, you know?" He yells as he stomps across the room. "When everything's so easy!"

When he flings himself on the bed, Susan thinks, is he crying? and when she realizes he is, she rushes to him, so jittery with worried surprise that she almost falls off the edge of the bed as soon as she sits on it. When she rights herself, she rubs her son's heaving back, offering him the age-old sounds of comfort, "Shh-shh-shh." It's almost like a mantra, and she doesn't know how much time passes until Sam heaves himself up into a sitting position, drags the heel of his hand across his eyes, and says in a ragged voice, "I'm such a baby!"

"So," begins Susan, her voice tentative, "I take it that was in reaction to—"

"The girls were getting so mad—it was like they thought all of us guys were big pervs!"

He shakes his head and exhales a quick puff of air.

"I mean, it's not like I haven't heard you and Dad when you've lectured me and Jack about the dangers of online porn—I haven't just heard you but agree with you! And how freaky is that?" His eyebrows crinkle, and he flares his nostrils, what looks to be a prelude to more tears, but he blinks hard, and none fall. "I can't say I haven't watched any, but the few times I have, it's just so—I mean, it's not the way I want it to be!"

He's folded his legs up and draws his arms around them, his chin resting on his knees.

"I can't believe I'm telling you this."

"You can tell me anything," says Susan and means it, although a part of her silently begs, "but you sure don't have to."

"Jacob's dad's got a bunch of old *Playboys* in their garage, and we've looked at those, but that's different, you know? I mean, you can use your imagination when you just look at pictures, but watching people fu— . . . uh, watching sex, it's just . . . super weird. What do you call those weirdos who get off on watching?"

"Voyeurs?"

A one-syllable laugh escapes from Sam.

"I could only think of *voyager*. But yeah, I don't want to a voyeur, like, to someone else's story. And how you've said that porn demeans women? There might be stuff that doesn't, but what I've seen—and really, Mom, I haven't seen that much—does. I mean, even though they're like the stars of the show, they really aren't, you know? And they're all so fake looking, like with these huge boobs." Shaking his head, Sam reddens and reiterates that he can't believe he's telling Susan this.

There's a long-enough silence that Susan thinks he's done talking, but then, almost wailing, he says, "Everything's on a screen! Haze wrote about moms being distracted by their phones, and it's true—something about a screen draws you in and kind of . . . puts you in a trance! You can shoot up zombies in a video game or blow up a whole village, and it's . . . and it is, like, exciting for a while, but for me, the more I play, the more I feel . . . well, sort of like there's less of me. Sort of like I'm not all there. And I don't want to feel like I'm not all there. I want to be here." He bangs his hand on the bed, emphasizing his words, and a moment later tips his head back and says to the ceiling, "Oh, God, I am such a weirdo."

"You're not a weirdo. You're a wonderful, sensitive young man."

Sam makes a face. "Like I said, a weirdo."

Susan smiles and gives his shoulder a gentle push.

"Come, on. Let's go eat some spaghetti."

27

Lois once posited the theory that age didn't bother her because she'd never been good-looking.

"I beg to differ," Haze had said. "You're a real glamour puss."

"I'm talking about *having* beauty, not just a beauty *routine*," said Lois, whose budget allowed for weekly hair appointments as well as decades-long subscriptions to both *Vogue* and *Harper's Bazaar*, and who, unlike Haze, didn't think "serviceable" trumped "fashionable" when it came to one's wardrobe. "I'll always take care of my appearance, even as I've never had that great appearance to begin with."

"Lois, you're a lovely—"

"No need to say anything," said Lois, raising a precisely manicured hand. "I'm not fishing here. I'm only saying because I was never thought of as pretty, I don't have to worry about losing my looks. Style's something completely different—I can be stylish into my hundreds, and therefore, age doesn't bother me."

"Don't achy joints and liver spots bother you?"

Lois frowned; she thought she'd been winning the argument.

"Well, of course," she said finally. "But I accept those things . . . that the body gets a little cranky."

Haze chuckled. "A little cranky!"

"You know what I mean. Just look at Janet Oakes—remember how pretty she used to be? And now it's so hard for her, trying to hang on to what she had but what's gone, always on this diet or that diet, slapping on so much makeup a clown would warn her to go easy."

Lois pretended to be offended by Haze's laughter but after a moment joined in.

"And then there's you!" she said finally, after taking a sip of her drink. "You were good-looking enough, but that wasn't your main calling card. *You* were your main calling card, and you're still you, so you don't seem to age at all."

Haze reached over the tabletop—she and Lois had been enjoying Sunday brunch at Zig's—to squeeze her friend's hand.

"The reason I don't seem to age at all is because you're so vain about not wearing your bifocals, *and* you're on your second Bloody Mary."

At the sound of a knock on her car window, Lois startles.

"Oh!" she says, transporting herself out of memory and into the present. She rolls down the window. "Oh, Caroline. Hi!"

"You okay?"

"Yes, I was just—" Lois unfastens her seatbelt and grabs her purse on the passenger seat—"I was just thinking about Haze."

"You were smiling," says Caroline.

Arm in arm, the two walk into the hospital.

Throughout her career, Mercedes had seen patients whose recovery or deterioration had baffled the medical staff. She believed in miracles, because she had seen them, but she also believed in the inevitably of death, and she knew that for Haze, the window through which a miracle might blow in had not just closed but had been double latched, and the shades had been drawn.

Now a small group is gathered in Haze's room, with the intention not to visit but to say goodbye.

"so weird," Sam texts to Elise, and after adding a crying face emoji, he presses send.

His word and picture message are terse, but they also convey his many feelings; it's weird to be watching Haze die, weird that she's an old lady but feels like a friend, weird that it's through her written words that he's gotten to know her, weird that he's not embarrassed to send Elise an emoji as well as tell/text her just about anything—and send it to her!—no matter how lame it makes him look.

"Haze," says Lois, striding into the room like a mayor greeting constituents. "Haze, I don't care if you're dying, you've simply got to open your eyes. I just got the cutest haircut, and I need you to scold me for paying too much for it!"

She sits on her friend's bed, an act that deflates all her energy and swagger.

"Aw, Haze," she says, taking her friend's hand and blinking back tears.

When Mercedes comes into the room, Caroline goes to hug her.

"Tina's coming by after work," she says. "She's doing an emergency surgery on someone's pet ferret."

"*Dios mío*," says Mercedes, and their exchange causes everyone in the room to laugh.

"Did you hear that, Haze?" says Lois. "A pet ferret! Who has a pet ferret?"

Haze's only response is a breath that's loud and weak at the same time.

"That's how you know, isn't it," Lois says to Mercedes. "By the way she's breathing?"

Mercedes nods. "One of the ways."

Now her words are like a switch flicking off light, and a gloom shadows the room as everyone strains to hear Haze's irregular breaths.

Mercedes excuses herself to tend to another patient, and Susan takes something out of her purse. "Mitch and I worked on this today," she says, unfolding a piece of paper. "It's the obituary we're thinking of running."

After she reads it aloud, there is a long silence.

"Well?" Susan says finally.

"It's okay," Sam says. "But it . . . well, it doesn't really capture her."

Susan stares at the paper. She's a little stung by the criticism (when doesn't criticism sting a little?), but it's a tiny scratch softened by the balm of her pride for Sam's astute words.

"You're right. Any suggestions?"

"Well, I think your lead sentence needs to be like . . . flashier," says Sam, and the balm of pride heats up in Susan, as if Vicks VapoRub has been smeared on her chest. "I mean, 'beloved columnist' is good, but I think Haze deserves more."

"Right on the money, Sam," says Lois, and after a moment adds, "how about 'beloved columnist and all-around good egg?'"

Typing the keyboard of her iPad, Caroline says, "'Beloved columnist, all-around good egg,' and—"

Sam joins her as she says, "radical hag!"

Laughter and occasional exclamations—"yes!" and "perfect!" and "beautiful!"—fill the room as they brainstorm on the obituary, Caroline furiously typing away.

By the time she reads aloud the final version, Mercedes has returned to Haze's room.

Lois smooths her friend's hair and says, "I hope you know it's not everyone who gets to hear their own obituary. Anything else you'd care to add?"

She wasn't alone in wishing that the patient would, in a final dramatic moment, open her eyes and wink or offer a thumbs-up, but Haze only breathes in a rattly breath.

The wall clock reads 8:34, but it feels much later, as if the weight of what's happening has leaned on time, pressed it into the future.

Sam has thought several times about telling his mother he should go—he's got a big test in precalculus tomorrow—but precalculus and his grade seem pretty inconsequential in the scheme of things. Now *calculus*, he jokes to himself, *that* would have been something totally different.

Lois is in a chair now; sitting on Haze's bed was too uncomfortable for her, and what with all her shifting around, probably not that comfortable for Haze, not that she'd notice. She's kept body contact, however, her hand first curled around Haze's inert fingers and now resting on her friend's forearm. Susan's checking her vibrating phone, but seeing Mitch's name and number, as opposed to Jack's, she returns it to her purse. Caroline too is looking at her phone and the message Tina has sent: "FERRET WILL LIVE. SHOULD I COME TO

HOSP?" and just as her fingers are about to type "Yes," she lifts her head, hearing a great gasping breath from Haze.

It's a sound that makes everyone lean forward, as if they've heard a clue and are waiting to hear what exactly it's a clue to.

The boulder that has been pushing time forward rolls back a little, and seconds are longer than minutes, which are longer than hours.

They wait and wait and wait, but there is no more breath from Haze. Still they wait, until Mercedes finally lays her hand on the old woman's throat and says what they all know.

"She's gone."

October 29, 2016
It is with great sadness we at the *Granite Creek Gazette* announce that the Radical Hag has left the building. Yes, Haze Evans, beloved columnist and all-around good egg, died last night at the Granite Creek Hospital after having suffered a massive stroke this past summer. Her full obituary as well as funeral details will be published tomorrow.

As readers of this paper know, we have been reprinting past columns of Haze's, with the hopes that she would recover to write new ones. Our hopes have been dashed.

Some of Haze's columns were folksy, some were funny, some were sad, some were controversial. My grandfather William McGrath hired Haze and gave her a free rein when it came to her columns, as I have tried to do. There were times when I thought, Oh my gosh, can I publish this? but I did so because I felt her readers, even if they vehemently disagreed with her, could handle whatever Haze put forth.

Some of the columns we've reprinted have gotten nearly as much response as they did when they were originally published, and it's been heartening to hear from all of you.

Haze always said, "It's an honor to be heard," and because we're days away from a historic election, we're reprinting two columns on the presidential candidates, the first one written last year, and the second one just three and a half months ago.

We've printed the recipes she included with each column, because we all could use a little sweetness right now.

Susan McGrath, Publisher

April 13, 2015

If I were a contestant on *Dancing with the Stars,* I don't think I'd be voted off first; in fact with the right partner, I'll bet I could cha-cha, rhumba, quickstep, and waltz into midseason. (Semifinals might be wishful thinking.) But I tell you, if there were an award given for Most Joyful Expression, I would have taken it—picture me dancing a hula, mixed with a cheerleader rallying the masses, topped off with an ape beating its chest.

Hillary Clinton is running for president! I get another chance to vote for her!

I cried hard back in 2008 when she conceded her primary loss to Barack Obama, but my sadness was tempered by the fact that history still was being made by the first man of color to run for (and then eventually win) the presidency. I've written many laudatory columns about the job President Obama has done, despite crazy—and shameful—conspiracy theories ("He's not an American citizen!"), racism (of course there's racism, when will we admit it?), and the obdurate unwillingness of Republican leaders to put American interests over party ones, but still . . . I was writing about a *man*.

I would like you men reading this column (c'mon, I know my male readership is vast) to imagine this: the country that you live in, the greatest democracy of all time, has always, in its two-hundred-forty-year history, been governed by women. All of its forty-four presidents and vice presidents, all of its members of Congress, all of its Supreme Court judges have been women. Oh sure, as we evolved, we

came to the enlightened opinion that maybe some men
were capable human beings and elected a few senators, a
few more representatives, and even a male justice or two to
help us run this country, whose very pledge acknowledges
ours as a nation that honors liberty and justice for all. All
being the extremely operative word, because really, fellas,
how would you feel to have been considered such second-
class citizens that you didn't even earn the right to vote until
well into the twentieth century?

How'd you feel, fellas, if as kids, in minus-ten-degrees
weather you wore trousers to keep your legs warm on
your walk to school but once inside had to take them
off because dress code demanded you wear impractical
dresses? How'd you feel if as a single man, you couldn't
get a credit card, but if you were married, you could, that is,
with your wife's signature? How'd you feel if you were fired
because you were expecting a child? How'd you feel if your
career options were limited because society told you, "men
aren't doctors/lawyers/scientists/mathematicians/music
conductors/CEOs" ad infinitum?

How, fellas, do you like those indignities? *Indignities* is
a good word too, because even though we've gotten rid
of some of them, many of these stupid rules, regulations,
and customs remain, their only purpose to strip you of
your dignity, your personhood—your personhood, which in
importance is secondary to your sex. And speaking of sex,
how would you feel if yours always made you a target? That
if you were out at night and robbed or raped, it'd be your
fault, because what are you doing out at night anyway?
That if you went to a party and some woman took you
into a bedroom and forced herself upon you, it'd be your
fault, because you were, after all, dressed in a tight T-shirt,
and oh my, those pectoral muscles of yours were such an
invitation! How would you feel if at your workplace your
bosses constantly made remarks about those pectorals
that made you feel uncomfortable, or worse, if they shoved

themselves against you in the copy room and threatened you with firing if you weren't "nice to me"?

So I am thrilled that Hillary Clinton has officially announced that she's running for a position she's as qualified for as any who might run against her in the primary, and (because I'm feeling so confident that it's our time, it's the world's time) for the presidency.

Please, fellas, throughout the upcoming campaign season, consider this candidate the way you would a male one. What are her policies? Are they more important than what she's wearing/how she looks/her tone of voice? Does she back up her ideas with facts and figures, or does she make grandiose, empty promises? Is she a fighter, albeit a fair fighter? Does she listen? What ideas does she have that will make not just your life work better but our country as a whole? And most importantly, would you like to have a beer with her? . . . Ha ha, remember when that was actually considered a serious enough question in 2000? (And look where that got us.)

Having written all my life, I have several times entertained the idea of writing a novel, but my ideas never took me further than the first couple pages or, in some cases, the first couple paragraphs. I couldn't seem to summon up the same energy for made-up people and plots as for real people and real life. This coming year is going to be such an exciting one, and I'm so glad to be a witness to it, to be able to write about it, to actually think that in a less than a year and a half, I might get to write about the first woman elected president and it won't be fiction.

IT'S TIME! TOFFEE BARS
    1 cup butter
    1 cup brown sugar
    1 egg yoke
    2 cups flour

In a bowl, knead all ingredients together. Pat in greased cookie sheet. Bake at 350 degrees for fifteen minutes. Remove from oven, and immediately pour one package of chocolate chips over uncut bars and wait 1–2 minutes. With a knife, evenly spread melted chocolate, and sprinkle chopped walnuts or pecans on top. Cut into small pieces so you can eat more.

July 6, 2016

When I was eight, I had my tonsils out, and I was told later that coming out of anesthesia, I remarked to the nurse looming in front of me, "But you're not fluffy like a real bunny rabbit."

That's a story lodged in the Evans family lore, one that always got a good laugh in the retelling, and one I, for a change, don't remember. Through the years, I've heard other people's post-op stories, the funny things said, the discombobulation felt.

To me, it feels as if we Americans have been in a communal surgery lately. The political arena is our operating room, and in it, politicians and a complicit media are trying to excise our common sense/dignity/commitment to facts. And as I struggle to get out of this anesthesia, I direct my befuddled comments not to a nurse but to Donald Trump: "But you're not presidential like a real presidential candidate."

As usual, the chamber of commerce put on a swell Fourth of July fireworks display over Kingleigh Lake, with a twenty-five-minute show that lit up the sky with pinwheels and comets and multicolored bursts of glittering confetti. A big crowd on blankets and lawn chairs had situated itself on the south hill, and Lois and I enjoyed cheese and crackers and wine with some of our book club members. It was a balmy, beautiful, festive evening, and I smiled as I eavesdropped on teenagers to my left as they oohed and aahed over the fireworks and each other, and I frowned as I overheard two old gentlemen to my right talking (loudly) about how thrilled they are that it looks like Donald Trump will be the Republican presidential candidate.

When he announced he was running last year and floated down that escalator like he was on his way to a shoe sale at Nordstrom, I wondered if I was watching an episode of *Punk'd*. I'll admit to getting a kick out of watching that shallow blowhard in the Republican debates. Because I didn't care much for his fellow debaters or their policies, his rude, pugnacious insults (Little Marco! Lyin' Ted! Low-Energy Jeb!) were a source of childish entertainment. I was certain that is how he would ultimately be regarded, as childish entertainment (what's he going to call someone next—Poopie Face?) meant for easy yuks (but certainly not for children).

But wrong I was; despite his verifiable cheating, lying, and false boasts, despite his denial of science and his debunked conspiracy theories, despite his rants against immigrants/women/anyone who disputes him, he's not only popular, he's beloved and revered, by an extreme(ly) passionate base, like the old men I heard swooning over him.

I don't know these two men personally, but I could see by their age and the World War II Veteran hats they wore that they were part of what's been called the Greatest Generation, a title I don't believe they, or anyone, have earned. Don't get me wrong. Of course I honor the bravery, industry, and we're-all-in-this-together unity of those (like my brother, Tom) who grew up in the Depression and fought in the war, but the superlative determines that the contest's over, that no following/preceding generation can be/was as great. How does that help us? Wouldn't it inspire us to know that the Greatest Generation is still in the making?

I'm old, and I don't have any children of my own, but I still look to the future, still get excited for all children: What's ahead for them? What'll they discover? How'll they make the huge differences our country, our world so desperately needs?

I'm scared but ultimately excited for those teenagers watching fireworks and their peers and the ways they'll help our upcoming President Hillary Clinton figure out how to make this world a better place for all, because, remember, the Greatest Generation . . . is yet to be.

THESE BROWNIES DESERVE BRAGGING
Preheat oven to 350 degrees.

- 3 ounces unsweetened baking chocolate
- ½ cup butter
- 1 cup sugar
- 2 eggs
- ⅓ to ½ cup flour (depending on how cakey you want brownies)
- pinch of salt
- ½ cup chopped walnuts or pecans
- 1 teaspoon vanilla

In saucepan, melt chocolate and butter over low flame. When completely melted, turn off burner, and stir in sugar. Set aside for 10 minutes. Beat in eggs, one at a time. Stir in flour, salt, nuts, and vanilla. Pour into a greased 8-inch-square pan, and bake for 40 minutes. When cool, cut into squares, and try not to eat all of them.

28

The genial and informal minister whom parishioners call Pastor Greg looks out at the mourners packed into the pews of St. John's by the Lake. He smiles, knowing they will wait for whatever it is he has to say, and he is grateful for their patience, which gives him enough time to swallow the lump in his throat.

"One of my," says Pastor Greg, but his voice is rusty, and he stops to clear his throat. He begins again. "One of my enduring memories of Haze Evans was seeing her in the back pew—that was her favorite seat—during one Christmas Eve candlelit service, laughing. It's not that I don't try to use a little wit in my sermons, but her laughter was more than I thought my sermon inspired. After the service was over and we gathered in the fellowship hall, I asked Haze what she had found so funny.

"'Check the program,' she said. 'See what the celestial beings are up to.'"

"I have a very efficient secretary, but everyone makes mistakes now and then, and when I finally got back to the parsonage that night, I went over the program and saw the typo that had caused Haze such mirth. Among the carols the congregation had been directed to sing was this one: 'Angels We Have Heard Get High.'"

Laughing with the rest of the congregation, Sam thinks *hold*. Listening to the choir sing "Morning Has Broken," he tears up, blinks hard, and thinks *discard*, and when his mother reads the eulogy and a wave of sadness, like a syrupy liquid, glugs through his body, he can't help but think *fold*.

Lame, he thinks next, wondering what he'd be thinking if he'd watched *Game of Thrones* or *The Walking Dead* the night before instead of some two-hour-long poker marathon.

But he can't help feeling that in the church packed with people, everyone is being dealt emotions from a big deck by a fast and tricky dealer. Throughout Haze's service, people laugh, cry, laugh again, sigh, cry again.

NOW SITTING WITH A GROUP OF FRIENDS (his entire English class showed up), after eating the luncheon put on by the church ladies, Sam can't say for sure what he's feeling . . . maybe grateful?

"Why are you smiling?" asks Elise, who sits next to him.

Sam looks down at his plate, and his grin widens.

"Are you thinking about how you want another one of those toffee bars?" says Elise, taking his plate as she rises. "Because I do—they're the bomb."

"If you're getting up, get me another brownie," says Jacob from across the table.

"Not your waitress," says Elise in a singsong voice, and Jacob's exaggerated wounded face makes Sam laugh.

"Chicks usually dig it when I talk like that," Jacob says in a serviceable gangster voice.

"If we're chicks," says Claire, "then what're you, a Peep?"

"A gross Peep," says Stacy. "Like one you find in the couch cushions way after Easter. Crusty and full of dog hair with all the sugar scraped off."

"A crusty Peep?" says Jacob, splatting his hand across his chest. "Girls, that hurts."

"Sorry you feel that way, *boy*," says Claire.

A crusty Peep, thinks Sam. I've got to write that down.

Since Radical Hag Wednesday, it's been Sam's nightly or sometimes afternoon habit (why, he wonders are *nightly* and *daily* words but not *morningly* or *afternoonly?*) to write down his thoughts and observations, his "columns." He seems to censor himself less when he writes by hand; words not easily erased by a click of a key seem more real to him, more permanent. Working at the *Gazette*, reading all those typewritten and handwritten words on all different kinds of stationery, has made him a fan of ink and paper, and he has started carrying a notebook in his back pocket. He already jotted down a few things when he was in the bathroom after the service, and when he gets home, he'll write more.

He sees Elise chatting with Lois and Mrs. Garnet at the dessert table. Sam didn't know that almost always there is a standard after-funeral menu of ham and turkey buns, potato salad, and coleslaw, followed by white and chocolate sheet cakes. Because of his mother's request, the desserts offered today were all made from Haze's recipes—almond crescent cookies, brownies, lemon bars, fudge, and toffee bars.

There are at least a dozen women, mostly gray or white haired, who skitter in and out of the swinging church kitchen doors. Previously, these devoted church ladies would have been invisible to Sam, mere figures to refill trays, to get everyone more of what they wanted, but now he's looking at them as real people who were once his age (although he finds that almost too hard to believe).

One woman trots back to the kitchen carrying an empty bowl, her apron strings tied around a trim waist, and Sam notices her legs (despite the ugly crepe-soled shoes she wears) are shapely and imagines what she was like—fifty? sixty? sixty-five years ago?—when she was his own age.

Get a grip, he says to himself, with a slight shake of his head.

"We're going back to school," announces Claire, and as she and Stacy stand, Jacob bolts up and says, "I'll go with you."

Sam stares openmouthed at Jacob, who has never been eager to get back to school.

With a slight shrug of his shoulders, Jacob raises his eyebrows, and his eyes dart to Stacy, a signal to Sam that "wherever this one's going, I'm going too."

He watches his friends thread their way around the cluster of round tables, Jacob's neck craned to give him more height because both girls are taller than he.

Sam's goal is to be six feet three inches, and at five feet eight, he's hoping for a growth spurt. His dad's six feet, and his mom's five feet seven (he knows that because they just measured themselves, Susan laughing and disbelieving that her youngest son had surpassed her in height and wanting definite proof).

"A lot of movie stars are shorter than you'd think," Lois had told him during one of their mutual hospital visits. "I liked the tall ones: Henry Fonda, Burt Lancaster, Clint Eastwood." Sam knew who the latter was but had to look up the other two, and after watching clips of them on YouTube, he rented a couple of their movies. And liked them.

"Here," says Elise, setting a small frosted square in front of him. "That's one of the last toffee bars, they're going fast." Sitting down she asks, "Where'd everybody go?"

"Back to school," says Sam.

"Losers," says Elise, "although I probably should do the same. I've got a test in biology, and the makeup tests are always harder than the regular ones."

She wipes a smear of chocolate off her lip and adjusts her purse on her shoulder.

"See you back at school today or tomorrow?"

"Tomorrow," says Sam, understanding how lips can be described as rosebuds.

With a nod, Elise says, "Cool" and "See you later then." She rushes out but doesn't get very far, turning around to tell Sam, "You look really handsome in that suit."

Sam watches her leave and pops the bar into his mouth. The pleasure receptors that have already lit up with Elise's words light up again.

"Scare all your friends away?" a voice asks.

It takes Sam a moment to chew and swallow.

"Guess they saw *you* coming," he says, looking up at his neighbor Harlan Dodd.

The old man laughs.

"I seem to have that effect on people. But only the ones I'm not interested in anyway."

"Would you like to sit down?" asks Sam. "Could I get you a treat?"

"I already partook," says Mr. Dodd. "I particularly enjoyed the fudge."

Dodd continues to stand, his veiny hands gripped on the back of a chair. Sam can tell he wants to say something, so he waits. Finally, the old man coughs and says, "Has your mother told you . . . has she told you if they'll be looking for a new columnist?"

Sam is surprised by the question, surprised that he hasn't wondered that himself.

"No, she hasn't."

"Well, if she's thinking about a replacement, tell her to get someone who's not such a flaming liberal. Those last two columns reprinted were off the rails."

"At least we didn't reprint the letters you wrote complaining about them," says Sam, a flush of anger rising in him. "They were *really* off the rails."

"At least I'm going in the right direction," says Mr. Dodd.

"Ever think your *right* direction might be wrong?"

That their words are equally huffy and petulant seem to surprise them both, and they almost, but don't, laugh.

"Can't believe you'd rile up an old man like that," says Mr. Dodd, for whom having the last word is important. "Anyway, tell your mother that I hope that she finds a good replacement—someone who has a little more sense."

"Haze had a lot of sense," says Sam, wondering, Doesn't this old asshole ever quit?

"I know she did," says Mr. Dodd. He leans and raps once on the tabletop, which seems to Sam a sort of jab in the ribs. "Haze Evans was *blessed* with sense."

Sam's gape is about to turn into a smile when Dodd adds, "Notice I didn't say what kind."

He pivots as easily as a pro basketball player, and Sam watches him until he exits and is surprised by his own low chuckle, even as he thinks, what a jerk.

Most of the tables are empty, although knots of people stand around talking, arms folded across their chests (in one column, Haze had referred to this as the Minnesota State Pose). Sam sees his mother talking to Jens Selby's mother in one such group and sees his dad coming out of the kitchen, bus tub in hand.

"Dad," he says, joining him at a table covered with half-filled coffee cups and saucers dotted with crumbs. "How'd you get roped into this?"

Phil gestures to the white-haired and bald church men who are helping their female comrades in the kitchen by bussing tables.

"Thought they could use some help."

"Okay, okay," says Sam, getting the hint. He gathers up several water glasses and places them in the plastic tub. "It was nice, wasn't it, Dad? I mean the funeral?"

Phil nods. "It was a *beautiful* funeral. The kind I'd like to have— good music, an officiant with an actual sense of humor, and eulogies that make you wish you knew the person being talked about a little better."

"I feel like I knew her pretty well," says Sam. The words surprise him, jumping out of his mouth like sheep out of an open gate. Dishes clatter as he sets coffee cups in the tub. "I mean, because I've read so many of her words."

Phil nods. "Your mother told me about how you discovered . . . well, about her grandfather and Haze."

A man with a silver handlebar mustache passes by with a full bus tub.

"Hope you know," he says, "that all helpers get their dibs on any leftovers."

"Great," says Phil. "Thanks."

"Dad," says Sam, "Dad, I would have told you too, but—"

"But I haven't exactly been someone you'd like to talk to," says Phil. "I mean *really* talk to."

"Dad, I—"

Phil's lower lip raises, pushing his whole mouth into an inverted smile.

"Just know," he says, after a moment, "that I'm glad you can talk to your mom. But also know that if you want to talk to me—about anything—I'm available. No, not just available—happy to do so. Honored to do so."

Sam clears his throat and says, "Dad, please. Get a hold of yourself."

They both laugh, and then Phil tells his son to grab another bus tub—what, does he expect eighty-year-old men to do all the heavy lifting?

Snow flurries aren't uncommon in early November, but they're still a surprise, and the group walking in them grumbles about winter's early arrival.

"We live on a corner," says Caroline, her arm tucked through Tina's. "Which means we've got twice as much sidewalk to shovel."

"I've got a snowblower," says the man Mercedes introduced to Sam as "my friend, James." "I'll come by anytime and help you out."

"No, I like the exercise," says Tina.

"I don't," says Caroline. "So come by anytime, James, and use the snowblower on *my* half of the sidewalk."

"If he doesn't, I will," says Lois. "I already plow out my whole block. I *love* using my snowblower."

"Oh my goodness," says Sarah, Caroline's mother. "I don't even know how to turn on ours, but thankfully, my husband does!"

Part of the small group piles into one of the few cars left in the church parking lot and extends an invitation to the others to come by that evening to Caroline and Tina's house to finalize their plans to say goodbye to Haze.

"There'll be Mexican hot chocolate," says Caroline.

"And I'm bringing churros!" says Mercedes.

Sam walks with his parents to their cars, parked near one another, and before Phil leaves, he reminds Sam of their billiards date tomorrow night (there's a pool table in the game room of Mac's condo, and they've been giving it a good workout). With a bow, Sam opens his mother's car door, and they laugh at his gallantry, but instead of getting in on the passenger side, he says, "I'm thinking maybe I'll head back to school. I'll walk there."

"Okay," says Susan. "See you later at home then."

After his parents drive off, the wind kicks itself up a notch, flicking a snowy gust at Sam, and he thinks he might have been a bit hasty in choosing his two feet over four wheels for transport.

But as he begins walking, the icy wind is less of an intrusion than an occasional wintry accompaniment. His mother has nagged at him all his life to dress for the weather, and for a change, he has. He wears his winter coat over his suit, and jammed in its pockets are gloves and a scarf, which he ties around his head, over his ears, and under his chin. He is not the least concerned about the dork factor; anyone whose opinion he cares about isn't around, and why not be warm?

He walks in the direction of his school and is only a block away when he gets another idea.

The snow flurries gradually peter out, which is a slight disappointment to Sam, who thought there was something not just atmospheric but romantic about walking, face tucked into hunched shoulders, in a swirling snow. Plus he liked the feel of it, of the air filled with motion and matter, of snow battering his face with streaks and dots of cold. It almost seemed miraculous, if you thought about it, how the skies could be sunny, be rainy, be windy, be foggy, be snowy, be whatever they wanted to be.

The sky, he thinks, the sky is a quick-change artist / with a whoosh of its cloak it's something that it just wasn't . . .

Take that, Walt Whitman, he says to himself, thinking of one of the American poets they've begun studying in English, and takes the scarf off his head and ties it around his neck.

It's a long walk, but not one that would cause blisters or frostbite, back to where he's going. He has turned on his phone after having silenced it at the funeral, and it has already chirped three times since he left the church. Maybe it was Elise, checking up on him? Or Jack? He couldn't believe how much he and his brother were texting each other lately; Jack never had time for him before, but travel definitely seems broadening . . . and maybe Sam's job at the paper is too? Whatever the reason, the Carroll brothers were communicating in a way they never had before.

Maybe it was Jacob, wondering what was up, or maybe it was Claire, or Stacy, or Kurt, or any of the people who last year were his schoolmates and this year are his friends. He'll check later.

The iron gate is open, and Sam walks into the cemetery.

The snow flurries have added only a tinge of white to the ground, not enough to change the prevailing grayness of the skies and tombstones. He's not sure why he's there—Haze isn't. She was cremated, and Lois, who is her executor, is in possession of her remains.

"She scattered Royal's into Lake Superior," she had told the group when they had assembled in Haze's hospital room the night she died. "In her will she asks that the same be done with hers."

Susan said she'd like to accompany Lois, and everyone in the room volunteered they would too, and it was decided that they'd drive up to Lake Superior that Tuesday, after everyone voted.

"Haze couldn't wait for Election Day," said Lois, "This way, she'll still be part of the celebration!"

"Can I still go?" Sam asked his mother later. "Even though I'll miss school?"

"If you're caught up on your homework."

Sam nods. "I could even try to get some extra credit. Yeah—maybe I could write a column for Radical Hag Wednesday. A column about saying goodbye to Haze."

"Goodbye to Haze," says Susan, her smile mischievous, "And hello to Hillary!"

WALKING DOWN THE MAIN ROAD, Sam steps to the side when he hears a car behind him, and when he turns around, he's surprised—and he isn't—to see his mother. She pulls her car over onto the gravel shoulder and gets out.

They greet each other with the same question: "What are you doing here?"

"I just thought I should spend some time with my grandparents," says Susan, and as she takes Sam's arm, he says, "I guess that's why I'm here too."

WITH LINKED ARMS, they stand in front of William and Eleanor McGrath's monument.

"Grandma was one of the lucky ones," says Susan. "She outlived her cancer prognosis by about"—she looks at the date carved into the granite—"oh, twenty-five years."

"Do you think," says Sam, "that they know? That where they are—if they're *anywhere*—they know Haze died?"

"Well, there are those 'near death' stories," says Susan after a moment. "The ones told by people who've come back after supposedly dying? About the white light and the feeling of being enveloped in love? And some people have said how their loved ones were there ready to welcome them in."

"Ha," says Sam. "I wonder what your grandma would think about welcoming Haze in."

"I don't know, I'd bet she wouldn't feel any jealousy or betrayal . . ." Susan shrugs at her son, who stares at her. "I think—or maybe it's that I *hope*—that where we, or our souls go, is to a place, or realm, or existence that's far bigger and understanding and forgiving than we can ever imagine. A place where . . . where love, *complete* love, presides."

After a while, Sam says softly, "That wouldn't be a bad place to wind up," and his words are nearly carried away by a wintry wind that's aimed its blast directly at their faces.

A bird swoops down from the bare branches of a nearby oak tree and into the branches of another.

"A raven," Sam says melodramatically.

Susan looks up at the tree.

"Uh, that'd be a sparrow."

They laugh, and like longtime dance partners, they turn at the same time, without words, and walk toward the car.

"Mom, do you think I could ask Elise to come tonight?"

"To Caroline's? Sure. Tell her I can pick her up."

"Won't you love it when I get my license?"

"When you get your license, Sam, I'm sure I will feel many emotions."

In the car, Susan turns on the ignition and the heat, and in the idling, warming car, they both reach for their phones, Sam to read his texts and send Elise an invitation, Susan to see if there are any work emergencies that need tending to.

Scrolling through her e-mails, Susan stops to read one.

"What?" says Sam, noticing her smile.

"It's from Jack."

"What's it say?"

"Copenhagen. I might just have to move here. The women are beautiful, especially Ella, who's from a farm in the Jutland and is staying at the same hostel (a hostel with a bar!—what do they think we kids are—responsible or something?). She and I played chess in the lounge, and she beat me. Really beat me, but she's so SMUK (weird word for 'beautiful,' but that's how the Danes say it) I didn't mind at all. I was going to head to Sweden tomorrow, but the reason for the changed plans is easy, and it's spelled E-l-l-a."

Susan looks up. "Aw, I was kind of rooting for the Italian astronaut."

"He sent me a picture," says Sam and holds his phone out.

"Oh," says Susan, "she *is* smuk."

The snow has picked up again on the drive home, and the windshield wipers make a rhythmic whomp-whomp sound. Sam unbuttons the top button of his coat and loosens his tie—did Elise really say he looked handsome in his suit? The heater blows a soft current of warmth at him, and he tips his seat back and shuts his eyes.

"Tired, honey?" asks Susan.

Sam shrugs. It has been a long day, but he's not really tired. He just wants to think.

How can a person *ever* have time to think about all the things there are to think about?

About Elise and how when she tucked back her dark, shiny hair, a tiny blue stone sparkled in the middle of her perfect earlobe, like it was winking at him; about Harlan Dodd joking with him; and about how he, Sam, might make him some of Haze's fudge and ask if he could interview him (would he dare ask the question he's dying to know the answer to: How'd you go from really thinking about things to being such a dickwad?); about that church choir and how those raised voices were somehow *magnificent*; about how he couldn't remember the last time he'd used the word *magnificent*; about understanding how the phrase *poker face* came to be after watching that televised tournament; about how Jacob had pointed out a bent-over old woman working in the church kitchen as someone whose groceries he carried and who told Jacob she had once been a skater in the Ice Capades. And did Elise say he looked "so handsome" or "really handsome" in his suit?

Sam wonders what Haze would think of her jam-packed funeral, or if in that "realm" where "love persists," nobody bothers to keep track of crowd size. Still, wasn't it a tribute to all the love she generated on earth?

Turning into the driveway, Susan says softly, "We're home," and inside the house, she yawns and tells Sam she's going to take a little nap before they go to Caroline's that evening.

Laughing as Cesar chases him upstairs, in his room Sam poses in front of the mirror—he wouldn't say he exactly looks handsome, but he does like how his suit makes his shoulders look broad and his waist narrow, well, *narrower*. Pulling down the knot of his tie, he stops himself, thinks maybe he won't change into his sweats, maybe he'll stay dressed up for a while—he read somewhere that a sci-fi novelist he admires always wears a suit and tie when he writes, believing it makes him and his work more professional.

He takes his phone, notebook, pen, and folded service program out of his pockets and flicking the vent of his suit coat, sits down at his desk, his dog settling at his feet.

His phone chirps, and he sees the message is from Elise. In response to his invitation, she's texted a happy face emoji and the words, "LOVE TO!"

Seconds after he sends back a thumbs-up emoji, he hears another ping. A text from Jack: "I'VE DECIDED: INTERNATIONAL RELATIONS, SINCE I'M SO GOOD AT THEM!"

The brothers' recent texts (and when they want to expound, e-mails) have been about everything from Jack encouraging Sam to at least *try* out for a team sport (to which Sam asked, "Does debate count?") to the likelihood of their parents getting back together (with Sam "hopeful" and Jack "doubtful," they both agreed to be "doubtfully hopeful") to Jack's simple condolences upon hearing of Haze's death, "So sorry, bro."

When Jack wrote how much he loved travel yet how excited he'll be to go to the University of Colorado Boulder, where he had been accepted and had deferred, Sam had texted him back, asking what he was thinking of studying, what kind of career did he want? And Jack's reply, "HELL IF I KNOW—AERONAUTICAL ENGINEERING?" had prompted Sam to text, "DON'T YOU HAVE TO BE SMART FOR THAT?"

"HA HA. LAW?"

"SEE ABOVE."

Looking at his phone now, Sam smiles. He doesn't doubt Jack would be good at international relations—at whatever he decides to go into—but for now he won't offer any advice or counsel. He turns off his phone and tosses it onto his bed.

For now he has to write.

EPILOGUE

November 11, 2017

Dear Haze,

In keeping with your tradition of wrapping up each year by writing down its highs and lows, I'm doing the same here, with a minor adjustment. It's not New Year's Eve, but it is a time for reflection, as it's been a year since we let your ashes fly over Lake Superior (almost taking down a dive-bombing seagull who thought we were throwing bread crumbs).

Here's how I'm honoring another of your traditions: I write (and I'm talking with a pen) regularly in a notebook. I don't address my stuff to "Dear Helen," like you did, but to another inspiring woman: "Dear Haze." Ha—not. I mean, I can write you this letter, but to address you in my journal would be weird, considering some of the things that occupy the mind of a normal, red-blooded fifteen-year-old player like me . . .

I'm not gonna spend a lot of time on the lows, because I don't want to (a) be here all day, or (b) puke in a public place. But it's bad, Haze. Everything seems jacked up—it's like there's a civil war brewing, with our leader-in-chief sending out crazy Us vs. Them tweets that do nothing to unite and everything to divide. There are all kinds of investigations and scandals going on, more insane gun violence, white supremacists and neo-Nazis not afraid to crawl out of the woodwork, all these men in power who turn out to be sexual predators, more weird weather that we're not supposed to do anything to fix . . . okay,

I've got to stop, Haze, because, to repeat (b), I don't want to puke in a public place.

So whaddya say we move on to the good stuff?

One, I've got a girlfriend, and coming in a close second, I got my driver's permit!

I wish you could have met Elise—I'm way out of her league, but she doesn't seem to notice. At least she hasn't called a ref over to throw me out of the game.

She's one of an octad (I just looked that word up) that sort of rose up from last year's Radical Hag Wednesdays. We meet once a week, and although it's not a writing or reading group, we do a lot of both, considering Abdi, Grace, and I like to write and like to share what we're working on. Fun fact, Haze: you weren't replaced at the paper. Instead Mom started "Open Door," a biweekly column that publishes anyone with a good story or strong opinion. Abdi's already published two columns, twice as many as Grace and I have. (Not to brag, but I've published four short articles, and the fifth'll be printed in tomorrow's paper. I know, I know, it pays to be the son of the publisher; still Mom assures me she wouldn't print anything subpar.)

A couple times we've met to write letters to government officials, even though we can't vote yet (according to Abdi, our congressman is "a real tool who would like my family behind one of those walls he can't wait to build"), and on the anniversary of Prince's death, we spent our time reading aloud his lyrics as we listened to a mix of his songs that Kurt had made.

Mostly we meet to vent, which is satisfying by itself, but even better when it's led to taking action, like when we caravanned down to St. Paul last January to participate in the Women's March. Stacy and her sisters had knit us all pussy hats (don't ask), and while the girls talked about how empowering it felt to wear them, I can't say I felt empowered—at first I felt stupid. But then, I don't know, I felt cool, part of something bigger than myself.

My parents were too young to be part of the protests in the

sixties, but my dad says his brother Tim was really involved in the antiwar movement and even got his head bashed in at the Democratic Convention in Chicago. I don't want to get my head bashed in, but I figure if you just stand by, you either get passed by or get trampled.

And speaking of my parents, it seems they aren't too old to remember some of the sixties slogans though, especially "Love Is the Answer"—and act on them: they're back together! It took a long time, and they both say a lot of work, but it boils down to my dad just started being less of a jerk and not afraid to tell my mom what he needed, and my mom, though not as big a jerk, started being less of one too and not afraid to tell my dad what she needed. Oh yeah, and then they both listened.

The six windows big as doors face south and will offer plenty of natural light when there's natural light to be offered, but for now the sun is hidden behind a dreary veil of gray and the second floor is lit by electricity.

Sam slowly swivels left and right in one of the many forest-green club chairs—he loves these chairs!—that are situated in various niches, and surveys rows of book shelves. A goateed man, his hands clasped behind his back, peruses what Sam bets is the poetry section. He swivels in the other direction to see a spiffed-out older woman place an oversize book in the arms of a young, disheveled friend? granddaughter? who pretends to stagger from the weight of the growing pile she holds, and Sam thinks, Organizing . . . or Personal Hygiene. Tapping his fingers on his notebook, he looks at another row of shelves and sees someone dart behind them. Was that Elise? His heart, which like a sedan had been doing its steady, serviceable job, revs up like a Ferrari.

A second later, his question is answered in the affirmative when Elise, her smile sheepish, reappears and waves. He holds his hand up but instead of waving back, waves her forward.

"I knew you were writing," she whispers, setting down a large case as she sits in the chair next to his. "And I didn't want to disturb you."

"You could never disturb me, *chérie*," says Sam in a suave French accent (or facsimile thereof), and in response, Elise, holding her hands to her heart, flutters her eyelashes.

"Besides," says Sam, "the article's done. I already e-mailed it to my mom."

"So what were you writing now?"

"A letter to Haze."

That Elise's expression isn't one of befuddlement is a testament to their relationship and that Sam feels comfortable telling her just about anything.

"I was trying to wrap up the year for her, you know how she always did?"

"Can I read it?"

"No."

"Then how about the article?"

"You can read it in the paper tomorrow," teases Sam. "Just know that I did mention the jazz band."

"And me in particular?" Elise teases back.

"Sure. I wrote about a whole page on how Elise Wahlberg's saxophone stylings take jazz to another level."

"Saxophone stylings," says Elise with a laugh, which causes the man with the goatee, now seated in a chair across them and reading not a poetry book but one on electronic day trading, to look up and frown.

"Wanna go to Irv's?" Sam whispers, and Elise nods.

On the still busy main floor, they stop near the circulation desk to read the "Celebration Events!" listed on a big erase board. Already in progress in the lower-level meeting rooms is a slide show presentation by a history professor on "Farmers and Furriers: The Founders of Granite Creek" and a talk by the owner of Sweet Buns Bakery and self-published author of the book *Apple Fritter Confidential*.

A story hour is in progress, and on their way out of the building, they pass the children's library, whose primary-colored decor is further brightened with clusters of balloons. Sam smiles and waves at the reader, but Shelly, the newly retired receptionist from the *Ga-*

zette, doesn't see him, too busy asking a semicircle of rapt children, "Is your mama a llama?"

FOR YEARS, Irv, the proprietor of the eponymous ice cream shop, had ignored customer pleas to serve Shamrock Shakes year-round and not just in March, in homage to St. Patrick.

"Some things gotta stay special!" said the man, who believed that gratification was sullied when it was instant and that coddling had overrun tradition. But when his wife, who loved the mint-ice-cream-with-a-secret-ingredient shakes, survived a cancer scare, Irv decided to offer them during November, Thanksgiving's month, in her honor. This was a heartfelt, but also savvy, move, as it brought in customers for whom an ice cream shop was not a go-to destination in wintry weather—so many customers that Irv decided that as long as the shakes were already green and therefore of the holiday season, he would extend the Shamrocks' run through December. His wife, who's been eyeing a new leather sectional at Schneeman's, is thrilled.

Sam and Elise hang up their jackets on the wall-mounted coatrack, whose hooks are shaped and painted like ice cream cones. After they've ordered, Elise carries the shakes, and Sam her saxophone case as they look for a table in the crowded shop.

"Yoo-hoo, Sam! Over here!"

Lois moves to the end of the booth so that Elise can slide in, and on the other side her companion does the same, giving Sam room— and a surprise that makes him nearly spill his shake.

"Mr. Dodd!" he says, placing his fountain glass carefully on the table. "I didn't know you two knew each other!"

"We don't entirely," says the old man. "But we're getting there."

Lois laughs at the look on Sam's face. "We're in the same ballroom dance class at the senior center," she explains. "We were dancing, what was it, Harlan, the foxtrot?"

"The Viennese waltz."

"Ah, yes. Anyway, I complimented him on both his dancing and on his recent column in Open Door."

Elise stops sipping her shake to nod and say, "We read that."

Sam says, "Yeah, we were both sort of . . . surprised by it."

After a mass shooting at an outdoor concert in Las Vegas, Mr. Dodd had written a column about the Second Amendment that asked, "What part of 'well-regulated' don't these gun nuts get?"

"I told him," says Lois, her eyes shining, "Harlan Dodd, you're turning into a radical old coot!"

Under the white hedge of his eyebrows, the man rolls his eyes. "Hardly," he says gruffly, and they can't help but laugh as he takes a sudden interest in his remaining shake, sucking up the last inch in a loud gurgle.

"So your mother told me you're writing an article about the big day, huh?" says Lois, giving Sam one of those conspiratorial winks of which old people are masters.

Swallowing a mouthful of creamy minty goodness, Sam says, "I am. And I quoted you."

"Oh, goody," she says. "Haze must have put me in at least 10 percent of her columns, and I've missed seeing my name in print. Well, except for in the police blotter."

SAM WOULD HAVE LIKED to give Elise a ride home, but in possession of her own permit, Elise declines the offer, eager to take over the wheel of her dad's SUV when he picks her up.

"Call me tonight!" says Elise, rolling down the driver's window. Sam, who had already started walking toward the *Gazette* offices, blows an exaggerated kiss, which, to his embarrassment, Mr. Wahlberg pretends to catch.

SAM DRIVES HIS MOTHER'S ACCORD (Susan yelling at him only once to "look both ways!"), and when they get home, his dad is in the kitchen, making dinner.

Little steps (coffee dates and long telephone conversations) had given way to strides (dinners at Zig's and playing tennis again) had given way to the leap that landed Phil back in the house, with both he and Susan committed to giving their marriage a second chance.

"What am I smelling?" asks Susan, unwinding her scarf.

"The Sundown's Famous CheeZee bites are in the warmer," says Phil. "And *my* famous barbecued meat loaf will be ready in a half hour."

Sam has had his dad's barbecued meat loaf (one of the few dishes in his repertoire) and asks, "Famous for what?"

Phil pretends to look wounded, and Susan laughs and says, "What's the occasion?"

"Well, the library opening, of course." After a pause, Phil adds, his voice sly, "And Cancún."

It had been one of those flukey turns of luck: one of Phil's customers mentioned that he and his wife would be spending Thanksgiving weekend on the road in their brand-new Class A motor home instead of at their time-share in Cancún, and Phil had said, "Wow, Cancún," and the satisfied customer had said, "Hey, since you gave us such a good deal, let me give you the keys!"

Susan and Phil do a little happy dance, which Sam laughs at but doesn't join. That'd be *way* too weird.

"I'm going upstairs," he says to the couple jumping up and down, and as he leaves the kitchen he hears his mom say, "This can be our honey *crescent* moon!"

HAZE'S PIRATE BOOTY BOX no longer holds the journal she kept while seeing Bill McGrath; that valuable historical property is kept in Susan's cedar chest along with crocheted linens her great-grandmother made, her wedding album, and her sons' baby books. Sam is welcome to almost everything in there (hands off the linen) as long as he returns it, but he is far less interested in the notations on his weekly infant growth chart and pictures of his parents surrounded by a brigade of ushers and bridesmaids in pale-blue tuxedos and magenta taffeta than he is in Haze's journal.

Sam has claimed the stained wood box that held it, and it sits on his desk, the repository for his own important papers—letters from *his* grandfather, his own writing that has been printed in the

Gazette, and some of Haze's columns and journal entries (which he hand copied) that are especially meaningful to him.

At his desk, Sam opens his notebook and continues writing his wrap-up letter to Haze, telling her about Jack's return from Europe last summer and how he claimed to have fallen in love about twenty times, "but Mila from Munich . . . *mein Gott.*" Jack is a freshman now at the University of Colorado in Boulder and is deciding whether to major in business or German.

Sam writes about visiting his grandfather in California and how his step-grandmother let him drive her pink (!) convertible down the Pacific Coast highway one day and all the way to Disney World the next.

He fills her in on how Elise has inspired him to take up an instrument and how his progress with the guitar is slow but steady, and he wishes his fingers were longer.

When he has nearly finished the letter, he opens the implement he uses when he writes as a different kind of journalist: his laptop. He clicks open his article that will appear in tomorrow's paper. He won't hand copy all of it into his letter to Haze, only the beginning:

> The grand opening of Granite Creek's new downtown library was a celebratory affair featuring music by the GC High School jazz band, door prizes, and speeches given by library board chairman Tanesha Williams and newspaper publisher Susan McGrath.
>
> When Mayor Elizabeth Gluck cut the ribbon, declaring, "The Haze Evans Memorial Library is now open!" a crowd of 143 (this reporter counted) teemed inside the main entrance.
>
> Lois Henson, a friend of the honored columnist, was heard to say, "Haze would have been thrilled to have her dinky little branch library named after her, but this would have sent her over the moon!"

Sam continues to write:

You always said "voice matters," and I know yours sure did. It mattered enough to all the people who voted to name the library after you (my mom says the runner-up was a far and distant second), and it sure mattered to our Radical Hag Wednesday group. We were just talking about you last week and how your voice made us want to use ours better.

"And we can't just be voices of the future," Elise had said. "We've got to be voices of the present." (Isn't she awesome?)

"Yeah," said Abdi. "Especially because there are hardly any sane ones left!"

And guess what—I'm going to see if we can start using one of the library meeting rooms. That'd be cool, wouldn't it, the Radical Hag Wednesday group getting together in the *Haze Evans* library?

Sam hears his mother calling him to dinner, and Sam calls back that he's coming, and then adds a P.S.

Haze, can you believe Lois was on a date with Harlan Dodd?

ACKNOWLEDGMENTS

I would like the following people to step up to the podium to receive their gold (24 carat) thank-you medals.

For incredible generosity and support: Scott Eastman, Kris Strobeck, Janice Veech, Jean Borgerding, Kimberly and Killian Hoffer, Susan Lenfestey, Elizabeth Zaillian, Peggy Erickson, Sandy Benitez, Dave and Ruth Wood, and Karen Schwartz.

For their efforts in making this book an international blockbuster: Erik Anderson, Emily Hamilton, Mary Keirstead, Rachel Moeller, Jeff Moen, Maggie Sattler, Shelby Connelly, Heather Skinner, Matt Smiley, Laura Westlund, and everyone at the University of Minnesota Press. And to Kimberly Glyder for your fantastic cover—thanks!

For being good relations whose reunions are never a chore: the Petersons, the Dynnesons, the Strands, the Rasmussens, the Larsons, the Hoekstras, the Steinwands, the Opdahls, the Gabrielsons, the Pietigs, the Raberges, the Klevens, and the Landviks.

For being good eggs and/or artists and/or inspirations: Doug Anderson, Catherine Armstrong, Jill Boogren, Stephen Borer, Michael Bradley, Belinda Cella, Sheila De Chantel, Kate DiCamillo, Judith Guest, Judy Heneghan, Jennifer Hezmall, Kim Hovey, Terry Kalil, Gabe Klem, Brian Motiaytis, Betsy Nolan, Vicci Pederson, Mary Rockcastle, Gail Rosenblum, Kirsten Ryden, Cathy Schlesinger, Julie Schumacher, Barb Shelton, Wendy Smith, Mike Sobota, Sarah Stonich, Faith Sullivan, Sandy Thomas, Mark Thomson, Greg Triggs, Cynthia Uhrich, Anne Ulseth, Pat Francisco Weaver, Greg Winter, and Brenda Young.

For so much: Charles, Har, and Kinga. Oh, yeah—and Pharaoh, Super-Mutt.

Finally, although she's not here to take her place on the medal stand, I'd like to pay tribute to the memory of my beloved mom, Ollie, whose donuts are still remembered with reverence by all lucky enough to imbibe, and whose paper-thin krumkake cookies were the world's best, no contest. She might have wondered why I didn't put more of her recipes in this book, but as I haven't been able to recreate the above-mentioned delights (or her crescent rolls), I decided to hold them in my memory, where they're so sweet but calorie- and carb-free. She would have chuckled over the book's title, even while muttering "uff da." She had strong opinions (not always loudly expressed because she was, after all, raised Lutheran), and she believed, like Haze Evans, like Paul Wellstone, "We all do better when we all do better."

Lorna Landvik is the author of twelve novels, including the best-selling *Patty Jane's House of Curl*, *Angry Housewives Eating Bon Bons*, *Best to Laugh* (Minnesota, 2014), and *Once in a Blue Moon Lodge* (Minnesota, 2017). She has performed stand-up and improvisational comedy around the country and is a public speaker, playwright, and actor, most recently in her one-woman all-improvised show *Party in the Rec Room*. She lives in Minneapolis.